RIM

A NOVEL OF VIRTUAL REALITY

Alexander Besher

HarperPaperbacks
A Division of HarperCollinsPublishers

HarperPaperbacks   *A Division of* HarperCollins*Publishers*
                   10 East 53rd Street, New York, N.Y. 10022

Copyright © 1994 by Alexander Besher
All rights reserved. No part of this book may be used or
reproduced in any manner whatsoever without written
permission of the publisher, except in the case of brief
quotations embodied in critical articles and reviews. For
information address HarperCollins*Publishers*,
10 East 53rd Street, New York, N.Y. 10022.

Grateful acknowledgment is made to the following for
permission to reprint material copyrighted or controlled by
them:

Excerpt from *Cult of Tara: Magic and Ritual in Tibet,* by
Stephan Beyer. © 1973 by the Regents of the University of
California, University of California Press.

"Pigs (Three Different Ones)" by Roger Waters. © 1977
Pink Floyd Music.

A trade paperback edition of this book was published in
1994 by HarperCollins*West.*

Cover illustration by Rick Leider

First HarperPaperbacks printing: March 1996

Printed in the United States of America

HarperPrism is an imprint of HarperPaperbacks.
HarperPaperbacks, HarperPrism and colophon are trade-
marks of HarperCollins*Publishers.*

❖ 10 9 8 7 6 5 4 3 2 1

For Nicholas who inspired the story

For Françoise who kept it going

and

For the Family Everywhere

ACKNOWLEDGMENTS

I would like to thank Geoff Leach in Japan, who was the first to discover *Rim* and who brought it to the attention of *MacPower* magazine in Tokyo, which serialized an early draft of the manuscript in Japanese. Geoff also introduced me to my Japanese literary agent, Kiyoshi Asano, who found a first home for my as yet unwritten first novel at the Crest-sha publishing company in Tokyo. I would like to thank Makoto Satoh, the editor-in-chief of Crest-sha for his patience and faith in the project.

Thanks to *Kyoto Journal*, which published the first English excerpt of *Rim* in Japan.

I am also grateful to Bill Gladstone, my American literary agent, and to Joann Moschella, my editor at HarperCollins West. To the many others, among them Joe Holzer, Christophe Marcant, Choni Yangzom, Renée Wildman, David Bunnell, Paul Saffo, Tom Peters, Bernie Krisher, and Leonard Koren, who offered support and encouragement along the way, domo arigato.

Alexander Besher
March 7, 1994
San Francisco

The Keiretsu Wars were bloody even in the virtual worlds. Some time before the Mega-Quake of '26 erased Neo-Tokyo from the Matrix, the first unsuspecting CEO was sitting in his New Nippon garden enjoying his 'trodes when he was downloaded by the enemy.

His Honorable Consciousness was captured in a bio-ROM and spirited away in a brocade box to be presented to the Lord of the Rim. The others fell just as rapidly. This was not widely known to the world. In the West, a few more years would have to pass before the scientific establishment accepted the fact that energy can be manipulated by consciousness.

Then there were only two keiretsu groups left—one that belonged to the Lord of the Rim and another inhabited by the Lord of the Dream. One drew the sword; one visualized the sheath over the sword. Which one was greater?

In this history, you must decide. But before you do, you must know that the world is not as it seems. Not any more.

For one thing, when Neo-Tokyo ceased to exist, something greater came into being. A new Matrix was born. Which one was more real, which one was more imagined? To travel from one realm to the other became the new form of commuting. To dwell equally in both Matrixes was highly prized. Eventually, as both worlds interfaced, all such distinctions fell away.

But before that occurred, before the ceremony of consciousness became a highly refined art form and before dreams became the most sought after commodity in the marketplace, there was a troubled time when the Keiretsu Wars appeared endless and when hope was feared as much as love was endured.

This is part of that story, a small part that I know well. This account is dedicated to my father, who is now a ronin in the realm of unknowing.

Trevor Gobi
from "The Keiretsu Monogatari"
("Annals of the Mega-Corporate Wars")
Vector 16, Matrix Two
Taihei 43 (2067 A.E.)

A Japanese tea garden, Neo-Tokyo, Autumn, 2025

The elderly Japanese man stepped with a purposeful stride toward the entrance to the inner garden. It was an exclusive residential district of Neo-Tokyo where members of the Imperial family and top corporate clansmen lived. The cuckoos were calling out in the pine grove that bordered Prince S.'s villa. Somewhere in the garden, wind chimes tinkled in the dusk. It was a lonely sound.

"Wait outside," the man commanded his entourage in a gruff voice. The four men in dark suits bowed and stood motionless as his grey kimono-clad figure paused for a moment, then swept through the 500-year-old thatched gate.

Two of them were the old man's bodyguards and they took up a watchful position at the threshold to the roji, their senses alert, but their bodies relaxed. The other two were his personal aides. One carried a briefcase containing the old man's backup consciousness, which he laid down between his feet wearily. His colleague lit a ginko cigarette and admired the tranquility of the grounds. It was difficult to believe that such peace was only minutes away from the frantic hubbub of the city center.

On the other side of the bamboo fence, the old man paused to admire a clump of yellow and white chrysanthemums. Such simple, breathtaking beauty. Despite the pain of the cancer that ate remorselessly at his insides, he breathed in the fresh, cleansing scent of the pines and felt momentarily invigorated.

The cancer was incurable, but that was a minor inconvenience compared to the struggles he had faced during the 83 years of his active life. And it would not stop him now.

Irregularly shaped stepping-stones zigzagged toward the small teahouse that lay at the end of the winding path. The moss was so green and so thick. For a moment, the color reminded him of the Mekong River that flowed through Indochina. Those were happier days; not more carefree perhaps, but exhilarating as he captured market after market in Southeast Asia. Days of empire building.

And thinking of the Mekong, how could he not remember Mai? Sweet lovely Mai, who performed every function of womanhood and femininity for him, offering her body and her soul, a young woman devoting herself to an old man. He could still smell the scent of sandalwood on her soft brown skin. . . .

The pine needles crackled under his step, and he noticed the thin wisp of smoke coming from the chimney of the teahouse. Mai was now behind him, along with everything else. All of his past lives, fallen like persimmons from a tree that no longer existed. It had been cut down and uprooted a long time ago, seamlessly obliterated by his thoughts, which were now racing toward the boundary where his next life awaited.

If all went according to plan, this would be the most important day of his life: the culmination of his career and the beginning of a new era for the House of Kobayashi.

He stepped up to the stone water basin, lifted the bamboo ladle and filled it with cool water that he splashed over his hands. He pulled a sheet of folded handmade paper from his sleeve, dried his hands, then turned to face the tiny "wriggling-in" entrance to the tearoom. This was the ritual entryway signifying humility and the transition from worldliness.

He doffed his wooden clogs on the stone, slid the diminutive screen door open, then, bending almost in half, crawled inside the cool interior of the tiny two-and-a-half-size tatami-mat chamber.

Through the slats of the bamboo window lattice, the late afternoon sun daubed what was left of its soft golden rays on the brown plaster walls. The man turned to face the alcove where a scroll of calligraphy hung. The thick black Japanese kanji ideograms were appropriate for the occasion, he thought.

> *"Seeing all the way into the universe,*
> *from what lies before you."*

A stick of incense was lit in the burner, a single chrysanthemum stalk minus its head was placed in a bamboo vase. Wait a minute, *without* its head? The man froze and stared at the stalk. Then suddenly, the yellow petals of the chrysanthemum appeared from the top of the stalk, a marvelous work of graphics, as splendid as the flowers outside. The flowers were on-line, of course. Mitsubishi mums.

In the fading light of the room, he heard the sound of boiling water, almost like a brook burbling in a forest. The charcoal glowed softly in the hearth under the kettle. To the side was the tea cabinet, with all the utensils ready for the ceremony.

He heard the host coming from the other entrance. The screen door slid open and the master of the ceremony wriggled into the small room. He bowed to the old man, who bowed back to him wordlessly. It was strange, the old man thought. He was so young to be such a master. A master of nothingness.

All his life the old man had struggled to amass untold-of riches, unheard-of power and influence, all of which was nothing compared to the power contained within the pale young man with the pencil-thin arched eyebrows and the burning eyes.

Those eyes did not need to meet his, yet they saw and absorbed everything.

They understood that the old man's power was at its zenith, and only one thing would bring him the peace of mind he desired: to control the Void that awaited him, to embrace it within his very being, and to incorporate it into the structure of his powerful worldwide organization.

This nothingness would ensure that he left his imprint behind after he was gone. It would be like the seal of his signature, which he would stamp onto everything he encountered, all his business affairs and all of his worldly relations.

The young man did not mind that he would be the medium for the transfer of this power, because to him, it personally meant very little. On this level, nothingness was just a game. On other levels, it had different effects. There were many levels of nothingness. The old man could not possibly appreciate that knowledge at this stage of his personal evolution.

The young man bowed and produced a small bundle wrapped in brocade. Holding it reverently with both hands, he laid it down on the mat between them.

The old man sat, transfixed. He did not dare doubt. He had seen the beta test himself. An entire rock, weighing four tons, from the Zen garden of the Ryoanji had been digitized from a distance of 400 kilometers using a Kobayashi K700 downsizer. He had the image stored in a file that he kept in an amulet around his neck.

When he first obtained this evidence, he studied it with a feeling of almost religious conversion. For him the image had the full weight, the look and feel of the huge boulder once buried in that famous Zen garden. If there was an illusion, it was that it once was a solid rock. Yet it was still a rock. It had rock essence.

The old man held his breath as the master unfolded the bundle. He removed the ceremonial glove and slipped it onto his right hand, almost casually. The understatement was powerful, refined. Then, with another curt bow, the young man began the virtual reality ceremony: *Vacharu-no-yu.* The new way of serving—and savoring—reality.

For tea traditionalists, this was an aberration, of course. They were hopelessly behind the times. For them, nothing could replace the original Cha-no-yu tea ceremony as it had been refined by the tea-master Sen Rikyu in the 16th century.

The fools! No wonder New Nippon was beset with strife

and with intrigues just as it had been during the civil wars in the feudal times. As for Rikyu, these new traditionalists even refused to confront the master in his current holocarnation.

Why, the old man had been served by Rikyu himself in this very tearoom, courtesy of a Kobayashi Chajin projector. Imbeciles! What would it take to convince them that the times had indeed changed!? Did they want The Great Generalissimo Nobunaga himself to appear and demand their heads?

The old man grinned several layers beneath his expressionless mask. He could arrange it for them. In fact, he already *had*. A number of cowardly keiretsu lords could attest to this fact—if only they were able to speak, that is. He had amassed quite a collection of their extracted consciousnesses, utilizing the compression technique that the young master had so expertly developed for him.

Neuro-netsukes, that's what the old man jokingly called them. Brain bonsai! He had a dozen figurines on display inside a glass cabinet. Let's see, there was the traitor Ono, who had secretly conspired against him with the Fuji clan of Osaka. Then there were his other prize pieces—Shigehara, Tamba, and Ikeda. Had they not declared themselves against the House of Kobayashi? Now they all were part of his priceless netsuke collection. Who else in the world could boast of playing host to such handcrafted houseguests!

Each of his former enemies had been transformed into a singularly unique work of art. *Miniatures, befitting their new status,* the old man chuckled silently at the thought. Tamba was a wild boar; Ono, for his insolence, a rat; and that slippery Ikeda, a fish writhing in a net. . . .

Such exquisite detail! Such pathos! There was such life and movement to them. They ought to be grateful that they had been permitted to evolve into fine art from the scum they were!

The old man caught his breath. He watched as the young master performed each delicate movement in the ceremony with other-worldly grace. From the way he handled the glove, almost like a calligrapher with a brush, to the way he drew the meta-ROM bowl from the stand and held it with reverence.

It was an old Kyocera ceramic bowl bristling with

holotropian chips, brown, almost black in color. Except for the bowl and the tea caddy, which was a Hitachi vacuum bottle, each of the utensils was a functional hologram, from the teaspoon to the ladle. Even the boiling kettle was a high-density mirage. Priceless!

The master now took a ladleful of water and put it in the bowl. He washed the tea whisk and replaced the ladle on top of the kettle. He emptied the tea bowl. He wiped the bowl with a cloth swab. He placed the swab on the lid of the kettle.

Finally, the moment of truth had arrived. The master unscrewed the lid of the Hitachi vacuum and the green glow of the virus lit up the room.

Incredible. So this was it. The young man had transported it himself from the source. *The unreal made real,* the old man sighed, as he contemplated its radiance.

The young man took out three spoonfuls of the green pixels, placing the virus into the Kyocera bowl. He poured a ladle of hot water into the bowl and whisked the tea rapidly. Then he took the tea bowl in his left hand and presented it with his gloved right hand to the old man.

The old man rotated the tea bowl just so, held it up, and peered into it intently. Through the green haze, he saw the mountains and rivers of old Yamato. He saw the virtual reality factories of New Nippon, and the coded vision of its people. He saw their aspirations and their fears, their allegiances and their longings. He saw the long scroll of their births and the incense clouds that shrouded their deaths. He saw the skies above New Nippon, grey and blue and green, and the weather pattern moving obliquely over the islands as it dissipated above the Inland Sea.

He saw everything there was to see from the moment the islands knew creation until the green froth of the tea covered them up again in the impenetrable present.

Yes, it was the present that was always impenetrable. The old man had known that truth for a long time, and he would take it with him to his grave. The most impenetrable moment, indeed.

He almost sighed, but it would have been bad form in the

face of this great gift. He held the bowl to his face, inhaled the fragrance of the mountains and the rivers and the sea and the fields, then drank it all down noisily, slurping his appreciation.

Nothingness never tasted so full.

The young man bowed. It was a moment he would allow to pass without comment. The old man had swallowed New Nippon, down to its very essence. Let him enjoy his fleeting glory. The virus was everywhere anyway, and no one could stop it now, much less control it. He had not bothered to mention this fact to the old man. How could he possibly appreciate that he did not exist?

That he never *ever* existed in the first place? But let us return to this innocuous dualism for a moment, and to the burbling of the tea kettle.

Every single moment was linked to every other moment. There was no separating anything. Every fragment was attached to every other fragment. Time and space, life and death, it was all so ephemeral. Digitized nothingness.

Gatay gatay paragatay parasamgatay bodhi svaha. Gone, gone, gone beyond, gone beyond even the beyond into full enlightenment. . . .

The ceremony of virtual reality was only just beginning. So let it begin.

ARROYO

U.S.-Mexico Border, Spring, 2027

It was a broiling day; the blue sky shot through with hot, white light like a shot of mescal chasing the worm down the throat. The man with the silver face waited on the U.S. side of the Mexican border between Tijuana and San Ysidro. He wore a long tan suede coat and a pentium-studded rasta cap.

He didn't have too long to wait. He'd been watching the hillside for about twenty minutes through the form-finder. The chaparral on the Mexican side was teeming with chi energy waves. Now the first figure stepped out into the open, followed quickly by five forms.

The U.S. immigration officers in the jeep were parked below in the arroyo. Chi waves undulated like vapors of shimmering heat. The man checked the form-meter: 35 hertz. *Not bad.* He spit. *Vamonos, amigos. Time to get on. Hayaku.*

He rose from his squat, popped the form-finder into a pouch clipped onto his belt, then ambled down the arroyo toward the waiting INS officers. Sure enough, he heard the motor on their jeep start up, purring like a cat. When the illegals touched U.S. soil, the purr turned into a growl and the machine leaped out of the hidden hollow.

The six illegals did not seem concerned. They walked almost casually toward the INS jeep that was racing toward them kicking up a rooster tail of dust. They made no attempt to hide themselves or to flee. The jeep screeched to a halt, and its sharp metallic reverberation echoed across the arroyo. The illegals just stood there, waiting.

A few of them laid their bags on the ground as the two INS officers slowly got out of the jeep. The leader of the group waved a greeting to the officers. "Hola! Konichiwa!"

One of the officers turned around when he saw the man with the silver face step out from behind a giant cardon cactus. "*What the——*?" he began, but was cut short. His system crashed in mid-sentence. His partner noticed the intruder at the same instant. But his reading was equally slow in reaction time, thrown off by the sudden onset of shutdown.

The illegals remained motionless, frozen in their reflexes. They were accessing this new development on their own terms. A lot of good that would do them. The wave was irreversible for all except the one who held the chi-absorber.

Everything within a radius of fifty yards that did not match the preset parameters for chi-compatibility wonked out like a shorted fuse.

"Welcome to the Virtual States of America," the man with the silver face said, bending over the erased forms. "Sorry to bust up your party," he added under his breath as he scanned their inert CPU units. "Just a few minor formalities, then I'll let you go."

The download was quick with the anti-virus protocol buffering him. Just in case they were communicable. He double-checked the reading on the meter. The two bogus INS officials were definitely superior quality in every way except one. These new arrivals had an interface on their consciousness processor that he'd never seen before. That was interesting. But one of the illegals was special. Very special.

He turned to one of the forms lying on the ground and turned it over with his foot. He had the face of a young man, about twenty-three years old. Close-cropped chestnut hair, a smooth complexion, a look of innocence on his even features. The man with the silver face patted him down, and brought out a driver's holo.

He switched it on. The voiceprint stated his name: Thomas Ferris. Date of birth: June 2, 2005. Address: 1862 Hollyoake Drive, San Diego. Occupation: Nanopharmacist, Western Labs. His medical records showed his latest immunizations, the most recent ones being for agoraphobia, depression, gastritis, and fear of death.

The man with the silver face smirked. *Gone to a lot of trouble for a mannequin, hombre.* Still, he had to admire the depth of detail that went into the droid. It was a Kobayashi from the neuralworks in Todos Santos.

"Okay, Mr. Ferris, let's see if you got anything to declare."

With a quick slash of the knife, he removed the box from the neo-cortex at the back of the head. Still squatting in the dust, he studied the board for a few moments; his eyes lit up. "Right on, Tyrone!" he exclaimed with pleasure. "Domo arigato, Mr. Sato!"

He dropped the board into the pocket of his long coat. Then he took a hit from his snuffbox, snorted, spit noisily, and glanced at the other forms lying on the ground. *Might as well go for it,* he thought to himself. They were all older models, not in great demand, but who knows—they might bring in some extra pesos.

When he finished gutting them, he had all their neural boards. Then he walked away without a backward glance, the spurs jangling on his lizard-skin boots.

"Many lives, Arjuna, you and I have lived. I remember them all, but thou dost not."

—*The Bhagavad-Gita*

BARDO ONE

SHUTTLE

L.A. Metro-New Narita, 2027

As Frank Gobi rushed through L.A. Metroplex to catch his noon flight to New Narita, his mini-cam Ray-Bans quick'corded a scene outside the duty-free shop.

He was late for the flight and out of breath, but he turned his head instinctively to witness the exchange of corporate energies. Two American salarymen were bowing to each other.

"Johnson-san, have a safe trip," the taller one in the three-piece hakama suit was telling his colleague. "Domo arigato, Smith-san," his friend replied.

Judging from their Midwestern accents, the two men were from Chicago. It was a blink of an eye, but Gobi was sure the scene was a take. If it was, he might replay it during one of his lectures. If he ever taught again, that is.

Strange though, he'd have to review the clip when he had more time. Their bows were crisply executed from the waist down, just so. Their hands, palms open and pressed stiffly against the thighs, were a tad too mechanical. Was there a new conservatism in the wind?

For the past three years, Frank Gobi had been teaching a course in transcultural corporate anthropology and organizational shamanism at the University of California in Berkeley, Tokyo University extension.

His students enjoyed these real-life case studies of the new business culture that was emerging in the region. Under normal circumstances, he would have been busy mentally cross-indexing the clip for possible use in the next edition of his interactive textbook, *TransRim Customs 3.0*.

But right now, Gobi couldn't care less about any of that. Just this morning, he had received some great sequences of dream-simulations from a colleague of his who worked as a trancetherapist in Johore Bahru in Malaysia. Fabulous stuff with all kinds of implications for the etheric body. But his spirit—his shen—just wouldn't rise to the occasion. Who could blame him?

He still saw his son's face on the chi box. They had projected Trevor's consciousness to him. He must be awake now and playing. What time was it for the boy? How could he know the difference between being cut off and being in two places at the same time?

For Trevor, it probably was an extended vacation. Like all ten-year-olds, he was thrilled to be in Gametime without any interruptions except for sleep. He even played in his dreams. There were dark rings under his eyes.

Gobi saw his son's mop of blond hair, razor-cut like a choirboy's, his blue eyes lighting up.

"Hi, Dad! I know you're probably really worried about me, but don't be. I'm fine. I know I can't get back to you right now. But it's okay, I'll come home soon. I promise. There're just a few more levels I need to complete before I can get out of here. You won't believe this game, Dad! There're all these weird things that come at you. Demons, zombies, gdons, ogres, all kinds of hungry ghosts. . . . It's like nothing else you've ever seen! Oops! I gotta go now! This is costing me!" He smiled wanly. *"You owe me a couple of thunderbolts, Dad! I love ya! 'Bye now! I'm outta here!"*

Trevor was his only child. Gobi was divorced and his ex-wife was a full-time artist who lived and painted in her studio in the Santa Cruz Mountains. So he was Mother Dad—or Daddy Goddess, as his ex jokingly referred to him. Trevor lived with him full-time. Until now.

Now he was living on-line at the Alta Bates Adolescent Virtual Reality Unit.

A voice interrupted his thoughts. "Dr. Gobi? This way, please." A Satori Airlines flight manager stepped forward to greet him as he reached the departure desk. She gave him a tight smile. It was polite, but tinged with obvious relief that he had finally arrived.

Her nameplate read *Claudia Kato*. She was a young, attractive, black-haired Japanese-American, dressed in a green latex kimono with the Satori logo stamped on the sleeves.

Gobi allowed himself to relax for the first time that morning. He'd made it. Everything would work itself out. He had to have faith. This was a test. What else could it be? Grief was like a laxative for the soul. He grinned at his own bad humor. Bad humor was good therapy sometimes.

"Sorry I'm late," Gobi apologized, as they walked briskly toward the boarding area for the spaceplane. "I had a bad connection from San Francisco."

They stepped through the swinging doors of the security corridor. "We have a few minutes before takeoff actually, so everything is fine," Claudia Kato said, as she eyed him curiously. She had expected a much older man. She didn't know many scholars in her line of work.

"Our in-flight artist on the Live Entertainment Channel only arrived a few minutes ago himself. He got caught in traffic," she said, making an attempt at light conversation. "They say this Butoh is very, very fine. He's a third-generation Living Treasure from Seattle."

"I look forward to his performance," Gobi bowed, as he handed her his passport. They were standing at the entrance to the spacewalk. The spidery vibrations faintly rattled the platform as the engines began to warm up the bioskins of the spaceplane.

Claudia slid the blue card through the optosensor and returned it to him after it beeped its approval.

His holo-foto materialized briefly. His eyes registered as red pinpricks on the air screen, identification positive. They did not reveal his pain.

Not quite done with the official check-in procedure, Claudia Kato gave Gobi a secondary scan. Her eyes moved over his body professionally, pausing occasionally to check certain points.

It was a low-level scan, Gobi judged, as he felt her tuning in to him. Very basic. He taught much deeper techniques to his freshmen students at Berkeley.

Still, it was an interesting sensation. She had a nice touch, almost like she was breathing gently on him from the inside. He allowed himself to enjoy the feeling of being processed by an attractive woman.

Gobi relaxed all his muscles as she deepened her probe.

She's archiving me, he thought, as he went with the flow; Dr. Frank Gobi, white male, mid-thirties, 165 pounds, trim and muscular, with close-cropped brown hair that was short but curly. He had an aquiline nose that gave him a profile like a Roman emperor on a coin, but without the haughtiness. Grey eyes that were dreamy, yet alert. Lips that were full and sensual. Smile wrinkles around the mouth indicating an open nature. Lines that were pulled down now by the gravity of a heavy heart.

Claudia paused, then continued with her routine face reading. The subject had a finely chiseled chin that tapered into a dimple, indicating willfulness, stubbornness, opposition to authority.

There was that teasing smile of his again. She smiled back and found that his energy soothed her in a certain way. It made her feel relaxed.

She studied him again. This was on her own time. Definitely an attractive man. Oops, she was responding to him sexually. *Better stick to the task at hand,* she frowned inwardly at herself, then continued with the official procedure.

Since she had joined Satori Airlines six months ago, Claudia had taken an airline security program to develop various body-centered psycho-sensitive skills. She had learned to frisk bioenergy fields. It was an accredited class designed by the Dale Carnegie School of Light Body Reading.

She now proceeded to read Gobi's hara. Going down the checklist, she found that the vital center located in the lower center of his torso was in balance with his physical, mental, and emotional energies.

For a few moments their focus merged. It was almost like . . . well, a cool fire that coursed through her body until it formed a warm energy pool in her own emotional center, on the fourth meridian level of the body's seven major energy centers.

Gobi realized, of course, that she was digging into all his personal—and even intimate—levels. He enjoyed it even though he knew it was a legal requirement of the Federal Aviation Administration. The way he felt, it was a welcome diversion.

"You're cleared, Dr. Gobi," she said, as she returned the passport to him with a smile.

"Anytime," he smiled back at her. "You've got a nice touch," he complimented her. "Very delicate."

She blushed. "Would you prefer the vegetarian or non-vegetarian section today?"

Food was definitely a second meridian issue as far as he was concerned. He had no appetite. But it was a three-hour flight to Neo-Tokyo and he would need all his strength when he got there.

"What are you serving in the V-section today?" he asked, still aroused by their accidental brush of energies.

"Let's see," she recited matter-of-factly, trying to recover her composure. "We're serving shiitake pizza, a Shogun salad with blue-green algae dressing . . . and complimentary Domain Suntory champagne."

"V-section is fine."

"Very good. By the way, sir," she paused, as her tone suddenly became grave. "Have you brought your PVI kit with you? It's a requirement for all passengers traveling to New Nippon—as I'm sure you're aware."

"Of course," he replied. His Psycho-Viral Immunization kit was in his briefcase. He snapped open the case and handed her the sealed kit.

"FAA regulations require us to run your kit through our preflight tester to make sure all the seals are intact," she intoned, popping the cannister into a pneumatic tube to be examined.

There was one last bit of business to run through—the most unnerving part of the check-in procedure for most passengers. It still gave Claudia a chill, no matter how standard or routine it had become in the twelve months since the Mega-Quake had struck New Nippon.

"As a passenger on Satori Airlines Flight 129," she said, reciting the preamble to the flight agreement, "you hereby agree to waive any and all personal liabilities against Satori Airlines for any potential neural, psychological, or physical damage that you might incur before or after disembarking at your final destination, New Narita International Airport, in New Nippon."

Gobi looked straight into the notary vidcam that automatically registered the scene. "Affirmative," he answered softly and turned away.

What rights did he have now anyway? The rights of the damned? Did ghosts have rights? Did Trevor have any rights? A heavy dark cloud settled on his heart. Did his own *heart* have rights?

"Your PVI case will be returned to you right after takeoff," she informed him after the lab light flashed its clearance. "I'll be your flight manager during the trip," she added.

"You'll need to take your vaccine an hour prior to landing in New Narita. I'll make a special announcement to remind all passengers to self-immunize at the appropriate time," she told him.

She handed him a boarding pass with a gold Satori emblem

embossed on the black lacquer strip. "Here you are, Dr. Gobi," she said, in a purposefully cheery voice now that the ordeal was over. "You're in Chrysanthemum Class, seat 6-A. If there's anything I can do to make your flight more comfortable, please don't hesitate to ask. I hope you enjoy your flight."

"Thank you," he said. But his words came out sounding hollow.

Trevor had been watching the news on the cube when the first reports of the 'Quake filtered in.

"Dad, they say it's like what happened to the dinosaurs millions of years ago." There was a worried expression on his pale, studious face. "Are we going to disappear too?"

"Nothing's going to happen," Gobi had said. "It's just a big cloud, that's all. When it lifts, we'll be able to see everything much more clearly. Everything's going to be all right. Don't you worry, kid."

But the cloud hadn't lifted for days. And when it finally did, there was a swath of radiant lights above New Nippon that had blinded all the sats. The communications links between the island nation and the rest of the world had been cut off without warning.

Gobi still shuddered inside when he thought about the weeks that followed. The scientists and seismo-psychologists of the Task Force were trying to piece together exactly what might have happened.

The early reports weren't helpful beyond supplying the sketchiest of details. Certainly, on one tangible and measurable level, the 'Quake had registered 11.2 on the Richter scale. But what that meant precisely, no one had any idea. It was like an invisible 11.2. You felt it, but it never revealed itself.

After putting Trevor to bed, Gobi stayed up till the early hours of the morning, glued to the set. Red-eyed, he watched as Bryan Ishimoto reported for PacRim 2 News from the Russian port of Vladivostok on the Sea of Japan. Vladivostok was the temporary headquarters for the emergency relief efforts being organized by the New U.N.

Ishimoto's hair blew against a laser-lit backdrop of the stormy sea. Snippets of agitated Russian, Japanese, and English were heard off-camera as the TV newsman gestured toward the dark expanse of water with the whitecaps of waves catching the reflection of the news crew's lightwebs.

"This is all we can tell you with any degree of certainty so far," Ishimoto announced in somber tones. "Seismologists are already referring to this event as the 'Mega-Quake of the Millennium.' The last catastrophic earthquake in New Nippon occurred almost a hundred years ago, back in 1923, with more than 100,000 deaths recorded. But this new 'Quake is . . . well, they're not commenting officially, but off-the-record, they're using terms like 'humanly incomprehensible' and 'the ultimate disaster' to describe what's happened."

Ishimoto's face was haggard as he glanced at his notes. "There's no mystery about the sequence of events that triggered the 'Quake. As you can see on your screen sim, the Philippine Sea plate slipped under the Eurasian Continental plate right here, exactly as predicted by New Nippon's network of seismo-sensors. Then it dragged the edge of this plate downward; and with a ferocity never known in the recorded history of earthquakes, forced it all back *upward.* . . ."

The newsman paused to blink his wide eyes. "Please bear with me," he pleaded to his viewers. "What we do *not* know at this time is the answer to the question: *What has happened to the world's most powerful city?* How could it have possibly *disappeared* from the face of the earth? So far, none of our satellites have managed to pick up any scenes of Neo-Tokyo, much less reveal to us the extent of the devastation in the Japanese capital."

Ishimoto paused again and cleared his throat. There was an agonized expression on his face.

"There is no other way to put it: *Neo-Tokyo is missing.* If that sounds crazy, it is." He shivered. "Beyond any doubt, this is the biggest mystery in the history of the world. Now stay tuned for the latest breaking reports coming your way on PacRim 2. This is Bryan Ishimoto, reporting to you live from

Vladivostok, headquarters of the International Earthquake Relief Effort for New Nippon."

Gobi flipped to another station. A New Age telechanneler was interviewing various Ascended Masters about the metaphysical significance of the Mega-Quake. The two guests, channelers for St. Germain and The Coming Buddha Maitreya, appeared to have different opinions on the matter.

Benjamin Dream, a solemn, white-haired Briton, cited the 'Quake as further evidence of the emergence of the Christ, who was reputed to be an unidentified Pakistani immigrant residing in the East End of London. "The Master Maitreya will make his first public appearance as soon as he receives an invitation from the world media. He shall reveal his True Light at that time."

Anna Seacliffe, a middle-aged channeler for St. Germain, leaned toward the view that the Japanese people had made a collective pact to withdraw from the outside world in order to work out their unresolved race issues.

"It's sort of a karmic housecleaning . . ." the small, dark-haired woman said, knitting her brows in concentration. She fingered a crystal pendant hung around her neck. "My dear children—for you *are* my children—do not lose faith."

Gobi killed the talk show and skipped back to the first cube report. He dove deeper into the satellite still life, trying to dig for further information about the disaster.

It was 11:59 A.M. on Wednesday, September 2. The AsiaSat meteorological report had indicated blue skies, no clouds, a sizzling thirty degrees in downtown Tokyo. The GNP was $730 billion; the Nikkei Index hovered at 60,000 points. Kyocera's new bio-plastics were the hot new growth stock. Emperor Naruhito was receiving the newly enthroned Russian Tsar, Nicholas III, at the Imperial Palace. The keiretsu mega-towers in the Marunouchi business district were humming with the usual activity. The Underground City, thirty labyrinthine stories beneath Tokyo Bay, was packed with a lunchtime crowd of 140,000 people.

Then, in a series of sudden crunching snaps and jolts, the history of the world was changed forever.

Especially when Neo-Tokyo reappeared three weeks later without showing any visible signs of damage.

No, those poor souls never knew what hit them, Gobi thought, as he entered the dim halogen-lit cabin on the Chrysanthemum deck of Satori Air's MLS-400 spaceplane.

The tilt-rotors were vibrating as he made his way to his seat. The craft would be lifting off any second now.

Gobi nodded an apologetic greeting to the passengers seated around him. Their faces, half-hidden in shadow, studied him without betraying any hint of curiosity. His arrival had done little to buoy their spirits, despite the chakra snacks and mood drinks they'd been served while waiting for him to board.

He looked around, admiring the peaceful decor. The beige carpet of the interior resembled the raked sand at the famous Ryoanji temple in Kyoto, its pattern of waves rippling around the bases of the heavy black leather swivel chairs.

At the head of the cabin was a blue neon Hokusai wave, which hovered like a woodblock hologram; it bore a message: *"Please fasten your seat belts. No negative thoughts please. Countdown to Liftoff: 02:32."*

Gratefully, he sank into the deep well of the chair and fastened his seat belt. Another three hours and he would be landing at New Narita.

What would it be like to interact with the Japanese he met in New Nippon? He'd have to relate to them on a different level, that's for sure. Certain topics were taboo, according to the travel advisories. Topics such as the 'Quake.

"Remember, you are exchanging business cards, not paradigms," the introduction of *The Business Person's Guide to Neo-Tokyo* proclaimed. Gobi found a copy of the booklet inserted in his seat pocket and flipped through the pages. It had been published by the New Nippon Chamber of Commerce for Satori Airlines, he noticed.

"Etiquette is no longer just a social or a cultural consideration; it is ecological and psychological as well," Gobi read.

"Please do not discuss the Great Earthquake of '26 with your Japanese hosts, or for that matter with any Japanese nationals you may meet during your trip."

What these handy little "official guidebooks" failed to mention was that a collective amnesia blanketed the consciousness of the entire Japanese people like ash from a volcano.

Western psychologists attributed this reaction to "a consensual hallucination on a mass scale—a collective psychosis," as Dr. Henry Bollington of the Harvard Medical School declared in the *Journal of Near Death Studies and Extrasensory Trauma*. Gobi had a copy of the article downloaded in his Ray-Bans. It was an interesting theory. But he wasn't so sure about it.

All this theorizing did precious little to explain anything, in Gobi's opinion, except perhaps the scientific establishment's reluctance to consider any viable alternative explanations. More than anything, how could modern-day science explain the actual *physical* transformation of the Japanese megapolis?

Those 300-story towers that hugged the New Nippon stratosphere were living ferroceramic colossi by day, but by night . . . Good God! There was not a sign of them anywhere. They dropped entirely from view, as though temporarily separated from the rest of the material world. Twelve hours later, they reappeared again, no worse for wear, as though they were pachinko balls that tinkled into being, like value-added nothingness redeemed each day at the shop counter for the modest prize of consciousness. Each day the game was repeated, and the player flipped the balls once more through the thicket of pins on the glowering face of the machine.

Gobi flicked on the mini-video deck on the armrest to watch the liftoff as the MLS-400 hovered above the tarmac. The picture of the dancing rotors looked like crazy brush strokes on rice paper.

As the image of those vibrations reached his body, he felt a sudden swift pressure in the pit of his stomach—the kind of feeling you got when you took a speedvator to the top of Azabu Century City Tower, high above the smog bank of the L.A. Metroplex.

Suddenly there was grey rain pelting his oval passenger window. A few moments of grey waves visible below in the rain, with a skeletal torso of a Hyundai mega-container ship heading for Long Beach, followed by a *whoosh!*—like a cold breath—which made the halogen beads flicker in the cabin.

Lulled by the spaceplane's vibrations, Gobi entered into a reflective trance as he focused on the diamond trail of a raindrop that splattered against the window. It hadn't been all that long ago. But then that's what they said about eternity. . . .

CLOUD HANDS

The light in the Berkeley dojo was an even off-white.

The students were finishing off their vai-chi exercises, their movements graceful and fluid despite the encumbrance of their goggles and the V-bands on their arms. Master Yang monitored each student individually. He appraised their form as they followed through with fluid motions. Gobi was doing Cloud Hands.

"Move slowly, breathe in time with the gentle breeze, merge with Nature in a healing rhythm," Master Yang encouraged him in his ear. "Head, shoulders, arms, trunk, legs, and feet moving as one, continuously, smoothly and restfully, as if you are swimming into a new and all-encompassing element, into a different time, a different space. . . ."

Gobi was in the Yang family compound in Shanghai with its crimson pillars and slate tiles, the sun beaming down on him as the children's dragon kites bobbed and weaved high in the sky. Master Yang stepped forward to correct him. It felt like the sifu had actually >touched< him. He corrected the angle of Gobi's arms and hands as he moved the cloud circles across his throat and lower abdomen.

"That's much better, my son," Master Yang said, smiling

through his sparse white beard as he stepped back in his black gauze-silk robe. "You're showing great improvement."

Gobi wound up his final moves and peeked at the time at the bottom of his left goggle. 1:58 P.M. In virtual time, it was approaching the Hour of the Tiger. They were in Shanghai in the year 1932, in the last years of the legendary Tai-Chi Master Yang Cheng-fu's life. No greater teacher ever lived.

Class was now over. Gobi bowed to the VR image of the sifu with his fists clasped against his chest, then pulled the headset off before the production credits began to roll.

The other students doffed their headgear and suddenly the group was transported back from Shanghai to Berkeley at the vai-chi dojo in the year 2027. Eyes still blinking, Gobi recognized the short tubby man with the salt-flecked brown beard who lumbered toward him. It was Hans Ulbricht, a friend of his who was a new physicist at the Lawrence Livermore lab.

"Ah, Frank, how are you?" the scientist asked, grinning affably. "I'm afraid I still can't get those clouds right. And the Golden Rooster Stands on One Leg, forget it! I'm never going to stand on one leg. You had lunch yet? Tell you the truth, I'm starving! Melissa's got me on a diet again. Care to join me for some dim sum? I know it's late, but I've got some time before my next class."

Frank Gobi smiled. He liked Hans. He liked his earthy humor and his ability to see the big picture even when it threatened to come down on his head. Hans believed in change, and if change didn't come, well, he'd see about that in his lab. He'd gone beyond most of his fellow scientists, who were still writing new fractals to describe the post-string theory of matter. Hans was definitely a mind-over-atom man.

"I'll nibble just to keep you company," Gobi grinned, as they fell into step together.

"Good, good," Hans said, gruffly expressing his approval. He glanced at his friend. "You are well? And Trevor, how's the boy?"

"Fine," Gobi answered. "We're all fine as can be, I guess. It's a fuzzy world."

"Ja," Hans grunted. "That it is. Who knows how to make sense of it?" He shook his head. "The more we learn about it, instead of becoming smarter we just become more confused."

They walked in silence from the campus dojo to Telegraph Avenue. Gobi pushed his bicycle along till they reached the Great Shanghai Iron and Steelworks restaurant, which served vegetarian dim sum. It was a favorite campus hangout.

"Ja," Hans said, as he poured some jasmine tea into Gobi's cup. "First, we have Neo-Tokyo, now this."

He nodded at the wall-cube, which was recapping the latest news about the Channel Emmanuel incident, now being called the world's first on-line virtual reality disaster.

Gobi glanced at the cube. He'd seen the clips last night and again this morning, and he had brooded over them. He saw the now familiar face of Patrick Bruce, with his blond dread 'trodes ablaze, intoning a Rasta Navaho prayer as he led his followers into the River Jordan. Patrick Bruce was considered by many to be the "Pope of VR," the title coined for him by *Popular Karma* magazine. An estimated 80,000 'trode-heads had followed him to Zion in the highest-rated tele-dunking ever. It was a mass immersion in the True Light.

"All is beautiful behind me, All is beautiful before me, All is beautiful below me, All is beautiful above me, All is beautiful all around me, For I-and-I have been found and everything is beautiful," Bruce chanted at the opening of the on-line VR baptism the night before.

By evening's end, 193 people across the country had died in freak accidents. Some had been electrocuted, while others had wound the 'trodes around their necks and accidentally strangled themselves in fits of ecstasy. Additionally, there were eighty-seven reported brain-deads whose systems had disconnected from Channel Emmanuel, and whose consciousnesses were lost in mainframe file-servers in Salt Lake City, Minneapolis, and Albuquerque.

After the sect's Angel Gabriel search program failed to locate the lost minds in any of the known nodes, Patrick Bruce declared that they had been embraced by Jah and were resting in the bosom of Marley.

Hans shook his head sadly. "What a tragedy. Still." He sighed, "It was like an accident waiting to happen. It's nothing though, compared to Neo-Tokyo. Now that, my friend, is a more dangerous situation than anything you can possibly imagine."

"How do you figure?" Gobi asked, as Hans took a bite of a mushroom shu-mai dipped in soy sauce.

"Urban dematerialization, my boy, that's the defining phenomenon of our times. Now Channel Emmanuel, this is a regrettable aberration. Neural technology gone awry. But an entire city that disappears for a twelve-hour period each day of the week?"

"What do you think is happening over there, Hans?" Gobi asked quietly, setting down his chopsticks. He fought a feeling of helplessness. If he didn't watch out, he could easily become depressed. There was a lot of that going around. The "Neo-Tokyo Flu," as it was called by the media. Maybe it was time to get another booster shot.

"Don't ask me where Neo-Tokyo goes, okay?" Hans gestured. "Shopping. To the movies. It takes a vacation. I don't know. I don't care. The point is, it vanishes from 7:00 P.M. to about 7:00 A.M. So what else is new?" He shrugged.

"How can you be sure that Neo-Tokyo actually disappears *anywhere?*" Gobi pressed. There, he had gotten that brooding feeling off his chest. "What if it's *us,* not *them,* that's doing the disappearing act?"

"Frank, Frank." Hans patted Gobi's hand patiently, a sliver of Tomales Bay fungus caught between his teeth. "Don't play armchair shaman, okay? Just listen to the facts. What's being affected here is not just physical space, that's obvious. It's about time, too. None of our infrared probes can penetrate Neo-Tokyo during the witching hour. But what we have been able to measure is the exact moment—the precise *nano-nanosecond*—when the city deconstructs and when it reappears twelve hours later."

"What does *that* mean?"

Hans collected his thoughts, then continued. "All that our fancy-schmancy instruments in the sky above New Nippon can tell us with any degree of reliability is that there is a gradual signal transduction of frequencies moving from their lowest to their highest potential."

"Which means *what* exactly? In fortune-cookie language, please."

Hans blinked at Gobi for a moment. "It means just this." He wrinkled his brow. "According to the data we're receiving, it appears that Neo-Tokyo is undergoing a state of flux on an atomic and subcellular level, perhaps as a result of being triggered by the earthquake. We don't know *why.* That is the big mystery, ja? The city is in what you would call a state of accelerated transformation into another energy matrix. Using the Pribram model. . . ."

"Karl Pribram? The brain as hologram?"

Hans leaned over and pinched Gobi's cheek with affection. "You *do* have some modicum of awareness left, after all. Ja, Karl Pribram, a mere neurosurgeon from Stanford, who picked up where Einstein's relativity left off."

Hans cleared his throat and began to recite: "*'Our brains mathematically construct concrete reality by interpreting frequencies from another dimension . . . '*"

"*'. . . A realm of meaningful, patterned primary reality that transcends time and space,'*" Gobi interrupted Hans to complete the famous theorem that everyone learned at school.

"Famous last words, no?" Hans laughed. "Especially when you think about our concepts of reality today, hmm? Look where they've gotten us. Some taro root?"

"The brain is a hologram interpreting a holographic universe," Gobi mused out loud.

"Genius, wasn't he? Isn't it?" Hans said approvingly, wiping his broad ruddy face and beard with a steaming towel.

"So where does that leave *time* then?" Gobi challenged his friend.

"Exactly. Where does that leave time?" Hans replied, as he pulled his timepiece from his vest pocket and studied it. "I have to be back in class in twenty minutes, for one thing. How about you?"

Gobi sighed. Both men felt the strangeness that underlay their conversation. Sharing the moment, they were aware that such strangeness was not out of place. It was becoming the status quo, the unknown making itself known in their lives.

"Strange," Gobi said out loud, as Hans read his mind and grinned. He nodded enthusiastically.

"Yes, time is just *another* illusion, my friend. Did you know there's a primitive tribe in Papua New Guinea—they've only just discovered credit chips—that believes the universe actually ended *millions* of years ago. All this," Hans gestured around the room vaguely, "is simply the fallout, the dust settling down *after* the Apocalypse."

He leaned toward Gobi conspiratorially. "Tell me something, Frank. You can tell me honestly. You're a big-shot specialist in dreamtime technologies. Maybe time *doesn't* exist—or, alternatively, it *does* exist, but it exists *simultaneously,* that is to say: past, present, and future, all at the same time, are just laid out on separate tracks. Then maybe Neo-Tokyo is skipping from Track 1 to Track 100, or to some other place that we don't even know about. . . ."

Gobi asked his friend gently, "What are you suggesting, Hans?"

Hans gave him a sly wink. "Do you believe in reincarnation? Tell me truly."

Gobi evaded the question. "I don't know. But I definitely believe in *weird* incarnation. Like yours, for example!" He laughed.

"Isn't that what you've been working on these days—reincarnation? Huh?"

Frank Gobi looked up at him without replying.

"Word gets around, Frank," Hans said, crumpling his napkin on the table and leaning back in his seat.

"I'm not sure what you're referring to," Gobi answered cautiously.

"It's OK if you don't want to talk about it." Hans grinned

at him again. "Melissa says you've been spending a lot of time at the Arboretum."

Gobi's eyes flickered imperceptibly, but his face remained blank.

"I don't mean to rock your boat," Hans prodded him. "Melissa's on the board of directors. She's my *wife*, Frank, she *confides* in me."

Hans' face suddenly reddened with embarrassment. "Ach, I'm sorry. I didn't mean to pry. I should have known better. You're not in a position to discuss your work. Of course not. Forget I ever mentioned this to you, OK?"

"Not to worry, Hans, there's really nothing to discuss." Gobi shook his head. "Honest. And you can tell that to Melissa."

"Ja," Hans said sourly, as he rose to go. "Sure, I'll tell her."

Outside on Telegraph Avenue where Hans and Gobi parted company, university students swam the sidewalks like tadpoles and the birds in the leafy, green trees were uncharacteristically silent.

Gobi watched the scene for a moment. He felt the strangeness still within him. He hurried down the street to where his bicycle was chained outside Moe's Bookstore. The feeling followed him like an invisible shadow.

BICYCLE KARMA

Gobi felt the wind in his hair as he bicycled across campus, carefully navigating around students who meandered on the path. *Channel Emmanuel, Neo-Tokyo, wherever the next twist in the spiral led to . . . the world would always continue. At least it did in one form or another. Didn't it?*

Meanwhile, the sunshine was warm, drowsy golden; students gathered in the plaza tossed solar frisbees, watching them glide in the lubricated air. A mood of lazy innocence took over as the late Indian summer afternoon wound down.

How much could Melissa possibly know? Gobi puzzled over the question as he whizzed past the Student Union building. He was sure he had been careful, but then again maybe he hadn't covered *all* his tracks.

Let's see, she had to be aware that for the past couple of years he'd been volunteering at the Arboretum of Light, a fifty-acre hospice located on the rugged Pacific coast north of San Francisco. She was on the administrative board. She saw him there all the time. She read the staff reports.

A couple of weekends a month, Gobi would offer terminally ill patients therapy sessions in neurolinguistic shiatsu bodywork. He had developed a technique fo clearing up energy centers in the body in preparation for the death experience. "You've got to unclog those chakras so your life energy gets to flow as smoothly as possible without getting you stuck in any past conditionings," he joked. "That's why you called me, right? I'm the Roto-Rooter man of the soul."

He also led a series of Clear Light workshops aimed at strengthening higher consciousness and self-awareness so that the dying person could remain as alert as possible at the exact moment of death. It was a yoga for the dying. And if someone requested his presence when the time came, he acted as a kind of midwife to assist them during their passage from this life to the next.

But none of the staff at the Arboretum realized that Gobi's work didn't stop there. He went a little further than anyone would have imagined. Sometimes he even crossed the line, like a neutral observer on the other side. And sometimes he even did reconnaissance work—what he referred to as "consciousness navigation."

It was a process he would never dare to reveal to anyone, much less to Melissa, for whom gossiping was a holistic art form.

Hacking the soul. That wouldn't exactly be considered spiritually correct by the transpersonal medical community, now would it? Was it karmically okay to be a voyeur of the transmigration of the soul? To be a witness of the *actual* process of spiritual evolution?

He could already hear the public outcry if his secret ever got out. *"Dr. Frankenstein, I presume . . . ?"* The mob would then ransack his laboratory, no doubt.

They might even discover some of the specimens of consciousness he had filed away!

Gobi had managed to download bits of flickering astral images: some beautiful, some terrifying. *That lovely girl, for instance. The one who died recently. What was her name? Ingrid. Her frail body had been eaten away by cancer, and she had lain wrapped in foul-smelling bandages. She had been so beautiful, so young! Then her own body cannibalized itself beyond recognition.*

But as soon as she passed beyond the seventh gate, as soon as her light slipped through the keyhole of the thousand-petaled crown of the Sahasrara channel, Gobi saw her rise like a beautiful dancer reveling in her inner nakedness.

Her breasts were now full and voluptuous, her eyes shone with a tender passionate gleam, and her golden hair flowed down her back as she made love to all the turned-on angels who flocked to her. She wore them out!

Gobi had used an entire roll to record the joy of her liberation. It was all on samskaric "film," of course. Those mental impulses left faint impressions on the primal negative, and he worked painstakingly to capture the dream.

Because, of course, it was only a dream. Once the soul of the deceased realized the truth behind the illusion—however horrific or beatific it might be—it moved on to its next stage without looking back. The movie was over when the credits of the past life ran out at the end of the reel.

Oh, yes, they'd crucify him for sure if they ever found out what he was up to! But one day—not yet, not yet, the time was not right—his contributions would be appreciated. Until then, he would have to continue to work clandestinely. Yet another pioneer who was ahead of his time, laboring in an unrecognized field. Just an anthropologist doing fieldwork in the afterlife.

No, Melissa was definitely not aware of the full extent of his research.

A thought suddenly hit him.

That didn't mean that someone who was a sensitive might not have picked up on it. Especially if they'd been anywhere on the premises when he was "traveling" with his clients. God knows, there were enough different workshops happening all the time at the Arboretum. But they'd have to be good— really good—to detect him.

He frowned.

Who?

TARA

Damn! He swerved to avoid a 'trode-head who appeared out of nowhere, following behind his guide dog. Gobi thought of them as guide dogs for the perplexed. Technically speaking, these guys weren't even legally blind.

They suffered from VR dyslexia—a form of extreme hand-eye disorientation resulting from excessive virtual tripping. They couldn't do simple things like tie their own shoelaces or place one foot ahead of the other. They had to wear corrective head braces and rely on guide dogs to get around.

Who-a-a-a-a-a-a-www!!! Ya-a-a-a-a-a-a-a-a-a-a-a!!!

His bike twisted sideways and hit a bump. Gobi lifted off the handlebars like an acrobat about to tumble across the stage. Up he went; everything hung upside down, then *whump!*

Gobi landed on his back and found himself staring up into the blue sky as faces circled around, a moving mandala of eyes, noses, eyelashes, mouths, and chins.

There was perfect stillness and silence for a moment, perfect equilibrium. He never wanted to move again. Nor was he certain he would be able to. He somehow couldn't connect his thoughts to the rest of his body. Get up! No such luck. Panic swept over him. Had he broken his back?

"Move aside, please, give him some air! I'm a doctor!" demanded an authoritative voice. The crowd stepped back instinctively.

Then she appeared. Green eyes framed by a waterfall of honey-golden hair. There was an alert expression on her face. She was bending over him and he could smell the sweet peach scent of her skin and feel her warm breath on his face. She wore a grey Tibetan jacket with rose-colored Vajrayana-style thunderbolts on its sleeves, and baggy Afghani guerrilla pants.

He felt her soft hand on his forehead. God, she was gifted! A warm, penetrating energy flowed down his neck, into his shoulders, and down his back. The pain and buzzing in his head began to drain away. She studied him closely, her look of concern changing to a confident smile.

"I think you'll live," she said, making a quick pass over his body with both hands, as if she were changing the sheets on a hospital bed. "Your skull is still in one piece and your internal organs don't seem to be damaged. That was quite a landing you made. I'm impressed!"

He still didn't want to get up. He wanted to remain here, beneath her goddess form with its wonderful healing properties. More than anything, he wanted to rest undisturbed beneath the gaze of those magnetic green eyes.

"Have we met before?" He managed a weak grin, marveling that he was now able to clearly express his thoughts again. "A past life somewhere?"

She laughed for the first time, and he wanted to record it in his memory forever. It was a golden, husky laugh with the timbre of sunlit pastures in the Sierras.

"No, I don't think so," she said. "Not that I can recall anyway. Can you sit up? Try."

"All right, but—what happened?"

"You didn't want to hit the dog," she replayed the incident to him as she helped him reach a sitting position with a single powerful pull of her hand. "But I don't think it would have bothered you to run over that student," she chuckled.

"Ow!" he groaned, as he felt his head. "You're right about that. Those 'trode-burners are a menace to traffic. Not to mention to themselves."

"I know what you mean," she said, offering him her hand

to shake. After working on him, her palm fairly sizzled with heat. "Hi, I'm Tara. Tara Evans."

"I'm Frank—" he began to introduce himself. "Frank—"

"I know who *you* are," she said. "You're Frank Gobi."

"That's right," he said, wondering. "Have we met? I thought—"

"You said past life," she interrupted him. "I don't know about that part. But I've attended a few of your lectures. You're very good. I like your work. I think you're on to something."

"Thanks," Gobi gasped as he attempted to stand.

"Here, let me help you. You took a nasty fall." Her grip was just what he needed to straighten himself. He braced against her for a few extra seconds, feeling the tautness of her waist until she swiveled away.

"I think you can manage on your own now," Tara smiled. "Go ahead, try taking a few steps."

He glanced down at the bicycle. Its front wheel was twisted. "I'm going to have to push this thing home," he said, lifting the frame off the ground.

"Do you have far to go?" she asked.

Gobi scrutinized her again, this time from a more objective upright position. She looked even more beautiful now that he could see her entire form. The baggy trousers and loose jacket only emphasized the gentle swell of her chest and the curve of her slender hips.

Tara Evans looked to be about twenty-eight. She was of medium height, and her long nose with its flared nostrils was in perfect proportion to her high cheekbones. Her lips were full and sensuous, her eyes an electrifying green set against translucent white skin. She had the sinuous build of an Indian dancer.

Gobi blinked. He had to glance at her again to make sure. Was it an optical illusion? One instant her face looked almost Nordic, but the next moment her complexion seemed much darker, almost African American or even South Asian. Whatever it was, he had never seen skin like hers. The pigmentation shifted quicker than the eye could see. Had he rattled something loose in his head?

"I said, do you have far to go?"

Tara casually acknowledged his male scan without any sign of self-consciousness, as though she didn't put much stock in it. Which meant that she either didn't take his interest in her seriously, or that she took it for granted. If she only lit up just a little, he thought, that would be nice!

"Um, let's see now," Gobi said, looking around. "How about as far as that cafe over there? Listen, you saved me from a concussion and probably much worse. I owe you a drink for your trouble at the very least. No, I insist. A cup of tea? Coffee?"

"I'm afraid you're exaggerating, Dr. Gobi," she smiled, revealing even white teeth. "You don't do *that* in your *work*, do you?"

"Please don't call me *doctor,*" he pleaded. "It makes me feel like I'm grading optical chips."

She laughed. "All right, I won't. If you call me Tara."

"But I do recall your saying that *you* were a doctor." he told her. "Whatever you did, it really helped. I mean that sincerely. I feel much better. Thanks."

"Thank you," she said. "Actually, I'm a doctor of chi kung and I also practice herbal medicine."

"A healer," he said.

"In a way. Mostly I help people to heal themselves. You're doing all right, I think. And I really ought to get going."

"No, please, don't go yet," he urged her. "I'm still a bit dizzy, to tell you the truth."

She tuned in to him now. It felt like a soft orgone current traveling across the two or three feet of space between them. It made him buzz inside.

"I'm supposed to meet somebody, but he's late," she told him. "All right, if you like. Let's go."

They walked toward an outdoor cafe where dogs patiently waited—as regal as statesmen and poets—beneath the tables while their human counterparts cavorted in the pleasure of the sun, sipping honey teas and algae cappuccinos.

● ● ●

They both drank bottled spring water from Bhutan.

Gobi petted a German shepherd that looked like Dostoyevski. He suddenly felt tongue-tied, almost shy.

"Nice doggy," he said. He favored the Russian realists.

"So," she said, detecting the change in his mood now that they were seated opposite each other. "What kind of a name is that? *Gobi?* Sounds like the Central Asian desert. The Silk Road. Teas and spices and Buddhist scrolls, all that."

The dog licked his hand. He looked up at her. "Well, yes. But the name's been shortened. I come from Huguenot ancestry by way of the Central Asian steppes. The name was much longer once upon a time. Something quite unpronounceable, from the Uygyur actually. It was shortened to Gobi."

"I can relate to that," Tara admitted. "My name's been abridged, too."

"Oh, really?" he asked. "We've got something in common then. What was your name originally?"

"It's rather a mouthful," she said. "My full name's Tara O'Shaughnessy Evans-Wentz."

"No!"

"Yes."

"No! I don't believe it," he said. "Any relation to . . . ?"

"Yes," she said.

"You're related to W. Y. Evans-Wentz? *The* W. Y. Evans-Wentz?"

"Yes, I am," Tara replied. "Walter Yeeling Evans-Wentz was my great great granduncle."

Gobi grinned. "I can't believe I'm actually sitting across the table from an honest-to-goodness Evans-Wentz. He's always been my idol. The first Westerner to introduce the *Tibetan Book of the Dead* to the West. His other books are classics, too: *Tibetan Yoga and Secret Doctrines. The Tibetan Book of the Great Liberation.* One of the early pioneers in East-West consciousness work." Gobi shook his head with admiration.

"He was a native Californian, too," Tara added. "From San Diego. Don't forget that."

"Is that where you're from?" Gobi asked, wondering.

"Mostly," she replied. "Great-Uncle Willy was sort of the

black sheep of the family, you know. He disappeared for years at a time in India and Sikkim. He was a scholar, but he was also on the path. He was a big influence on my father, who sort of took after him. I was raised in Tibet during my early years."

Tara took a sip of her water. "That was after the fourteenth Dalai Lama returned to Lhasa, when Tibet became independent again. They needed all kinds of Western aid to help the Tibetan people rebuild their country. The Chinese had left it in pieces. My mom was a health-services professional. My dad helped build the Tibetan software industry up from scratch. He was a programmer at Microsoft, but as they say, he found tantra."

"What a wonderful childhood that must have been!" Gobi exclaimed.

"It was," Tara agreed. "In a sense, it was almost like coming home again," she said, biting her lip. "I mean, with Great-Uncle Willy's historical connection to that part of the world. We were really received with open arms by everyone, including the Dalai Lama."

"You met the last Dalai Lama?" Gobi marveled.

"Of course, I did," Tara said. "I'll never forget Tenzin Gyatso as long as I live, even though I was just a little girl, maybe five or six years old. He used to slip me little Tibetan sweets in the shape of different gods and goddesses." She laughed. "He called me Little Durga, after the Great Cosmic Goddess, because I was so full of energy, running around all over the place, turning everything in the Potala upside down."

In a tone that she could not possibly mistake for scholarship, Gobi said, "I'd say you're more of a Kwan Yin—a goddess of mercy."

"You're exaggerating again, Dr. Gobi!"

"Frank. Call me Frank, remember?"

"Frank." She stared at him, the green energy of her eyes twinkling with humor. "Well, there you have it. My life story."

"Hardly," he said. "You grew up in Tibet?" He didn't want her to stop. He wanted to keep listening to her voice.

"Yes, until I was eight or nine. I went to university at UC Santa Barbara. I studied Chinese chi kung energy healing and I got a license in herbal medicine. I used to practice on my mom and dad a lot."

"Oh? How are they?"

"They're both in great shape, full of energy and vitality. They even had another child, my little sister, Devi. She's twelve now."

Tara drank from her bottle of spring water. "And how about you? You don't exactly look like a crusty academic," she prodded him.

"Well, I'm pretty busy, between teaching and writing. I do a little consulting on the side for companies that have a budget for corporate enlightenment. That pays for all of my expensive habits—like traveling, doing research, and meditation."

"That's expensive all right," Tara agreed, jokingly. "Especially meditation."

"That's right. It's amazing how much the cost of meditation has risen these days. I can barely afford it."

She laughed. "So are you married?"

"I used to be divorced."

"Oh, so you *are* married." Her eyebrows rose.

"No, I'm single again. I've been married twice. I have a ten-year-old son who lives with me. Trevor. He's a great kid."

"Is he anything like you?" Tara asked, smiling with her green eyes.

"Oh, I hope not! Funny you should ask though. He has an expression: 'Like father like son, only son is more devious.'"

"He sounds quite profound for his age."

"He's just a kid, but he sort of acts like a cranky Zen master at times." Gobi grinned. "You know, he'll give me a whack at the side of the head whenever I need it. Figuratively speaking, of course."

"I'd like to meet him some day." Tara smiled. "He sounds like a bright boy."

"I'm sure he'd love to meet you, too. . . ." Gobi began. He was already building up to the next rung of conversation. *"Er, how would you like to have dinner with us?"* he was about to ask her, when she sat up and waved at someone walking toward them from across the plaza.

As the man approached, Gobi saw that he was a Tibetan, in his thirties, on the short side, a bit stocky. He was dressed studiously in a grey Savile Row suit with a starched white shirt and a striped cravat tied in an Oxford knot. He wore heavy-frame glasses and his black hair was slicked back from his forehead. He could have been a visiting lama or an exchange student.

Noticing the sparkle in Tara's eyes when she saw him, Gobi's heart sank a notch. Damn. Could he be her consort? The man was smiling broadly. He radiated good cheer, good will, and, yes, if Gobi wasn't mistaken, a certain knowing intimacy. Gobi was already feeling a twinge of jealousy.

"This is Dorje Rinpoche," Tara said, as she introduced them. "Frank Gobi."

"How are you?" The Tibetan nodded, displaying a set of square, white teeth. "Very pleased to meet you," he said with a slight Anglo-Indian accent.

They shook hands, and Gobi felt somewhat relieved. Dorje Rinpoche's handshake was open and compassionate. If there was tantra between Tara and the Tibetan, well, Dorje wasn't holding it against Gobi's obvious romantic interest in her. It was all fine, the handshake seemed to say. Nothing is exclusive.

My God, the Tibetan had read him accurately, but without any negative judgment! Embarrassed, Gobi flushed. Tara laughed at his obvious discomfort, and he felt silly.

"You haven't been waiting long, have you, Tara?" the Tibetan asked her in a deep voice.

"No, Dorje, Frank and I were just getting acquainted. Well." Tara turned to Gobi as she rose from the table. "I've got to get going. It was really nice meeting you. I hope you fix your bike. And try to be more careful around pedestrians who're stumbling in the darkness."

"Wait a minute," Gobi said, riding anxiously. She was slipping away from him. "You said you had a chi kung practice somewhere? How do I contact you? I mean, for a follow-up visit?" he tried not to stammer.

"A follow-up visit?" Tara asked, perplexed. Dorje Rinpoche grinned at him. "Oh, I think you'll be fine," she assured Gobi. "I'm afraid I don't have an active practice at the moment. I'm on . . . sabbatical. I'm doing some postgraduate work," she added, exchanging glances with Dorje.

"Are you on-line somewhere? How can I reach you?" This *was* silly. She was going to leave, and he had no idea how to get in touch with her again.

"No, I'm not on-line anywhere," she told him. "At least, not in that way. But I'm sure our paths will cross again. I have a feeling they will."

"You don't have a beeper on you?" he asked, his heart sinking.

"Good-bye, Frank! Remember, there are no accidents—at least," she smiled, "unintentional ones."

He watched her walk away with Dorje through a crowd of students, her golden hair catching the sun, then suddenly darkening as though it had absorbed all the light.

ASHOK

Hi, Trevor, I'm home!"

Gobi stood in the hallway of his Victorian flat on Oxford Street. The house was quiet, but he heard Juan's radio tuned to Spanish music in the kitchen. Their Salvadoran home-supporter was cooking dinner.

"Oh, hi, Mister Frank, you're home," Juan said, a smile crossing his broad face when he saw him enter the kitchen. "Tofu enchiladas okay for tonight?"

"Si, muy bueno," Gobi grinned. "Sorry to keep you this late, Juan," he apologized. "I got tied up on campus."

"No problem. Trevor's in his room now," he nodded.

"Doing his homework?" Gobi asked hopefully, slipping on a pair of comfortable old cotton-soled kung fu slippers.

Juan made a face. "He says he finished that already."

"Right."

They both laughed.

"Why don't you go on home?" Gobi told him.

"You sure?" Juan asked. "If you got some work to do, I can feed Trevor his dinner before I go."

Gobi slapped him on the back. "We'll be okay. Vamonos!"

Juan smiled, setting the dish of enchiladas on the counter by the quartzwave. Then he undid his apron, and got his bag from the kitchen table.

"One minute maximum in the oven," Juan warned him. "I'll see you in the morning, Mister Frank. 'Bye!"

Gobi stood in the kitchen until he heard Juan call out, "Buenos noches, Trevo*rrr!*" There was no reply. And then the door closed behind him.

Gobi went to his son's room and knocked. No answer. He turned the doorknob slowly and stood in the doorway.

Trevor sat in the hatch of his V-board, which was mounted on its mother-platform. Feet in the stirrups and clutching the small U-shaped wheel in front of him, he was taking it through its winding paces on the swiftly moving conveyor track. His helmet was on and Gobi could see the blinking red lights on the inside of his visor screen.

Trevor had a wild smile on his face, as though he had just outrun the Triborgians and was roller-coasting down to the finish line in Finisterre. But he could have been anywhere in Gametime for that matter. He might be riding with Beowulf and Hrothgard on the way to slay the monster, battling the enemy forces in the Mahabharata epic adventure game, or jousting with his pals somewhere on King Arthur's turnpike.

Trevor's handle on-line was the Kundalini Kid. That suited him—"kundalini"—the vital life force that erupted from the base of the spine to hyperactivate the entire nervous system.

When he wasn't linked to the mother-system, Trevor could detach the board and use it manually in an outdoor rink like the one they had in Berkeley at Interfaceland. If Gobi didn't put his foot down, the ten-year-old would easily spend seventy hours a week V-boarding.

"Hey, Trevor, I'm home," Gobi whispered, but his boy

didn't hear him. He wanted to touch his cheek to let him know he was there, but he was afraid to interfere with the program. It made him uneasy with all those neural connects buzzing inside Trevor's helmet. For an instant, he thought of Channel Emmanuel, but he quickly dismissed the thought. This wasn't a funky bible-thumpin' VR after all, this was a world-class Satori system.

It wasn't time to reel in Trevor anyway. Gobi would give him another twenty minutes, then he'd post him a message to come in. And be sure to wash his hands before supper.

Gobi checked his chi box for messages in his office down the hall.

"Have you hugged your poltergeist today? This could be you!" the announcer declared in an exuberant voice.

It was a junk vista advertising a Club Midori vacation. To Gobi's surprise, it showed him and Trevor walking down the beach at Ixtapa. How did they manage that? Then he recognized the dolphin T-shirt Trevor had been wearing during their last vacation to Cabo San Lucas. The neighborhood travel agent must have bought the footage from Baja Holidays and superimposed it over Ixtapa.

"Now you and your son can enjoy a wholesome family vacation at Club Midori Ixtapa with free airport transportation and other Club Specials."

He skipped the other coupons in the value-pak: *Angelina's Cafe & Catering, 50% off all salads. Free bee propolis . . . Complete interactive dental exam from the comfort of your own home. . . . Wow! Free Jungian dream analysis with one-hour $35 crystal healing . . . North Coast Fêng-shui Geomancers: Any Two Rooms & Hallway $45.95. . . .*

The news icon flashed. *A newspaper delivery boy was pedaling a bicycle at full speed, then tossed a rolled-up paper onto his front steps.*

Gobi said, "Bulletins."

Then he sat down in his armchair to watch the *New York Times.*

● ● ●

National Telecommunications and Information Administration Investigation into Channel Emmanuel Disaster Continues. Bogota Bashing in Caracas. Secretary of State Lanier Confers with Republic of Alaska Foreign Minister on Virtual Rights to Mt. McKinley. Free Japanese Government Renews Lease to Island of Bermuda. French Farmers Dump Tons of Pixels on Ministry of Agriculture Mainframe in Food Protest. World Health Organization Report on Nippon 'Quake Leaked Before Melbourne Meeting. Shocking Discrepancies, Claim Scientists.

Gobi clicked on the last item. He'd had enough of Channel Emmanuel for the time being. Time for a Neo-Tokyo update.

"It's too soon to jump to any conclusions about the stabilization of the psycho-ecosphere of New Nippon," declared Dr. Olaf Fluegelhorn, president of the American Seismo-Neurologists Association.

"The situation is still in flux there and we feel it is too early to lift the World Health Organization's quarantine of the Japanese islands. I'm sure there will be a great deal of debate about this in Melbourne, and that is the right forum for this discussion. It's premature to be discussing the normalization of ties at this time," the scientist continued.

"Why, even their government is still temporarily operating out of Nassau. You don't see them packing up to go home. No, there are still too many unanswered questions," he declared. "But nobody seems to be asking the really tough questions, in my opinion. What if it *is* some sort of unknown virus? What if it manages to spread to other countries? This is a national security matter. The president knows about our concerns, and I'm sure our delegation will make that an issue when we meet in Australia next month at the WHO conference."

Gobi scoffed. *Humph.* No one knows what it is, yet it's become a major rallying point for the far right, the far middle, and the far left. Everyone reacting in a mental knee-jerk fashion. Why don't they just send in an intelligence team, and check it out? So far, limited travel to New Nippon was permitted despite the quarantine. But nobody stayed past sunset. They were all out safely on the last spaceplane.

"Check personal messages," Gobi instructed, noticing the blinking icon. There was a message on his business line that had been downloaded in the morning. "Message one," he ordered.

"Moshi-moshi. Gobi-sensei? Good morning, this is Kiyoshi Kimura of Satori Interactive." The Japanese man in the elegant Ralph Yamamoto suit bowed so low that Gobi was able to admire his samurai topknot. "We met once at the NNETRO open house." That must have been at the New Nippon External Trade Organization office party in San Francisco a year ago.

"Hayashi of Toshiba Intel introduced us, if you recall. We discussed the consciousness deficit in the new line of *vachuru* products."

Sure, Gobi remembered. He was the dapper Japanese who wore a spicy thirteenth-century aftershave; what was the scent called? Eau de Genji. Yeah, sure. How could he forget the guy? Kimura asked a lot of questions about a lot of things, especially about his work at UC Berkeley. It was no secret that Satori had a major endowment at the university.

Pause, a brush up on the smile. "Hai, Gobi-sensei, I would be honored to meet with you to discuss a consulting project we hope you can do for us." He blinked. "This is short notice, but if you are free, can you meet me tomorrow afternoon at the Hotel Naniwa Nob Hill? On the thirtieth floor in the Plum Room. Would 3:30 P.M. be convenient?" He bowed again. "Please confirm with my office if this is agreeable."

Gobi leaned back in his chair and swiveled around. He thought for a moment. Normally, the Japanese weren't that pushy. They liked to take their time and make their arrangements carefully. If Kimura wanted to see him tomorrow, it must be important. He checked his schedule. His last class ended at two. He could make it.

"I'd be delighted to meet you tomorrow afternoon as you requested, Kimura-san." Gobi flashed his most professional smile as the message was relayed on the return loop. "See you then."

Time to get to work, he sighed. He would have to get briefed as fully as possible before the meeting.

Satori was a heavyweight client. Gobi had never actually consulted directly for them before, although he'd once done some intuitive analysis for one of their subsidiary companies on an R and D project. What had it been? Oh yeah, assessing some cruelty-free software.

He leaned back again and put his feet up on his desk. "Okay, Ashok, let's do a search," he said out loud. Ashok was his Akashic Reader, a personalized information access system connected to the Global Omni-Net.

"How about starting with a company backgrounder for the Satori Group?"

Ashok emitted his usual low gurgle as he began to scour the Net.

Gobi went back down the hall to the kitchen, passing Trevor's room. The kid was still rolling on his skateboard chassis. OK. Another ten minutes, then it's back to pedestrian life, Kundalini.

Gobi fixed himself a mug of Bengal cha and sauntered back to his workspace. He sipped the spicy brew as he slipped back into his chair. "What have you got for me?"

Ashok paused. "Would you like the neurons-on tour, Dr. Gobi? If so, kindly slip on your Satori goggles at this time. Otherwise, you will receive a 3-D version of this report on your screen. What is your preference?"

"Okay, hang on, Ashok, let me grab those eye-suckers." He rummaged around his desk. One of these days, he'd have to sort out the mess. Books, cassettes, diskettes, gizmos he'd forgotten he ever had, techno-fetishes collected from his travels. There they were. He picked up a streamlined visor with an infrared connect to the system. "Going on-line, Ashok," he said, adjusting the set on his head. "Give me a sec."

"Very well, sir."

$$\Sigma \text{o} Z!$$

Ashok was already flashing the holo-title from Satori's latest annual CD-ROM report, which was entitled "A Tour of the Satori Group, 2027."

"Very good, Ashok, let it roll," Gobi said, as he began to concentrate on Ashok's info-junket.

"Satori Group, with estimated annual revenues of 3.2 billion New Yen, is one of the biggest keiretsu conglomerates in the world," Ashok announced, as he ran a stream of images from the report.

"Its virtual multimedia entertainment and information divisions rank among the top fifty companies on the Nikkei-Fortune 500 list. Among other things, the 'retsu operates an international space airline with the motto 'The Enlightened Way To Travel.'"

Gobi found himself boarding a Satori spaceplane, then he was quickly downloaded in a comfortable seat taking off. But Ashok was giving him the economy-class tour, so it was a roller-coaster clip. Suddenly he was looking down at a topographical grid of a shimmering metropolis, its skyscape zooming all around him.

"Satori is perhaps best known for its vast holdings of 'Unreal Estate' in the virtual dominion of 'Satori City™.'"

The light of the metropolis radiated beyond the neon of imagination. It glowed like a stained-glass consciousness within his mind. It was more than image or even symbol. It was compressed presence, a silence that shouted at you. Gobi felt like he had swallowed an entire city.

"Slow down, Ashok," Gobi ordered. "I'm getting a little discombobulated here."

"Sorry, sir." Ashok said, then continued.

"Satori City, better known as 'Virtuopolis,' or 'Virtualopolis,' was developed in the year 2017 by the Satori Group as the world's first on-line VR city. In terms of its actual tsubo-acreage in Cyberspace, it is equivalent in physical size to the island of Manhattan. Virtuopolis offers fully-equipped virtual reality office buildings—VR-rises—with discrete cells for short- or long-term lease; interactive convention centers; pay-per-use R and D labs in all the major nano-industries, from desktop cold fusion plants to bio-

origami pulp processing facilities, to name just a few applications."

Gobi neuro-scrolled his way through vast hallways teeming with iconographic representations of live on-line office workers. He passed PVWs—Personal Virtual Workspaces that looked much like the office cubicles of yore—boardrooms, public domain virtual workplaces, paradigm lounges, encryption-secured conference sites, and offices for transient consultants, as well as free intellectual zones with readylinked global library and data resources.

Thundering Toshiba! There was even an electronic watercooler located in a neutral site. Judging from the avatars, it was a spot for informal get-togethers for company personnel who might otherwise never get an opportunity to mingle.

So far this was nothing more than the standard Satori office tour to attract corporate, government, and university sector tenants. Enough of that.

"On the cultural side," Ashok went on, *"Virtuopolis houses most of the world's leading museums—from the sweeping collections of New York's Metropolitan Museum to the Louvre in Paris, Taipei's National Museum, the Hermitage in St. Petersburg, Amsterdam's Rijksmuseum, the Uffizi in Florence, the Tate Gallery in London, not to mention the important smaller venues like the Picasso Museum in the Marais section of Paris and the Groeninge Collection of Flemish art in Bruges."*

Here Gobi was able to inspect a multistory series of museum icons. He could enter any gallery he chose to view paintings or other artworks. This was a holo-visual scan. If he had the time, he would have been able to spend an entire afternoon browsing in any wing that interested him. A perfect thing to do on a rainy afternoon.

"Give me Dreamtime now please, Ashok," Gobi requested, as he leaned back in his chair again.

"Dreamtime, one of Satori City's most popular sectors, includes a holographic construct of the Angkor Wat in Cambodia, the ancient temple of Knossos on the island of Crete, a neural version of the Olmec temple complex at

Teotihuacán, as well as its famous replica of the Forbidden City in Beijing. . . ."

Zong! He was in the cobbled courtyard of the Hall of Supreme Harmony gazing up at the throne of the Son of Heaven. Then, in a sudden switch of perspective, he was on the throne looking down at rows of prostrated mandarins and high officials with their peacock-feathered caps touching the floor.

By the balls of Eunuchrama, *he* was the Last Emperor!

"Er, *slow down,* Ashok!" Gobi urged his Reader. The pace shifted, but the images persisted. He gritted his teeth.

"Every major international film festival in the world, and their entire archives, are live on-line in Satori City. Twenty-four hours a day. Tele-tours and bookings can be made through Satori Tours and Satori Presents outlets using your Visa, Rim Express, Mastercard, or Satoricard."

"Skip that part," Gobi ordered.

"For families going on vacation, Virtual Disneyland offers several Matrix levels of clean family fun—and, of course, there's the ever-popular Gametime that's full of challenging VR adventures for the kids," Ashok recited. *"But if you want real thrills, Everest Magic will provide you with your own personal AI-sherpa to help you climb any peak in the world—from Mt. Everest to Annapurna to Mont Blanc. And you can adjust the height and danger level to your personal specifications.*

"OK," Gobi said. "Enough of this virtual press kit." He removed his visor and rubbed his eyes. "Whew! I get the idea!" He took a sip of tea to get grounded again.

"All right, that's the official line," he said. "Now what about the press? Are there any current clips on how Satori is really doing? An opposing view perhaps?"

A few moments passed.

"It appears that *Offshore Networking* fits the bill, sir," Ashok said finally. "There's a rather challenging article by Bob Hoff. He's their chief investigative reporter. Hoff has won the Noam Chomsky Journalism Award for the past three years."

"Fine, get him on."

Hoff's craggy face, with its penetrating robin's-egg-blue eyes and bushy eyebrows appeared on the cube.

"Good evening . . . Mr. Gobi. Thank you for joining me. And now to my special feature report on the Satori Group. . . . Because of its unique decentralized corporate structure, the Satori Group has been able to manage its global business empire with relative ease despite the obvious disadvantage of having its corporate headquarters in Neo-Tokyo, which has been all but inaccessible since the Mega-Quake. There, overall corporate strategy and new product development continue to be charted by the company's visionary founder and chairman, Kazuo Harada.

"But there are some problem areas developing for the Satori keiretsu," Hoff went on. *"Due to the downturn in the economy in the last quarter, occupancy in Virtuopolis, the group's flagship property, is estimated to be only around 45 percent. The unused sectors have been dubbed the 'Wasteland' by investment analysts who are skeptical that Satori can recover its lost ground in the face of advancing competition, particularly from one of their leading rivals, the Kobayashi Group."*

Hoff shifted in his seat. *"We posed that question to Action Wada, Satori's Vice-President of Operations, who spoke to us from his office in Neo-Tokyo."*

The clip showed a man with a steely build dressed in a dark blue Intel power suit. A fancy stud all right, but a cybercrat through and through. Gobi knew the type, their arrogance barely disguised as efficiency.

"Mr. Wada, let me ask you about the Wasteland, if I may," Hoff began.

"That is your *term, not ours,"* the Japanese interrupted angrily. He spoke a standard English seasoned with a slight but noticeable New England accent harkening back to the R and D hub of Route 128. *"It is not uncommon to have a few downsectors on the system,"* he continued. *"By the way, that figure you just cited for on-line usage is incorrect. Our Nikkei-Nielsen audits indicate a virtual occupancy/usage rate closer to 56 percent, which is very respectable."*

"What comment do you have about reports that colonies of squatters occupy unused portions of the VR-rises in the so-called 'warehouse district' of Virtuopolis?"

"Those are unsubstantiated rumors and sensationalistic stories that we deeply regret," Action Wada replied, his face darkening further. *"We do have some unauthorized entry into Virtuopolis, of course, but it's very limited, maybe one or two percent. As for squatters, not a chance. Our nodes are all monitored. Satori City can assure its customers of the highest quality on-line security to be found on any system anywhere."*

He faced the camera squarely.

"You are safe on our digital streets." He smirked. *"Not like in New York or Los Angeles."*

"No data muggings, no piracy, no hacking, is that it?"

Action Wada nodded curtly. *"As I have already said, our system is foolproof."*

"But what about reports of terrorism in the financial vectors?" Hoff pressed him. *"We have heard, for instance, that a branch of Interface Investments and Securities was recently sabotaged and all its assets drained."*

"Lies, lies, lies," Action Wada scowled. *"That is the terrorism of rumormongers and the innuendo of the media, nothing more. I have no further comment to make."*

Hoff's talking head reappeared on the screen.

"Mr. Gobi, stay posted for more on this story in our three-part series on the travails of the Satori Group as it seeks to adjust to the changing marketplace. This is Bob Hoff reporting for Offshore Networking *magazine. Until the next issue."*

"HEY, DAD!!!"

Gobi spun around to see Trevor, his blond hair tousled, his hands rubbing his eyes. "When'd you get home? I didn't know you were here."

"Hi, Son!" Gobi smiled, giving his boy a hug. "I didn't want to disturb you. You looked pretty busy."

"I was boarding, Dad."

"So I noticed."

"I found this way-cool place. But it's not in Gametime. . . . I found a way to patch through to it, though."

"Wait a minute. Stop right there!" Gobi exclaimed, a grim look on his face. "How many times do I have to tell you to stay inside? You don't go *out*. You stay *inside* the system, OK? It's not safe to be boarding God-knows-where."

"But . . ." the boy protested.

"No buts. You stay in. Or you stay off. Got it? You want to get grounded in realtime? *It's not safe, Trevor.* End of discussion."

They were going to have to butt heads again, but Gobi was determined not to back down on this critical point. God, Channel Emmanuel was making him jumpy. He could really feel it now.

Trevor looked at him, openmouthed, then turned around and left the room.

If that's the way his Dad felt about it, all right. But he wanted to tell him about that place the guy on the screen was talking about. What did he call it? The Wasteland.

KIMURA

Thank you for coming, Dr. Gobi," Kimura said after the kimono-clad waitress left, sliding the screen door closed behind her. She had brought them tea and rice cakes. The two men exchanged and then studied each other's meishis in respectful silence.

They were in a private Japanese tearoom on the top floor of the Hotel Naniwa Nob Hill. Koto music played softly in the background as they sat on tatami mats at a low lacquer table.

From a large picture window, you could see the towers of the Golden Gate Bridge peeping from under the heavy futon of fog. Hovercraft skimmed across the grey water like daddy longlegs.

Gobi read Kimura's card: *Kiyoshi Kimura, Vice President, Marketing, Satori Interactive North America.* At the bottom of the card, he noticed there was a real-time readout of Satori's activity on the 24-hour Global Exchange.

10067 93-. The stock appeared to be dropping.

"Just a temporary downturn, I'm sure," Gobi remarked. The green tea was hot and tasty. He smacked his lips in appreciation.

Kimura poured more tea into his cup.

"Business could be better," he frowned. "Projected bookings for Satori City are down 22 percent already for the next period. The Channel Emmanuel disaster has damaged the confidence of people in vachuru," he said, using the Japanese word for VR. "So many people—ah—disconnected."

"So desu ne," Gobi nodded. What did Kimura want to discuss with him? Eventually, he would get around to it. Gobi noticed Kimura's socks when he stretched his legs out on the tatami floor. They were a shiny gossamer material that glowed unnaturally. For some reason the socks unnerved him.

"Have you ever visited Satori City, Dr. Gobi?" Kimura asked.

"Umm, not recently," Gobi replied, not wishing to offend his host. "I've taken the quick tour, though."

"It's quite safe, you know," Kimura said defensively. His next remark came out of the blue.

"Perhaps you've heard that Procter-Gamble is planning to pull all its advertising from the 'I AM' show?"

"No, I wasn't aware of that," Gobi answered, genuinely surprised.

'I AM' had a clever gimmick, he had to admit. Every week you got to be a different historical or contemporary celebrity. You could take your pick from the menu: Einstein, Madame Curie, Mick Jagger, Lady Murasaki, Stradivarius, young Tolstoy, Julius Caesar, Ronald Reagan, or the Prisoner of Wenda, today's hottest teen holo-throb.

You merged into their consciousness and saw the world through their eyes. You might watch 'I AM Sadaharu Oh,' who was one of the historical Japanese Zen baseball players. And you got to hit a homerun, too. *Bop!* It was a pretty hot concept actually.

"Our highest-rated program and it is in danger of being cancelled," Kimura stated matter-of-factly.

"You're kidding. Why is that?"

"There is a vachuru backlash," Kimura pursed his lips, using the Japanese word again. "Consumer fundamentalism. Very dangerous."

"Consumer fundamentalism," Gobi repeated. The idea seemed strange to him.

"Yes. Back to ordinary reality. Before vachuru."

"I see," Gobi said.

"You must understand, Gobi-sensei. VR has grown to be a 13 trillion New Yen industry. If vachuru is crippled, Satori is severely damaged."

"All because of the accident on Channel Emmanuel?" Gobi asked. So this was one of the major ripple effects. Of course. Why didn't he think of that earlier?

"Channel Emmanuel," a sneer appeared on Kimura's face. "That's *Sensulogic,*" he scoffed dismissively. "Third-rate sim. Not much better than *Gogglerama.*"

"I suppose not," Gobi replied, feeling rebuked.

"Look," he said, uncertain where this was leading. "It sounds like what you really need is an aggressive information campaign. Highlight all the built-in safety features of Satori City, and gradually the public will rebuild its trust in VR. There's a cycle to everything. It'll all come around again. You'll see." He tried to sound encouraging.

"I'm afraid it's not quite that simple." Kimura looked up at Gobi. "In this industry if you are not prepared to move fast and anticipate the blow of the enemy, you cannot hope to survive. And one thing we *do* know is that Satori City is being targeted."

"But . . ."

Kimura raised his hand. "We have many sources of information available to us, Gobi-sensei." He affected a confidential tone. "May I speak frankly?"

"Of course," Gobi responded warmly. "Rest assured that everything you tell me is under complete nondisclosure."

Kimura bowed, perhaps with a tinge of cynicism. "Very well then. I can tell you this. We have reason to believe that Channel Emmanuel was a test run. The real target is Virtuopolis."

Gobi was stunned. He felt immobilized by what he had just heard. Was Kimura being *literal* or was he speaking in some sort of corporate allegory? Channel Emmanuel was part of a deliberate campaign to discredit VR in general?

"To destroy Virtuopolis is the goal of our enemies. And we have many enemies who will stop at nothing. Not just here, but among our own keiretsus as well. You know the Kobayashi keiretsu?"

"They're number two after Satori, aren't they?"

"They want to be ichiban," Kimura held up a finger. "Number one."

"You're suggesting that *they're* behind this? They have some plan to bring you down?"

"Suggesting is one thing." Kimura smiled. "Proving is another. Yes, they would like to absorb Virtuopolis. If they can't, they would like nothing better than to destroy us." He smiled cynically again. "Imagine," he continued, "Satori City, one of the world's greatest on-line monuments, swallowed up by a creeping jungle of algorithms. Perhaps to be uncovered one day by a future explorer, and hailed as a remnant of a lost digital civilization. . . ."

Kimura rolled his eyes. There was a trace of whimsy there, but more menace.

"That's unbelievable!" Gobi exclaimed. "How can anybody possibly expect to get away with attacking Satori City?"

It was Kimura's turn to act surprised. "That's the easiest part, Dr. Gobi," he said. "We have received intelligence indicating that some Channel Emmanuel-style accidents may occur in Virtuopolis in the near future. After that, it should be a simple matter for lobbyists to press for the closure of Satori City on the grounds that it poses a 'safety risk' to the public."

Gobi listened in disbelief. "Why don't you inform the authorities—or better still, put out a consumer alert?" he demanded. "If you've got any information about an impending terrorist threat, you *must* do something!"

He shuddered. An incident in Virtuopolis would be like Channel Emmanuel magnified a thousand times. Thousands of people, maybe *tens* of thousands might be affected. Men, women—and children. Gobi froze when he thought of Trevor V-boarding out on Gametime. Something clamped on to his heart and wouldn't let go.

"Inform the world? But that's *exactly* what they would like us to do," Kimura sneered. "Have us spread rumors about our own demise! Have *us* advertise the dangers of Virtuopolis to the end user! How poetic!"

The Japanese sipped his tea noisily. "No, that would be impossible. And I'm afraid we can't turn to *your* authorities either."

"Why not?"

"There are those in your country who would like nothing better than to shut down Satori City for 'security reasons' while they carry out a long and thorough investigation of our system, one that would no doubt include the disassembly of Satori's proprietary VR technologies."

Kimura shook his head. "The result would be the same. We would be forced to close down. And Satori City would die a slow death as our technology became more and more out-dated. No," he sighed. "I'm afraid none of these scenarios offers us any viable options for countering our enemies."

"Aren't you going to do *anything?*"

"We could strike first, Dr. Gobi." Kimura raised an eye-brow.

"How do you propose to do that?"

"Say, a preemptive move. We could announce the tempo-rary closure of Satori City ourselves—*before* we were forced to do so."

"I don't understand," Gobi scowled. "Wouldn't that have exactly the same effect you were just talking about? It would set off a wave of bad publicity against the Satori Group."

"On the contrary," Kimura replied with a smile. "We could announce major plans to upgrade our system. We could offer our customers newer and more sophisticated features. This is a much more honorable solution, I think. It is credible and, best of all, it could buy us time."

"Let me play the devil's advocate," Gobi interrupted. "I

assume you're interested in my opinion, or you wouldn't have invited me here this afternoon?"

Kimura bowed in agreement. "I am anxious to hear your opinion."

"You mentioned a potential consumer backlash. And the growing public fears about the hazards of virtual reality?"

"That is correct," Kimura nodded.

"Well, then, no matter what kind of system upgrade you're planning, you would still face the same old problem. And the same threat. That won't change. It will *still* be waiting for you whenever you decide to reopen for business."

Kimura had been listening with his eyes closed. He now opened them. His pupils were like polished black go stones. "No, Dr. Gobi, perhaps I should explain a bit more," he said in a smooth voice.

"This upgrade that we are considering, it is *not* about virtual reality. It is about the next stage. It is about what comes *after* virtual reality. Post-vachuru. Wakarimasuka? Do you understand? We will be the first once again to introduce a brand-new standard. A technological breakthrough. And *no one*—none of our enemies or competitors—will be able to oppose us."

Gobi mused; there was still something missing here. Almost like Neo-Tokyo, he grimaced to himself. Sorry, bad joke.

"Let me understand this," Gobi said finally. "You're going to introduce a *post*-virtual system and *relaunch* Satori City?"

"Hai," Kimura nodded again. "So there should be no challenge from the anti-virtual lobby. It will be a new, clean technology."

"You have this new technology now?"

Kimura's voice dropped ever so slightly. "We are still working on it. It is almost there. There are a few remaining . . . challenges."

"So." Gobi sought the right words to complete his sentence. "What can I possibly do for you then? I mean, how can *I* be of service?" He laughed feebly. "I'm not even an engineer! I don't do virtual, I don't do post-virtual!"

Kimura looked at him thoughtfully, almost regretfully.

"We don't need engineers," he said finally. "We need you."

Even the fog felt feverish to Gobi. It had a serrated edge that scraped the top of Nob Hill before spilling over in strips of white gauze onto California Street.

Maybe he *was* feverish. After his meeting with Kimura, Gobi hurried to catch the trans-Bay maglev back to Berkeley. He had to get away as quickly as possible. He felt sick, dizzy, disoriented. His heart pounded and cold sweat soaked his body.

It wasn't possible, was it? What Kimura had shown him? If it were possible, then the meaning of everything he had ever held to be true was changed forever. All the rules were different now. Correction: There were no rules anymore.

Nob Hill was crawling with tourists at this half-twilight hour. Russian aristocrats rode past in horse-drawn carriages. Rowdy groups of wealthy Greater Chinese businessmen milled about in front of glitzy Hong Kong-style hotels with atrium lobbies, preparing to head down to the Grant Avenue restaurants in New Chinatown.

Laughing and cheering, a group of Latin-Americans hung on to a cable car as it clanged up California Street.

An aborigine—nearly naked, with long, dark legs—strode up the steep hill clutching a didgeridoo. As he passed Gobi, he spun around and rasped something at him. His red-rimmed eyes burned with fever. Gobi stepped back, startled. "What?"

The aborigine laughed and said, *"It's steep both ways, mate"* in a deep Aussie accent. When Gobi looked again, the figure was gone.

Ding-ding-ding-ding-ding!

Gobi ran up to a cable car that was lurching down California Street toward the Embarcadero terminal. He leaped onto the sideboard, grasped the pole, and took a deep breath. Opening his eyes, he saw the ivy-covered Transamerica Pyramid building in the Financial District below.

The cable car picked up speed as it passed the tacky neu-ron swirl of New Chinatown. Iridescent Chinese ideograms hovered above Grant Avenue like multidecked kites, and the cacophony of Hubei pop music and synthesized riffs of the Peking Opera buzzed in the air like sizzling rice soup.

When the cable car screeched to its final stop at the Embarcadero, Gobi jumped off. As he hurried down the stairs to reach the rapid-transit terminal, he passed a group of chant-ing Hare Nixon cult members. They had shaved heads and wore their trademark orange robes. *"Hare Nixon, Hare Nixon, Hare Nixon, Hare, Hare. . . ."* Their voices echoed deep inside the tunnel.

Gobi heard the hissing of the trans-Bay maglev rising on its tracks. He had just enough time to slide his BART card through the slot and slip into the carriage before the doors locked behind him. The maglev jerked forward as it turned a corner in the transparent tube.

Whoosh! The water in the bay was an opaque sludge-green. A juvenile sea lion had wandered too close to the underwater tracks in search of plankton; it tumbled backward as the maglev shot past it in a streak of light. The creature's startled reaction reminded Gobi of the expression on his own face when Kimura had shown him the future. It was a future that had no past and no present. It didn't need either.

Gobi's pocket 'shiba beeped. He ignored it. He had the feeling it was Kimura trying to reach him. They wouldn't let go of him that easily. Not after what he'd experienced.

He glanced around the carriage, which was nearly empty. A couple sat inside a private sensu-sound Shikibo unit zipped down to their waists, like a small Alpine tent. They were tightly squeezed together, their legs dangling from the base of the portable amphitheater. Their feet jerked from time to time as if they were practicing dance steps on an invisible dance floor.

Next to them, a skinny young Latino with a goatee was lowriding on his brain waves. His shades were uplinked to his headset and he was obviously tripping. Gobi had seen it before—all the physical moves that mimicked the motions happening somewhere else in V-space.

God, was it happening already? The Transformation? It seemed the only person who *wasn't* linked to something was a wild-looking mountain man who shared the same bench with Gobi. He wore a broad-brimmed leather cowboy hat and was bare-chested except for a leather vest. *Holy shit! Was that a ferret sitting on his shoulder?* Yes, sir, it was. Like a good San Franciscan pet, it even sported a gold earring.

Gobi noticed that the man's arms had long bloody scratches where the ferret's sharp claws had dug into him. Gobi sniffed the air. *Whew!* The smell of animal musk was overpowering. *Ugh.* It was going to be a long ride.

The mountain man finally spoke. "Aincha gonna answer that thing, mister?"

Gobi's 'shiba hadn't stopped beeping. "No, I'm not."

The mountain man grinned. He was missing some front teeth and his face was lined with deep furrows. "Them things bring you nuthin' but trouble, don't they, mister?" He raised a small flask to his mouth and took a drink. His breath smelled of cheap shochu spirits.

"Want some, Norman?" He offered his furry companion a sip from his open mouth. "This here's my pal Norman Rockwell. He's a ferret, man. Same family as a mink or a marmot or a weasel," he explained proudly.

Gobi didn't say anything. The man grinned again and pointed a grimy finger at Gobi's beeping pocket. "They must want you pretty bad, huh? Wha'd you do? Run off with the boss' wife? Hee! Hee! Hee!" he chortled.

Gobi just stared at him.

"Fucking shit," the mountain man said, wiping his mouth with his hand. "What you suppose they're doin' in there?"

The couple in the Shikibo had their legs twisted together. The man's right thigh suddenly jerked over the woman's lap.

"You think they're actually *doin'* it?" the mountain man asked with a smirk spreading across his unshaven face. "Wow, they must be *fuckin'* or somethin'! That's something else, man!" He encouraged the couple as he took another swig from his flask. "Way to go, man! Fuck yer brains out!"

Moving spasmodically, the couple slid off the seat and crumpled to the floor, still tangled in their tentware.

Gobi jumped to his feet. Something was very, very wrong.

"Hey, look at *tha,* dude!" the mountain man muttered, pointing at the lowrider, who was beginning to twist around in his seat. "He must be OD'ing or something. What the fuck do you think's goin' on, man?"

As the drunk staggered up, the ferret jumped off his shoulder and scampered away.

"Unhhhhhhhh . . ." The lowrider let out a groan.

"Jeezus!" Gobi exclaimed. "He's having a seizure! He's foaming at the mouth!"

Gobi knelt down beside him and carefully removed his shades. The lights were still blinking, but the man's eyes were rolled upward with only their whites showing. His body frantically pumped up and down on the floor. Gobi tried his best to restrain him, but the effort was too great.

"Lend me a hand here!" he cried.

"Hell no!" the mountain man screamed as he retreated to the rear of the carriage. "What if he's got somethin' contagious I might catch?! He don't look right to me! I ain't touching nobody! You fuckin' crazy, man!"

A rasp escaped from the lowrider's throat as his breathing subsided. Gobi pried open his mouth to give him CPR. He worked as fast as he could, alternating deep breaths with sharp thrusts against the young Latino's abdomen. The rasping started up again like a slow leak, but then it stopped for good.

"He's gone, man! He's gone! There ain't nothin' more you can do for that dude!" the mountain man wailed. Gobi felt the lowrider's pulse. He was stunned. *Nothing.* He couldn't believe it. The man really *was* dead.

Gobi turned his attention to the couple on the floor. It looked like they were still struggling inside their portable tent, trying to claw their way out.

Gobi rushed over and unzipped the unit down the front.

But he stepped back and let out a scream when he saw what was inside.

The young man and woman had their eyes closed as if they were in deep slumber. A 'trode-cable hung between their foreheads. They had been neural-connected, like lovers sharing a dream. But not any longer.

Looking up at Gobi with his pinprick black eyes was Norman Rockwell, the ferret; one of the wires he'd been gnawing was still caught between his sharp little teeth.

The mountain man stepped up and leaned over. With an agility that surprised Gobi, he lifted his pet off the two bodies and slipped the animal under his arm.

"I think you might want to answer that phone now, mister," he suggested quietly. The maglev pulled into the Berkeley BART station. As soon as the hydro-doors swung open, the mountain man stepped out onto the platform and hurried off in the direction of the exit.

Gobi brought the beeping unit up to his face and unsnapped its compact screen. The picture sizzled and Kimura's face materialized.

"Dr. Gobi," the Japanese began without further greeting. It was as though their conversation in the teahouse had barely been interrupted. "Our worst fears have just been realized." His mouth was a tight slash against his face. "Satori City has crashed. A number of sectors have suffered heavy damage. There have been numerous casualties. We suspect sabotage. I'm afraid you really *must* help us now."

NIGHTMARE

Even long after the nightmare was over, Gobi was still unable to reconstruct the actual sequence of events that occurred that night. He tried to call home from the BART platform. Juan must have left already for the day. That meant Trevor was home alone.

"Come on, Trevor! Pick up the phone, for God's sake!" he

shouted into his 'shiba. *"Come on! Come on! Come on!"* But there was no answer.

He could recall only fragments of the nightmare, but they were extremely vivid: The deep blue of the twilight sky above the Berkeley hills as he walked out of the BART station. The man sitting in the cafe window with his head on the table, his headset dangling to the floor. A small group of people who must have been sharing a multiplex Shikibo. Their bodies lay sprawled at a bus stop as if a carnival tent had collapsed over them. In the middle of the street, a delivery van and an automobile had collided. The van bore an RVD sticker. It had been on Remote Virtual Dispatch. The driver of the car had been killed on impact.

It was useless to try to get a ride home, so Gobi ran as fast as he could. It was five blocks down Shattuck, dodging people who were milling around in confusion. He passed Vine, and was about to turn on Oxford for the final leg home. At the corner, he stopped cold in his tracks.

He couldn't believe his eyes. A guide dog was dragging the body of a 'trode-head down the street. The leash was still tied to the man's wrist. Gobi attempted to calm the dog as he undid the leash, but he couldn't stay with the student whose mind had been blown. He had to leave him lying there on the sidewalk.

What was happening!? Fighting back his panic, Gobi sprinted the next few blocks without pausing for breath.

He unlatched the gate and took the stairs three at a time till he reached his front door. He unlocked it and stepped inside the dark hallway. A kitchen light was on. Trevor sat at the table eating a bowl of cereal.

"Hiya, Dad," the boy looked up at him with a grin. "You're home."

Gobi blinked. The table was empty. A flashback from this morning. They had been joking together before Trevor went off to school.

"Trevor!" Gobi called out anxiously. His heart pounded like it was going to explode. It hurt not from pain but from anxiety.

He ran to Trevor's room and opened the door. There he was, his boy, hunched forward on his V-board, his arms hanging at his sides, his feet clad in twill hiking socks. Trevor was never happy with his socks. He was so finicky about them. He didn't like regular cotton socks because they developed little cotton squeegees inside the toes after they'd been washed once or twice. And he didn't care for the way the elastic dragged down around his ankles. So he wore heavy wool hiking socks all year 'round—spring, summer, autumn, and winter. . . .

Gobi shook his head as the flood of trivial thoughts engulfed him, offering him a fragile solace. Then the dam burst. *"No, Trevor! No, Trevor! No, no, no, no, no. . . ."*

He fell to his knees and cradled his boy in his arms. He sobbed as he inhaled his son's skin, the musty smell of his hair, and he kissed the cold cheeks, now wet with his tears. He kissed them again and again, and he wept as the world was carried swiftly away on the shoulders of a flash flood.

ALTA BATES

Frank . . . Frank . . ."

He felt a gentle tugging at his sleeve. Gobi looked up, dazed. For a moment he didn't know where he was. He recognized the familiar face of Hans Ulbricht. Behind the portly figure of his friend stood Hans' wife, Melissa, a worried expression on her pinched face.

He looked around. They were in the waiting room of the Alta Bates Hospital outside the restricted area of the Adolescents VR Unit.

"Frank," Hans addressed him softly. "You need to get some rest. You've been here forty-eight hours already. Let us take you home." Hans exchanged glances with his wife. "Trevor's in good hands," he added, wanting to reassure Gobi.

Gobi was wide awake as soon as he heard his son's name. There were over fifty kids in Trevor's ward. But Trevor was one of the lucky ones. Some of the other children were more brain dead than he was. Trevor had been placed on a neural support system. Part of his head had been shaved and his frontal lobes were connected with clips and 'trodes to a bed-side unit that was networked to the Neural Emergency Task Force file-server in Atlanta.

Strange, Trevor looked like he was dreaming. But some-where, *somewhere,* he must have still been boarding in deep V-space. From time to time, his legs jerked and his eyes rolled in his head as the computer graphics spilled over in vivid colors. The eeriest thing was the game score. It appeared out of nowhere on the screen, an apparent residue of the crash. It was frozen exactly where Trevor had left off in mid-game.

But where *had* he left off? And where was he *now?*

Eight hours after the madness began, Gobi found himself in a private lounge at Alta Bates. He waited along with other anx-ious parents and relatives to speak to physicians and health officials. He wore a name tag on his chest.

"Ah, you must be Trevor's father. Hi, I'm Dr. Winston." A lanky middle-aged physician with sandy hair peered at his sticker. He glanced at his charts to make sure. "It's Trevor Gobi, right?"

"That's right, I'm his dad. How is my son, doctor?"

"Your son is in stable condition." Dr. Winston held his hand up cautiously, as if to discourage any unwarranted opti-mism. "He's still in a coma, like the other children, but he seems to be holding his own. Let's say we're guardedly hope-ful."

He nodded toward a sofa. "Why don't we sit down for a moment?"

The two men sat. The doctor fiddled with the VR goggles and neuroscope that hung from his neck.

"What's wrong?" Gobi asked anxiously.

"You've already received the briefing from Dr. Wolinsky, I believe?" Dr. Winston probed Gobi.

"Yes, I was there." Gobi's voice trailed as he recalled the session.

At a hastily arranged conference to brief the families of the children, a hospital spokesperson had provided an initial report on the situation. *"First, I've got an announcement to make,"* Dr. Wolinsky said, leaning over the podium. *"The President of the United States has just declared a national emergency. He has ordered the Neural Task Force in Atlanta to coordinate the effort and to work with their counterparts abroad on spearheading an international rescue effort."*

He paused before continuing. There was a stark silence in the room. *"Now I'm going to share a few details with you that we've been able to piece together so far about the crisis. They're still sketchy, so please bear with me. And we still don't know exactly what went wrong, but we're working on it."*

Dr. Wolinsky cleared his throat and looked at his notes. *"This is what we know so far. Apparently, there was a systems-wide breakdown in three of the most downloaded sectors of Virtuopolis, which, as you know, is operated by the Satori Corporation. Gametime, the children's game environment, was hit the hardest at 4:56 this afternoon, followed minutes later by Adult World and Karaoke Country."*

He adjusted his glasses; his voice broke slightly. *"An estimated 8,042 neural disconnects have been reported by forty-three countries so far.*

"Of that number," Dr. Wolinsky coughed into the microphone, *"we have reports of 648 adult fatalities due to cardiac arrest resulting from the shock of disconnect. That figure is now being corroborated."* He raised his eyebrows. *"Approximately 3,800 children have been trapped in twenty-eight virtual game environments, on about forty game levels."*

He pursed his lips. *"So far, no children have perished."* He shook his head in amazement. *"We don't know why they've survived while the adults suffered fatalities. The children's neurological systems are still functioning. They remain in varying degrees of coma. I'm not going to mislead you. It's an extremely dangerous situation. But there's still hope that they will be able to pull out of it."*

The tension in the room spilled over as one of the mothers broke down. *"My baby, I want my baby!"* she wept.

"I assure you that our neuroprogrammers are working around the clock to raise the stricken sectors," Dr. Wolinsky declared, after the woman had been tended to. *"There's an intense international effort going on. In the United States alone, all the neurologically affected children are having their brain waves collectively monitored by the NETF network in Atlanta. We're getting updates on their condition every hour. . . . We'll be keeping you posted."*

"Just tell it to me straight, doctor." Gobi fixed his eyes on Dr. Winston. "What are his chances? Fifty-fifty? Less?"

"You have to understand, Mr. Gobi," Dr. Winston replied cautiously. "I'm a neuropathologist by training and this is an area of trauma we're not exactly familiar with." He sighed. "I realize this is an extremely difficult situation for you. I'm a father myself. Thank God, my daughter is only a year old or else she might have. . . ."

"I'm terribly sorry, Mr. Gobi." The physician caught himself in midsentence, his face reddening. "I didn't mean to say that. I just put my foot in my mouth, I'm afraid."

"That's all right, doctor," Gobi waved him off. "Never mind about that. Just tell me about Trevor's condition."

"He's in theta," Dr. Winston answered, after a moment's hesitation.

"Excuse me? I didn't quite catch that." Gobi shook his head. "What did you say?"

"Your son is in a coma, but his brain waves are transmitting at a theta frequency. Somewhere between five and seven hertz."

"He's *what?*" Gobi looked perplexed.

"Let me explain," Dr. Winston said, holding his hands up as if he were illustrating a lesson in a classroom. "There are four bands of brain waves." He ticked off the fingers on his left hand. "There's *beta,* which is your normal state of waking consciousness. There's *alpha,* which is the equivalent of, say, a deep state of relaxation or concentration. Then there's *theta.* It's a deeply internalized state, Mr. Gobi. You'll find a great deal of production of hypnogogic imagery occurring in this state."

"Hypnogogic imagery?"

"Better known as creative reverie," Dr. Winston explained, apologetic. "It's a lucid dreaming state located just at the point between consciousness and deep sleep. Your son is in a very creative space right now. At least we know he's not in *delta.*"

Gobi frowned and shook his head again. He couldn't believe he was hearing any of this.

"Delta is associated with deep sleep and other similar unconscious states," Dr. Winston continued kindly. "Your son is generating a lot of rather interesting graphics on the monitor," he added as an afterthought.

"Graphics?" Gobi repeated, incredulous.

"Yes. Mostly spirals and mandala images. He wouldn't be doing that if he were in delta, I can assure you."

"Wait a minute. Are you telling me that Trevor is technically in a state of so-called 'creative reverie'—but that he's in a *coma?"*

"Exactly," Dr. Winston nodded. "I know it sounds crazy. We don't pretend to understand it . . . I mean, medically speaking. If your son were in an ordinary state of trance or reverie, he could come out of it at any time. But he *can't* in this case. At least, he can't do it at will." Dr. Winston coughed nervously.

"Another thing," the doctor added. "We don't know just how long Trevor—and the other children who are in a similar situation—can sustain their current level of neurological activity. Our support equipment is taking care of their normal brain and bodily functions. But. . . ."

"But what?"

"There's something else occurring that we're also baffled by," Dr. Winston said, avoiding Gobi's eyes.

"What do you mean something's happening? What is it, doctor!?"

Dr. Winston lowered his voice. "This is most peculiar. Highly unusual. I'm not sure I can even begin to describe it to you." He rose to his feet, suddenly showing his weariness. "Why don't you come with me to see Trevor? You can have a look for yourself."

The doctor led him through the swinging doors into the emergency VR ward.

Gobi walked past a series of small white tents. He saw nurses entering and exiting through flapped entrances. Young children appeared to be asleep inside. It didn't seem like an emergency ward so much as a place of spiritual retreat. There was even some meditative background music.

Gobi glanced at Dr. Winston wonderingly. He hadn't expected this—this *refuge*. But maybe that's what it was like in the recovery ward when death arrived during visiting hours, flowers in hand.

"So you hear it too, then?" Dr. Winston asked, relaxing his features for the first time since Gobi had met him.

"It sounds like some kind of a Gregorian chant."

"As near as we can tell, it's a mix of some sort from the devotional songs of Hildegard von Bingen. Are you familiar with the music of Hildegard von Bingen, Mr. Gobi?"

Gobi looked at him blankly. He knew who Hildegard was, of course, but his thoughts were jumbled. He was still in a state of shock.

"Wasn't she a 12th-century mystic and composer?" Gobi asked. "During the Middle Ages? In Germany?"

He suddenly stopped. "What do you mean by *as near as you can tell?* What's this music got to do with anything? Anyway, don't you know what you're playing in your own ward?"

Just then a hauntingly beautiful phrase of music hovered in the air like a fragment of stained glass. Both men were totally absorbed by the sound.

"That's just it," Dr. Winston replied, glancing back at him. "We're *not* playing any music in the wards. We don't even have a sound system! It's the damnedest thing. Come on, your son is over this way."

They stopped in front of a man who was standing in the middle of the hallway. "Ah, professor! There you are!" Dr. Winston exclaimed.

He was a small gnome of a man with a fringe of white hair around his bald head. He wore thick glasses and a rumpled, brown velvet suit with a round collar and a lace ruffle at the sleeves. He aimed his recorder at the ceiling as gingerly as if it were a starter's pistol.

"I'm sorry, you were in the middle of recording?" Dr. Winston asked.

"It's all right," the gnome said. "I've set up microphones everywhere."

"This is Professor Heinrich Mueller from the San Francisco Conservatory of Music," Dr. Winston said. "Mr. Gobi is the father of one of the children here."

Mueller nodded. "Definitely Hildegard. Beyond any doubt," he remarked in a thick German accent. "How do you do?" he nodded at Gobi. "I'm very sorry about what's happened to your child. But this music, it's something of a miracle, *ja?* We must all admit."

"We must all admit *what?*" Gobi asked, still at a loss.

"Professor Mueller is an expert in medieval music, Mr. Gobi," Dr. Winston explained. "He's been recording this music ever since we first noticed it a few hours ago."

"Would somebody *please* tell me what is going on!?" Gobi pleaded. "Professor?"

Professor Mueller blinked, then pursed his lips as though pondering a weighty question. "Oh, dear," he said finally. "You don't know about this then? You haven't told him yet?" He turned to Dr. Winston.

"We're still sort of patching our way through all of this," Dr. Winston admitted apologetically. "They're trying to make sense of it in Atlanta. All we know is that they're picking up this music everywhere. Over the entire network."

Gobi stared at him. "You must be joking."

"We think it may be some sort of bleed-through from Virtuopolis," Dr. Winston added. "They're trying to run a check with the music programming department of Satori City, or what's left of it. But so far it's still a mystery. Baffling."

"Ubi tunc vox inauditae melodiae," Professor Mueller murmured, a look of rapture passing over his cherubic face.

"What did you say?" Gobi asked, still staring at him.

"It's a line from a letter written by Volmar, a monk who served as the private secretary to Hildegard von Bingen. When she was on her deathbed, Volmar asked: *'Where then is the voice to this unheard melody?'*"

"Here we are." Dr. Winston held the flap open so Gobi could enter the tent. "Your boy's inside. After you."

Gobi's heart skipped a beat as he gazed upon his son's sleeping face. Trevor looked like a child having a dream. His eyelids fluttered and his breath escaped his half-opened mouth like a little stream in the woods.

The neural headset was connected to the bedside monitor and the 'trodes buzzed incandescently. Mandalas grew from seeds and sprouted mandala branches on the screen as they exploded in concentric octaves of color.

Trevor's face was deathly pale.

Dr. Winston put on the goggles and felt Trevor's pulse. He shook his head and removed the neuroscope from around his neck and handed it to Gobi along with the goggles.

"Here, take a look at this."

Gobi brought the goggles to his eyes. Trevor, himself so white, was radiating incredible waves of color. Deep reds, orange hues, blues, yellows, greens, and violet poured from his body. The entire area around his bed was drenched in ripples of light.

Gobi removed the goggles and looked up at the doctor with a stunned expression. "What is it? What's going on?"

Dr. Winston stood behind him with his arms folded. He rocked on the balls of his feet, deep in thought.

"It's truly amazing," he said, as he donned the goggles to check the neuroscope once again.

He turned to Gobi. "Your son is in what we'd call a state of heightened trophotropic arousal. That's evident from all the parasympathetic changes—the reductions in his heart rate, blood pressure, sweat excretion, striated muscle relaxation, as well as the synchronized cortical rhythms."

"Doctor, please!" Gobi pleaded with him.

"I'm sorry." Dr. Winston shook his head. "I guess what I'm trying to say, Mr. Gobi, is that neurologically speaking, your boy is in a state of heightened consciousness normally associated with profound Zazen meditation and yogic states. All his brain waves match up with the existing template for the so-called 'awakened mind.' These are all the traditional signs of what the medico-spiritual literature describe as 'enlightenment.' From a clinical standpoint, of course."

"What . . . what exactly are you saying?" Gobi spluttered.

"I'm saying, Mr. Gobi, that if your son were conscious right now and able to relate to us through our ordinary form of reality, we'd probably find ourselves in the presence of a fully enlightened being. But since he *can't* communicate with us directly—or rather, since we can't communicate with *him* through *our* normal channels of sense perception—we will never be able to know his true state of mind."

Dr. Winston bit his lip and sighed. "You see, Mr. Gobi, we'd have to be enlightened ourselves in order to understand what any of this means. But we're not. I'm afraid we're rather a long way away from that. If we were, perhaps none of this would be happening right now. It's a paradox."

He laid his hand gently on Gobi's shoulder. "Come on, we should go now. Let him rest. We'll let you know if there are any changes in his condition."

THICK FACE, BLACK HEART

Why don't you come home with us, Frank?" Hans Ulbricht gently prodded Gobi. They had found him in the hospital lounge, stretched out on one of the couches.

"Frank!"

"Oh, hi." Gobi looked up at Hans and Melissa and smiled weakly. He'd been in a half-dream state for the past few hours, seeing in his mind all those vivid colors that were leaking from Trevor's energy centers. His own consciousness felt as if it were being swept away on the current of a mighty river.

"You're right. I should get some rest. If you'll just drop me off at home, I'd appreciate it."

"Are you sure you want to be by yourself?" Melissa pressed him.

"I'll be all right. Don't worry about me."

They drove him home to Oxford Street. Before he got out of the car, Melissa leaned over and asked, "Is it true, Frank? What they're saying?"

"Is what true, Melissa?" he asked, still half-asleep.

"About the music," she said, "in the VR ward."

Poor Melissa. He looked at her with compassion. He couldn't bring himself to be irritated by her needling curiosity right now, although his nerves were certainly stretched past their limit. He was beyond exhaustion.

No, she was just expressing her normal pushy need to know. It was all right. It was part of being human, too. *Thick face, black heart,* the Chinese called it. Some people were born with it. It was in their nature.

"What about the music, Melissa?" he asked kindly.

Her face looked more pinched than ever. She said, "They say it's changing. From Gregorian chants to something else. To something evil. You've heard it, haven't you, Frank? What's it like? *Frank?*"

He got out of the car, slammed the door shut, and walked up the stairs to the front door.

He didn't look back.

Juan met him at the door. "Oh, Mister Frank!" he cried, and hugged Gobi. "I'm sorry!"

"It's all right, Juan," Gobi told him.

"I didn't know what to do!" Juan cried tearfully.

"It's not your fault," Gobi said, feeling his own grief weigh on him. He felt like the man in one of those old China coast lithographs showing a criminal being led through the streets with his head protruding from a wooden cangue. His crime was pasted on the board for all to see: *Not present when son crashed in virtual world.*

"He just won't leave!"

Gobi blinked dully at Juan. "Who won't leave? What are you talking about?"

"The other mister. I try to tell him you're not at home! You're at the hospital. I tell him call back, but he no listen! He's still here!"

"Juan, *who* is still here?"

"He!" Juan's frightened eyes looked down the hall toward Trevor's room.

Gobi stepped briskly down the hall. As he passed his study, he noticed the wall cube was on, glowing. Behind, in the kitchen, the extension cube was also on.

Gobi opened the door to Trevor's room.

The room was dark except for Trevor's cube, which was switched on like the other sets. The man standing in front of the screen turned slowly and flickered. He nodded almost imperceptibly when he saw Gobi enter.

"Dr. Gobi," he said with a bow. "My name is Akira Wada. I'm so sorry to be intruding. Your servant said I could wait here."

He moved as fast as the graphics would allow. He stood in front of Trevor's V-board, which was parked at the foot of the bed.

The man nodded thoughtfully. "This is your son's equipment." He looked up at Gobi. "Very high quality."

"Action Wada?" Gobi was too surprised to protest the holoid's presence in his house. He'd obviously been teleprowling on the premises.

"You know who I am?" the Japanese holoid asked with a faint smile. 'Action' is my nickname because I am supposed to get things done. Not always, I'm afraid," he laughed lightly.

Gobi nodded. He remembered Wada from his background search on the Satori Group. He had pulled the file on Wada's interview from *Offshore Networking* magazine. "You're the Vice President of Operations for Satori Corporation, aren't you?"

Action Wada blinked at him. "Actually, Dr. Gobi, at the moment I am the Acting Director of the Satori Corporation."

"What's happened to your chairman, Kazuo Harada?" Gobi asked bitterly. "I suppose he had to resign after what's happened. To 'save face' for the corporation. Isn't that how it works?"

"No, he has not resigned," Action Wada's form crackled at the joints and then reintegrated. "In fact, he has disappeared."

Gobi paused to take that in. "Well, he's going to have to take full responsibility for the breakdown of Virtuopolis. I can promise you there's going to be hell to pay! And I'm not just talking about damages!"

Action Wada waited for Gobi's outburst to subside. Then he continued. "When you met with our representative Mr. Kimura in San Francisco, we were not sure whether you would agree to work for us or not. I regret that Mr. Kimura did not present you with all the necessary facts."

Gobi felt a familiar chill course through his body. "What do you mean? He showed me the demo for your so-called 'post-virtual' environment. You could have fooled me. If it's not some sort of an elaborate hoax, it was pretty convincing. What was Kimura holding back?"

"I must tell you the real reason we wish to employ you, Dr. Gobi." Action Wada took a step closer to Gobi.

Gobi noticed a slight blemish of fractals, like stubble, on Wada's chin. His eyes looked a little too wide-orbed. Was he wearing turbo-contacts? Gobi's sixth sense told him the holoid had some extrasensory features built in for remote intelligence-gathering. Was he picking up stuff in the rest of the house while they were chatting here?

"Our chairman disappeared in Neo-Tokyo shortly *before* the crash of Satori City," Action Wada said confidingly. "We have reason to believe the two events are related. The fact is, we need you to help us locate him. We need your, ah, *expertise* in such matters."

"My expertise?"

"Intuitive investigations are your specialty, are they not?

You are known to be—what is the term?—a 'consciousness detective.' You investigate phenomena involving states of altered consciousness. Well, consciousness is the business that Satori is in. We've built our reputation on it."

So *that* was it. Gobi had to laugh. They were shopping around for a private eye. An on-line Philip Marlowe. They needed a Continental Op to find a missing person in a city that was missing half the time. It was almost a letdown, really. But he was glad to get to the bottom of it.

"I don't do that kind of work anymore," Gobi replied cautiously. "I did in the past, but that's ancient history. I'm strictly involved in academe these days. R and R. Research and Regurgitation. I'm sorry, but I'm really *not* your man, Mr. Wada. You need someone else. Have you tried Kroll & Kawasaki Associates? They have operatives everywhere. They're very good, I hear."

"No, I don't think so, Dr. Gobi," Action Wada persisted. "Contrary to your expressed opinion, I believe that you are *indeed* our man. I wouldn't be here otherwise. I assure you."

"I *told* you, I quit being a private investigator years ago," Gobi repeated. "I do a little corporate consulting now and then. A little R and D, a bit of product analysis, some scenario planning. That's the extent of it."

Action Wada grinned. "Yes, I've heard about your recent research efforts on behalf of Shiseido-Dior. You did a reading on their new line of 'karmic cosmetics.' Correct me if I'm wrong: *People with skin trouble have something sticking to them from a past life.* They were cruel to animals, abused them, or tortured them in some way, and that negative behavior has left a residue on them in *this* lifetime. But they can, if they so choose, balance that karmic pH factor with an application of this revolutionary skin cream from Shiseido." Wada chuckled. "That's wonderful! Really ingenious!"

Gobi looked at him stonily. "Animal cruelty leaves a mark on the abuser. It seeps through people's genes karmically. And it affects the sensitivity of their skin. This fact is gradually becoming better known." He paused. "I thought my report to Shiseido was supposed to be confidential."

"Please don't misunderstand me, Dr. Gobi," Action Wada protested. "I have nothing but the greatest respect for your—ah—bold intuitive approach. It's—it's truly *profound.* What can I say? Besides, that product is selling extremely well, isn't it? What's it called—'Karmic Cleanser?' So your vision has been vindicated where it counts most—in the marketplace."

"Thanks," Gobi said dryly. "And now, Mr. Wada, if you'll excuse me. I'm really quite exhausted."

Action Wada didn't miss a beat. "No, I was thinking more along the lines of the work you did—not *too* long ago, if I'm not mistaken—for Ono NeuroIndustries." His eyebrows lifted inquiringly. "A case involving a missing person? There seems to have been a string of them lately. Does the name Ono ring a bell? Yasufumi Ono, the president of Ono Neuro? You came out of your self-imposed retirement to tackle the case. May I ask why?"

Gobi's face hardened. "I can see that you're remarkably well-informed, Mr. Wada," he conceded. "I won't mince words with you. The case you're referring to was a rare exception for me. Please believe me when I tell you, I haven't handled anything like that in years. Anyway, if you know *that* much, you ought to *also* be aware of the fact that I was unable to solve it. I never did find the man."

Action Wada rotated on the balls of his feet as he studied the furnishings in Trevor's room. His gaze returned to Gobi after he had made his sweep.

"Perhaps you didn't go far enough, Dr. Gobi?" he suggested. "I don't mean to be harsh, but perhaps that's been your trouble all along?"

Gobi eyed the holoid with mounting irritation mixed with dread. "What do you mean by that?"

"Let me ask you something." Action Wada blinked at him. "Why did you give up your career as a private investigator? You were on the cutting edge, yet you chose to retreat to the ivory tower. Yes, you're doing brilliant work. You're highly respected in your field. But it's all *theoretical.* You could have gone *further.*" He sounded reproachful.

"Like where?" Gobi felt the dryness in his throat and the

familiar pressure building around his windpipe. So it was all coming back to him again, full circle.

"You could have broken through, Dr. Gobi—*to the other side,*" the holoid hissed at him from another time and place. "The whole world is on the verge of something new. Soon it will be part of the mainstream. But you were a pioneer. What held you back? You were *so* close."

Gobi closed his eyes. He had been close once. But that was a long, long time ago. *Her name was Kimiko. He had just hung his shingle out above an Italian bakery in North Beach:* <u>Frank Gobi, Private Investigations. On-Line, Off-Line, Out-of-Line Searches. All Inquiries Welcome.</u>

She had walked into his second-floor office on Green Street one afternoon like the young Japanese heiress that she was. Her father had a medium-size robotics factory, doing mostly offshore assemblies of Japanese cars out of Phnom Penh. "Hello," she said, flashing him a smile that made her strand of white Mikimoto pearls look like synthetic baubles by comparison. He beamed back at her.

Her black hair had the shine of the finest obi silk, and the dimples on her face suggested other surfaces on her body whose curves he was tempted to investigate. "My name is Kimiko Ono. I'm a student at the Art Institute?"

She had a way of appending question marks to her statements that endeared her to him even more.

"Yes?"

She had no way of knowing it, of course, but she was one of his first clients. Gobi was a gumshoe fresh out of the Berkeley Psychic Institute. He'd done some fêng-shui work, a little geomancy here and there. He had located a few missing objects, dowsed a bit, recharged some power spots that had lost their potency, performed some intuitive projections for business plans. He was a rising star among Rim P.I.'s, but he had never been involved in an attempted murder case before. Not before Kimiko came along. She changed his life forever. She made him jump from the void into the fire.

"Someone is trying to murder me?" she told him demurely, as though she were worried about a run in her stockings. Not that she wore stockings. Kimiko had long bare legs, almost translucently white. The light handmade slippers on her feet made Capezios look like Birkenstocks. A black latex Stormy Leather corset cradled her hips like one of the Black Ships entering the port of Kanagawa during Commodore Perry's forays into feudal Japan. Her breasts peeked out of her bodice almost like an afterthought. The look was of decadent innocence—or of depravity lost, depending on your point of view. Gobi wasn't sure what his was at that moment.

"Someone is trying to murder you?" he asked, trying his best to stifle a smile. He had done a quick probe when she sat down. She was clean. There ought to have been a knot of fear in her second meridian if she'd been dealing with a death threat or if somone were stalking her. And if someone had attempted something—even on the subtext level of intent, a continent away—there would have been the telltale fingerprints on the sheath of her fifth auric layer. But there was nothing. Only the swell of a passionate calm, which Gobi took to be evidence of her own exuberant nature.

"I am my father's only heir?" she said. *"I have no brothers or sisters? He has not adopted a male heir to succeed him. He is a very nontraditional Japanese, you see? Now my father's business is growing and he has many enemies. It is quite a good sign, actually. Ono Industries is becoming quite well known in the world."*

"Yes?"

"It is a known fact that certain competitors wish my father to merge his business with theirs. The keiretsus, *you know."* She flashed him another wide smile, as though he didn't really know. *"They are big complex alliances, more like the old clans than like businesses. They are always challenging one another, absorbing one another. Growing. Fighting. Absorbing."*

She crossed her legs, two sensual stalks of a flower arrangement. *"So desu ka?"* he said to her, seriously in awe of her beauty.

"Oh, you speak Japanese?"

"Sukoshi. Just a little."

"Hmm," she said, as if considering him from another vantage point. Her lips, which were painted a rich russet shade, opened like dark clouds to reveal the tip of her salmon-hued tongue. She flicked it at her lips nervously.

"The keiretsus," he prompted.

"If my father has no direct successor, he is more likely to accept a merger offer. Negotiations are not going smoothly. I am a natural target for assassination, neh? My father is worried. He says I need protection."

"You're a student at the Art Institute? Is that going to help prepare you to take over your father's business? Shouldn't you, ah, be enrolled at the Harvard-Keio Business School, or some place like that? What I mean is, Miss Ono, do you really believe that you pose a threat to your father's business rivals? What do you do *at the Institute anyway?"*

She leaned over and pulled at the strings to her furoshiki handbag. They came undone easily and she removed a small package from the bag. There was an intense gleam in her eyes as she undid the wrapping. *"This is some of my work,"* she said. *"You know origami? Paper sculpture? Thousand cranes. Little crabs. You can make many different things?"*

"Yes, I'm familiar with origami," he said, bemused as she showed him her collection of twisted paper creatures.

"These are bio-origamis," she said. *"They are like folded pieces of consciousness? And you can twist them into different thought forms. My father is very interested in this process. It is a talent I have. My father believes that robotics and bio-origami have a bright future together."*

"A bright future together?" Gobi asked, as he stared at a little rooster made of red and white paper. His mind was suddenly blanking out and he was seeing images—algorithmic faces and bodies, neuro-binaries that rushed helter-skelter along skeletal frames, movement and thought coinciding.

"Intelligent wood pulp," Kimiko giggled. *"Robots that live on a piece of paper. Interactive milk cartons. Crazy things! I don't worry about that. That is my father's business."*

It was true. She wasn't worried about anything. She was recession-proof and naturally worry-free, as far as he could see, except for her complaint about being on somebody's hit list. She didn't act scared though. It remained a complete abstraction to her. "What exactly do you want me to do for you, Miss Ono?" he asked.

She studied his face for a moment. He could see her thoughts coming at him from different angles, trying to picture this, conjecturing that. She brushed the long, black hair from her face, then reached out with her hand and touched his shoulder. She urged him forward just a bit. He came around the rest of the way on his own. As she savored his kiss, she said, "I must tell you, I never mix business with pleasure. It just comes out that way. I want you to make love to me first. Then you can save my life, Mr. Detective-san. Can you do that for me?"

"In that order?" he asked, tasting the stillness of the typhoon before it whipped his body apart.

"In that order," she said. "But you can choose the position."

He had chosen the first position, but she had chosen all the rest after that. And even when he had come to believe her story, it was too late. But not too late for him to have fallen in love with her. A wild once-in-a-lifetime love, the kind that consumes you and brands you a gypsy or a gigolo or both. Basically, she paid him to make love to her and then to act as her bodyguard. But he never took the latter part of the job too seriously. He dismissed it as being just part of Kimiko's kooky mystique. She got messages all the time. Strange-looking Japanese guys on mopeds would deliver packages to her in the cafes. Or she'd hand them big envelopes stuffed with her latest bits of neural menagerie. She'd smile at Gobi and say, "Birds and lions. Crocodiles. No problem."

The problem was, he had allowed himself to become too involved in the romance and had forgotten about the business. Late one evening, around midnight, they found Kimiko's body *in a laundromat on Upper Grant, stuffed inside the dryer, panty hose wound tight around her throat, sheets and pillow-cases and lacy underthings buffering her as though she had made a crash landing in a barrel of lingerie.*

Gobi had been trying to call her for the past two days but had gotten no answer: "The Mitsubishi Bell customer you are trying to reach is currently unavailable. . . ."

"Did you know the girl?" Detective Wong asked him when he showed up at the Grant Avenue Wash & Dry. "We found your card in her bag. It was kind of hard to read. She had twisted it up in a funny shape, sort of like a valentine's heart or something."

"Did you find any other origamis?" Gobi asked. The homi-cide inspector was a young guy and he was doing everything by the Newton.

"No, what other origamis?" Detective Wong asked as he scribbled on his pad. He looked worn out in the soapy glare of the neon—like he'd seen it all before. The names and the bod-ies and the murder weapons had been changed, but the motives were still the same.

"Little rabbits, roosters, cranes, that kind of thing?" Gobi couldn't bring himself to look at Kimiko through the glass hatch of the dryer. Not that he could see her face anyway; the inside of the porthole was draped with her long black hair.

"No, sir. Nothing like that. Only your card, all twisted up. Care to tell me about it? You got any ideas about who might have killed her? She's a New Nippon national, according to her I.D. Kimiko Ono, age 22," Detective Wong said, peering into his screen. Gobi saw her face in the detective's high-res hand, two-by-three inches, so oddly unfamiliar to him at that angle, and he felt his stomach lurch.

Detective Wong studied Gobi's meishi card. "She was your client, Mr. Gobi?"

"Yes, she was." He felt choked inside.

"Did she tell you about receiving any threats to her life?"

Gobi shook his head. He felt sick to his stomach, ashamed and nauseated. He had let her down. Kimiko, that poor little rich dreamer; so she hadn't been dreaming after all. That was *when he decided he wasn't cut out for the job. He bailed out in a heavy funk. It took him three years to get his head together. He traveled around the world. He lived for brief periods in India; in Bali; in Boulder, Colorado; in St. Petersburg-on-the-Neva. He decided to go back to graduate school. One day he was cleaning out his closet and found a little origami in the breast pocket of one of his jackets.*

Kimiko must have stuck it in his pocket without telling him. It was pale blue and green and it looked like a little heron standing on one leg. He held it in the palm of his hand, almost afraid that it would fly away.

"Hi, Frank, I hope you're well?" He heard Kimiko's musical voice as clearly as if she were standing before him. "If you find this, it must mean that I am—chotto—well—you know. Otherwise, I planned to recover this message from your very nice jacket before you discovered it. I wish I could hold you or something, neh? Grrrr . . ." she growled like a tigress, then laughed. She said more seriously: "Don't blame yourself for my death, Frank! You've got to forgive yourself. Not your fault. But I want you to promise me one thing. If my father ever needs your help in the future, you must help him. For my sake. You may not know it yet, lover, how good you are. How good you can be if you let yourself go. Because that new world is going to be opening up soon, you know. You know it is! And you're standing right on the edge of it all. Not everyone is. I knew right away you were special." She giggled. "My special Kimiko sense told me. Oh, P.S., watch this."

The origami suddenly began to reshape itself. He smiled despite himself. It was a variation on the Fluttering Phoenix, one of Kimiko's favorite love arrangements in bed.

"Mister Frank!?" Gobi heard Juan's voice call to him anxiously from the hallway. Gobi's thoughts recoiled back to the present. Action Wada's holoid still swayed on the balls of his feet, a grin frozen on his face. But the light in his eyes had somehow dimmed.

"Go-bi . . . ?" The name slurred off Wada's lips like syllables of water. Gobi stepped past the scroll-like image and swiftly left the room. He found Juan at the end of the hallway, his ample form trembling in his colorful Guatemalan shirt.

Juan had his ear cocked outside the door that led to Gobi's private meditation chamber. His personal Zendo was off-limits to everyone, including his housekeeper and his son.

"Juan, what's the matter?" Gobi asked.

"The other mister, I see him enter your room just now!" Juan's eyes were wide with alarm. "The mister you are talking to in *there?*" He nodded in the direction of Trevor's bedroom. "¿Es posible, señor?"

"We'll see about that. Gracias, Juan."

Squaring his shoulders, Gobi slipped off his shoes and strode into the six-mat room of yellow woven tatami reeds. Action Wada barely turned around as he entered. "Ah, Dr. Gobi," the Japanese said, glancing at Gobi's stockinged feet. "I hope you don't mind if I keep mine on?" He chuckled. "I don't think it makes much difference in any case. My shoes are in Neo-Tokyo."

"Seen enough, Wada? How about if I show you where the bathroom is. I could flush you down the toilet."

"This is where you do your work, Dr. Gobi?" Wada looked at him coldly. "I mean, your deep work?"

There was a zabuton mat in the center of the tiny room with a turquoise and plum round zafu pillow on it. It faced a small altar with a 19th-century Thai Buddha sitting on it, its gilt long since worn off. A smaller Japanese Buddha, a dark cast-iron Manjusri, the Buddha of Wisdom, held court at its feet. An incense burner contained ash that had grown cold. A bronze Tibetan bell stood silent nearby. A brass bowl with a single azalea floating in the water stood as an offering.

How long had it been since he last sat here? Since the nightmare that had led him to Alta Bates?

On the wall, which Gobi had plastered himself, hung an ink-brush painting, a copy of Sengai's 18th-century *Circle, Triangle, and Square.*

"If you like, I can arrange to obtain the original for you,"

Action Wada said thoughtfully, studying the painting. "It's hanging at the Idemitsu Museum in Neo-Tokyo."

"What would *you* know about anything that's original?" Gobi retorted. "You're a projection of a projection of a projection."

Action Wada laughed heartily. "Very good, Gobi-sensei! You are right! When you are everywhere, you are practically nowhere. But let's talk business now."

"What do you want from me? I told you I'm not interested."

Again, Action Wada looked at him coldly. "I wanted to see your base of operations for myself." He sniffed the air. "Very refined vibrations. Good for classical trancework. You learned the Balinese technique? Maybe Burmese? You are accustomed to working with intermediaries? You call on some of their 'nat' spirits?" He rubbed his hands. "Good, good." He turned to Gobi. "But I can see where you would end up with unreliable information if you rely on such primitive intelligence-gatherers. It's a long way from Mandalay, Dr. Gobi."

"Spit it out, Wada."

"Dr. Gobi, no offense meant—"

"I said spit it out."

"Very well. I have seen where you work. And the impression I am left with is this: 'Failure now may be more enjoyable than success later,' as the saying goes. I don't think you really *want* to succeed."

"Meaning what?"

"I can see how your search for Ono would have ultimately led you nowhere. Your—ah, *studio*—is too far removed from more powerful energy channels. Dr. Gobi, your only hope of finding anyone is to come to Neo-Tokyo yourself. In person. To start from there. Incredible energies have been unleashed since the earthquake. You can use them to your advantage."

"I have no intention of traveling to Neo-Tokyo. Or any place else, for that matter."

"Perhaps you will reconsider. I have taken the liberty of booking you on tomorrow's flight, a first-class ticket on Satori Airlines departing at noon from L.A. Metroplex to New

Narita. You will be met at Narita by one of our operatives. He will be at your disposal."

"Something tells me we're not speaking the same language. I'm not planning to go to Neo-Tokyo. I'm not interested in looking for your chairman, Kazuo Harada. My son is in a coma. He may—," Gobi's face flinched. "I may lose him at any moment. I'm staying here with him. That's final."

"That's precisely why you mustn't waste any more time, Dr. Gobi. Your son's life depends on it."

Gobi moved up to the holoid. He peered into those cordless sockets of tele-optic energy. "What did you say? My son's life depends on it? My son's life depends on what?"

"Find Kazuo Harada. He has the missing source code for the new post-VR Virtuopolis that will jump-start Satori City. He can override the crash. That will restore your son and all the thousands of others who are hanging on by a slender thread of consciousness. If you don't cooperate with us—I don't need to tell you what will happen. It's up to you."

"What's the catch?"

"There is no catch." Action Wada's eyes were level with his. "What is your answer?"

Gobi had never punched out a holoid before. Wada's image flickered. The high-definition pixels glopped and the look of astonishment was worth the price of Gobi's admission to Neo-Tokyo.

Gobi only missed him by about 4,000 miles or so. But hell, it *still* felt good.

BAD CHI

Gobi scowled. So Melissa had been right all along. Her "thick face, black heart" instinct had sniffed out the evil that was snaking its way through the corridors of the Adolescent VR Unit at Alta Bates.

What had happened to those beautiful inner harmonies of that medieval mystic Hildegard? *'De Verginibus.'* O wonderful

*creatures, gazing upon God, with beautiful features, uplifted
by the dawn, blessed virgins high-born. . . .*

He grimaced. What *was* that sound!? Couldn't they turn it
off? There was an awful refrain of pigs rutting and snorting
and scarfing up what could only be described as the offal of
human existence. He listened to it closely. They really *were*
pigs! He wasn't imagining it. It really *was* happening.

Gobi walked past the white tented units where the children
were filed away like cocoons. Doctors and nurses hurried past
him with vacant expressions. No one stopped to ask him what
he was doing in the ward. They were wrapped in a darkness of
their own—one they could not possibly diagnose.

That suited him. He wanted to see Trevor one last time in
private, to say good-bye to him before he left for Neo-Tokyo
in the morning.

Gobi slipped into his son's tent. He bent down to kiss him
and caught his breath. He saw Trevor as if from an elevated
bird's-eye view, lying on the cot down below, all wired up,
the shaven lobes of his skull raw and chafed where the elec-
trodes had been implanted. His pale blue eyes were open, but
they were fixed blindly on the ceiling.

Those must be his brain waves, Gobi shivered, as he gazed
at the monitor by Trevor's bedside. A swirling lava lamp of
colors boiled on the screen like a hallucination that the cat had
dragged in. It was a collective collage of some sort.

Was *that* what it looked like? The Big Dream? Thousands
of children all across the country were being tracked and monitored by the Neural Emergency Task Force in Atlanta. *And it
looked like a bad acid trip?* Was there some unresolved karma
here from the last century?

"Trevor," Gobi whispered. He felt his son's brow. It was
hot and moist, as if a tropical storm were raging under his
skin. His blond hair was soaked with sweat.

"I don't know if you can hear me or not. This is Dad. I
want you to know that I love you. I'm leaving on a little trip.
I'll be back soon. I . . . "

But he couldn't continue. The tears that flooded his eyes
were mixed with rage. *What had they done! WHAT HAD THE*

*BASTARDS DONE? It was a genocide of the soul. They had
shorted the consciousness of thousands of innocent people—
men, women, and children. Not even the surge protector of the
Satori VR system had been able to save them. Whoever was
responsible would pay dearly for their crime.*

Gobi's eyes blazed with anger. He took a deep breath, then
bent to kiss Trevor good-bye a final time. "'Bye now. I'll be
back before you know it. I promise. Remember, wherever you
are, we'll always be together. Hang in there, champ! I'm
counting on you."

Out in the ward, Gobi bumped into the German musicologist,
Professor Heinrich Mueller. The gnomelike man was fiddling
with his recording equipment. He did not look very happy.

"Ach, it's you, Herr Gobi," Professor Mueller sighed.
"These animals, they are the pits. *Ja?*"

"What's going on, professor?"

The pigs were now storming the VR ward's airwaves,
sniveling, snorting, and rooting. A crash of electric guitars
reverberated as a pipe organ stitched a counterpoint to their
burrowing grunts. A rasping voice began to sing:

> *"Big man, pig man, ha ha charade you are. . . .*
> *You got to stem the evil tide, And keep it all on the inside.*
> *Mary you're nearly a treat, Mary you're nearly a treat,*
> *But you're really a cry. . . ."*

Professor Mueller swore darkly. "It's a composition by Die
Rose Fliegen . . . by the Pink Flies, Mr. Gobi." He waved his
hand limply in the air. "Better not ask."

"It's *Pink Floyd,* professor," a woman's voice corrected
him from the rear. "They were an English rock group from the
last century. I believe this is a track from an album of theirs
called 'Animals.' In fact, I've just downloaded it from the
Library of Congress archives to study it in its entirety."

Professor Mueller blinked at her myopically. "Young lady,
you certainly know your pigs, that is all I can say!"

Gobi recognized the voice immediately, even before he
turned around. "Tara!" he exclaimed.

"Hello, Frank," Tara said, as she touched his arm, her green eyes lighting up to see him. "How are you?"

Gobi felt immediately comforted. The pain in his heart began to drain away, slowly but surely.

So there *was* some light in this world after all. And it was a blond wearing a Tibetan jacket, baggy Afghani pants, and the sweetest smile this side of the San Andreas Fault.

"What are *you* doing here?" Gobi asked in amazement.

At that moment, Dorje Rinpoche, the young Tibetan lama, rounded the corner. The suit and tie he had worn on campus were gone, replaced by a maroon robe with a long fold tucked at his shoulder. He was studying some notes.

"Ah, Gobi is it?" Dorje acknowledged when he saw him. "What do you make of this? Could it be a line from one of the animal tantras?" he turned to Tara. " *'Big man, pig man . . . ?'*" He squinted at his writing through his thick glasses.

"No, Dorje, as I was just telling the professor here, those are rock lyrics from, let's see now," Tara checked her readout. "The year was 1977," she replied. "That was an important transitional period in the world-consciousness movement."

Dorje thought for a moment. "Would that be part of the Uranus-Neptune conjunction? A middle phase, before the nineties acceleration?"

"That's right. Shift-time."

"Hmm, that's interesting, Tara!" The Tibetan grinned. "The pieces are coming together, I think."

Tara's green eyes returned to Gobi. "Your son is here, isn't he?" she asked gently.

Gobi felt the raw pain grab his heart again. "Yes. He was one of those who got caught in the wave."

Dorje looked at him with sudden interest. "Your *boy* is here? In this ward?"

"Yes. But what are you two doing here? Do you mind telling me?"

Dorje exchanged glances with Tara. "Perhaps we ought to have a talk with him," he said quietly.

Tara took him by the arm. "Why don't you come with us, Frank? I have a small apartment near here. I can fix you something that will make you feel better." She read his pulse with two fingers pressed against his wrist. "You could use a shot of chi after what you've been through. We'll fix you up, then we can talk. Okay?"

She drove them in her old Toyota Garuda hatchback down the seedy stretch of Telegraph Avenue. "I sometimes use this route as a shortcut," she apologized to Gobi. "I live up in the Berkeley hills. We'll be there in just a few minutes."

They passed a string of boarded-up shops, then slowed at the corner of People's Park where the street people were camped out, untidily crossing back and forth across Telegraph. A gaunt, dreadlocked Jamaican stepped up to their car at the traffic light: "Hash, grass, acid, mescaline, six-pack o' Jolt?"

Tara rolled up her window, shaking her head. "No thanks," she mouthed through the glass. Then she nodded out the window for Gobi's benefit. "Look, dogs," she said.

"Dogs?" Gobi wondered. He saw them, a pack of strays, a few still wearing their guide-dog harnesses. They were sniffing around a dumpster. One of them jumped out with what looked like the remains of a burrito, the glint of tinfoil in its mouth. A German shepherd sat on its haunches on the curb, scratching itself.

"They must have become separated from their owners after the Satori City crash," Tara said. "It's sad, isn't it? I hope the animal-control people round them up soon."

"'Trode-heads," Gobi said, sitting up.

"They must have really burned out their brain cells," Tara agreed. "It must have been terrifying for them when they crashed."

"No, Tara, over there," Gobi pointed at the corner of Channing. "Slow down a second."

"What is it?"

"See that group of guys?"

"What about them?"

"They're 'trode-heads. But they're not with their dogs."

Dorje sat up in the back and began to take notice. "He has a point, Tara. They seem to be getting around without any problem. Don't you find that odd?"

"Are you thinking what I think you're thinking?" Tara asked him.

"I don't know. Maybe," Dorje replied. "It's possible."

The car slowed to a halt as the group of brain donors shuffled past them on the sidewalk.

One of them turned when he noticed the Toyota and began to approach the vehicle. He had a limping gait, greasy overalls, and a bristling headset of 'trodes arranged in the dread manner. He brought his face to the windshield and peered inside, his hands wrenching the wipers in a sudden anguished reflex.

Gobi saw the gnashing teeth and the drool and for an instant he thought he saw the eyes, like gutted-out membranes computing their own darkness. The 'trodehead let out a sudden howl that alerted his buddies. His companions stopped and began to lumber toward the Toyota.

"I think we'd better get going," Tara said, as she gripped the steering wheel. "Get off!" she yelled at the interloper, who had wriggled onto the hood of the car, his arms stretched across the windshield in an embrace.

"*Mooooo,*" he moaned.

"Jeezus, they're heading this way!" Gobi warned as five or six 'trode people approached their stalled car, jerking their feet as they walked.

"That's it!" Tara said, as she stepped on the gas. They carried their unwelcome passenger a block down Telegraph before Tara made a sharp right and screeched to a halt. The 'trodehead slid off the hood and bounced to the ground.

Tara burned rubber all the way up Durant. "Whew!" she exclaimed. "That was close."

"I don't believe this," Gobi said, shaking his head. "I'm sure I've seen that guy someplace before."

"Well, he certainly was drawn to you," Tara joked. "I think he wanted to go home with you!"

"Now I know where I've seen him!" Gobi remembered. "I thought he was dead!"

"How's that again, Frank?" Tara asked, glancing at him with concern.

"The afternoon it happened. The crash. I was rushing to get home from the BART station. It was terrible. People were dropping like flies everywhere." He grimaced. "Then I came across this guy."

"Which guy?"

"This 'trodehead. His dog was dragging him on the street. He had his leash tied around his wrist. I did my best to help him. I got him off that leash. But the rest of it—" Gobi shook his head. "I could have sworn he was dead!"

Tara laid a hand on his shoulder.

"Perhaps he *was* dead," Dorje said somberly.

"What? What did you say?" Gobi said, staring at Dorje.

"Have you ever heard of the 'ro-langs,' Gobi?"

"What are you talking about?" He looked at Dorje sternly.

"They're a type of zombie. There are different categories."

"Zombies? What do you mean zombies? Like zombies from Haiti?"

"No, Gobi. From Tibet."

Tara parked her Toyota Garuda in front of a shoe-box-size driveway with a sign that read "Don't Even *Visualize* Parking Here."

Tara lived on a narrow lane on a wooded hill overlooking the Berkeley campus. Her flat was at the bottom of a long flight of stairs.

"Come on in, but take off your shoes first," she told him. Dorje was already untying his shoelaces.

Gobi stepped into a tiny studio with a hardwood floor. There was a low Japanese table by a sliding glass door that opened to a small moss garden.

"I'm afraid this is it," she said, giving him the instant tour. "There are some mats on the floor over there. Why don't you two make yourselves comfortable?"

She touched his shoulder. "Meanwhile, I'm going to prepare a little herbal tonic for you. It'll make you feel much better."

"Don't go to any trouble," he said.

"Don't worry, I won't." She smiled again and disappeared into a tiny kitchen behind a beaded curtain. Her feet were bare. Gobi felt funny, as if he had seen her in the nude. But it was enough for him just to watch her move like a dancer across the polished floor.

Dorje was arranging some zabuton cushions on the floor. "Sit," He patted one of the pillows.

Gobi noticed a little altar in the corner. The gold figure of a Tibetan goddess sat on a lotus throne. She held a lotus blossom in her left hand. Her open right hand rested on the knee of her right leg, which she was extending as if she were about to step down from her pedestal.

Gobi recognized the gesture to be the universal wish-granting mudra. The smile on the goddess' face was directed as if at some invisible supplicant.

"Tara," Gobi declared.

"Yes?" she called from the kitchen.

"No, this is a Tara figure. She's the goddess of compassion, isn't she?"

Dorje laughed. "Don't forget, she's also the Cheater of Death and the Prolonger of Life."

Gobi sat wearily on a mat. "So," he said, "tell me about your rolaids."

"Ro-langs," Dorje corrected him. "You must know your ro-langs, Gobi, if you are to defeat them."

Gobi eyed him warily. "What kind of a lama are you anyway? Red-Hat school? Black-Hat? Or what? How come you know so much about zombies?"

"I'm a Yellow-Cab lama," Dorje gave him a broad grin. "I drive a taxi."

"He's not kidding," Tara joked, as she brought in a tray with a pot of the chi kung tonic she had prepared for Gobi. "Dorje's main qualifications for driving a cab are that he doesn't have a valid driver's license—it expired in a former life—and he's a terrible driver," she teased her rotund friend. "How many yaks did you mow down on the Friendship Highway before you left Tibet?"

Dorje rolled his eyes. "Road kill one day, reborn as Norwegian philologists the next. It's the never-ending cycle on the Wheel of Life." He laughed uproariously, his belly shaking with mirth beneath his robes.

"Oh, Dorje, you're too much!" Tara laughed. She poured Gobi a bowl of nasty-looking brown liquid. "Here, drink this," she instructed. "This will give you a nice lift."

"Whew, what is it?" Gobi asked, making a face as he sniffed the brew.

"It's called 'Tame the Charging Bull,' and it's highly recommended for fatigue, burnout, insomnia, and chronic depression. It'll tonify your middle burner, regulate your chi, stabilize your exterior, and strengthen your lungs, spleen, and stomach. Any more questions?"

"Just one. Do I really have to *drink* it?" he groaned. "Can't I just inhale the fumes?"

"I'm afraid not, Frank. But I promise you won't regret it."

"To your health then." Gobi drank the bitter tonic down to the twigs at the bottom. "Ugh!

"Now," he continued, as a sudden ray of light began to sort through the rubble of his brain stem. "Let's try this again. Where were we?"

Gobi's head was buzzing softly. He was pleasantly energized. His middle burner certainly felt tonified, no question about it. His eight vessels and twelve chi channels felt like they were in the best shape they'd been in in years. He was ready to face the world again.

He glanced at Tara, who sat with her right leg folded over her left thigh in a half lotus position. Her eyes were almost closed. The oil lamp that flickered on the altar cast shadows that made her features appear darker than they were a few moments ago. Her nostrils were flared. What a striking face, he thought.

Her green eyes opened and focused on him and he felt the tingling sensation at the back of his head intensify.

"You asked if I was a Black-Hat lama or a Red-Hat." Dorje smiled at Gobi, breaking the silence. "Actually I'm a programmer. That's my real profession. I only drive a cab part-time."

Gobi focused on the stocky Tibetan who sat cross-legged in front of him, lightly fingering a string of beads.

"You're a programmer?" Gobi asked in disbelief. "A *computer* programmer?"

"With Shambhala Software. It's a small start-up company based in Yarlung Valley, near Lhasa."

"Dorje is too modest," Tara interrupted. "He's developed a new systems architecture called Tantrix. Perhaps you've heard of it?"

Gobi shook his head. "No, I haven't. What is it?"

"It's a Tibetan virtual reality imageering system," declared Dorje good-naturedly.

"A *what?*"

"The Tibetans have historically had a long tradition in visualization, Frank," Tara explained. "They were naturally very quick to adapt their tantric visualization techniques to VR applications."

"Tara's father helped Tibet's software industry get started at the turn of the century. Without him we would still be spinning prayer wheels." Dorje nodded gravely.

"Nonsense, Dorje," Tara disagreed. "My father just helped with the basics. But it was all your own initiative. Your *own* hard work. Your work, and the work of all the other lamas at Shambhala Soft."

"What are the applications of your system?" Gobi asked.

"It's not for the mass market, I'm afraid." Dorje smiled at him. "Let us just say, it's intended more for the advanced meditation end user."

"What he means is, you have to be *initiated* first," Tara added. "You can't just pick one of these units off the shelf and use it."

"What kind of units are you talking about?" asked Gobi, still mystified.

"Consciousness processors," Dorje said, as he clicked off one of his beads.

"Consciousness processors?"

"That's right," Dorje said. "What word processors were to the verbal mind in the early days of personal computing, these consciousness processors are to the human consciousness."

Gobi turned to Tara. "He's kidding, isn't he? This is one of his jokes?"

"No, Frank, he's not kidding. He's telling the truth," Tara's green eyes assured him.

"You mean to say, he's not kidding about those zombies either?" he challenged her.

"The ro-langs?" Dorje asked, his eyebrows climbing. "But you saw them yourself this evening. There are plenty of them that are not yet visible to the human eye. They're beginning to spread everywhere. They're in the system. They must be stopped."

"They're in the system? Wait a minute, you don't mean . . . ?" He sat up rigidly. "Is there some connection with the crash of Satori City?"

"The ro-langs are a kind of virus, Gobi," Dorje said, tapping his foot with his hand. "A VR virus. But the virus is crossing over into human consciousness. That is the problem we're facing."

"I think you'd better tell him about Tashi Nurbu," Tara told Dorje. "Better start at the beginning."

"Very well," Dorje sighed. "But that is not his real name. He has no real name. Hell has no real name. It just *is,* you know. It just is."

TASHI NURBU

That is the most amazing story I have ever heard," Gobi exclaimed, after Dorje had finished his tale.

"Tashi Nurbu is a dugpa, a lama programmer who practices the black arts," Dorje said, smoothing the folds in his robe. "He joined our order as a small child. His mother was Tibetan, but she had been raped by a Chinese soldier from the People's Army. When they were retreating from Tibet, they committed many atrocities. His shen, his spirit, was tortured from a previous existence. But he was very gifted at writing code. He advanced rapidly. His dark side did not appear until much later." Dorje frowned. "I should have foreseen that. That was my failure."

"He was Dorje's personal assistant," Tara added. "But he was already scheming when he began to work at Shambhala Soft. We learned that afterward when we reconstituted his V-mail to New Nippon. He thought he had vaporized all traces of his communications. And he had. But Dorje was able to call it up again. It told us a lot."

"You see, Gobi," Dorje said wistfully. "He stole the most advanced version of Tantrix we had at the time, which was Vajra 4.0. But the program wasn't quite finished yet. It had some rather unpleasant bugs, but he stole it nevertheless. It was his karma to steal it."

"We know he's been peddling it to the highest bidder. He's been leaving a trail."

"A trail?"

"The virus," Dorje said. "And now it's spreading all over. It's mutating."

"So that's how it got into the Satori City system? He sold it to the Satori Corporation? Did they know what they were buying?"

"He presented it to them as the next step beyond virtual reality," Dorje replied. "Which is what it is. That's what they were looking for. As a bridge to Satori City 2.0, the post-VR version."

"But he's moved on now," Tara interrupted. "You see, Tantrix is infinitely adaptable. It has many other features beyond consciousness simulation. In the wrong hands, it could be used to dominate the world."

"I can see how there would be a lot of buyers for that," Gobi agreed. "I can think of a few myself."

"Imagine," Dorje said, as he spread his hands open. "Does

the fish in the ocean realize that it is swimming in water? Does it have any *conscious* awareness of being immersed? Of course not. It accepts that as its natural state. Tantrix is like that ocean. It is a template that can be imposed upon the consciousness of the world, altering all awareness and perception. No one would be the wiser for it. Or even question it. It would become our new collective reality."

"It sounds like the Big Brother myth to me," Gobi sniffed.

"Believe me, Big Brother is just a little brother compared to this," Tara retorted. "They're not even blood relations."

"But how does it work?"

Dorje glanced at Tara. She nodded back. "I think we're on the same wavelength, Dorje. Go ahead and tell him."

"Very well," Dorje said. "It works this way, Gobi. What Tantrix does, in fact, is it *digitizes* consciousness."

Gobi let this thought sink in. He heard the tinkling of wind chimes in the garden, where a breeze played through the trees. *It digitizes consciousness,* he mused. *How alien, yet how familiar that landscape seemed. It's been a long time coming, hasn't it? How did the line in the song go? "This must be the place I waited years to leave. . . ." Alice in Wonderland meet Alice B. Toklas. Lotus Sutra meet Lotus 1-2-3. Here we go 'round the mulberry bush. . . .*

"Where is Tashi Nurbu now?"

"Ah, Gobi," Dorje smiled at him. "There's the rub. We believe he is somewhere in Neo-Tokyo at this time. Operating under an assumed name, of course. What name does he go by these days?" he asked Tara.

"He calls himself Sato," she replied. Then she became serious. "Frank, Tashi Nurbu has got to be stopped if this madness is to be contained. You can see the chaos that's already spinning out of control all around us. But first, we've got to neutralize the virus. Can you help us?"

"Help you? How?" Then it hit him. He felt the tingling at the base of his skull suddenly transfer to the fourth meridian around his heart. It *pinged!* open and he knew the answer, but there was something he couldn't quite put his finger on. And he needed to be certain about it first.

"Wait a minute," Gobi squirmed on his cushion. "There's something funny here. You *know* that I'm going to Neo-Tokyo tomorrow, don't you? *That's* why you invited me here."

He desperately wanted to trust those green eyes again. But his face was grim. "This isn't an accidental meeting, is it? None of it is. You've set this up. You've already figured me into your plan. But *how? How* do you know so much about me? And what do you *really* want?"

His energy suddenly felt depleted, as though whatever chi he'd had shooting up and down his spine had reached stasis again.

"If you're going to use me, you're going to have to tell me everything," he said hoarsely. "And I mean *everything*. Or else you can take your damned virus, boil it, and swallow it till you choke."

"Frank," Tara said. "I can see how you would get upset. But it's not what you think. We're not using you, we're . . ."

"We're *accepting* you," Dorje suggested cheerfully. "On our team. Look at it that way."

"That may be *your* way of looking at it," Gobi scoffed.

"Frank—," Tara's eyes pleaded with him, but he cut her short with an angry look.

"How did you know I would be going to Neo-Tokyo?" he asked accusingly. "Have you been spying on me?"

"Not exactly," she answered.

"What do you mean by 'not exactly'?" he demanded.

"Dorje was monitoring Satori's internal channels. When Kimura in San Francisco suggested to the head office in Neo-Tokyo that you be hired as a private investigator, that flagged you for us. Especially when he said you had what he called the 'requisite abilities.'"

"What abilities?"

"Obviously it was something that interested them very much. We tried to pull the Satori file on you, to see what it was, but it wasn't on-line. Which meant that it had been hand delivered to Neo-Tokyo. When you use a courier to transmit hard copy, Frank, you know it must be hot."

"Hmm," Gobi wondered. "I can't imagine what that might be. So you began to check me out. Why were you so interested?"

As Dorje stirred on his cushion, he twirled a large silver-and-turquoise ring on his forefinger. "We were expecting some major activity on the Tashi Nurbu front. The virus was due to manifest at any time. Sure enough, it did. In the form of the ro-langs."

"How?"

"We had reports of some early ro-langs sightings." Dorje glanced at Tara, who had become noticeably pale and sad. She was beginning to rock back and forth slightly on her zabuton cushion.

"They were beginning to appear in some of the more remote game sites," Dorje continued after a moment.

"Which game sites?" Gobi asked, a feeling of foreboding setting in.

"In Trek Land," Dorje went on. "That's the Himalayan portion of Gametime. Around the simulation of Sikkim and Bhutan. They were moving down from the highlands. Soon their presence would become more widely noticed. When they ran into groups of trekkers."

"Yes, and—?" Gobi sat up, listening raptly.

"That's when Satori realized they were in big trouble and had to do something fast before any bad publicity got out. The last thing they wanted was for the world to hear they had a runaway killer virus in Satori City."

"What did they do?"

"They sent a team of virus killers into those sectors. Neural ninjas. They weren't going in for any mercy killing, Gobi. They were going in to mop up, eliminate the problem, and get back out again."

"So what happened?"

"They never got out."

"How do you know that?"

"We found their remains."

"*You?*"

Tara stopped her rocking, and a tear trickled down her cheek.

"No, not me, Gobi," Dorje said quietly. "Tara's younger sister, Devi. She was up there trekking. She was the one who alerted us to the first signs of ro-langs on the trails. She found what was left of Satori's crew."

"You see, Frank," Tara turned to Gobi, her face glistening. "I know what you must be going through with your boy cut off some place in Gametime. That's where Devi is, too. She was there when it crashed, Frank. She's there now."

"But why didn't you tell me, Tara?" Gobi asked, laying his hand on hers gently.

She smiled, wiping a tear away. "You might have accused me of manipulating you then."

Dorje leaned forward. "Nothing is ever so simple or so direct, Gobi. As the artist said, 'Can 500 paintings be created in one single stroke?'"

"I'm sorry," Gobi said. "I should have trusted you. I *did* trust you. I guess I just didn't trust myself."

"It's all right, Frank," Tara replied. "We understand each other now. That's the important thing."

"All right," Gobi said, turning to Dorje. "Tell me about this virus. Tell me how I can nail this ro-langs."

"Are you sure you are willing to undertake this challenge, Gobi? It may cost you your life."

The Tibetan lama looked him in the eye, as though he were reading Gobi his karmic rights. *It is your move. It is your decision. You move. You decide.*

"What do I do?"

"Very well." The lama bowed to Gobi. "I can see that you are ready. Would you like to receive initiation in Vajrayana VR? To be initiated into the Way of the Virtual Warrior?"

With a lightness that surprised Gobi, the lama sprang to his feet to fetch a black leather case that resembled an old-fashioned doctor's satchel. Opening the clasp, he brought out an object wrapped in velvet. Gobi watched curiously as Dorje revealed a small handheld prayer wheel mounted onto a wooden handle. There was a little leather thong attached to the cylinder along with a tiny lead weight to facilitate in the spinning of the device.

Winking at Gobi, Dorje settled back in his place on the mat and crossed his legs. "This," he said, "is a 'mani.' It is loaded with the latest version of Tantrix, Vajra 4.2, which I've just completed. Don't worry, it's a bug-free version. Please keep your mind clear. The rest will just come to you. You will know by the images you see everything that you need to understand. Nothing more is necessary."

Gobi glanced at Tara. She had already settled into a full lotus position, her feet anchored on her upper thighs. Her eyes were closed. Her fingers were in the mudra of downloading nothingness. Her breathing was deep but regular.

"Ready, Gobi?" Dorje asked.

He nodded as he got himself as comfortable as he could get in a semi half lotus, feeling the flow begin.

Dorje began to spin the prayer wheel and to chant. Right away, Gobi realized it was no ordinary mani. The hard drive was built into the cylinder that contained the sacred syllables of the Om Mani Padme Aum sutra. As Dorje cranked the wheel faster, the program loaded, caught, and fired up.

Gobi closed his eyes. Vivid flashes of snow-capped mountains and a cobalt sky already burned into his brain. *Zap-zap-zap*. His third eye opened like a V-mailbox rapidly filling with visual messages.

In the back of his mind somewhere, he could hear Dorje's guttural tale of the ro-langs and the virus—both one and the same—unfold throughout the history of consciousness, before the history of consciousness, and beyond the history of consciousness.

"Rgyal po gau pa la 'di'am de wa pa la'i mtshams su / dpal o tanta pu ri'i gtsug lag khang yang bzhengs te / de ni ma gadha'i phyogs cig na mu stegs byed kyi rnal 'byor pa sngags kyi nus pa grub cing drang po'i rang bzhin can na ra

da zhes zer ba zhig yod cing / de ro langs kyi dngos grub sgrub pa la grogs lus stobs che zhing nad med la lus la dpa' bo'i mtshan ma dgu yod pa. . . ."

He was standing on the ledge of a great and immense monastery, staring into the blackness of a valley littered with rocks and bones. He was speaking in Tibetan. Dorje stood before him. But it did not look like Dorje. He was an old wiz- ened monk, toothless, dressed in a worn but patched robe, greasy from the spluttering of the many butter-lamps burning in the monastery halls.

Gobi did not recognize himself either. He was young, handsome, his hair was black and long, he had on felt boots and carried a whip. He had ridden his steed, like the wind on fire, to the monastery from whence the Old One had sum- moned him.

Gobi's mind spluttered, too. He was in the service of— which king, was it? Gau-pa-la or De-wa-pa-la? At any rate, he was not like this Old One who kept grinning at him like one of the human skull goblets from which the monks drank their barley grog.

"You are a heretic," the old monk addressed him. "Yet I invite you to act as my assistant in an exorcism."

"The exorcism of what?" the young warrior asked, feeling the nails of the wind rake across his face and hearing the prayer flags fluttering wildly from the pole above him.

"Of a ro-langs."

He shivered when he heard that name. It was common knowledge that the living dead were animated by the gdon, the primordial spirits of darkness who once ruled the rooftop of the world. Dri-gum-btsan-po, seventh in the lineage of the ancient kings, had been possessed by an evil gdon spirit, which drove him mad and caused him to fight with his minis- ter, Long-ngam.

In his own village, near Skye-rgu-mdo in Khams, was a house that a wealthy family once lived in. The head of that family was a much beloved man, generous of heart and boun- tiful in spirit. When he died, his family grieved so long that they failed to bury him in the appointed time. It being the dead of winter, they stored his body in a shack behind the main house.

Two weeks later, the man's son heard noises in the shack. He peeked inside, and, lo and behold, the corpse of his father was slowly moving. The boy ran to a nearby encampment of nomads and told them what he had witnessed.

When they arrived at the shack, the door had been splintered open. The ro-langs was moving toward them in a stiff-legged gait, his tongue waggling and his hand gesturing for them to come, come, and not to be afraid. . . .

The nomads threw Buddhist images and board-bound books at the ro-langs, but it kept on walking. They drew their short swords and hacked at its limbs. This did not slow the zombie. They cut both arms off at its shoulders and it still waggled its evil tongue. Only when one of the nomads swung his mighty sword and decapitated it, did the ro-langs finally fall over.

The nomads left after they had assured the boy that the monster was truly vanquished. Not so! As soon as they had departed, the ro-langs rose again, headless and without its arms. Its skin, blood, flesh, and bone had all been viciously attacked, and still it drove itself forward.

The boy, being keen of wit, thought to himself: "This must be a mole ro-langs! Only if its secret mole is pierced will it finally be laid to rest!" He ran to his mother and asked if his father had a mole anywhere on his body, and, if so, which part? The mother recalled that there was one unusual mole on her husband's back, just below his left shoulder.

The boy took a knife and carefully circled the ro-langs, which even now shuffled toward him, its breath rushing from its headless stump in a bloody spray. The boy waited and then struck. He plunged the blade into its back, just where his mother told him the mole was located. The ro-langs keeled over, twitched, and entered the Void.

"Since it already is a corpse," the old monk explained to the young warrior, as though he had just read his mind, "you can never kill a ro-langs. You can only cause it to 'brgyal-ba'—to 'fall over.'"

*The Old One lectured to his selected assistant.
"Remember, there are different types of ro-langs. First,
there's the lpag-langs, or the skin zombie. Then there's the
khrag-langs, the blood zombie. Then the sha-langs, or the
flesh zombie. Then the rus-langs, the bone zombie. All these
ghouls can be felled by placing your hand on top of their
heads. Only the rme-langs, which is the mole zombie, requires
the piercing of its mole. The rme-langs has a special name.
We call it the Rimi."*

*"Why are you asking me, a heretic, to assist with your
exorcism?" the young man asked.*

*"Because you display the nine characteristics of the dge-
bsnyen. These are the signs of the perfect apprentice to the
nagspa."*

"Which signs are those?"

*"Foremost among them are truthfulness, sharpness of
mind, lack of guile and deceit, physical strength, and knowledge of all the arts. These render you fit for the mantric
realm."*

*"And what do I get if I assist you in the ceremony?" the
young Tibetan asked, eyeing this living mummy in lama's
robes.*

*The old monk cackled. "You are a heretic. You may keep
the corpse of the ro-langs, which will turn into gold. Cut off
its flesh down to the bones. Do not spend the gold on
improper things, like barley beer and prostitutes! If you use it
for your own livelihood and for deeds of virtue, then whatever
flesh you cut off the corpse in the daytime will be replenished
at night, and it shall last forever!"*

"And what shall you obtain from it, oh learned nagspa?"

*The old monk chuckled. "Not for you to know! Will you not
be satisfied with your reward of golden flesh? Or do you seek
riches beyond your knowing? Will you not assist me as my
dge-bsnyen, my son?"*

*The young man glanced at the darkness, which was riding
over the entire valley, packing away the Peaks of the Gods in
its saddlebags, the wind stinging the memories of the day with
the fierce lash of its whip.*

"When shall you be requiring my services as your dge-bsnyen?" he asked casually.

The old monk chortled gleefully, his voice rising in the wind. "Not in this lifetime! There will be many more turns of the Wheel before I call upon you! You will know it when the time comes!"

The young man shivered as he looked down into the gorge. The wind howled, echoing the old monk's laughter, which sounded to him now like the tinkling of bells and the murmur of prayers and the spinning of a thousand prayer wheels.

He did not see—and neither did the old monk—the dark figure standing in the doorway, listening intently to the words exchanged between the Old One and his newly recruited dge-bsnyen. Satisfied that he had heard everything there was to hear, the dugpa silently slunk away.

"Which lifetime might that be?" Tashi Nurbu wondered. He would have to plan accordingly.

Gobi opened his eyes. Dorje had stopped whirring the prayer wheel in his hand. Tara now opened her eyes as well. They were a translucent green, the shade of the snow algae that grows on the rocks above the snow line of Mount Kailas.

With a smile on his face, Dorje wrapped the mani in its velvet cloth and carefully placed it back inside his satchel.

"So, Gobi," Dorje asked him with a twinkle in his eye. "Did you see anything?"

Gobi slowly came to, savoring the present moment, as if he had just chanced upon it, a single bead in a rosary stretched across time.

"I . . . I don't know. I'm not sure. What version of Tantrix did you say that was?"

Dorje laughed. "It was 4.2."

"It was amazing. Whatever it was." Gobi rubbed his face with his hands.

He looked up at the Tibetan lama. "You get all that just from *spinning* that thing?"

Dorje laughed again. "It's all in the wrist."

"What a trip." Gobi rubbed his eyes.

"You see, Gobi, you and I *are* fated to work together. This is an appointment that was set a long, long time ago."

"It *does* seem incredible. Is it really possible?"

"Ah," Dorje said. "You are wondering about the Wheel. Its many spokes. And the turning of the axle. You know what Krishna told Arjuna in the Bhagavad-Gita, don't you? *'Many lives, Arjuna, you and I have lived. I remember them all, but thou dost not.'"*

Now it was Gobi's turn to laugh. "Sometimes it feels like that," he agreed. Then he grew serious.

"You expect me to find Tashi Nurbu somewhere in Neo-Tokyo. Or to confront this virus face-to-face. This . . . 'Rimi.'" *There,* he had named it. "But how am I supposed to destroy it?"

"Very simple, Gobi," Dorje said, as he reached inside the folds of his lama's robe. "With a phurbu." He handed Gobi a ritual Tibetan dagger with a three-edged blade. "With this."

TAXI

Come, Gobi, it's getting late. I'll drive you home now. My cab is parked outside," Dorje told him.

Tara walked them both outside. She stood in the doorway, barefoot, clasping her arms around her, and shivered. The fog was rolling in.

"You will be careful, won't you?" she asked Gobi.

"I'll try," he said, and took a step toward her. She offered him her cheek, but he kissed her mouth instead. The kiss lingered. It was not the most passionate kiss he had known, but before it broke off, a kind of warmth began to spread between them.

Dorje was waiting at the top of the stairs.

Tara sighed. "You're very nice, Frank," she demurred. "I could feel from the beginning that you've got a very strong sexual side to you."

"I do," Gobi admitted. "If there's a place for it." He looked at her hopefully.

"Mmm," she murmured. "I'm flattered that you think I'm attractive."

As if given the right cue, he moved toward her again, but she slowed his advance with the brake pad of her hand.

"Is . . . is Dorje your boyfriend?" he asked, pulling back.

She laughed lightly. "Oh, no. He's not. We're too close for that."

"I'm sorry, I was just wondering."

"Don't be sorry, it's just that—"

"It's just that—*what?*"

"You need to conserve your *yang,* Frank," she laughed as she rose on her tiptoes and quickly kissed him on the mouth. It was a hit-and-run.

"I beg your pardon?"

"Come on, Gobi," Dorje called out, as he held up his keys and jangled them.

"You're going to need it where you're going." Tara pushed Gobi on his way.

"My yang? My male energy?"

"That's right," she said. "Your yang, your yin, and everything in between."

"Gee, thanks," he said. "I'll have to pick up some ginseng at the airport."

She slipped a small envelope into his hand. "Here are some Fo-Ti pills. Good for jet lag, or if you make love too much and dissipate your male essence."

"You think of everything, don't you?"

"You'd better go now, Frank. It looks like Dorje's becoming impatient."

The Tibetan lama was coming down the stairs to collect him.

"I'm coming, Dorje," Gobi called to him. He weighed the envelope in his hand. "You're sure there's enough in here for both jet lag *and* lovemaking?"

"That depends on how far you get," Tara teased him. "Come back to us safely, Frank."

"'Bye, Tara."

"'Bye, Frank."

He ran up the stairs.

"At last," Dorje chided him when he reached the street. "Climb in," he said. "Welcome to Dorje's Tantric Taxi."

Dorje's hand drummed on the dashboard. "Do you mind if I put on some music?" he asked, eyeing his passenger as he adjusted the rearview mirror.

"No, go ahead," Gobi replied absentmindedly. He sat, wrapped in thought, in the back, occasionally bouncing on his seat as the thirty-year-old Chevy Isuzu gave its springs a workout on the winding road.

He was still trying to put the pieces together. Dorje's handheld prayer wheel had a much deeper quality than the demo Kimura had shown him. Kimura's post-VR program had obviously been derived from an earlier version of Tantrix. The one that Tashi Nurbu had sold to Satori. The look and feel were the same, but it didn't have the same inner resolution and real-time transcendence that Vajra 4.2 had.

And besides, Satori had changed the platform. Spinning prayer wheels weren't that user-friendly. You had to take too much on faith.

Kimura had handed him a package containing what looked like a folded Japanese yukata robe. "Please put it on," Kimura had told him. "You have worn yukata before?"

"Of course I have," Gobi had said, as he slipped his arms into the billowing sleeves of the wavy-pattern blue yukata. He felt like a guest who had just checked into a Japanese inn. "Here," Kimura said, presenting him with an obi belt. "When you tie it closed, the bio-circuits will activate and the down-load will begin. The sensors are woven into the material. We call this fabric 'Neurayon'. Of course, we plan to release it in different formats: cardigans, sports jackets, a complete line of post-VR sportswear, in fact."

The rush of images was breathtaking, but they were nothing like Dorje's handheld unit. There was a distinctly commercial

gloss to them. Kimura explained they were outtakes from vari-
ous "I AM" show episodes in the making. Goofy lowbrow
comedy things like "I AM Jimmy Durante's Nose," which
actually had a kind of giggly Gogolian whimsy to it; historical
fantasies like "I AM Napoléon's Hand," this being the view of
the Battle of Waterloo as seen through the open buttons of the
French conqueror's military tunic; and the cushy soft-porn
titillation of "I AM Madonna's Bustier."

But it was the "I AM Trapped in the Black Hole of
Calcutta" clip from the "Famous Historical Massacres"
episode that had spooked him so badly. The shifting and
groaning and the stench of piled-up bodies had been too much
for him. He had almost passed out. "I'm not sure we're going
to run that one," Kimura confessed. "It's really for a niche
market."

"What's that music, Dorje?" Gobi asked, suddenly sitting up.

"Oh, that?" Dorje replied, fiddling with the dial. "Let's see
now." The screen was fuzzy with grey resolution and the
sound crackled as it scattered from the different speakers in
the cab.

> *"You're my I Ching love, baby*
> *Changing all the time*
> *You're my I Ching love, baby*
> *Changing all the time*
> *I thought I had you covered*
> *But I haven't got a dime*
> *Well, I love you three times, baby*
> *But it's hard to draw the line*
> *I love you three more times, baby*
> *But it's hard to draw the line*
> *I know I got to get Creative*
> *'Coz I'm about to lose my mind. . . . "*

The 'trode-DJ came on a moment later. "*And that, for all*
you ghosts out there, is a blast from the past, Huey and the

Hexograms, broadcast live to you from the Wasteland NetFM, don't panic! And I'm yours truly, your ghoulish DJ, King Alfonso Aserioso, still managing very well on my life supports as you can see, thank you . . . (chuckle, chuckle) . . . We got some 'trodes still functioning down here in the studio, but we can still use some volunteers' . . . brains! Just kidding! No, I'm not. Anyone wanna share any of their few remaining neurons with us, we'll accept anything you send, any handouts, even from you burnouts out there! We'll even take loaners! And while you're at it, hey, would any kind soul upload us some vasopressin, it's lonely down here with just a few brain cells hangin' around. Okay now, let's see what the cat drug in. It's request time at Mailbox Central."

The talking-head DJ wore a jester's cap with bells. There was a spiral tattoo on his forehead and he was wearing a thick pair of Unagi neurospecs. As he spoke, his tongue flicked out of his mouth sibilantly, and his mouth wobbled on its spent stem.

Leaning over the front seat, intently focused on the dashboard screen, Gobi saw that the 'trode-J's lips were sewn together with coiled rings except for a tiny budlike opening through which his tongue extruded.

"That's King Alfonso Aserioso," Dorje explained, as he glanced back at Gobi. "He's a real character. No, I take that back. I'm not sure just *how* real he is."

He looks like a weasel, Gobi thought. He could see Alfonso was a hybrid. Half of him came out of a postmodern primitive's toolbox, while the rest looked like it had been scratched together from an old interactive Sonic the Hedgehog chip set.

"Yes, but where's he *broadcasting* from? The Wasteland NetFM, what's that!? I never heard of it."

"It's a pirate radio station. From Satori City," he replied.

"Satori City?" Gobi was stunned. "But how's that possible? Satori City is supposed to be down! It crashed."

"There are a few pockets left," Dorje informed him. "Strictly illegal. They burrowed in before the crash. They're mostly squatters in a place called the Wasteland. They must have made provisions for themselves, set themselves up in advance. You know, like earthquake preparedness. Not a bad idea in a Virtual Fault Zone like Satori City."

"Do the authorities know anything about this?"

"Hard to say." Dorje snapped some gum. "Want some?" He offered a stick to Gobi. "Bach's Flower Remedies. Take one. It's Rescue Remedy flavor. It helps me drive. Prevents accidents on the road."

"No thanks. Answer my question, Dorje. Does anyone know there's a group of survivors broadcasting out of Virtuopolis?"

"Even if they did know, there's no way to reach them. This is strictly a one-way communication. And they've been losing power in the past few days. Their signal's getting weak."

"I don't believe this!" Gobi exclaimed, as he watched King Alfonso adjust the visor on his jester's cap.

"Okeydoke, excuse the noncommercial interruption," King Alfonso beamed. *"Or as they say in Neuro-Nippon, 'I'm O.K., you're karaoke.' Now then, who's up at bat?"*

"Hi, Alfonso, this is Phil." A pimply youth with reddish-green hair appeared on the screen. His cheeks were hollow, there were dark rings under his eyes, and he appeared to be breathing belaboredly, like an asthmatic on-line.

"Hi, Phil, what can we do for you tonight?" Alfonso asked. *"I mean, we can't fly you home on United, obviously, but what's the next best thing?"*

"I'd like to . . . dedicate a song to my girlfriend, Norma?"

"Okay, kid. Where'd you say she is?"

"In Cleveland. We were tripping together in V-town, but we got separated during the crash. She made it back though. But I'm still here. . . ."

"Gee, that's tough, kid. Hang in there," King Alfonso commiserated. *"She oughta hear this, we're still your favorite radioactive station! What's the message, Phil, to your darling Norma?"*

"Norma, I miss you babe. Wherever you are, take care of yourself. I love you."

King Alfonso wiped away a tear with a multicolored

hanky. "I couldn't have put it better myself, guy. And hey Norma, hey Norma! A big kiss to you from all of us stranded freaks down here. Now what's the song, dude?"

"Well," On-Line Phil said, "since you're playing oldies tonight, how about 'Monkey Me, Monkey You,' by Goin' Ape?"

"You got it, Toyota, we're gonna spin that platter for you, then we'll be back with lots of other messages from another bunch of dearly beloveds to their dearly beloveds who're in different time zones, different mind zones, not to mention different erogenous zones. There's no accounting for taste, right? I can see our lines are jammed. OK, Phil, this is from you to Norma in Cleveland. . . ."

"You gotta monkey mind but I don't mind 'coz I'm a monkey too . . ."

"Dorje, this is unbelievable!" Gobi marveled. "It's simply unbelievable!"

The Tibetan honked at a stray guide dog that yelped as it ran across the road, its harness dragging behind it.

Dorje held the door open for Gobi at the curb outside his house.

"Thanks for the ride, Dorje," Gobi said. "Take care of yourself."

"You'll do fine, dge-bsnyen!" Dorje grasped him by the arms.

"I don't even know how to *pronounce* that word," Gobi protested, "much less what's expected of me."

"Don't doubt yourself, Gobi," the lama told him solemnly. "It will all come back to you. Have faith."

"You should open up a franchise," Gobi said to him fondly, as he walked up the stairs to his house. The porch lights were off and it was dark inside the Victorian.

"Good night and Godspeed, sir." Dorje bowed as he climbed back into his cab and drove off.

The house seemed totally empty. Juan had gone home. A Satori courier pack with Gobi's ticket to Neo-Tokyo sat on the kitchen counter. He opened it and scanned the itinerary. He noticed a light on the cube.

Gobi turned and gave the command: "Messages." Then his knees buckled.

There were dark circles under Trevor's eyes and his mouth moved soundlessly until the words caught up with it. They were coming from very far away. The message had been left on his unit at about the same time Gobi had visited Trevor at the hospital. How was this possible?

"Hi, Dad! I know you're probably really worried about me, but don't be. I'm fine. I know I can't get back to you right now. But it's okay, I'll come home soon. I promise. There's just a few more levels I need to complete before I can get out of here. You won't believe this game, Dad! There're all these weird things that come at you. Demons, zombies, gdons, ogres, all kinds of hungry ghosts. . . . It's like nothing else you've ever seen! Oops! I gotta go now! This is costing me!"

There was a knowing smile on Trevor's face that was very familiar to Gobi; it was his collection-time look. Trevor was always good at keeping accounts.

"You owe me a couple of thunderbolts, Dad! I love ya! 'Bye now! I'm outta here!"

BARDO TWO

"The Orchestra is small,
and plays the role of
doppelgänger."

—*Wolfgang Rihm*

BUTOH

With his Ray-Bans clicking away, Gobi counted twenty-seven passengers sitting in Chrysanthemum class. The flight to Neo-Tokyo was less than half full, but it was rich in flora and fauna. *Mostly Rim carpetbaggers and keiretsu types,* Gobi concluded as he scanned the cabin.

His 'Bans were programmed to pick up any interesting clips that might fit into his interactive textbook on the new Rim culture. At this rate, he'd have to load another cartridge.

Wth the exception of the lovely Miss Claudia Kato, the Satori flight facilitator wending her way down the aisle with the drinks cart, it was pretty much a yang crowd on board.

There were a couple of Greater Chinese arms dealers, noticeable in their sharkskin suits of grey shantung silk. Flaunting jade rings the size of Kowloon and Seiko-Rolexes loaded with the latest Hsinchu Park circuitry on their pudgy wrists, the GCs looked more like rich uncles on holiday from Singapore than they did merchants of death.

There was a contingent of American 'retsu-jins on board. They were dressed in those boldly understated Ralph

Yamamoto suits that corporate lifers tended to favor, the kind that came with a built-in paper shredder in one pocket and a satellite linkup and com-center in the other. Come to think of it, the suits were probably leased from AT&T.

Miss Kato was busy serving drinks to the passengers. Gobi watched, fascinated, as she bent over in her tight latex kimono, her hips swaying in the aisle. He could tell that she was going to have a difficult time with this crowd.

One of the North Koreans on board—a traveling salesman from Pyongyang, judging from his Kim Jong Il memorial bouffant hairdo—was already drunk and rapidly getting red in the face. He'd be stripping down to his long underwear and demanding his karaoke any minute now. In the meantime, his fingers were busy trying to figure out the combination to Miss Kato's obi.

She smiled ingenuously at him as she removed his hand from her rump and moved on. "Mian hamnida," she told him in Korean. "I'm sorry."

Not all the passengers fit the commercial profile. There was that pair of California healers, for instance. They wore diaphanous snow-white parkas and had long golden hair, curly beards, and cherubic smiles. Their duty-free bags were probably filled with smudge sticks, crystals, and medicine cards.

Well, God knows, there was plenty of healing and channeling to be done in New Nippon these days.

And then there was that gargoyle cowboy sitting right across from Gobi. He'd been nodding and grinning at Gobi for a while now.

It wasn't that he was dressed in a cheap white Issey Miyake suit from Sears and lizard-skin boots; nor was it the fact that he radiated Mexican yakuza from a maquiladora border town—a Tijuana-gumi syndicate, more than likely—that gave Gobi the creeps.

No, it was his *face*.

Gobi had never seen a body-modification job quite like his before. (*Click-click-click,* went Gobi's 'Bans.)

This hombre had a silver web of chains draped across the

entire left side of his face. It hung from above his left eyebrow all the way down to his lower lip like a veil stapled to his skin.

The gargoyle grinned at Gobi. "Carlos Morales. Pleased to meet you man," he said. "Care for a snort?" He offered Gobi a few grains of white shabu crystal from his gunmetal case.

"This shit'll get you there faster 'n the plane does," he boasted.

"No thanks," Gobi politely declined. "I'm Gobi, Frank Gobi," he introduced himself. "You heading over to Neo-Tokyo?"

Silver Face took a hit of the shabu. "'Scuse me . . . Wheew. . . ." he said, grinning as he sniffed the crystal up his right nostril. "Yokohama-mama, man . . . good stuff."

He extended his hand to Gobi. Gobi noticed a blood-red stigmata on his hand like a paste-on tattoo, but it was holo-grammed. Definitely a Tijuana-gumi appliqué. And the gold ridgework on his teeth, a sure sign of a yakuza dental plan.

"Nice to make your acquaintance," Morales said. "Yeah, I got some shobai over there. *Bi-zhi-nesu* as they say. Yourself?"

"I'm in market research," Gobi replied.

Morales barely restrained a laugh. "Yeah, *right.*"

"And what line are *you* in, Mr. Morales?"

"*This* line," Carlos said, as he brought out his case to sample some more shabu. He waved the snuffbox in the air. "Excuse me a sec while I powder my cortex. You sure?" he offered his goods to Gobi once more.

"I'm fine. I might smoke some spirulina once in a while, but that's about it."

"I can dig it. Yeah, well," he said, as he held back his silver curtain with a dainty gesture of his left hand. The chains tinkled. His right eye was dilated, but it was focused on the stage in the center of the cabin. He nodded. "Looks like it's Butoh time."

It was the in-flight entertainment. The Butoh dancer had slipped onto the stage unnoticed. He was already dangling upside down above the center dais with a muted spotlight shining on him.

The Butoh's feet were firmly planted in the overhead stir-rup. His head was shaved and his smooth body was naked except for a latex fundoshi loin strap. White chalk coated his entire body.

Gobi checked the program. It was a piece called "Silent Body Language," a classic Butoh study on motionlessness. It would run for about two hours, he guessed, or at least until they got into New Nippon air space. Passengers were already beginning to nod off. Butoh had that kind of tranquilizing effect, as medical tests had shown.

Gobi watched the Butoh hang upside down for what seemed like a few minutes, but it could have easily been much longer. The Butoh's bright black eyes were reticulated like an old-world chameleon's. You couldn't tell *what* he was focusing on. But Gobi had a strange feeling that he was staring at *him*.

It was *so* strange. The white-chalked mouth opened like a bud, revealing the black cavity of his mouth. Then the Butoh's face exploded.

What happened next was like a freeze-frame thawing out in Quick-Time.

Gobi felt the unmistakable blast of chi release across the cabin like greased molecules spinning out of control. The Chinese arms dealers bobbed their heads—a row of Lucky Fatty dolls bouncing on their springs. Claudia spun around on her feet. She first surveyed the damage on the Butoh stage, but the very next moment she glanced in his direction. To see if *he* was all right? What was going on?

Carlos hunkered down as the chi wave reached them. The lights in the cabin flickered, then went out. Confused and frightened voices began to cry out in the darkness.

The spaceplane shuddered and groaned, and the cabin suddenly tipped over in free-fall like a roller coaster skidding off its rails.

Would it end like this then? With people screaming, each of their lives compressed within their screams, until the final blackness reclaimed them? It was strange, but Gobi felt a whirlpool of calm in the third meridian around his hara. *No matter how fast it happens, you're always ready,* he realized, as he began to slip out of the seventh meridian at the top of his head. Just making himself more comfortable. *There . . .*

Then the lights came on just as suddenly as they went out, the halogen beads crackling their illumination. The falling plane landed in an invisible net. It steadied. A collective *"Ah!"* rose from everyone's lips.

"You all right, hombre?" Gobi felt a hand on his shoulder. It was the Latino yakuza.

Amid all the screams and groans, he was a cool one, the one with the silver face.

"I . . . think so," Gobi answered, as he brought himself back into his body awareness. "What . . . happened?" His breathing, so measured a few moments ago, now caught up with his heart, which was beating like that of a rabbit running down the road with auto headlights bearing down on it.

"I think it was a systems failure."

Gobi drew himself up unsteadily. "Of the plane?"

"Right. *His* system, too, I reckon," Carlos replied, indicating the Butoh, who hung like a twisted paper match above the matchbook stage.

Claudia Kato moved briskly toward the stage. One of the Americans joined her. He must have been an engineer, judging from the way he surveyed the damage. "Look, he's a droid!" he declared. "I don't get it." He turned to Claudia with a puzzled expression. "This guy's a *droid?* Did *you* know that? What's going on here, Miss?"

She was flustered for a moment but still in control. "Management's been introducing a line of entertainment droids on certain flights," she replied hesitantly. "But they usually perform only in the karaoke cabaret section. I wasn't informed about this. There must have been a last-minute switch. I can't understand what happened."

"Looks like your droid blew up. We're lucky to be alive," the American said angrily.

"What do you make of it, Harry?" one of the engineer's

colleagues asked. A small group had gathered around the stage.

The engineer knelt beside the Butoh and peered at the hole in the droid's head. "Hard to say, Jack. It looks like his brain's shorted. But why would it explode like that? Maybe a defective part. I don't know. There will have to be an investigation," he said. "I've never seen this model before. I can't tell which droidworks he's from."

Her mouth drawn tightly, Claudia Kato studied the flight-control reader clipped to her waist. It took her a minute to digest the data on the screen.

She finally raised her head to address the passengers. "I regret to report there's been a systems malfunction on board. Satori Flight 023 is now proceeding safely once again," she announced. "But a change of course has been ordered by Flight Control. We will not be landing at New Narita as planned. Instead, we will make a detour at Space Station Seven. Passengers will go through their immigration formalities, and you'll overnight there. A shuttle service to New Narita will be provided in the morning. We will be landing at Station Seven in approximately fifteen minutes. Thank you for your cooperation and understanding."

"Station Seven, man!" Carlos winked at Gobi with his dilated right eye. "That should be fun."

Gobi had heard about Station Seven, of course. But he had never imagined that he would transit there.

The Latino leaned toward Gobi with a handkerchief. For one single ridiculous moment, Gobi believed he was about to wipe a smudge off his nose.

Instead, Carlos plucked something from the headrest, a few inches from Gobi's face. "I don't think you want to prick yourself on this little sucker. He unfolded the handkerchief and flashed its contents.

"What the hell is it?" Gobi asked, as he scrutinized the tiny dart. It was almost invisible to the human eye.

Carlos sniffed it as if he were savoring its bouquet. "Hmm," he sighed at last. "This is what you would call a 'Snow Goddess.' Or a 'fukiya,' in the lingo. Guaranteed to put you to sleep nice and easy. The way it works, it just freezes your system till the old ticker . . . you know, your heart, stops beating for a very long time."

He chuckled. "You know anyone who'd want to take you out so bad they'd put a droid on board with a taste for tetrodotoxin? Not a bad aim either. A little bit lower to the right and you'd be sashimi." He paused. "I'd say the second shot would have taken you out if his mouth hadn't blown. That's where he fired it from, you know."

"Who are you, Mr. Morales?" Gobi asked under his breath, as Claudia Kato began to move in their direction.

"Let's just say, we may have some common interests," Carlos replied enigmatically. "Now let's enjoy the rest of the flight, shall we?"

"Are you all right?" Claudia Kato asked, but she was looking at Gobi. She glanced at the folded hankie in Carlos' hand.

"Just a little nosebleed, Miss." Carlos brought the handkerchief to his face and sniffed into it. "Nothing serious. I'm still in one piece. Not like our friend up there, eh?"

STATION SEVEN

Gobi caught his breath as the Satori space shuttle approached the revolving white cylinder of Space Station Seven. Set against the ornate blackness of deep space, its twenty-eight levels were illuminated by spotlights.

He had called up the Baedeker's entry on his Ray-Bans data base. The facility had been built in the year 2018 as a showcase for the Kobayashi Corporation, one of the world's biggest and most powerful postindustrial groups.

The top levels were an exact replica of the tower keep of Osaka-jo, the famous castle built by Toyotomi Hideyoshi, the all-powerful kampaku who ruled Japan in the sixteenth century.

It had a hotel, the Station Seven Intercontinental, that was listed in the *Suntory Book of Records* as being the first orbiting luxury hotel in the world. The 350 rooms included three large convention halls. It was a special favorite of Japanese honeymooners, who were prevented from traveling abroad by the New Nippon quarantine.

Perhaps most noteworthy, Station Seven was a legal gateway to New Nippon. It was the only entrepôt that Japanese citizens were permitted to travel to during the daylight Matrix hours.

Among its main attractions were its space golf course, its orbiting hot springs, and Matsu, the country-style Japanese restaurant that was rated four stars by the *Guide Michelin-Seibu*.

The space station was in geosynchronous orbit 280 miles above Neo-Tokyo. Reentry into the earth's atmosphere via a space taxi took forty-five minutes. Supposedly, that was even quicker than reaching downtown Neo-Tokyo by maglev cab from New Narita.

Gobi blinked and the Baedeker's page turned.

Station Seven had another distinction. It had provided a refuge for the directors of some of New Nippon's biggest keiretsus, those allied to the Kobayashi Corporation, when the Mega-Quake of '26 struck. For six months, an elite corps of corporate daimyos and their closest retainers oversaw their global interests by remote control from their space-station refuge.

When it was judged to be safe, they returned home aboard their armada of Mitsubishi Galaxy stretch space limos.

All except for one of them. Reportedly, he refused ever to set foot on earth again.

Ryutaro Kobayashi, the 84-year-old founder and CEO of the Kobayashi keiretsu, had long been rumored to be seriously ill. The Kobayashi Group maintained an entire wing for their master and lord consisting of 30 suites on the top three levels of Space Station Seven.

There was a momentary jolt as the Satori space shuttle landed on the receiving platform. Looking out of the porthole, Gobi saw that they were being lowered to the inside deck of the space station.

Carlos Morales peered over his shoulder. "It's a big ship,

ain't it?" he remarked. "Big enough to get lost in. I'd advise you to lay low while you're there. Don't go wandering about." He winked his gargoyle eye. "People have been known to disappear, if you know what I mean."

The air-lock doors opened and the canned air of the space station flooded the cabin.

Claudia Kato was in her official Satori Airlines bowing mode at the shuttle doorway. She delivered a crisp forty-five-degree bow to each passenger as they disembarked. "Thank you for flying with Satori Airlines. We regret any inconvenience. Domo arigato."

As Gobi reached the doorway, she bowed and whispered to him. "Please take care, Dr. Gobi. I will be contacting you soon." On the upswing of her bow, she awarded him a mechanical smile. "Have a pleasant stay on Station Seven. I hope you fly again with us soon."

"Thank you," he nodded, as he stepped out onto the deck. He walked briskly toward the immigration line. Three men stood there watching the passengers alight.

One of them stepped forward when he saw Gobi approach. He looked Eurasian with his high Slavic cheekbones and Mongolian eyes. He was in his mid to late thirties, with a slender build and a burnt-ivory complexion that looked like Japanese paper on a shoji screen left out in the sun too long.

His thoughtful black eyes studied Gobi through a pair of rimless spectacles. He was dressed in a tailored Mao tunic of shiny black ramie silk.

His two Japanese companions were providing the muscle of the party, Gobi could see that. Their eyes followed their boss' instinctively. One had close-cropped black hair and whispered into a data link clipped to his collar.

"Dr. Gobi? Dr. Frank Gobi?" the Eurasian addressed him in what sounded like an indefinable accent. Siberian-Japanese? Austro-Vietnamese? He couldn't quite place it.

"Yes?" Gobi answered.

"Passport, please." It was an order, not a request. Quick,

brief, methodical. The niceties—or their opposite—would come later.

Gobi handed him his U.S. smartport and the Eurasian held it in his hand briefly. It buzzed a positive I.D. He must have a bar-code reader hidden in his palm. Gobi noticed the green light pulse on a signet ring that bore the Station Seven insignia he had seen emblazoned on the ship: a writhing dragon chasing the pearl of wisdom.

"I'll have to ask you to step this way, please." The man pointed to one of the immigration lines that was not in service. His two associates closed in behind Gobi and escorted him through the exit door, which slid open automatically.

"May I ask what this is about?" Gobi asked the Eurasian. They had stepped into a courtyard with stone lions and an artificial skylight.

The man's smile was as cold as the white marble floor. "My name is Axel Tanaka. I'm the chief of security here on Station Seven. There are a few questions I'd like to ask you in my office."

"Please sit down."

Axel Tanaka's office was tidy, but in a cluttered sort of way. A potted fern wilted in a corner as it received its last rites from an overhead infrared. A videoscape of the Mekong River flowed against a dense jungle backdrop that buzzed with insects, birds, and hooting monkeys.

Through the porthole, framed by inky space, Gobi could see a slice of East Asia with the Sea of New Nippon and the Japanese islands. How many more hours, he wondered, before that image shifted? Meanwhile, the mirage still held.

"Now then," Tanaka said. His desktop was smoky glass. As he settled behind it, a portion of the glass cleared and he made a selection from a row of icons that appeared at his fingertips. He touched one and pursed his lips as he began to read.

He glanced up at Gobi. "Dr. Francis Gobi. Professor at the University of California in Berkeley, Tokyo University extension." He raised an eyebrow. "In para-anthropological studies? That's interesting."

"It's a new field," Gobi shrugged. "But I don't think you're interested in my academic credentials."

The Eurasian raised his hand. He leaned back in his seat and reached for a box inlaid with mother-of-pearl. He opened it and offered it to Gobi. "Cigarette? It's Marlboro Faux, 'twice the tobacco, none of the nicotine.' Biogenically grown aboard a Kobayashi space plantation, just one of our many enterprises. In case you don't know, Kobayashi is one of the top ten keiretsus in the world."

"No, thanks. I don't smoke. I don't drink. And I don't eat. So if you don't mind. . . ."

"Neither do I," Tanaka said, as he shut the box and pushed it away. "It seems you and I have similar tastes."

"Now where have I heard that before?" Gobi wondered out loud. "Mr. Tanaka, I think you'd better tell me what's on your mind. I like your office. It's got a great view. But I'm sure you've got other things to do."

"Please, Dr. Gobi . . . it's not often that we have someone of your stature visit our space station."

His tone was suddenly more conciliatory. He bowed his head, but he was still reading from the file. "Dr. Gobi, I see that before you became a professor, you were a—," he looked up with a smile,"—a private investigator? Is that right?"

"That was a long time ago," Gobi replied dryly.

"Dr. Gobi, I won't mince words. Kobayashi would like to retain your services."

Was he joking? The smile still played on Tanaka's face, but his expression was as serious as that of a go-player pondering the next move on the board.

Gobi smiled back. "What is it you would like me to investigate?"

Tanaka's eyes were remarkably cool. "You could call it a murder," he said. "In some cultures it might be considered that."

"A murder?"

"Yes, Dr. Gobi, the murder of a droid. You see, that droid

on the space shuttle . . . he was one of ours. From the Kobayashi droidworks at Todos Santos in Baja California. An advanced model, you might say. We're understandably concerned about what happened."

"But the droid short-circuited," Gobi responded. "The power surge was what caused the plane to lose its power. It was pretty scary there for a while."

"I imagine so," Tanaka smirked. "It must have been a harrowing experience. But the droid did *not* short-circuit."

"What?"

"Take a look at this. This is some of the data we recovered from the in-flight recorder. It was automatically transmitted to us right after the blast occurred."

Tanaka swiveled around and aimed an infrared beamer at the wall panel. The Mekong River tableaux vanished and Gobi found himself looking at the blurred white outline of the cabin on the space shuttle. Was it really only an hour or so ago that it happened?

"This is the moment of impact," Tanaka explained. "The details aren't clear, of course. But this is our analysis of what transpired."

A series of numbers appeared at the bottom, followed by a succession of cross sections of the Satori spaceplane rotating in a three-dimensional axis.

"That's the image of a neuronal blast moving across the cabin," Tanaka said. He double-clicked on his infrared pointer. "The epicenter of the blast was clearly around the droid's head. See?"

Gobi saw an electromagnetic swirl, like an orange-brown cloud, hovering above the white husk of the Butoh's skull.

"But the actual *source* of the emission—which is what *triggered* the blast, Dr. Gobi—originated elsewhere in the cabin."

"Meaning what?" Gobi demanded.

"Someone zapped the droid. Detonated his head, in fact. With a remote chi-blaster."

"You're saying he was neutralized?"

"Neutralized, Dr. Gobi? That's a curious expression to use." Tanaka looked at him oddly. "The strange thing is, as best as we can make out, the blast originated somewhere between rows seven and twelve."

"Yes?"

"Wasn't that around where *you* were sitting?"

By the time Gobi got to his room on the eighteenth level of the Station Seven Intercontinental, he was fuming, but in a cool and dispassionate manner.

Tanaka had just been toying with him, that's all. It had been nothing but a fishing expedition. That—or a provocation. Or both.

Gobi shook his head. He'd have to try to fit the puzzle pieces together later.

He laid his briefcase on the Chinese table in the foyer and glanced around the suite. Hodgepodge. An African sculpture from Benin stood beside a Korean chest. A Louis XIV gilt mirror hung on the wall. Two tubular Binendum chairs upholstered in black leather nodded at each other monochromatically across a white marble coffee table.

Through the open door to the bathroom, he saw more white marble, a deep tub, a cylindrical shower stall, and a row of mini holo-videos so he could ruminate as he shaved.

He took a few steps toward a raised alcove and held his breath. The paper shoji doors slid open to reveal yellow tatami mats on the floor and a lacquer table with zabuton pillows arranged around it.

In the corner of this traditional-style Japanese room was an alcove with a fuzzy ikebana arrangement that hovered in the Matrix. Peonies in space.

But what took Gobi's breath away was the picture window that opened to the darkness of the void. The stars were sprinkled like diamonds studding a dream; down below, as though resting on a velvet case of haze, lay the nondream that was Neo-Tokyo.

He would leave Station Seven first thing in the morning. There was a shuttle at 8:30 A.M. He'd be at New Narita by 9:30 A.M. when Neo-Tokyo would be well into a brand-new cycle—9:30 A.M. TCT (Tokyo Consciousness Time).

And then that evening where would he be? Inside the Dream, or whatever it was. And what dream was Trevor trapped in right now?

The reality of that thought suddenly gripped him.

Gobi sighed. He was exhausted. Time to freshen up.

He stood beneath the thundering pulse of the shower. His thoughts raced against each other like alternating currents.

Okay, Gobi, he told himself, as he shook the water off his face. *Time to take a little inventory. Rinse out the left brain.*

Someone tried to kill you. Exhibit A: The poison-tip dart. What did that silver-faced Mexican yakuza call it, a 'fukiya'? He would know about such things, right? He probably shops for his little poisons at the Fugu Barn. Who IS that guy? Why did he warn me? What does he want from me?

He could still see the shiny nib of the dart embedded in the headrest of his seat. A shiver ran through him. *Okay, Gobi, get that out of your system, you old dog. There, cough it out. Let it flow off your body like water and wash down the drain. Fear's gone.*

He stared down into the dark drain, then clicked his thoughts back on.

Someone neutralized the Butoh droid before he got another chance to take you out. Assuming it was the droid. Which is a fair assumption, considering the trajectory of the chi-blast and the way it sought out the heat of the projectile as it ejected from the droid's mouth.

A few conclusions so far: Someone doesn't want me to reach Neo-Tokyo. On the plus side, I have a guardian angel looking out for me. A bodyguard.

I guess that balances things out a little, Gobi mused, as the hot needles of the shower stung his body. He was beginning to feel reinvigorated. *Okay, time to do the right brain now.*

He switched on the cold water and stood there for a full three minutes. It was like standing beneath an icy waterfall. His nerves were racing, his synapses firing away.

Why would anyone want to prevent me from reaching Neo-Tokyo?

Is it to keep me from locating the missing Satori chairman? Is it a keiretsu thing? A rivalry?

Or is it more serious than that? Is it meant to keep me from finding Tashi Nurbu and terminating the Tantrix virus?

He stepped out of the shower and grabbed the plush terry-cloth towel from the rack. He began to dry himself. He saw his reflection in the steamed mirror, a fuzzy figure. He saw a muscular chest, strong forearms, a stomach, if not exactly washboard hard, at least it wasn't a dashboard yet. His legs taut and wiry from bicycling and swimming. The dark apostrophe of his sex.

Or was that a question mark? Hmm, he could use a little goodwill in that department.

He found a razor and cream and began to shave his face with sharp, precise strokes.

Concentrate, Gobi. You're not out of the woods yet. Why would Tanaka bait you like he did? Think!

He laid the razor down on the marble sink and stared into the mirror.

Thank you, O Honorable Right Brain, he smiled at his reflection.

Of course! Tanaka knows you didn't take out his precious Butoh. But he also knew what the Butoh was there to do, didn't he? It was their droid.

No, he wanted to learn two things. First of all, he wanted to discover how much I already knew. Did I know the droid was out to kill me? I think Tanaka knows the answer to that. Of course I didn't. I wouldn't have just sat there waiting for it to happen. Would I?

No, what Tanaka really wants to discover is: Who is my secret protector?

Because whoever it is, they're here right now. Somewhere on Station Seven.

Gobi stared into the mirror and sighed. *Well?* And the mirror replied, ‘llsW

CLAUDIA

Gobi splashed on some Samadhi after-shave, it had a tart nirvikalpa aftershock that made his sixth meridian tingle. He slipped on a white terry-cloth bathrobe with the Kobayashi coat of arms sewn on it. Then he stepped into the suite.

It took a moment for his eyes to adjust. The halogen lighting had been dimmed. He saw that housekeeping had laid out the futon bed on the floor of the Japanese room. It loomed invitingly like a soft billowing cloud a couple of hundred miles above the streets of Neo-Tokyo.

He could use a nap. He would just push off from here on one of those clouds. . . .

Two hands suddenly emerged from beneath the futon, followed by a silky waterfall of black hair and the rippling intensity of her eyes. He felt like a leaf caught in the current, twirling this way and that, but still obeying the will of the stream.

"Miss Kato . . . " he began, and then his eyes blinked. "You're out of uniform." For some reason he couldn't think of anything else to say. He suffered from a sexual shyness that some women mistook for tenderness, which it *was,* but he had to overcome the awkwardness of his self-consciousness first.

"You don't mind?" She raised her arms. Claudia Kato had beautiful breasts. They were small, ivory, perfectly formed, born of a thousand ukiyo-e wood-block prints, with erect nipples and dark aureoles that floated on the mounds like velvet lily pads.

"I let myself in," she explained. "I couldn't call you on the house phone. They would be listening."

Her eyes settled on him. "You were in the shower. I've already showered. The futon looked *so* comfortable . . . "

He looked around for her clothes. He couldn't see any, just her Prada-Rei Okubo saddlebag on the floor in the corner. She was a mystery woman, all right. The kind that he liked. Especially now.

"You don't have to explain anything." He touched her face. "You're very beautiful. Very, very beautiful."

"Why don't you sit down?" She patted the futon beside her with a smile that told him they understood each other perfectly.

He sank to his knees, and cupped her face with his hands as he kissed her. *"Umm,"* she said, as she tugged at the loops of his belt.

His robe came open and he felt her hand—cool but warming to his heat—caress his skin. She traced the muscle of his chest and abdomen until she discovered what she was looking for.

She stroked him as he lost himself in the intoxicating musk of her breasts, nuzzling and biting them lightly, then again more greedily with his teeth. Her body had a slightly salty taste that made him hungry. He buried his lips in her breasts again and under her arms and then down to her lower belly.

Umm, she was shaved down there, smooth, slick, oily, and delicious. . . .

She sighed as she ran her hand through his hair, then pushed him backward on the futon.

He kicked off the covers as she climbed on top of him, a conch shell seeking the solid shelter of a rock. He felt the succulent pressure build as she slipped him inside and rode him on the waves *away* from the shore.

He opened his eyes. He was now disappearing deep, deep inside her. She rode him hard, urgently, and scraped his sides with her nails like a coral reef push-pulling the tide. He didn't mind the burning sensation. He didn't mind being caught in the angry crosscurrent and forcibly dragged to the sandy bottom, where he drowned in the black whirlpool of her thighs.

"You're a good lover, Dr. Gobi," she told him afterward.

"I think you'd better call me Frank," he said, as they lay side by side on the futon. "You're wonderful, too."

"Thank you." She leaned on an elbow and flicked him under his chin with her tongue, then slipped it inside his mouth again. *"Frank."*

He laughed. "You're welcome, *Claudia.*"

"I had a feeling you wouldn't mind if I came to your room," she said, sitting up. The silhouette of her body was beautiful, the curve of her breasts, the line of her back that led to the soft pillow of her buttocks.

She leaned over and kissed him. Then she made a sudden move as if to rise from the futon.

"Wait a minute, where are you going?" he asked her.

"To get dressed," she said, as she picked up her bag and padded on bare feet toward the bathroom.

"You're leaving?"

She paused. "It's 6:15 Frank. I've made a dinner reservation at Matsu's for two at seven. Do you like Japanese food?"

He sat up. "You have a *reservation* for *dinner?*" he asked, frankly amazed.

She rummaged in her bag and brought out a hairbrush. "I'm always hungry after making love," she said. "Aren't you?"

Gobi followed her and lingered at the doorway. "Tell me something," he asked her. "Do you work for Action Wada?"

"No, I'm the Shiseido lady," Claudia replied, as she applied some lipstick. "You can come in, if you like."

She dug into her bag and found her outfit. She slipped into a sleek black latex miniskirt with a studded belt that hung low on her hips. Her low-cut top revealed the swell of her small but shapely breasts. Gobi saw the unmistakable impressions of her nipples through the tight latex.

"I'm a little out of the loop here . . . " he began.

Claudia put a finger to her lips. He watched as she removed a few hairpins from her purse. She twisted the head of one hairpin and a jet stream of white noise filled the bathroom.

"This will take care of any bugs," she advised him. "Now we can talk."

"Oh," he said, and then continued. "Someone from Satori was supposed to meet me at New Narita. Now we've been rerouted to Station Seven and I. . . ."

"It's all right, Frank," Claudia answered. "I'll see to it that you get to Neo-Tokyo in one piece."

"Someone tried to kill me, you know."

"I know. Don't worry, it won't happen again," she assured him.

"How did that droid get on board?"

"The real Butoh never made it to the flight. There must have been a switch made before he got to the airport. The important thing is, *you're* still alive," she touched his chest and allowed her hand to rest there. *"And* well."

"Thank God you were there to stop him."

A funny look crossed her face. "You mean it *wasn't* you?" Gobi frowned.

Claudia giggled, but it came out sounding more like a purr. "Frank," she said to him a moment later in a husky voice, "there's been a change of plan that you should know about."

"Yes?"

"We believe we've located our missing chairman, Kazuo Harada."

"Where is he?"

"We have reason to think he's being held right here on Station Seven."

"What!"

"Come on, get dressed," Claudia told Gobi. "We can discuss the next move over dinner."

Matsu's was the four-star restaurant on the fifth level of Station Seven. It had a thatched awning at the entrance and an old-fashioned waterwheel that splashed as it turned.

"It's unreal, isn't it?" Claudia said, as Gobi peered through the glass wall of the restaurant into the dark trough of the Pacific Ocean.

New Nippon should have been there. Right there. In that spot. But it wasn't.

To the west, Gobi could make out the Korean Peninsula, its bright outline shaped like a ginseng root. That illuminated coastline must be Siberia, as it wound it way up north to the

Sea of Okhotsk. He stared into the darkness again. The islands of Honshu, Kyushu, Shikoku, Hokkaido, and the scattered go-stone islands of the Inland Sea were all missing.

So strange. He sighed as they stepped into the foyer of the restaurant.

"I assure you, Miss, I called in my dinner reservation earlier this evening," boomed a British accent. A tall Englishman in a safari suit winked at them as the flustered Japanese hostess searched through her reservations list.

"I'm sorry, sir, I can't find your name anywhere," she apologized, a smile frozen on her face.

"Chadwick. Simon Chadwick," the Englishman insisted. "I suggest you look under *'Chadu-wicku,'* dear, you might have more luck."

The hostess wiped her brow with a lace handkerchief plucked from the sleeve of her kimono.

The Englishman appeared to be in his mid sixties. He stood slightly stooped at six-foot-two, had a sunburnt complexion and white sideburns that grew like a pair of moccasins at the sides of his head. His greying hair was slicked back carelessly to reveal a furrowed brow with a long bridged nose and brown eyes that dogged you like a pair of English spaniels.

When he smiled, he revealed a gap between his yellowing teeth. That was nicotine from the last century, Gobi deduced. His safari suit probably dated back to that period, too.

"Chadwick's the name," the Englishman said, as he thrust his hand at Frank Gobi. "But it's Simon to you and the young lady. How'd you do, my dear?" He nodded at Claudia.

"I always find these four- and five-star places to be utterly snobbish, don't you? They make a huge fuss if you don't book at least 15 hours in advance, and they always expect you to be 'suitably attired,' whatever *that* means," Chadwick scoffed. "Personally, I never know *where* I want to eat until the last minute. And I'd sooner wear a bone through my nose than a black tie. I think *all* restaurants should have a section for nudists. I mean, why not? There are more and more naked people in the world. It's discriminatory."

Chadwick's eyes widened. "I say, are you two newlyweds? A whole load of them came in on the noon shuttle from, you know," he whispered, "down there."

"Oh, I'm a travel writer, by the way," he went on, without waiting for a reply. *"Chadwick's Notable Travel Guides* and *The Lobby Review*. It's a newsletter that reviews the most unique hotel lobbies in the world. That's why I'm up here at Station Seven. On assignment, don't you know? Perhaps you've seen some of my special issues? Here you are."

He spilled out a few miniature editions from the pocket of his safari jacket and handed Claudia several booklets. One was entitled *The Use of Tundra as a Motif in the Lobby of the Irkutsk Hilton.* Another read *Complimentary Fetishes at the Togo Sofitel.*

"I crank them out the old-fashioned way," Chadwick explained. "Desktop publishing. I'm the last of a dying breed, I'm afraid. Everything's getting so bloody virtual these days. It's virtual *this,* virtual *that.* Nowadays people seem to have this compulsion to anthropomorphize absolutely everything," he spat out. "Why, you'd think a paperback was nothing but a hardcover book in shorts!"

He was clearly getting heated.

Claudia exchanged an amused look with Gobi, who rolled his eyes.

"Thank you," Claudia said, accepting the copies. "These look very interesting. I'm not acquainted with your work, Mr. Chadwick, but now I *will* be."

Claudia spoke in rapid Japanese to the hostess, who nodded and bowed.

A pair of menus appeared in her hand as she led the couple to their table.

"They shouldn't be too long in seating you, Mr. Chadwick—even without a reservation," Claudia smiled at him in passing. "I've fixed it for you."

"I say!" the gangly Englishman rocked back on his heels. "Astonishing."

● ● ●

Claudia and Gobi were soon seated at a rickety table on ancient tatami in a secluded corner of what had originally been an early 20th-century Japanese inn.

The furnishings had been transported piece by piece from some island in the Inland Sea, according to the legend of Matsu's, which was recounted in English and Japanese calligraphy on the back of the menu.

"Imagine all this existing in space, hundreds of miles above Neo-Tokyo," Claudia said, as her legs slid under the table. Their feet touched and they smiled at each other.

"It really *is* unbelievable," Gobi agreed.

A ruddy-faced waitress dressed like a country maid in baggy blue mompei pants brought steaming towels. Gobi breathed in the heat as it opened the pores of his face.

He looked up at her. "All right, Claudia. Do you want to tell me about it?"

Claudia removed one of the pins from her hair and laid it on the table.

"We have information that Harada, chairman of the Satori Group, is being held somewhere on this station," she said. "Possibly in a suite on the 28th level, which is Ryutaro Kobayashi's private floor. Those floors are off-limits to the public."

"Do you have any way of confirming it?"

"That's where *you* come in."

"What do you expect *me* to do?"

"We'd like you to corroborate this information by establishing contact with Mr. Harada."

"How?"

"Through a telepathic linkup." Claudia studied him. "Can you do that?"

He looked at her curiously. "I'm not sure."

Claudia drummed her fingers on the table impatiently. "But you're one of the best. That's why Satori hired you, isn't it?"

"It's not so easy," Gobi said. "A linkup would depend on various factors. Such as his mental and physical condition. Whether or not he's under sedation, and, if he is, what sort of drugs they're using on him. That would really have an effect on his brain waves. Some drugs are more difficult to break through than others."

He continued to think out loud. "The physical environment is important, too. Where he's being held—and whether or not there is any active field of interference around him."

Gobi paused. "If I can establish that it *is* Harada in that suite, how are you going to get him out?"

"Frank," she said very quietly. "There's something else I should tell you."

"What is it?"

"If Mr. Harada is being held prisoner here, it may be difficult to get him out *in time*. That may have to wait for later."

She played with the oshibori washcloth, which had gotten cold, folding and unfolding it.

"What do you mean it might be difficult to get him out *in time?* In time for what?"

She looked up. "We have perhaps forty-eight hours at the most to raise the downed sectors of Virtuopolis. If we *don't* get the system up by then, we risk a permanent disconnect of users who are still on-line. At the moment, there's a backup system keeping the neural connects on hold. They're on *hold* now. But the system cannot last much longer."

"Only forty-eight hours?" Gobi looked at her stupidly.

"I'm sorry, Frank," she told him quietly. "I know that your son is among those who got caught in Gametime."

"So what can we do?" Gobi replied in a hard voice. "I'd say forty-eight hours doesn't give us a hell of a lot of time. Does it?"

"There *is* something, Frank," she whispered, as she leaned toward him. "Something that only *you* can do."

Gobi had a feeling he knew what it was, and there wasn't anything he could do about it.

They had him where they wanted him.

"I say, bon appetit!" the English-accented voice resounded. "You two lovebirds are in the thick of it, aren't you? Sorry to interrupt."

Gobi and Claudia both looked up, startled.

Simon Chadwick stood behind the Japanese hostess, who was leading him to a table at the rear of the restaurant.

"Thanks for putting in a good word," the Englishman smiled at Claudia. "I've been promised a lovely table by the window. They say the view of New Nippon is absolutely unforgettable from up here. Enjoy!"

CASTLE KEEP

The elevator door opened on the fourteenth level of Station Seven and Claudia and Gobi stepped out onto a floodlit tarmac enclosed in a giant transparent bubble. Green nets strung like interstellar webs cast giant shadows on the brightly lit deck of the indoor driving range. A dozen or so Japanese honeymooners in green Kobayashi leisure suits practiced their swings in the galleries. The sound of their arcing golf balls was a long drawn-out *whack!* that echoed in the climate-controlled environment.

Gobi and Claudia sipped a mineral water at the sports bar as they watched several bobbing figures of golfers in space suits beyond the giant bubble. Mini oxygen tanks were affixed to their belts and their white faces were lit up inside their helmets. Space caddies trailed behind with ziplocked bags containing their clubs.

They heard popping sounds as the hydraulic clubs connected with high-velocity balls that trajectoried into the floating black hotels. "It's a miracle of space engineering," Claudia explained. "This is the world's first golf course ever laid out in space. Those holes are orbiting garbage-compactor units designed to emulate black holes. They'll eat anything you throw inside them, including trash."

"Let me get this straight," Gobi said grimly, changing the subject. "You want me to download Harada's consciousness, then transfer it to another medium?"

"You've done it before. It shouldn't be that difficult." Claudia swiveled around in her chair to face him. "Should it?"

"Like I said, it all depends on how much material is being downloaded. If you're downloading the consciousness of a village idiot, it might not be that complicated. With Harada, I don't know. He's supposed to be a genius."

"We're only interested in *one* thing."

"What's that?"

"We need the key that was used to encrypt the source code for Satori City 2.0. Chairman Harada has it. It's our missing link, Frank. Get it for us and we can jump start Virtuopolis. That way, *everyone* gets liberated. Your son. *Everyone.*"

Claudia tinkled the ice in her glass. "The key is 16 characters long. We've tried every possible combination. But it's no use. We need to get it directly from him."

Gobi stared at her. "That would be like trying to find a needle in a haystack."

"You can do it, Frank."

Gobi watched as the golfers and their caddies returned to the space lock area. They were coming back inside. Beyond them, a green net completely encircled the gravity-free ten-acre course, securing it to the mother ship.

"How did you find out?" he asked her.

"Find out what?"

"About my research. It was supposed to be a secret."

"The Satori Corporation has *always* been interested in DNI. Direct Neural Interfacing is the next step. You were one of the people to watch, an up-and-coming expert in the field. The list wasn't *that* long. One day you may even win the Nobel prize for your contributions to meta-science. Would you like that?"

Gobi ignored her flattery. "How did you get *inside* my research?"

Claudia smiled. "If I tell you, will you cooperate?" She paused. "Very well, I won't torture you. If you want to know, I'll tell you."

"I'm listening."

"Does the name Fujimura mean anything to you?"

The name drew a blank. Gobi shook his head. "No, who is he?"

"He's no longer with us, I'm afraid," Claudia replied. "He's moved on to the Great Beyond."

140 ● ● ● Alexander Besher

Fujimura? Of course. The young Japanese student who suffered from advanced leukemia. He had come to the Arboretum and specifically requested to join Gobi's healing circle. And when the time came, he asked Gobi to help guide him through the bardos of the after-death plane. Fujimura had been one of Gobi's first successful downloads.

"I see that you remember him now," Claudia observed. "He worked for us, Frank. He was a volunteer. You did a good job with him. He thanks you."

"How would *you* know about that? I was with him when he died. He couldn't have told you anything."

"Primitive technology, I'm afraid," Claudia replied. "We used a Ouija board to communicate with him. He confirmed your download. Now you know. Come on, drink up. We'd better get moving. There aren't any golfers out on the course now. This would be a good time to do what we came to do."

"Look, Frank," Claudia addressed him in an exuberant manner, her arm locked in his. She was a tourist pointing out the sights of Station Seven from the viewing gallery.

"Ryutaro Kobayashi's private offices are on the twenty-sixth and twenty-seventh levels. His private apartments are on twenty-eight. Do you see that block of windows with the rosy glow? That's where he lives. They say he's got quite an art collection up there."

Claudia's face beamed, but she kept her voice low. "We suspect Harada is being held on the twenty-eighth level. See the fourth suite from the end on the left side of the cylinder? That's the one. Suite 2802."

She paused. "So that's where we'll be heading after we get suited up."

Gobi suddenly turned pale. "Wait a minute. We're not going to leave the golf course, are we?" he asked, startled. "I thought you said we were just going to try to pick up his neural traces from *within* the area?"

"Don't worry, you won't drift off into space," Claudia assured him. "I've got something to deal with that." She patted his hand. "Relax, Frank. This is a resort, not a prison. There aren't any bars or barbed-wire fences. We can slip out of the perimeter easily without being detected. We'll squeeze through at the farthest end, where the web is attached to the ship. It'll be almost like slipping under a volleyball net." She brightened. "You'll see."

"I've never gone scuba diving, much less space-walking."

"It'll all go very smoothly, I promise you. You'll download Harada. Then you'll transfer him to me. I'll take over from there." She let her hand rest in his. "Afterward we can spend the evening relaxing, Frank. There's a wonderful spa on board with an orbiting hot springs. I'll even give you a massage. I give terrific massages."

He felt a familiar tingling in his second meridian. She had left her imprint on him there.

"Come on," she said, draping her arm around his waist. "Why don't we play a round of golf?" She smiled. "Who knows, you might even get a hole in one."

Gobi and Claudia were both outfitted in ultralightweight blue Kobayashi space suits. "It's my first time out," Gobi confessed to the attendant at the counter who handed them their bag of clubs. "I've never played space golf before."

"Beginner's luck!" the young Japanese in the white T-shirt and pants reassured him. "Just follow regulation. Stay inside course. Keep radio on. Any problem, we send lifeguard right away. This is Kondo-san," the young man nodded at an athletic-looking Japanese man in a black space suit with two-toed tabi footgear.

"He number one lifeguard. Neh, Kondo-san?" The young man laughed.

Kondo grunted something in Japanese, then turned and walked away.

"Friendly fellow," Gobi remarked.

The attendant laughed. "He number one black belt in space. No problem!"

"I think we're ready," Claudia said, nodding at the space lock hatch. "Let's go, Frank."

The Japanese called after them. "Please remember, oxygen

in tank last forty-five minute. But please come back after thirty minute, okay? Please enjoy."

With that admonition, the attendant released the switch from behind the counter and the space lock hissed open. Claudia and Gobi put on their black-tinted bubble helmets, clamped them down, and stepped into the waiting chamber.

Claudia gave the attendant a thumbs-up sign. The space door now opened and they both stepped into the illuminated blackness of space.

Claudia floated out first. Gobi followed her. He felt a sudden surge of excitement. A strange feeling of recognition rose in him. *Weightlessness must be very Buddhist,* he decided. *Like emptiness, it can be navigated.* He chuckled. *Who knows, maybe I was a cosmonaut in a former life?*

Claudia turned around. "You okay, Frank?" She studied his moves. "Hey, you're a natural!"

"Surf's up." Gobi grinned, as he floated up beside her.

"We'll practice a few strokes in the warm-up area over there at two o'clock," Claudia told him for the benefit of any-one who might be listening in on their channel. Then she pointed in the opposite direction, to where the green net was attached to the ship.

Gobi looked up. Beyond the giant floating net, the cylindri-cal spokes of Station Seven looked like an ocean liner bearing down upon survivors in a lifeboat.

He saw the warm glow of Ryutaro Kobayashi's private apartments on the twenty-eighth floor. Now something began to happen inside him, a process he couldn't explain. It was something new. An uneasy surge of adrenaline began to shoot through his system. It felt grey and sticky like cobwebs on a branch caught in his face.

Then he understood. It was data. Filtering into his aware-ness. He was receiving a signal from somewhere, but it was too faint to decipher.

Try hibernation breathing, he told himself. He began to take very shallow but extremely absorbent breaths like Master

Yang had taught him. His heartbeat began to slow automatically. His energy began to focus into a tiny pinprick in his solar plexus. *Absolute conservation of chi, Gobi. Then your shen can leave your body and travel.*

Now he was in a working altered state. His consciousness preceded him, like an Indian scout on an astral plane.

He scanned the perimeter. Then he heard the voice, at first it was faint, but it was familiar and recognizable. It was the voice of his shen.

The way is clear. But evil lies ahead.

What evil? Gobi asked his shen. But his shen—now way ahead of him—did not respond. That was one of the difficulties with this form of yoga. There was a time-space lag between the higher and lower planes. Master Yang told him it took twelve years of proper training to perfect the kata.

Claudia waved him onward. He was surprised at how easily he could keep up with her now. At first he kept drifting in the wrong direction, but he soon learned how to navigate in the waters of the void.

They soon reached the perimeter of the course. A quick inspection revealed that the security web was a relatively simple construct. It was attached by a wire held by rings riveted into the skin of Station Seven, up and down the entire length of the ship.

By lifting the netting, you could easily squeeze your entire body under it—and you were out.

Claudia secured their bags of clubs to one of the rings. Then, like a fish wriggling out of a net, she took a deep breath, constricted her body, and slipped through to the other side.

As they ascended, their bodies blended into the space shadows.

Following Claudia's example, he activated the magnetic wristskates she had given him and ran them along the surface of the ship. What a strange sensation. It was like having maglev runners that enabled you to skate in any direction without breaking contact and drifting into deep space.

Halfway up, he began to pick up the signal again, the one

he had heard earlier. His shen was relaying the voice to him. It was the sound of a siren calling from a distant place beyond the space wind. Beckoning him.

He felt a tingling in his arms and legs, in his torso. His scalp prickled inside his black bubble helmet.

There was a look of astonishment on Claudia's face as Gobi passed her on the way up. He glided past several floors of hotel rooms. In one, he saw a naked couple on the bed making love; in another, a sad-looking man sat alone on a Louis XIV chair. In one suite, the holo-set had been left on, but the room was empty. The game figures hovered in a still-life limbo, like a family of ghosts waiting for the occupants to return.

Gobi's pulse quickened. It was coming from there. He heard the music clearly now. She was standing in the window waiting for him, her arms outstretched. It was a figure of a woman dressed all in white. Her eyes were like glass vacuum tubes, lit. Her hair was the color of copper and her face was copper, too. Her robe flowed around her shoulders in deep Grecian folds.

He stopped, transfixed, on the opposite side of the glass. When the color of her eyes turned green, her song became an endlessly spiraling message. The music was composed entirely of pastel geometric symbols that flashed rapidly into his brain stem.

It was a download. A solid charge of data that imploded somewhere deep in his skull.

Whatever information the song contained, he could not begin to grasp right now. It was definitely nonverbal. He could not translate it on a verbal level, much less understand it rationally. But he knew it could be activated.

Correction: He knew that it would activate itself at the right moment.

Claudia was at his side. She peered into the window to see what had captivated him. The woman in white was gone, the room empty.

Claudia made a face that said, *Let's not waste time!* Then she gave him a startled look when she saw the remote look in his eyes. *Are you okay?*

But Gobi was following his shen now. He was already there, at the approach to the upper levels of the space station where Ryutaro Kobayashi maintained his keiretsu headquarters.

He heard his shen speak with its inner voice. *Where the evil awaits you.*

They had arrived at the Kobayashi castle keep. There was no other way to describe it.

There was even a moat of sorts. This was a broadly indented channel designed to capture and deflect any stray meteors that might smash into Kobayashi's inner sanctum.

The sweeping eaves of the tower with its gilded tiles evoked a 16th-century Japanese castle in space. The windows of the Kobayashi apartments were protected by reinforced ferroceramic beams built to withstand not just the spray of meteorites, but the barrage of laser fire as well.

Castle above, town below with its hotel suites, shops, and restaurants. It was a medieval city 200 miles above the earth.

Claudia was about to cross the moat over to the twenty-sixth level. Gobi grabbed her by the shoulder and shook his head. She shook her head in consternation. *What is it now?*

Gobi pointed out the central tower to Claudia. On either end of the gabled roof, their lips curling in defiance, two Korean gargoyles waited for intruders to step into their trap.

Hateya. *Mercenary guardians from an ancient and powerful bestiary,* Gobi's shen informed him. *Menace. But not the evil. That you will find on the other side.*

Claudia shook her head. She didn't understand. Gobi gestured to her, *Watch this.*

He reached inside the Velcro pocket of his space suit, which contained a supply of golf balls. He brought out a couple and activated their detonators. He took aim at the central window of Ryutaro Kobayashi's apartment and hurled the two balls with all his might.

Claudia cringed. *What are you doing!*

The balls flew into the perimeter of the Kobayashi palace

quarters. A moment later, they evaporated in puffs of popping light. Sure enough, the hateya figures sprang into action, firing lasers through their open mouths.

Claudia braced herself against the replica of the sixteenth-century castle wall. They were trapped. They could not continue forward, they could not turn back. The slightest movement would trigger another round of fire.

For the first time, her eyes showed panic. Several layers beneath the lacquered coolness, she lived in fear.

Gobi was accessing data in another zone now. A pastel shard of geometry danced before his eyes. He recognized it as part of the download from the woman in white. He studied it. It was a hologram with an infrared scope. Through it he could analyze the working mechanism of the two hateya guardians.

He saw the laser triggers inside their grimacing mouths. Good, they could be disarmed. He knew what to do. He broke off bits of the hologram. It was digitally pliable. Pink and puffy pieces of liquid gel broke off and floated like quicksilver. He manipulated them into a couple of balls.

His eyes focused on the beasts, Gobi sent the spheres scuttling toward the hateya. As soon as they reached them, they broke off like putty and clogged the firing mechanisms.

From Claudia's perspective, Gobi looked like he was performing some sort of a ridiculous mime. A Noh dance from out of time.

She shook her head again. *What was he doing?*

The invisible hologram that danced in front of Gobi's face began to grow larger. It now manifested as two parallel lines, which he grabbed on to.

Claudia watched in horror as Gobi unsnapped the safety link of his tether and began to drift across the moat toward the Kobayashi levels.

Any second, she expected the laser bursts to atomize his body. But the hateya's guns lay silent and Gobi floated across the divide.

● ● ●

He was on the other side of the moat, within the inner perimeter of the castle, just outside the long latticed windows of the Kobayashi apartments.

The hologram crackled. He followed its direction, turning to the left. His eyes were at the level of the windowsill. Nothing here. An empty office with a wall of blinking computers. In another room, a lounge, he saw several Kobayashi technicians sitting around drinking green tea and chatting.

Moving onward, he saw long dark corridors with spotlights illuminating objects inside glass display cases.

A suit of samurai armor, complete with sword, helmet, and a face-guard bristling with white horsehair whiskers. A Tang dynasty celadon jar. A 2,000-year-old piece of Jomon period statuary, its empty eyes focused. Other modern objets d'art. Paintings. A Matisse. A de Kooning. A Jackson Pollock. A Picasso.

Wait a minute. That case right there by the window, a few inches away from his face. Something was not right. He hovered for a moment. There were three glass shelves with rows of netsukes, little figurines carved of ivory.

Except that these weren't made from ivory. They were some sort of archival storage devices fashioned to look like netsukes. Here was an oni, a demon with the claws of a crab, an expression of horror imprinted on its face. There, an ascetic wrestled with a demon on a lotus leaf. A wild boar caught in a trap. A rat. A fish writhing in a net . . .

Gobi suddenly understood. *My God, these are human psyches on display!*

His shen now spoke, calmly and in a detached manner. Gobi had to remind himself that objectivity for the shen was of a higher order. It did not denote insensitivity. It was merely the distance between the astral and the mental planes.

The hologrammatic algorithm you received on the way up is a subatomic utility program. Use it to decode this evil. Yes, evil has its own special algorithm . . .

Now the shen addressed him as though it were a tour guide showing him around the Museum of the Damned.

If you will look this way, please. Regard the texture of this drama. It is a karmic folly. These are the souls of men—not their shen, which is their spirit—but their souls. You understand the difference? They have been frozen in time.

Here, within each netsuke, you will find enough storage space to imprison each compressed thought that a person might have had in the past twenty years . . .

Enough! Gobi shuddered to the core of his being. *What was the square root of such horror? Who collected these figurines? This was truly darkness on a mega-karmic scale.*

He shivered again, then was reminded of the time by Claudia, who was waving at him frantically from across the castle moat.

Gobi checked his watch: *twenty-two minutes left. Must get to Suite 2802. Running out of oxygen, running out of time . . .*

Gobi skated to the end of the gallery where he could see some lights burning.

Claudia had specified the fourth suite from the end. He drifted toward it and hovered at floor level. It was a large suite. The lights were turned down low. What caught Gobi's attention was a tray on the bedside table holding various medications.

In the adjoining room, which was brightly lit, a burly man with a crew cut sat in a chair playing a handheld game. Bodyguard.

Gobi's eyes traveled back to the darkened room. He could not see inside it very clearly, but there was a figure lying on the bed. He couldn't tell whether it was a man or a woman. Was it Kazuo Harada? He'd try to pick up something, perhaps some stray vibration.

Then the door opened and Gobi received a shock.

The two healers from California walked into the room. Gobi recognized them from the L.A. Metro flight. They were still wearing their snow-white parkas, with their long blond hair and curly beards. The second healer carried a briefcase, which he set down on the side table and opened.

He removed a pair of crystal wands and ran them over the field of the bed like a Geiger counter.

Then Gobi received another shock.

Standing behind the two healers, expressionless, was Axel Tanaka, head of security for Station Seven. He was holding an electronic box.

One of the healers suddenly turned toward the window where Gobi was watching. It was a split-second intuition that caused Gobi to duck. He felt the man's inquisitive gaze travel out the window and dissipate into space.

With his back to the wall beneath the window, Gobi had to consider all his options. He had to move fast. For all he knew, these two healers were hired can openers. They might have the same idea that Gobi did—to probe Harada's psyche to come up with as many sectors of consciousness as they could, like forking pineapple slices from a can.

On the other hand, whoever was lying on the bed was in a very bad way. Gobi didn't have enough opportunity to determine if he were drugged or not. The life signs he picked up were virtually nil. The man was dying. That was obvious. But the two healers couldn't simply siphon the consciousness out of him. They had to stabilize him first.

That's what they were doing now with the crystals. Gobi could feel their powerful buzz even outside the room.

As soon as they had him stabilized, they would open him up. He'd have to make his move right away.

Gobi floated up to the windowsill again. A field of light glowed above the body of Kazuo Harada and a cord of light emanated from the top of his head.

It was now or never.

Gobi ran his chi like a powerful current through each of his 72,000 vital nadis, those spidery filaments of life energy. Blood, wind and prana breath now raged up his central channel, shooting up through the crown of his head till it connected with the soft liquid light that was escaping from the dying man's seventh meridian.

Even if he wanted to, it was too late for Gobi to turn back. The download was swift and furious. No time for delicate interactions.

>>>Now!<<<

The lights in the room blew out. Gobi was out of there in no time flat.

The Korean gargoyles were serene, their lasers mute. As soon as Gobi crossed the moat, Claudia stepped out of the shadows and floated up to him.

Her eyes were wide. *Did you get it?* She had seen the flash of light on the twenty-eighth floor.

Gobi nodded wearily. He felt drained yet full at the same time—full with the download of the stranger's consciousness. At this stage, it had the awareness of a prenatal being. It did not yet comprehend the world into which it was moving.

Gobi's chi held the foreign consciousness in its umbilical light. *Soon enough to be born,* he thought.

Claudia patted him on the shoulder. *Congratulations.*

Then she pointed at the gauge on his oxygen pack. It was in the red danger zone. Eight minutes of oxygen left.

He nodded. They both fixed their wristskates onto a groove in the wall and kicked off.

When they reached the giant green net, Claudia held it open while Gobi slipped through as if he were sliding down a chute.

As soon as Gobi was halfway through, he realized that something was terribly wrong.

He felt a tremendous pressure around his chest. The pain was so intense that he blacked out for a moment. As he came to, he saw that he was being relentlessly squeezed through the net. He wondered fleetingly if he might have strayed into the path of a machine. A winch?

On the other side, he realized what was happening. The vise that gripped him so mercilessly belonged to a powerful pair of legs. He was being squeezed in a scissors hold.

Now he saw the man's face. It was the Japanese lifeguard Kondo. His eyes were as cold and black as polished go stones. As they flicked toward Gobi's chest, his hands ripped off Gobi's oxygen-pac. *Aargh!*

Gobi began to black out again. Suddenly Claudia appeared, holding one of the hydraulic golf clubs. Gobi watched in slow-motion as she brought it down like a Japanese katana sword. *Whack!*

Kondo's head jerked back and Gobi was able to float away like a deflated balloon, his now-useless oxygen tube dangling behind him.

Kondo lunged at Claudia with both hands slashing like a pair of cleavers. She parried with her left and right forearms, then released a low kick at his groin. He somersaulted out of the way, and kicked back on the rebound. He connected with her ribs. Claudia was hurled back toward the net.

Kondo now drew a shuriken from his sleeve and aimed it at her. The miniature buzz saw ripped through the net. Claudia was enfolded for a moment in a straitjacket of green webs, then vanished into the blackness outside.

Gobi was on the last of his recycled CO_2. *Keep breathing hibernation-style,* Master Yang urged him. *Don Main Far!* It was a command he heard as though in a distant dream. *Your body must be completely transparent to the flow of chi.*

Kondo's impassive face peered into the smoky black bubble of Gobi's helmet. The lifeguard now began to drag him away into the golf course. *Where was he taking him?*

From the corner of his eye, Gobi saw an object spinning closer. From this range, he could make out the intricate mechanism of one of the orbiting mini black holes.

Gobi felt the sizzle on his suit as the compactor began to heat up its suctioning element. Kondo had him in a headlock and was drawing him toward the black hole. Another inch more.

Suddenly it was all over.

Kondo released him. He even appeared to be bowing to Gobi, graciously, like a greeter at a cheap nightclub.

At first, the black hole sucked only a quarter-size piece out of Kondo's helmet. Then the rest of his glass bubble cracked.

Claudia's form had been perfect. Parking the fully loaded golf ball on its geosynchronous tee, she swung the hydraulic iron and connected. The ball had sailed into space and detonated about a half-inch beneath Kondo's cortex.

The blast spun him around on his heels. He had plummeted to his knees, his face in the hole. More than half of him was now gone. He was a black hole sandwich.

Claudia floated up to Gobi and propelled him gently forward, one hand on his lower back and the other gripping his shoulder.

She paused to insert her oxygen tube into his helmet and he breathed in pure salvation, as much as he could stand without choking.

They arrived at the space lock and she buzzed them both inside the chamber.

Gobi looked up at her limply from the bench where she helped him recline.

Claudia looked so beautiful to him at that moment. Removing her helmet like a kendo fencing instructor at the end of a session, she shook her long black hair out and ran both hands through the silky waterfall.

She gazed down upon him with eyes that betrayed both sweet concern and profound relief. "Rest," she urged him gently.

He gulped the lemon-flavored air greedily for a few minutes. "I'm okay now," he said, as he rose from the bench. "Thanks, Claudia." She kissed his forehead tenderly. "Gobi, I love you," she whispered.

"Did you enjoy your game?" the attendant asked after they had returned their gear to the counter. He stared at Gobi's ruptured suit and his broken oxygen canister without comment.

"It was just like you said," Gobi replied. "Beginner's luck."

ONSEN

The orbiting gondola baths came and left every few minutes from the Spa Deck. The hot springs traveled the aerial tramway course around the central cylinder of Station Seven.

Dressed in a pink floral yukata robe, Claudia waited anxiously for Gobi to join her. He was late.

Now she saw him approach the platform wearing a dark blue happi coat over his green yukata. He wore zori on his feet. She couldn't resist a smile. "You look like a pilgrim," she said. "Or a yakuza."

He had brought his Ray-Ban shades out and placed them on his face.

"I was worried about you," she said. "What happened?"

"Oh, I went up to the room to get these."

"Sunglasses? Am I missing something?" She looked around. "This is not exactly Miami Beach."

"How about Guam?" He grinned. "Or the Solomon Islands? Waikiki?"

"Are you okay, Frank? I don't get it." There was a puzzled look on her face.

"When I was in the locker room, I passed the steam room and I saw some yakuzas sitting around inside."

"So?"

"Nothing. They were wearing shades, that's all. Reminded me of mine. I guess this space station must be a home away from home for them, huh? They come up here to vacation from the Golden Triangle."

She slid her hand up one of his open sleeves and felt his upper arm. "Don't be so impressionable, Frank. What are some yakuzas to you?"

"They bring out the bad boy in me, I guess, Claudia."

"You *are* strange!"

The spa attendant approached them and bowed. "Konbanwa. We close hot springs 11 o'clock. You are last customers, neh?"

He caught hold of their gondola. It swung to a momentary halt. "Hai, dozo."

They climbed aboard.

When the space hatch opened, the gondola jerked forward on its leisurely forty-minute orbit around the space station.

"Only the Japanese could dream up a gimmick like this," Gobi remarked in admiration. "An orbiting o-furo. An astral onsen. This is really ingenious."

"Oh, look!" Claudia exclaimed. A shooting star streaked by in a bright flash, like a jeweled fan being suddenly opened and shut.

"I thought this would be a good idea." Claudia leaned forward to kiss him on the lips. "Take off your yukata."

"'Aye-aye, cap'n," he obeyed.

She had already hung her yukata on a hook. "Come on, I'm going to soap you over there," she said, pointing to a small stool on the tile floor beside the sunken tub.

Her body was a perfect sculpture in ivory, slender but with curves in all the right places. She bent over to fill the plastic bucket with water from the o-furo, and he caught his breath. She was so beautiful.

"Oh, Frank," she said when she turned around and saw him. They embraced. She felt his hardness and played with him while he kissed her neck.

"You *are* a bad boy."

"And you like it, right?"

"I *love* it!" she laughed. "I'm going to miss you."

"You are, huh?" he said, as he soaped her back. His hands traveled down her back and felt the globes of her derriere. "How much?"

"A *lot*," she breathed into his ear as he let his fingers glide down the lubricated third rail of her shaven vulva.

"Sit down," she ordered. He lowered himself onto the tiny stool on the tile floor. The water sloshed over the tub as the gondola hummed forward.

She sat down on him and he was inside her again. *God.* He bit her neck. *He was going to miss her.*

"You like being a bad boy, don't you, Frank?" She nibbled on his ear.

"If it means doing it to you like this," he replied.

"Oh!"

"And like *this,*" he added for good measure.

"Oh!"

They kept it up for a couple of kilometers. Although the windows inside their gondola were steamed from the o-furo, Gobi noticed a Japanese couple perk up and stare at them as they passed a cocktail lounge on the ninth level of the space station.

"I didn't know you could see into these things," Gobi remarked, somewhat surprised.

"Mmm," Claudia sighed, as she slid off him. "It's part of the ambience of this place."

"I'll say."

She rinsed off, then filled a bucket and splashed his shoulders with hot water.

"Ow!"

She laughed. "It gets much hotter than this, you know. This is nothing."

"I know."

"This will get you nice and relaxed though. Just like I promised you. You were wonderful up there, Frank. I'm so proud of you. Do you have it?"

"Have it? Have what?"

Claudia stopped pouring. "You *do* have the Kazuo Harada download, don't you, Frank? Our chairman's consciousness? You *did* succeed?"

"I forgot to tell you."

Claudia stood in front of him. "Tell me what, Frank? Tell me *what?*" Her voice suddenly hardened.

"It wasn't Kazuo Harada. But I think you already knew that."

"You went up to Suite 2802, didn't you?" she asked him in a carefully measured tone.

"Sure I did. But it wasn't Harada in there. It was somebody else."

"It wasn't?"

"Oh come on, Claudia. Of course, it wasn't. It was a much older, much sicker man. It was Ryutaro Kobayashi. He was on his deathbed."

"You downloaded Ryutaro Kobayashi?"

"Don't act surprised. You knew that when you sent me up there. That was the real plan all along, wasn't it? This puts a new spin on industrial espionage, Claudia. It's one for the books."

She turned around to get her yukata from the hook. When she faced him again, she was holding a laser pistol the size of a penlight.

"I'm sorry, Frank," Claudia said. "It's time to get out of the water now. You're going to get all wrinkled."

"I'm surprised at you, Claudia," Gobi said, not sounding surprised at all. "You look like you're aiming something nasty and probably quite deadly at me."

He stepped toward her.

"I'm warning you, Frank. This is no loofah. You're right about that."

"But I thought you *liked* me. You told me you loved me not even an hour ago."

"That's right, Frank. But this is business."

"Oh, dear," he sighed. "That ugly word again. It always crops up when you most expect it but least deserve it."

"Sit down over there," she waved the gun at the swivel chair by the window.

"Now tell me, Frank, when did you get wise to me?" she asked him, almost regretfully.

"When I saw those yakuza in the locker room."

"What was it about them exactly?"

"I suddenly remembered my good old Ray-Bans. May I?"

"Don't try anything funny, Frank. Don't try anything stupid either."

"I promise."

"Go ahead," she waved the gun again. "Put them on if they make you feel better."

"Thank you." He reached for the 'Bans and slipped them on. "I ought to mention these aren't ordinary sunglasses, Claudia. They're prescription AI-lenses—with an on-line data base, among other things."

"So?"

"I've been researching a book. So I've got these things programmed to record anything that might prove useful to my work."

"Yes?" she replied cautiously.

"Well, I completely forgot that I was wearing them during the flight."

Gobi smiled when he saw a look of understanding cross her face. "You finally get it?"

"You recorded the entire flight?"

"That's right."

"When you went up to your room to get them, you played everything back?"

"More or less. I fast-forwarded," he admitted.

She smiled. "You *are* clever. What did you see?"

"It's not what I saw actually. It's what I figured out afterward."

"And *what* did you figure out, Dr. Gobi?" The smile played on her lips without any commercial interruption.

"You took the Butoh out." He paused. "But you weren't the *only* one."

Claudia looked out the window. "That's very interesting. But there isn't much time, Frank," she said. "You had better wrap up your story. We'll be getting back soon. And you've still got to do *this.*"

She brought out a small box with wires and clips attached to it. He looked at it. "That's what you want me to download Kobayashi into?"

She nodded. "Yes, Frank, it's a bio-ROM."

"It's fancier than the drive I use. Nice, Claudia."

"You were saying, Frank, that I took the Butoh out, but I wasn't alone?"

"Yes, you should have seen the look of surprise on your face. I can play it for you sometime if you like."

"That won't be necessary."

"That's what almost brought the plane down, Claudia. You and Silver Face. Who does *he* work for? I figured him for some maquiladora henchman from across the border. He had his chi-absorber inside his snuffbox. He aimed at the Butoh at just about the same time that you took him out with *your* Okidata bottle-opener. That was quite a blast zapping through the cabin. That, plus the droid fireworks afterward. Hell, even that Latino yakuza was surprised. I bet he's not used to that much recoil."

"For someone whose life was saved, you don't sound too grateful," Claudia chided him.

"You saved your own neck, too."

"Ah so?"

"My 'Bans told me so. If my 'Bans tell me so, they tell me so."

"All right, story time is over now. Time to get to work."

"Oh, the Butoh fired at me, all right. But that was his first shot. His second shot was programmed to take *you* out of the picture."

"Me? Why?"

"Because, Claudia, you were the only one on board who could reroute the spaceplane to Station Seven, which was the plan from the *very* beginning—and the reason I was booked on that flight."

She sat down across from him. The smile on her face was drawn tight like the string of a samisen. "You have sixty seconds, Frank. But I do commend you. You *are* very good."

The gondola was coming around the bend on the aerial course. A few more kilometers and it would reach the platform.

"Those two healers on board the flight," Gobi told her, "they were my tip-off. I saw them in Kobayashi's suite. I must admit I thought they were going to download him first. I believed you when you told me it was Harada up there. The man definitely looked very ill. Like he was dying. Now I'd have to say, they were just a couple of faith healers commuting to work. They'd been treating Kobayashi for a while now. Flying to Neo-Tokyo. Catching the shuttle from there to Station Seven. Nice work, if you can get it."

Claudia was fiddling with the bio-ROM. "Just put this band around your forehead," she told him. "The clips attach to your ears. This should only take a few minutes."

"But Kobayashi was failing fast," Gobi continued grimly. "He didn't have much time left, did he? And you people knew it. You wanted me to get to Station Seven at the same time they did. So I could download the poor bastard before he croaked."

"That's enough Masochist Theater," Claudia snapped. "Do the transfer. *Now.*"

Gobi shook his head. "You're not going to kill me, are you?" he asked. "If you kill me, there won't be too much left to download."

Her smile chilled him. "That's where you're mistaken, Frank. This is a new technology that you probably haven't heard about. This is a DNI 350 Professional Downsizer. It can digitize the brain waves of a dead person within two hours of their death. The choice is yours. Dead or alive."

"Now what do you say?" she asked him, with an expression that said *I love you but I'll kill you in a minute.* He had to admit that *yes,* it *was* in her nature.

"Have you heard the one about the two Zen acolytes?"

The gondola was approaching the perimeter of the 18th level.

" . . . so one of them said to the other, 'Take my roshi. *Please.*'"

Claudia shook her head. "Good-bye, Frank." She twisted the cap on the pen-gun. "I'm sorry."

Funny, how calm he felt.

Something snapped. The gondola jerked and swung wildly. Gobi grabbed Claudia's wrist and twisted it hard.

She dropped her gun.

"Claudia," Gobi said in his most earnest voice. "Listen to me. I'm not saying let bygones be bygones, but the cable connecting this gondola to the ship just snapped. We're heading out into space."

One after the other, the gondolas slowly slipped off the ribbon of cable that ran through the aerial posts of the tramway.

The tall, gangly figure in the Kobayashi golfer's suit watched as the capsules scattered in different directions in space. Then he slowly turned around and headed back toward the netted area of the golf course.

Over his shoulder, he carried a bag that contained his hydraulic golf irons along with another useful appliance—a high-powered space crossbow armed with explosive shuriken powerful enough to cut through a two-and-a-half-inch steel cable.

He drew his bag inside after he slipped through and made his way back to the golf deck.

It had been an excellent round. Yes, indeed. A jolly good show.

Gobi peered out the window at the roof of the gondola. A loop of cable still dangled from the jaws of the gripping mechanism.

Claudia studied the frayed ends of the wire. "Looks like a fifty-caliber shuriken. It would *have* to be to cut through steel like that."

"No wonder they call them hot springs." He sat down on the stool and opened the mini-fridge. "Well, let's see, as long as we're going for a little ride, we may as well check out the refreshments. What have we got? Hmm, two large bottles of Asahi-Heinekens and a bag of dried squid. How long is that going to last us before help arrives?"

"How much oxygen do we have left?"

"What flavor?" he rummaged in the back of the refrigerator, where he found some spritzer canisters. "Deer antler oxygen. Bear claw flavor. Whale gall flavor. *Ooh.* It says here, tiger testicle flavor. Are these aphrodisiacs or what? Is this legal? This is a very decadent mini-bar."

Claudia sat down on a stool beside him and wrapped the yukata around her tightly. She looked out into the blackness of space.

"You mind telling me something, Claudia?"

She turned. "What?"

"Why didn't you just use your little DNI Downsizer, or whatever you call it, on Ryutaro Kobayashi yourself? Why did you have to drag me into it?"

"Couldn't get access, Frank. You saw the security up there. It had to be direct. You were the only one listed in the phone book capable of doing a remote transfer."

"Ah . . . well, better luck next time."

Claudia continued to stare out the window, preoccupied.

"What's that!?" she said suddenly, looking up.

A pair of headlights shone in the distance. Whatever the craft was, it was approaching their gondola on the starboard side at about sixteen knots.

It was an old space trawler, a sorry-looking beat-up piece of space junk. It looked like a Chinese-make *Long March-12* shuttle picked up from a used-shuttle lot in the New Shenzhen Special Economic Zone in South China.

As it swept into view, Gobi and Claudia could see that it was painted with psychedelic colors. Its surface was pock-marked and dented from long contact with meteor showers.

The ship seemed to be trailing a long drift net. The net was filled with an assortment of jettisoned space garbage and other unmentionable effluents dumped by commercial shuttles and satellites in contravention of the International Anti-Space-Dumping Act.

An array of sensing and tracking monitors bristled on its roof. The radar was turning their way.

"What's the name on the ship?" Claudia demanded. Her old spirit was suddenly coming back.

"Well, I'll be damned!" Gobi exclaimed. "If it isn't the *Greenspace II!*"

GREENSPACE II

Captain Jesse Korkoran and Tomoko Kikuchi, Jesse's first and only mate on board the *Greenspace II* space trawler, pulled up alongside the derelict gondola.

"Well, well, what have we got here, Tom?" Jesse chuckled, as she brought her craft to a stop 50 yards away. *"Shee-it!* Would you believe that! It looks like some folks have been takin' an o-furo in space! I'm jealous!"

"Makes *me* homesick," Tom replied, sitting up. "I could use a good soak."

"Well, what do you think, honey?" Jesse asked, as she looked at Tom fondly. "Should we find out if they need some help, like, you know, scrubbing their backs or something?"

Jesse was about 36 years old. She had close-cropped salt-and-pepper hair and a husky, musky, and muscular body. She'd been captain of the *Greenspace II* for six years—three of them with Tom Kikuchi, and she'd never seen anything like this before.

Her first mate and lover was a young Japanese woman—Tomoko, or "Tom," as she preferred to be called by her friends as well as her enemies. She was a petite hunk with short platinum hair and a little ruby-studded nose ring.

Tom had been with Nissan for about eight years until she quit in protest over a toxic cosmetics spill over the Aleutian Islands. She'd been piloting a space lab shuttle for Shiseido scientists who were developing a new strain of bio-blush in the weightless atmosphere of space. There had been an accidental release of the stuff over Alaska.

Then, in a freak accident, a passing shower of asteroids had carried the bio-vapors into the earth's atmosphere. The result was a new species of pink polar bears.

That's when Tom saw the light and dropped out of the commercial space exploitation game. She'd met Jesse in a bar in San Antonio and they'd been together ever since.

Now they happily trolled for space trash together and kept a sharp lookout for any illegal dumping of biotech substances and other toxic wastes by greedy corporations in outer space.

Jesse hit the ship's loudspeaker switch. "Ahoy there!" her deep voice reverberated against the gondola. "This is Captain

Jesse Korkoran of *Greenspace II*. My partner and I request permission to come aboard and soak our tushes."

Claudia and Gobi's transfer to the *Greenspace II* had gone as smoothly as possible under the circumstances.

Jesse had backed her ship up against the door to the gondola. Then she opened the hatch and released what looked like the hose of a giant vacuum cleaner. It connected with the cabin door on the gondola.

Frank and Claudia had simply stepped on board the *Greenspace II*.

"Hi, folks. We normally use this tube as a pooper-scooper for all the shit we've got floating around in deep space. I hope you don't mind coming in the back door."

"You saved our lives," Claudia told her gratefully, as she looked around the cabin.

"Shucks, and I thought you were going to get all emotional on me." Jesse smiled. She gave them her hand. It was a bone-wrenching handshake, but it was warm and friendly.

They had to steady themselves in the weightless environment.

"I'm the captain of this derelict," she told them. "This here's my first mate, Tom."

"How do you do?" Tom said, as she smiled shyly at them.

Holding on to a handgrip on the wall, Claudia looked around the cramped deck and living quarters. Some escaped charts floated in the corner of the cabin, along with a few empty cartons of take-out Chinese food.

"Sorry about the mess," Jesse apologized. "The maid comes in on Tuesdays."

A tiny strip of paper floated by Gobi's face. He brushed it away. "From a Chinese fortune cookie," Jesse explained, as she grabbed it. She glanced at the fortune and grinned. "It says here *'You will be experiencing a minor revelation soon.'* Well, well."

Jesse let the fortune float away. "Can we get you anything?" She turned to Tom. "We got any coffee for our guests?"

"'Aye-aye, cap'n." Tom gave her a mock salute. She asked Gobi and Claudia. "You want a cappuccino?"

"Thanks!" Gobi replied, then he asked, "You have cappuccino in space? And Chinese food?"

"Well, we're pretty well stocked up here," Tom confessed. "Our usual tour of duty lasts about three weeks. Three weeks up in space, then two weeks on earth."

"Yup, we've got all the comforts of home," Jesse said proudly.

Claudia was staring at something that floated amid the clutter in the top corner of the cabin.

She gazed at both Jesse and Tom with a new understanding. "I see what you mean," she said.

Tom blushed as she grabbed at the nine-inch doubleheaded ribbed object that had caught Claudia's eye. She stuffed it inside a drawer, but it began vibrating so she had to switch off.

"Sorry about that," she said, her face reddening.

"Think nothing of it," Claudia said with a widening smile. "I'm extremely grateful to be here. My name's Claudia Kato, by the way. This is Dr. Frank Gobi."

"I don't want to get personal, but you two make a habit of hot tubbing in outer space?" Jesse inquired. "It's a terrific idea, but, if I might ask, how did you two launch this thing off the ground without spilling anything?"

"Oh, no, it was nothing like that," laughed Claudia. "We were involved in a little accident."

"That's right," Gobi explained. "This is one of the orbiting hot springs at Station Seven."

"No kidding!" Jesse said, finally understanding. "So you two were at Station Seven, huh? You work there or what? They've got a pretty clean facility, no complaints. Not *too* much dumping. But there's been some weird shit going on there lately."

"No, we don't work there," Gobi replied. "In fact, I'm bound for New Narita in the morning. And Claudia works for an airline. We were overnighting at Station Seven, and we were enjoying the hot springs when the tramway cable snapped. That's how we ended up here. That's the whole story."

"Wow," Tom said. "You're really lucky we came by."

"That's an understatement." Claudia gave Gobi a look.

"Okay, now that we've got you two escaped lovebirds back in the cage, what would you like us to do with you?" Jesse asked. "Return you to Station Seven? I'd better let them know you're safe and sound. I'm sure they'll be relieved to hear it."

Jesse frowned. "Anyone else out there that needs rescuing?"

"I don't think so," Claudia said. "We were the only ones in the spa at the time. We took the last scheduled run."

"Lucky thing then," Jesse said. "I'll go ahead and radio in."

"Wait a second, where are you bound?" Claudia asked Jesse, putting her hand on the woman's shoulder.

Surprised, Jesse put the transceiver down. She looked up and down at Claudia, whose thin robe lay slightly open at the front. Claudia made no attempt to pull her yukata closed.

Jesse could see Claudia's breasts and they looked fine to her. Definitely a nice-looking woman. "Hmm, what have you got in mind, honey?" she said in a soft voice. "Don't you want to get back to base?"

"Well," Claudia persisted. "It's not really a top priority for me. So where did you say you were heading?"

"We'll be touching down in New Zealand in three days. Don't you want to get off at your stop?"

Jesse's warm brown eyes were pouring over Claudia's curves. Tom observed the exchange with an amused expression.

"If it's all the same to you," Claudia said. "I'll just stay on board and get off in New Zealand with you. I've always wanted to see New Zealand."

"Yeah, and I bet New Zealand has always wanted to see you, too." Jesse nodded. "Let me ask my partner here if we've got enough rations for three—or is it four?" Jesse turned an inquiring face to Frank Gobi. "You got an itch to stay on board yourself, mister?"

"Oh, no, by all means make it three," Gobi said. "As I said, I'm bound for New Narita in the morning. You don't mind dropping me off at Station Seven, do you?"

"For you, sport, anything." Jesse nodded. Then she searched her lover's face for approval. "My partner's got to vote on whether your friend stays though. What do you say, Tom?"

Tom was at the espresso machine filling some cappuccino tubes with scalding espresso. The steamed milk was more difficult.

"Hey," she said, smiling at Captain Jesse Korkoran, "some extra company can't hurt. The more the merrier, right?"

"It's settled then," Jesse boomed, as she slapped her hands together. "We'll put the old zeal back in New Zealand."

Gobi sipped his cappuccino. "Hmm, excellent brew," he thanked Tom. "Arigato."

"Do itashimashite," she replied in Japanese and bowed.

Jesse was piloting *Greenspace II* back to Station Seven. The space station was coming into view again with its gleaming cylinder and multi-levels of hotel rooms and offices.

Jesse had radioed in with the news that she was returning with one of the hotel guests who'd been stranded in an onsen cabin that they'd picked up in space.

Station Seven Control thanked *Greenspace II* and authorized the landing. When Jesse inquired about other wayward gondolas, Station Seven replied that half a dozen had already been retrieved by search teams, while a few others were still on the loose.

As far as Station Seven knew, everything was under control. *Come on in,* Greenspace II.

Claudia was holed up in the toilet. She was going to wait it out until Gobi was dropped off.

"Well, good-bye, Frank," she said when they made their farewells. "I want you to know there was nothing personal in what I did back there. I truly respect you. I'm sorry if I hurt you in any way."

Then she whispered, "Are you sure you want to go back there?"

"Why not? Why shouldn't I?" Gobi asked.

"I don't want to put ideas in your head or anything, but aren't you forgetting something?"

"What am I forgetting, Claudia?"

"You've downloaded the consciousness of Ryutaro Kobayashi. And that can be a dangerous thing."

"You don't mean someone may want to kill me for that, do you?" Gobi asked her mockingly. "Anyway, who's going to know about that—except you—and you're on your way to New Zealand."

Claudia lowered her voice. "There's still time. Give me Kobayashi. You could become a very, very rich man, Frank. A very, very rich man."

"Somehow, coming from you, that doesn't motivate me very much." He smiled sadly.

"Oh, well." Claudia shrugged. "I tried. I'll see you around, Frank. Maybe sometime."

"Maybe."

She kissed him on the cheek.

Jesse and Tom couldn't help but follow the exchange. "Your girlfriend is in some sort of trouble, Gobi?" Jesse asked after Claudia locked herself in the benjo.

"She's not my girlfriend," he replied.

"She's not your girlfriend? *Hey, you're all right!*" Jesse said and slapped him on the back. "You're an okay guy."

"I'd watch out for her if I were you," Gobi suggested.

"Oh, baby, that's not going to be a problem, believe me. I'm a card-carrying butch and she looks like a femme to me."

"Yes, a femme fatale," Gobi answered. "Don't say I didn't warn you."

"You warned me, you warned me."

They were coming in for the landing on Station Seven. The docking hatches were open and he could see the interior deck with the Satori spaceplane parked in the corner of the hangar.

"Can I ask you something?" Gobi turned to Jesse, who was navigating the junk trawler.

Jesse had parked the drift net outside the space station. The escaped gondola was caught in its mesh and Kobayashi crews were on their way to retrieve it.

"How we doin', Tom?" Jesse checked with her copilot.

"Locked into descent and 2 minutes, 43 seconds till landing."

"Good." Jesse turned to Gobi. "Whatch' you want to know?"

"You said you noticed that some strange things have been happening on Station Seven recently. What did you mean by that?"

"Well," Jesse replied, "we picked up some bodies in our trawling nets a while ago. No personal identification so we don't know for an actual fact that they were from here, you understand? We found them mixed up with the other flotsam and jetsam that we usually pick up on our route."

"Who were they?"

Captain Jesse hovered above the open deck of Station Seven. "Okay, Tom? Lay her down as neat as you'd diaper a baby's bottom."

"'Aye-aye cap'n," Tom responded, as she gunned the engines into reverse for the descent.

Jesse turned to Gobi. "I said they were bodies, Gobi. I didn't say they were human."

She cut the engines. "Got any final questions, professor?"

"But they *looked* human?"

"Like you and me. There were three of 'em, two guys and a woman. Men were, let's see now: Latino looking. About 30 years old, brown hair, brown eyes, trim, 160-165 pounds, 5'10-5'11". Woman was Oriental, early 20s, kind of femme, nice slender build, attractive."

"But they were droids?"

"Yup. But nothing like I'd ever seen before. I mean, they had no mechanical parts. Nothing clunky. They were smooth but natural looking. They had birthmarks, stuff like that— super lifelike. One of them even had a driver's license from San Diego. I remember that 'coz I thought that was pretty weird."

Jesse unclasped her seat belt and rose to her feet. Gobi was quiet for a moment. The Kobayashi crews slowly approached the shuttle in their emergency gear.

"What do you think they were doing in space?" Gobi asked her.

"Search me," Jesse said. "I don't know. Once Tom and I determined they weren't human, we notified headquarters about our discovery."

"And?"

"We radioed on an open channel, you know—"

"Hi guys!" Jesse waved at the maintenance crews who were rolling a ladder over to the shuttle's hatch.

"Anyway, we got a message from Station Seven pretty fast. They said they just happened to pick up our signal and wanted to let us know that 'those mannequins,' as they put it, were from Station Seven, and could we please return them? They sure would appreciate it."

"How did they explain the droids being in space?"

"They didn't, really. Said something about their being test dummies for that outdoor golf course they were developing at the time—that they must have gotten through the safety nets, but that's what they were testing anyway, safety, etc."

"And you bought that?"

"Hey," Jesse said, poking her finger in Gobi's chest. "As you can see, we don't exactly have the facilities to carry around a bunch of stiffs on board. No offense to *you*, though. So we dropped the dummies off like we were asked. They were mighty grateful to us. We even got a case of sake from what's-his-face, their chief of security, for all our troubles."

"Axel Tanaka."

"Tanaka. That's the one. The same guy that's waving at us right now from the upper deck. See him? Let's wave back. Hi, there, Axel!"

Gobi stared out of the shuttle window. Tanaka came down the stairs to meet them. Following right behind him were his two musclemen.

Jesse advised Tom, "Better stay on board with Princess Charming, toots, you don't mind? Just in case things get touchy."

"No problema, cap'n," Tom grinned as she opened the hatch.

"I won't be long, sweets." Jesse wriggled her heavy hips out of the hatch. "You comin', professor?" She turned to Gobi. "There's a little welcoming committee waiting just for you, I'd imagine."

"I'm right behind you," Gobi replied.

Jesse took a deep breath of the hibiscus-flavored air and climbed down the rungs.

She was a handsome and stalwart figure, with her salt-and-pepper hair, broad shoulders, and indigo jumpsuit. At 160 solid pounds, with her hands on her hips and her muscular arms extended, Jesse looked every inch the tough space commander.

"How's it going, Tanaka?" she greeted him.

"Captain Korkoran, welcome to Station Seven," Tanaka said. "I'd like to thank you on behalf of the Space Station for returning the passengers safe and sound, and for retrieving the gondola. Excellent work."

Gobi climbed down to the deck. He felt a little naked in his bare feet and the light yukata he had worn in the spa.

"Whatever we can do to help out," Jesse said. "It's our pleasure. But you stand corrected, Mr. Tanaka. I'm only bringing you back a single passenger—the professor here."

Tanaka and his men exchanged glances. "I'm afraid I don't quite understand," Tanaka said to Jesse. "Dr. Gobi and Miss Claudia Kato were on board together when the gondola broke away from Station Seven. Surely, when you rescued Dr. Gobi, there was another person on board?"

"I'm afraid not, Mr. Tanaka. Just this gentleman here in his birthday suit. I don't know about any Claudia Kato."

Tanaka frowned. "There must be some misunderstanding then. Hashimoto," he addressed one of his men in a guttural tone without turning his head from Jesse and Gobi. "What does the log say?"

Hashimoto lifted his data link from his holster. He punched into it and read from the screen: "There's a record here of two guests, a man and a woman, boarding Gondola 8 at 22:56 P.M.

for the final scheduled run." He looked up at Gobi with eyes like charcoal briquettes waiting to be lit.

"So you see, Captain Korkoran," Tanaka said, with a sinister edge to his voice, "there must have been some error made in your accounting when you executed your rescue operation. Perhaps Hashimoto might have a quick look on board your craft. Our management would be most embarrassed—not to mention find itself in legal trouble—if one of our guests simply disappeared from Station Seven. You understand our position."

Hashimoto had already begun to climb the ladder up to the cockpit of the *Greenspace* shuttle.

Jesse said, "No one's making any mistakes except you, Mr. Tanaka. And no one goes on board without my permission. Under the charter of the Space Convention, *Greenspace II* is a protected craft with full diplomatic immunity."

"Perhaps we can discuss this matter later on in my office, Captain Korkoran," Tanaka replied with a curt smile.

"Chotto," Tom said to Hashimoto, as she met him at the top of the ladder. She had a space harpoon aimed at the soft part of his neck. "Going somewhere?"

Hashimoto froze. He backed down several rungs and scowled up at Tom.

"That's better, big boy," Tom said. "This harpoon's for snaring oversize parcels of garbage dumped into space. I guess you fit the bill."

Hashimoto's face darkened as he backed down to the deck. He turned to Tanaka for further instructions.

"It's all right, Hashimoto. Stay where you are," Tanaka ordered.

"A wise move, Tanaka," Jesse said, nodding her head in approval. "I like a man who thinks with his brain instead of his prostate. And now, if you'll excuse us, we've got to get back to work, so we'll be just moseying along. Professor," Jesse said, as she turned to Gobi. "Everything here to your satisfaction? You can still come along with us, if you like. The offer stands."

Gobi raised his hand to her. "Thanks, Captain. I'll be fine. I'll always be grateful to you both."

"You sure now?"

Gobi saluted her.

Wth a nod of her platinum-fuzz head, Tom called to Gobi, "Hang loose, mongoose."

"All right then, boys, I'll leave you to your business. Adios." Jesse turned around and climbed back up the ladder. She winked at Tom as she got inside the shuttle and closed the hatch securely behind her.

"Well, Dr. Gobi," Tanaka said, as they backed away from the craft. "You seem to have a habit of popping up wherever there is trouble."

"Maybe it's just a coincidence."

"I don't think so," replied Tanaka brusquely, as they watched the psychedelic-painted scow lift off the deck. "I prefer to regard it as a form of negative synchronicity myself."

HOUSE OF TENGU

Was it a form of negative sychronicity after all? Gobi tossed and turned on the geosynchronous futon in his suite and wondered about Tanaka's remark. How appropriate it now seemed!

Like a narcoleptic struggling to *a) stay awake or else b) remain fast asleep,* Gobi was undecided about what to do with the download. Waking or dreaming, the challenge was the same. The abducted Kobayashi consciousness had come to a full simmer just beneath the fourth meridian of Gobi's heart. His ribs were burning like forget-me-not coals in his chest.

Gobi groaned as his heart caved in.

This was the longest that he had ever retained another's prana. Two life-streams had been joined: Gobi's and Kobayashi's together.

Theirs were now Siamese karmas. They were twins, blood brothers, chi-brothers. Or was he just kidding himself?

Suddenly, there was an opening within an opening and Gobi's system felt the shock of the Kobayashi data. Actually, it energized him like a kundalini rush.

Gobi lay helplessly on his futon, soaking the bedding with his sweat as the data danced on his chest. He saw little electric blue explosions erupt from his yukata and he thought his heart would melt, but it had its own built-in surge protector and he survived their dual death.

Little tengus, Japanese cyber-goblins with long, red noses and a cackling laugh, ran 'round and 'round the tatami-room. All Gobi could do was watch them, a prisoner of their pyrotechnics.

By morning, the Kobayashi energy was simmering back into place, receding into his heart again.

Gobi rested briefly. Then the pain began anew. Was it his pain or Kobayashi's? He laughed at the absurdity of that thought. What difference did it make? Then he realized that the pain came to him as a guide. It was like a hands-on manual for the care and feeding of his temporary guest. It held all the secrets, and all the strategies for managing his successful confinement.

Master Kobayashi's pain, and you will master him. Master your own pain and you can forgive yourself for what you've done.

For what you are doing.

Gobi fell asleep at last. Deeply.

He was sitting in his private eye's office above the Italian bakery in North Beach. Seeing clients, the way he'd learned in psychic P.I. school: feet up on his desk, an eye-mask covering his eyes, in a deep trance, listening to a Hemisync tape from the Monroe Institute playing on his headphones. First, a pre-Native American spirit dropped by to pick up the rent. Then came a T'ang dynasty noblewoman who was missing her precious jade brooch. Then an Italian woman from the sixteenth century who suspected her husband of having an affair with an eighteenth-century maid. Then he shuffled in. An old Japanese guy in a ratty, plaid overcoat, with a grimy scarf around his neck, and a greasy fedora that looked like it had been dunked in a vat of tempura oil. This being a lucid dream,

Gobi recognized him right away. He had yellow rheumy specks in his eyes and a death-rattle sound in his throat.

"What can I do for you? Gobi asked.

The way the Japanese stared at him so intently, Gobi knew that he knew. At least, he must have suspected something on some level.

"It's a missing person's case," the old man said finally.

"Yes?" Gobi waited.

The old man's eyes darted around the office as though he might accidentally find what he was looking for just lying around in one of the corners of the room. Then his eyes settled on Gobi again.

"A man is missing. I wish to find him."

"Does he have a name?"

The Japanese man played with the brim of his fedora nervously.

"Can't remember exactly."

"Well, how do you expect me to locate him if you don't even know his name?"

The old man sighed. "It comes and goes."

Then he smiled. "Yes, I've got it now. That's it. Kobayashi, Ryutaro. Can you help me find him, sir?"

DEPARTURE

Time to go.

The first limo to New Narita was due to depart in 45 minutes. The 1,001 scalding needles of the shower revived Gobi. After he blasted himself with icy water for another 60 seconds, his right and left brain got reacquainted. The hellishness of his nightmares from the previous night had temporarily receded.

Now there was a clear space in his forehead, like a television monitor on neutral. Gobi dressed quickly, picked up his briefcase, and strode down the corridor to the elevator.

The Limo Deck was on Level 22. Gobi didn't have a

reservation, but he didn't really need one. He slipped the flight concierge a New Yen token and got bumped to the head of the standby list.

The Nissan space limo seated 24 passengers. It was a sleek Z-12 model that made the trip half a dozen times a day until the final shuttle at 4:00 P.M.

Gobi got himself an espresso and a cinnamon kelp stick from the snack bar for a quick breakfast. He also picked up a hard copy of the *Mainichi Daily News,* beamed that morning from Neo-Tokyo.

The headline read: *"Lost Japanese Soldier Discovered in Cambodian Jungle 35 Years After U.N. Peacekeeping Mission."* Gobi sat down and waited for boarding to begin.

It looked like a full flight. There were a few business types, three or four honeymooning couples, and a few foreigners like himself. He studied them for a moment. They looked like gaijin salarymen heading back to their home offices.

They don't look too happy to be going to Neo-Tokyo, he thought. But who can blame them? Not only do you have to be a workaholic to get a paycheck, but your body completely disappears at the end of the day. Phew!

One of the gaijins, a young Australian with blond hair and a prefab suit, eased himself into the seat next to Gobi's. "Mornin' mate," he said, as he slid his briefcase under his seat. "They should be boardin' us in a few minutes, I reckon. Which 'retsu you with?" he asked.

Gobi raised his eyebrows and shook his head.

The Australian grinned as he offered his hand. "Say, how d'you do? I'm Sandy Findehorn. From Melbourne. Hope you don't mind my pryin'. It's sort of a game with me whenever I travel. Tryin' to guess the professional affiliations, you know. Helps me pass the time, breaks the ice."

"I'm Frank Gobi, from San Francisco," he said, shaking the young man's hand.

"Pleased to meet you, mate. But say no more, I'll do the rest. *Mitsubishi.*"

"Sorry."

"Daihatsu."

"Sorry."

"Shiseido-Palmolive."

"That's three strikes, I'm afraid."

"Damn. And I'm usually the one having the drinks bought for me." Findehorn grinned. "Guess it's not my day." He paused before continuing, "So what's your blood type? You an A? Detail-minded thinker, are you?"

"No."

"You're definitely *not* an O."

"You got that part right." Gobi kept up the chatter with the hyper Australian, but he had his eye on the athletic-looking Japanese who was riding the escalator down to the waiting area.

It was Hashimoto, Axel Tanaka's right-hand man from Kobayashi security.

The data link on his belt beeped as he crossed the lobby to the check-in counter. He exchanged a few words with the flight concierge and glanced down at the list of passengers for the shuttle.

"Damned if you're a type B—you look arty, but there's somethin' else about you."

"Sorry, Findehorn, you struck out again." But this time it was Gobi's turn to miss the cue.

The Australian had been intently watching Hashimoto as well. To Gobi's surprise he suddenly rose from the seat, mumbling, "Catch you later on board, mate."

Findehorn picked up his briefcase and rapidly strode over to the boarding area, where he attempted to board the Z-12. One of the attendants politely blocked him from entering the dock. He pointed at his watch. Findehorn ignored him and tried to push his way on anyway.

The activity at the gate caught Hashimoto's attention. He nodded at two men waiting in the wings and the three of them approached the Australian, who was engaged in a heated discussion with the flight staff.

"Look, I've got to get on now and take my medicine, don't you understand. Doctor's orders!"

When he saw Hashimoto closing in with his two men,

Findehorn shoved the attendant aside with his briefcase and ran toward the escalator.

"Stop him!" Hashimoto shouted.

Halfway up the escalator, with Hashimoto and his men barely ten yards behind, Findehorn turned around and threw his briefcase at his pursuers.

He reached into his jacket and everyone froze.

Hashimoto and his two men crouched as Findehorn pulled out a test tube and held it high. "I'm warning you, this is a highly explosive substance! This entire ship will be destroyed if you take another step!"

An otherworldy stillness filled the departure complex. Only the throbbing vibrations of the Z-12 shuttle in the take-off area broke the silence.

Gobi watched the inevitable.

Findehorn held the vial high as he faced off Hashimoto and his guards, who were a dozen steps away and rising on the escalator.

Standing with his back to the upper lounge, Findehorn could not see the man waiting for him at the top of the escalator. It was Axel Tanaka.

A light flashed in Tanaka's hand and Findehorn went over the side. He dropped the vial and Hashimoto leaped forward to catch it.

For a second, he actually held it in his hand, but then it slipped through his fingers and fell to the lobby floor. The vial burst and spilled its contents on the floor.

Gobi felt a powerful tremor shake the entire lobby like a small earthquake. The newspaper rack fell over and all the copies of the *Mainichi News* shattered. But there was no aftershock.

Tanaka walked over to him. "Do you have anything to declare, Dr. Gobi?"

Gobi looked back at him before replying. "Only one thing. Sayonara."

It was a relief to finally get on the shuttle. The Z-12's tilt-rotors began to thrash louder and louder as the passengers hurried on board. The flight had been delayed 20 minutes as Kobayashi security mopped up. There had been another arrest, a Papua New Guinean who was attempting to smuggle some exotic birds to Neo-Tokyo.

What did Tanaka mean by 'did he have anything to declare?' Gobi wondered. *Did he know about his secret stowaway? About Ryutaro Kobayashi's consciousness?*

Gobi felt the sensation again, like heartburn, around his third meridian. That's where he had stashed the consciousness of the old man until he figured out what to do with him next.

He had visualized putting him inside a strongbox filled with back issues of the Scientific Nipponian *and* Nikkei Business Week *to keep him occupied. The Takarazuka all-women's theatrical troupe. Even a cable channel.*

Ryutaro Kobayashi had no idea his consciousness had been downloaded, much less that he was, if not technically dead, then holistically in a state of limbo.

But Gobi didn't know how much longer he could keep this up. He had never gone this far in any of his previous DNI experiments. The stomach cramps around his hara were becoming intense.

Gobi heard a familiar nasally voice. "Why, if it ain't the professor! The world's gettin' smaller and smaller, ain't it, doc? Now that's a scientific fact."

The silver filigree of chains rustling against his cheek, Carlos Morales, the Latino yakuza, eased himself into the seat next to Gobi.

"Whew," he said, as he settled in. "Looks like I made this buggy just in time. I was runnin' a little late. Not as late as our late friend back there, though, huh?" Carlos laughed. "It's a tough racket."

"What is?" Gobi looked at him sourly. He wasn't sure he was happy to see the Latino. Maybe he was just superstitious from the last time they flew together.

"He was a runner, man. But from the wrong side of the tracks. Some chickenshit-gumi from Queensland. Think they're smart; don't deal the big boys in. Greed will get you every time, quicker than cholesterol, amigo."

The Z-12 was moving away from Station Seven. Gobi could see the green net of the golf course and the white castle with the imitation 16th-century stone walls.

"The yaks use the station as a transshipment point for brain ice from the labs in the Triangle. They don't like it when other people muscle in. They think they own the market. It's a turf thing. The Kobayashis kindly accommodate 'em. You might say they have a trade deal."

Carlos paused. "'Course, there's always *new* shit comin' in." He laughed. "You know, like Shit 4.0. . . . The Aussies been dealin' with the West Coast boys. That's what got our friend in trouble back there. Did you hear the pop? Good stuff. Ah, what a waste."

Carlos leaned over at a Japanese businessman who was staring at the silver chains on his face.

"Hey, watch you lookin' at? You tryin' to pick me up or what? Chotto!"

The Japanese turned away, horrified.

"Yeah," Carlos continued. "The Japanese hacker zokus have been developin' a taste for this new line of shit, fresh out of Silicon Valley. Blows you away, man. Literally."

"What is it?"

"Ever hear of San Andreas 8.0?"

Gobi shook his head. "No."

"An ounce of San Andreas goes for about 500 New Yen, uncut. Cut, you can take it 10 times further."

"What does it do?"

"It's a synthesized hit of the San Andreas Fault."

"You're kidding."

"It's so new even the U.S. Surgeon General's not hip to it. It's not against the law in the states yet. But it's hot in New Nippon. It's one of our fastest-growing exports. Care to try some?"

"Excuse me, gentlemen." The Z-12 facilitator walked up to them with a tray. "Would you care for some champagne?"

"Me and my friend are talkin'. Don't interrupt." Carlos grimaced and opened his mouth to reveal all his teeth, his root canals, the Moorish-style goldwork and the West Hollywood-style porcelain caps.

The attendant backed away in a hurry. "Hai."

"Here," Carlos said, as he dropped a vial into the breast pocket of Gobi's jacket. "Save this for when you need to blow something out of your head. It's like a hit of Dreamtime nitro, man. They don't call it San Andreas for nothin'. Go ahead, man. I insist."

The attendant returned a few moments later with a look of pained politeness.

"We will be in reentry in about 10 minutes. Will you gentlemen please take your PVI serum now? It is required by law."

Gobi nodded. "Thank you." He removed the PVI kit from his briefcase. He broke the seal and got out a small glass vial of the psycho-viral inoculation drink. A few Japanese salarymen sitting nearby smiled and bowed when they saw him.

Gobi snapped the glass nipple of the vial and sucked the serum down with a small straw. It tasted sweet. "Aren't you going to take yours?" he asked Carlos.

Carlos shook his head. "Not me, man. This is my poison." He opened his snuffbox and stuck a shabu stick in his mouth and sucked on it.

He looked out the window.

"Whaddya know, professor? New Nippon."

NEW NARITA

Giant raindrops fixed themselves like eyelashes to the oval portholes and blinked. A greyish-green pall hung over the rice paddies. The bay looked like a squid with a brackish tarpaulin tossed over it. Kelp farms moored together in checkerboard fashion bobbed on the ribbed ripples of the tide.

The Nissan space limo was still for a moment after its runway landing. Then the door swung open and the passengers began to descend onto the rain-swept tarmac. Figures in Day-Glo ponchos and slick black rain boots stood outside the circle with their flares. The flight attendant bowed to each passenger as they got off the shuttle.

Gobi and Carlos followed the stream of passengers as they crossed the tarmac. They walked toward what looked like some stairs leading into an inflated tent of a building. Thick plastic sheets stretched the length of the terminal; a yellowish chemical light filtered in.

Gobi felt like he was walking through a hospital ward.

Small, silent groups of people were huddled inside the terminal. Gobi wondered if they were travelers or whether they actually lived there. Even the steaming counters of the kelp and noodle stands looked like food-distribution centers. People lined up holding chawan bowls and chopsticks, waiting for their turn.

The conversation now rose like a dizzying hum. It sounded as if the main power supply had broken and that all this talk was being fueled by some emergency generator.

Gobi had finally arrived. He felt a little lost. He didn't know if anyone from the Satori Corporation would be there to meet him.

After all, he had been scheduled to arrive the day before.

How would he get downtown to the Satori headquarters? How did anything work around here? Or did it?

Gobi looked into the faces around him, hoping to connect with them. They were human beings. They had gone through God knows what. They *still* went through it every day. Not to mention every *night* when the Matrix shifted. But he would find that out for himself.

Some of the people in the terminal felt his gaze and responded, offering whatever they could. A glimpse. But into what? Gobi noticed that many of them were not even Japanese. There were South Asians and Southeast Asians— Indians, Pakistanis, Bangladeshis, Filipinos, Indonesians, Malaysians, even Turks and Mongolians.

The poor immigrants still came in search of a better life. Could their lives really be that hopeless in their own lands? Perhaps to disappear into the unknown was preferable to facing the horrors of the familiar.

Gobi noticed a curious thing. The clothes that people wore here seemed to be inflated. There were inflated shoulder pads, chest pads, haramaki belly bands, and knee pads. In fact, most of them looked like they were wearing inflatable cells outside their bodies. What kind of a fashion was that, Gobi wondered? What did it mean?

"Shit, it's a quake, man!" Carlos cried out at the same moment that Gobi felt the sharp tremor.

A rippling wave indented the inflatable floors and walls of the terminal building and the inflated people bobbed in disequilibrium. Those who lost their balance and fell to the floor rebounded to their feet.

"Fuckin' *weird!* They're wearing *air bags!*" Carlos exclaimed, after the shock subsided. "That does it, I'm gonna buy me one of them bouncin' suits soon as I get into town. Right off the rack."

They saw the purple sky through the transparent vinyl tubing you squeezed through at the exit. They stepped outside into an incredible din of taxis, scooters, and a jumble of padded hover-rickshaws; crowds of Japanese milled about everywhere.

Giant neon billboards flickered their green, red, and blue advertising grids above the confusion on the ground. Dirigible air-buses loaded with passengers rose from various depots as they headed toward different destinations throughout the city.

Standing on the curb, Gobi took his first breath of Neo-Tokyo. It electrified him. His nostrils felt like they were sucking in microwaved particles of grit. He sneezed, then went into a hacking cough. He would have to relearn how to breathe, that's for sure.

In the meantime, the ion-singed air filtered into his brain. He saw a dark parabola turn different shades of green, then a spark of bright yellow. The colors that rushed to his brain were a vivid information pink and a bright cyber blue.

That's when the delayed neural adjustment began to occur. It was overwhelming—almost too much for Gobi's sensory input. He had no idea that a person could live, much less move and breathe, in an environment so heavily charged with energy. Even the sensation of having the Kobayashi download in his gut was nothing compared to this.

The whole atmosphere percolated furiously. *Flux in crisis.* That was the only way he could describe the second-by-second energy shifts happening all around him. His body trembled. How could anyone withstand the energy without collapsing?

Gobi glanced at Carlos. How did he manage? He had not taken his PVI, yet evidently he was unaffected by any of this neurological seesawing. It was almost as though this Latino yakuza were somehow inhuman.

Carlos grinned at him as though he read Gobi's mind. "It's all in the head, cojone. You'll learn that here. A bit of this, a bit of that. Ain't none of it what it seems."

He brought out his shabu case and sucked on a crystal stick. "I told you I got my own poison, bro."

Gobi felt the vial of San Andreas 8.0 in his breast pocket. "You sure about this stuff?" He brought it out. He felt like he was on a pharmaceutical safari.

Carlos told him seriously, "Let me give you a word of advice about the 8.0, man. You'll *know* when it's time to use it. When you start to feel those tremors *deep inside*. That's when you know it's time to drop the shit. It's the best-known antidote to the Flux in the world."

"Why are you giving me this?" Gobi asked him. "I don't get it. Why should you care what happens to me?"

Carlos punched him playfully in the hara where Kobayashi's consciousness was beginning to stir in the rare atmosphere of Neo-Tokyo.

"Who said I was looking out for *your* interests?" Then he looked up and said, "Hey, amigo, you didn't tell me you were gonna be picked up at the airport by a samurai."

YAZ

The Japanese dude looked like he was bodysurfing over the air-bag people. He wasn't dressed like any of them, Gobi noticed. He had a samurai haircut with a topknot and a blue shaved pate above his forehead. He was small but wiry looking as he danced up to Gobi in his funny baggy pants and cotton-soled kung fu shoes.

The sam was wearing a baggy vest, too, with a row of video buttons down the front in a winking collage of changing cartoon mangas. He had a canvas duffel bag slung over his shoulders with what looked like a bamboo flute sticking out of it. He wore a pair of swords in his sash, a long sword and a short one.

"Doctor Gobi?" he inquired, after checking the shashin of Gobi's face, which he held in his hand. The same glance measured Carlos up and down. His politeness had a sharp edge to it.

"Dozo yoroshiku." Gobi bowed.

"Welcome to Neo-Tokyo," the man announced in flawless but slightly accented English. "My name is Yasufumi Sakai. I work in the public relations department of the Satori Corporation."

He presented his card with both hands and bowed again. The holo-meishi flickered as Gobi accepted it. "Domo," he said once again to the strange-looking Japanese.

"Please call me Yaz."

"All right, Yaz. Call me Frank, okay?"

"Okay." He bowed. "Frank-san." He paused before he continued. "I will be your escort in Neo-Tokyo."

Then he added, "We have been expecting you yesterday. But your flight had technical difficulties?" He exhaled thoughtfully. "And you must transfer at Station Seven?"

"That's right."

"So desu ka?" Yaz's eyes lingered for a moment on Carlos.

"This is Señor Morales," Gobi introduced them. "We were on the same flight from the U.S. We also happened to travel on the same shuttle from Station Seven to Narita."

"Moshi moshi." The Latino waved at Yaz. His silver chains tinkled.

There was a trace of amusement on Yaz's face. "Ah so,

you speak very good Japanese." Then he asked him with an air of helpful concern. "You have made arrangements to reach Neo-Tokyo? Someone is meeting you?" Yaz glanced about the crowded sidewalk.

"No, I'm travelin' solo," Carlos drawled. "Any chance you can give me a lift? I sure would appreciate it. Tell you the truth, I left my Nihongo in the barrio."

"Ah," Yaz apologized with a bow. "I deeply regret. Only have room for single passenger."

"Only one passenger? What're you riding, a skateboard?"

Yaz lifted his left arm. As his sleeve fell, Gobi saw a gauntlet affixed to his forearm. "Tomo!" he barked into it. "Koi!"

A few moments later, one of the most incredible-looking bikes Gobi had ever seen roared to the curb with its full thrusters on. It was a Haniwa Mag-1000.

Gobi had only seen one in a Neiman-Seibu catalog. It had fuzzy power steering and a sidecar. It was also bi-navigational, which meant you could ride it on a normal road, but when you got on the maglev freeway, you could really let it rip.

"Dozo." Yaz gestured to Gobi. "This is Tomo," he said, as he patted the bike on its head. "My bullet-horse. He will carry us into town. Please climb aboard."

Tomo's recessed, infrared eyes registered Gobi's body grid. As it did so, it automatically adjusted the sidecar seat to accommodate Gobi's long legs. Damned, too, if its two radar ears didn't prick up and its head swivel as it checked the traffic. It even let out a sort of whinny.

Gobi climbed into the sidecar and stashed his briefcase beneath the seat. "Well, this is where we say sayonara, I guess," he told Carlos. "Good luck."

"Hey, wait a minute, how do I get into town, man?" the Latino protested.

"For the regular traveler, that is the best method," Yaz said, pointing to the depot of dirigibles.

There were lines of air-bag people waiting to catch the helium buses into town. Some of the buses were lifting off, while others hovered above the tarmac in the parking lot. Those loading passengers had their inflated stairways dangling to the ground.

"That way, huh? Don't bust a gut neither of you," Carlos huffed, as he began to walk to the helium-bus terminal, his garment bag slung over his shoulder.

Yaz slipped a samurai-style motorcycle helmet over his head and climbed onto Tomo's saddle. "Your own helmet is on the dashboard," he advised Gobi.

The machine roared to life and danced above the street for a second. Then, in an almost elegant high-stepping motion, the maglev bike began to maneuver through the arrival lanes into a bloodshot Neo-Tokyo morning.

"Yo," Yaz ordered when his steed reached the turnoff. As he let its reins out, it took off like a bullet.

"I have notified the office that you are on the way," Yaz told him. "They are expecting you."

Within minutes of leaving New Narita, they were racing through a densely packed suburb of interconnected geodesic villages built on either side of the maglev freeway. There was a transmitter inside Gobi's helmet as well as a navigational eye that allowed him a 360-degree scan.

Stacks of elevated rice fields hovered like playing cards that had been shuffled and frozen in midair. Traffic moved smoothly with maglev vehicles and trucks cruising at speeds of about 200mph.

Although Gobi's helmet was air-conditioned, he could still taste the acrid flavor of ions that seemed to have escaped some giant grill buried beneath the ground's surface.

Sure enough, immense mounds dotted the landscape as far as the eye could see. Gobi guessed that these were underground cities.

The freeway suddenly dipped. To Gobi's surprise, they were now traveling through the guts of one of these mound cities. The elevated maglev freeway had suddenly become a transparent artery.

They flew through a tube at a height about 30 stories above base level. All along both sides of the tube were rows of internal high rises. These high rises were spread-eagled over a series of parks and urban work-play centers.

Dirigibles were circumnavigating throughout the open core of the moundopolis.

Gobi could see the passengers holding on to hand straps on their way to work, smashed together in a rush-hour embrace.

As far as Gobi could tell, the residents of the inner city were dressed differently from the air-bag people he saw on ground level. The men were dressed more like Yaz was. Some had samurai-style hairdos; others wore their hair in braids and loose skirtlike pants with designer amulets and jewelry.

The women were dressed in skirts and tubelike upper garments crisscrossed by sashes. Their preferred hairstyle seemed to be a horizontal bun decorated with ornamental pins.

Children on their way to school hurried along with backpacks on their backs. There were dogs on the streets, little white spitzes and miniature red-haired Akitas.

Shops had open storefronts and a variety of goods on display, from fruits and vegetables to electronic items. There was an almost communal feeling. Gobi even recognized the wavy sign for a neighborhood bathhouse.

Yaz did not slow down for any of the tube exits and instead bore down on his maglev steed till he looked the very image of a Mongol rider on a blood-sweating pony as he raced across the steppes.

The transparent tube they were racing through suddenly did a 90-degree climb.

Now they popped out of what looked like a giant manhole cover. A powerful jet stream lifted them straight up—Gobi felt like a cork bobbing on the spume of a whale.

He caught his breath. They had finally arrived in downtown Neo-Tokyo, the circuit-board heart of the Rim.

Gobi saw wave after wave of towers.

Some of them were 500 stories tall, soaring to a point almost above the earth's atmosphere.

He saw the famous Aeropolis sky-rise, much larger than life but no different than the postcard image that was famous all over the world. Like a skeletal Mt. Fuji constructed of living tubes, it was a man-made volcano that pulsed and breathed in an awesome symmetry of life and death. Half a million people lived on its top floors, and commuted from one vector to another.

Birth, life, and death were elevator buttons pressed at random, Gobi mused, like a person philosophizing in a dream. *Life forms exchanged energy and DNA as readily as they did business cards.*

When you got off on the 230th floor, you were not the same person that got on at 101. On the 403rd floor, you emerged as another totally different being. Yet the energy behind the transformation remained the same, between all the floors, and among all the beings.

It was the same energy that brought you to the top, and the same energy that dropped you to the bottom of the shaft.

That was Gobi's vision, which he input in a nonstop stream of data; it both terrified and energized him.

He now heard a high-pitched wind reverberate in the canyons. But it soon sputtered into the growling echo of Yaz's Haniwa speedster as its turbos coughed down to a cruising altitude.

They coasted down the brightly lit strip of the historical Ginza Boulevard, with its quaint designer-boutiques and the centuries-old Kabuki theater.

Tomo, the maglev horse, whinnied as Yaz brought it to a stop outside the sleek Satori tower with its world-famous logo.

"Hai, Gobi-san, we have arrived," Yaz said, as he climbed off the saddle.

"The board of directors is waiting for you upstairs in the conference room."

SATORI

Gobi stepped inside an atrium that seemed to be overrun by rain forest. He paused, uncertain of which way to go.

"Frank-san."

"Yes?"

"This way, please." Yaz pointed toward the curtain of water in the center of the lobby.

Gobi looked up at a waterfall that plummeted from the summit of the Satori tower, a full 30 stories above the lobby.

Jungle vines, trees, palms, and bushes were growing everywhere in riotous abandon. He could see clouds moving on the upper levels.

"Into the waterfall?"

"Hai." There was a playful smile on Yaz's face. "Please."

Gobi followed his Japanese guide across the suspension bridge that led into the falls. A cleverly concealed deflector shield kept them from getting drenched.

It was like stepping inside a tropical aviary. Flocks of brightly colored parakeets darted among the trees, chattering as they flew. The shriek of macaws, parrots, and mynahs echoed raucously in the atrium.

A shimmering curtain of indigo butterflies fluttered like organic saran wrap, then dissipated into the mist before his very eyes.

The bridge led into a private lobby inside the core of the waterfall. There, a narrow glass cylinder awaited them, its door open.

"Step inside, please," Yaz instructed him.

The elevator ascended through a pulsating shower of foam. Gobi understood it was part of the ritual purification for arriving guests.

"This waterfall imported from Brazil," his trusty tour guide informed him.

"So desu ka?" Gobi had, in fact, noticed a plaque in the lobby that read: *"In Memoriam, Iguaçú Falls, Paraná, Brazil, 2006 A.D."*

"So this is *Kazuo Harada's* world-famous *Satori Building*," Gobi said, verbally highlighting the key words as he initiated a quick search through his Ray-Bans' data base.

□□□□□□□□□□□□□□□□□□□□□□□□□□□□□□□

*(Click!) Biodata: **Kazuo Harada**, born January 26, 1946. (Click!) The photo shows the famous man, with his white mane and designer glasses.*

(Click!) Cross-Index Satori Building, Ginza four-chome, Chuo-ku, Neo-Tokyo, New Nippon. (Click! Exterior/interior shots)

At the turn of the century, when it became apparent that the Brazilian rain forest was irreparably damaged, **Kazuo Harada,** chairman and founder of the Satori Corporation, mounted what became known as the "Emergency Rain Forest Airlift." *(Click!)* This was one of the most daring botanical rescue missions in the ecological history of the world.

More than 80,000 hectares of surviving, but doomed, rain forest were shipped to host countries around the world for transplanta- tion. A small patch of it *(Click!)* found its way into the atrium of the Satori Building, which was now officially designated a "global preserve."

This airlift marked the beginning of a new chapter in Kazuo Harada's life. It was his philanthropic, or "Boddhisatva period," as it came to be known among keiretsu historians. *(Click! On Time magazine cover, "Kazuo Harada—The Global Shaman," June 2, 2002)*

Shortly afterward, the Japanese multime- dia tycoon began to concentrate on develop- ing consumer products whose purpose was to raise the human consciousness to what he called the "next level of human and planetary evolution."

He has described that vision in his best-
selling book *One Planet, One Product. (Click!)*
Source: The Dow Jones Imidas Almanac, 2009
□□□□□□□□□□□□□□□□□□□□□□□□□□□□□□□

Gobi could have gone on accessing Harada—he was just
about to download his listing from the "Who's Who in
Service to the Earth" directory—when the elevator arrived at
the top floor.

Yaz had noticed the amber script inside Gobi's Ray-Bans
and had pressed in even closer to sneak a look. There was
nothing worse than having someone trying to look up your
nose when you were downloading data. That was Gobi's
major complaint about the system. It was almost as bad as
having someone read the newspaper over your shoulder.

Gobi smiled at Yaz as he slipped the glasses into his breast
pocket and they reached the 30th floor.

"Dozo." Yaz held the elevator door open for him. They
were now out of Brazil and back in New Nippon. Gobi found
himself in a small Japanese-style rock garden beneath a
domed skylight.

Two Satori security men dressed as Japanese gardeners
approached them. One held a rake, and the other a pair of garden shears. They bowed to Yaz. He bowed in return and
handed over his two samurai swords to one of them.

After bowing to Gobi, they scanned him with their hands.
They were very good, he thought. Their energy was just
right, crisp and blue. It was a high-quality sixth-meridian
reading.

Finished, they bowed again and went back to raking the
white gravel and clipping the hedges in the Japanese garden.

A metallic-grey door slid open. They stepped into a conference room lit only by a circle of spots recessed in the ceiling
above a trapezoid table.

Eight people—a mix of Japanese and foreigners—sat
around stiffly in high-backed chrome chairs.

When Gobi walked in, Action Wada said, "Welcome to
Neo-Tokyo, Dr. Gobi. We meet in person at last."

Action Wada sat stiffly at the center of the table. Physically, he seemed more compact than Gobi remembered from their initial on-line encounter. He wore a crushed Egyptian papyrus shirt and a white designer Vesuvio suit. His forehead was wider and his shoulders broader than his holoid had projected. But his eyes were no less probing.

"The last time we spoke we had a rather poor connection, as I recall." Wada grinned wickedly as he rubbed his jaw in a mocking but forgiving gesture. "Please sit down."

A Satori aide stepped out of the shadows to draw a chair for him. Gobi sat and looked around at the collection of faces that observed him in silence.

"I'd like to introduce our board members." Action Wada nodded at the assembled group. He waved his hand. "George Weber, director of the Americas . . . "

The patrician-looking white-haired American winked at him in a folksy manner and said, "Glad you could make it, Frank."

Wada went down the line. "Tetsuo Miura, director of Satori's human resources and robotics division . . . " A smiling Japanese man bowed.

"Hyacathia Wong, director of the Greater China division . . . "

She was a dynamic-looking woman in a jade-green jumpsuit with a carved jade figure of Kwan Yin on a heavy gold chain around her neck. She nodded.

"Kubota-san, head of the Satori Institute of Technology, which is our think tank . . . " The diminutive man with the dark circles around his eyes jumped up in his chair like a panda that had been jabbed with a fork.

"And to your left, that's Yuki Abe, director of Satori's multimedia networks division. That covers everyone, I think."

"How do you do?" Gobi nodded back at everyone, but his eyes were still on Abe.

The multimedia networks division? Gobi reflected, trying to remember his Satori backgrounder. *That includes Virtuopolis, doesn't it? That must mean Yuki Abe is responsible for the operations of Satori City.*

Gobi studied her for a moment. She was an attractive woman in her late 30s or early 40s. She was dressed in a mauve Yamamoto silk suit and wore a strand of white pearls around her pale throat.

The graphics were astonishing, Gobi thought. *Genuine Mikimoto quality. The only way anyone might guess they were look-and-feels was that she had a nervous habit of touching them with her fingers. Her pearls rippled when she did that.*

"I'm sure that Dr. Gobi appreciates the urgency of our need to locate our chairman," Action Wada reiterated for the benefit of the board members. "Regrettably, his own son was among those trapped when Gametime crashed."

The burly Japanese gave them all a moment to cluck and nod sympathetically at Gobi.

"Yuki," Action Wada's voice suddenly ricocheted in the boardroom. "Would you give us the latest status report on the situation in Satori City?"

"Not good, I'm afraid," Yuki replied in an even voice. "Time is running out for the three sectors. Six governments—the United States, France, Greater Britain, Germany, Greater Russia, and India—have sent teams of neuroprogrammers to work on site at our central node on the Isle of Man. So far they've been unsuccessful."

She paused. "Our VR interface remains impenetrable. We estimate that unless Virtuopolis is stabilized, we will reach the point of no return within 18 hours. That's when the first tier of users is projected to go into Omega."

"Omega?" Gobi's voice came out harsher than he expected.

"I'm very sorry. . . ." Yuki's head bowed for a moment. "Omega signifies systems termination. When that occurs, there will be an automatic reboot of Virtuopolis and all the consciousnesses on-line at that level will be erased."

"What's the termination count right now?" Action Wada asked bluntly, swiveling around in his chair to face her.

"It's up to 712," Yuki answered. "All those terminated were adult end users, between the ages of 18 and 82. Most of them were engaged in sexual activities in Adult World at the time."

She cleared her throat. "Currently, 3,816 children remain in different stages of coma, most of them between the ages of 4 and 16."

"Thank you, Yuki." Action Wada turned away from her. "Now—"

"There's just one more thing, Wada-san."

Wada swiveled around in his chair again. "Yes, what is it?"

Yuki hesitated.

"You have something you wish to add?"

"There's been a new development," she said finally.

"Well, what is it?"

"I'm not sure how to explain it. That's part of the problem."

"Please try," Action Wada remarked wryly. "Go on."

"I will have to show you some video footage instead. . . . It's still being analyzed. We picked this up from a small hospital in eastern Siberia, near the town of Yakutsk. It was captured by a security camera."

Yuki aimed her remote player at a blank monitor. The picture crackled to life.

Gobi saw a row of beds with children hooked up to portable VR units. The quality of the facility was not nearly as good as the Adolescent Unit at Alta Bates. The time on the clip showed 04:12:02 A.M.

"Watch this," Yuki said. "The third bed from the end. The small child. A little girl. About eight years old."

There was no one in the ward except for the children, who were dreaming in their on-line comas. No nurses were present on the floor. Suddenly, there was a slight, barely discernable movement on the bed Yuki had pointed out. Thin arms emerged from a hospital tunic, fingers clenched like small claws.

There was a gasp in the boardroom from Hyacathia Wong.

No one else uttered a sound. Gobi watched, transfixed. He heard Action Wada's chair swivel tightly.

It was the face of a bird in flight until its eyes opened. Where were the eyes of the child? Her hair was brown, curly, her face sweet as golden sunlight, but her eyes were erased from the screen. They did not register. The legs jackknifed now out of the bed. Bare feet on the linoleum, the smock hanging down to her ankles. The child paused, glancing at her sleeping companions until she recognized one. A friend. "Verushka, Verushka!" a tiny voice called out.

Gobi felt a chill run down his spine. These were the first words spoken out of a coma. But *which* was the coma? Which state of dreaming was closest to the awakening?

The child now wandered down the length of the room, disconnecting all the children from their neural-supports. One by one, the dreams displayed on the monitors were extinguished. Her task completed, the child sat on one of the beds and waited.

04:19:32 A.M.
Fast-forward.
04:22:008 A.M.

"It starts now," Yuki's voice, sounding muffled, interjected. Everyone remained silent.

One, two, now three children began to stir. They were joined by the others. They gathered together, compared their wounds, rubbed their foreheads, their hands, stuck out their tongues.

They saw the flash of something white at the far end of the hall. A stocky woman in a nurse's uniform—dark hair, dark eyes— stood there as the children began to move toward her. Her feet were frozen to the floor. She could not move, much less speak. One of the bigger boys, in the front, waggled his fingers at her. . . .

Yuki clicked her unit and the monitor went blank. George Weber's trembling hand brought out a cigarette case. He lit a nonfilter gingko bidi and inhaled deeply. "Shit," he said. The rest of the group sat in silence, thinking about what they had just seen.

Finally, Action Wada spoke: "What happened to the children, Yuki?"

"They were discovered walking in the woods near the village."

"And?"

"The people in those parts are still very superstitious. After they discovered the body of the woman, there was a meeting of the council of elders. They consulted their shaman."

"Yes?"

Yuki bit her lip, then clicked again. "This is a clip from the shaman's speech at the meeting of the elders."

The Chukchee shaman stood in the center of the Satori boardroom in his pelts and furs and bones. He wore an oracular mirror tied to his right shoulder. *"This enables me to see in the worlds beyond,"* he spoke to them, his words translated instantaneously. *"It also enables me to capture the lost souls of the dead."*

He touched the plaits and pendants and ribbons that were sewn to his costume. *"These are my tails and wings; they help me fly to the black mountain of darkness. There I flew to meet with the children who once inhabited their second bodies. They told me they had been robbed. Evil spirits roam in their place. The children demanded that they be returned. But the evil spirits refused. 'Let the children come back from the Afterlife Place in the bodies of wild dogs,' they laughed at me.*

"I reported back to the children. My spirit-goose and spirit-snipe carried me for many long hours to the kelet house where the spirits of the children rested. 'In that case,' the children told me, after I conveyed to them the thoughts and words of the evil ones, 'you must take your two-headed pike to wreak out vengeance on the hungry ghosts.'"

The Chukchee shaman shook his two-headed pike. *"Let no man or kelet doubt the will of the She-Eagle, who brings justice and death to all beings. Do not be bashful in death, nor too proud in life."*

The Chukchee lowered his pike. *"O children of the Chukchees, Buryats, Gilyaks, and of the Yenissei Ostyaks, fear not, you will be avenged. And you will return to your true selves."*

Yuki clicked off the shaman. "Shortly afterward, the eleven children found walking about 'in coma,' as they say, were destroyed and their bodies burned. Unfortunately, the local doctor was unable to perform any autopsies except on one of them."

"What did he find?" asked Kubota.

Yuki looked ashen. "Technically, the body was already in a state of rigor mortis. It had been dead for at least seven or eight hours before the villagers apprehended it."

"Jeezus Christ, Action," George Weber spoke. "None of this had better get into the papers. We'll be ruined for sure."

Yuki replied, "It's a remote village. We've been able to control the media on this. The local authorities have understood our concern. And we have expressed our gratitude to them accordingly."

Weber lit another bidi. "You should have paid the bastard what he wanted, Action—none of this would have happened."

"Please, George," Action Wada replied, eyeing Gobi apologetically. "This isn't the time or place—"

"Well, what's *he* here for then? I mean, you're going to do *something* about this, aren't you, Dr. Gobi?" Weber asked him pointedly.

"About what, Mr. Weber?" Gobi inquired.

"Jeezus Christ, Action, how much have you told him!?" Weber rolled his eyes in exasperation.

"Enough, I think, for him to begin to look for Chairman Harada."

"Right, Harada. But have you told him about *Sato? He's* the bastard that sold us a bill of goods."

"Action." Weber glared at the Japanese across the table. "If this thing in Siberia is a taste of what's to come, we can all go back to peddling instant ramen. Do you understand what I'm saying? I mean, have you seen the value of *Satori stock* lately?" He spluttered. "They're trading it short against betel nut futures on the Bombay Stock Exchange, for Chrissakes!"

Action Wada raised his hand. "You've made your point, George. Thank you."

"Well, what are you going to *do* about it then, goddamn it!?"

"Dr. Gobi is eminently qualified to handle this," Wada said quietly.

"Is he now?" Weber asked as he lit another bidi. He blew the smoke at Gobi. "So, professor," he challenged him with a sneer. "You got a Ph.D. in sniffing auras, right? You know about Sato?"

Gobi looked back at him from across the table. "You mean the Tibetan?"

After the meeting in the conference room, Action Wada approached Gobi. "I'm afraid I have underestimated you, Dr. Gobi," he said ingratiatingly. "Can I have a private word with you in my office?"

"Can I have a private word with you in mine?"

Action Wada blinked at him, then a broad grin appeared on his face. "Excellent. A man with a sense of humor carries an invisible sword in a sheath. It can be drawn and used at any time."

"A man who speaks in aphorisms is making hay while the sun shines."

Action Wada frowned. "I'm afraid I'm not acquainted with that saying."

"Sun Tzu. It's in *The Art of Jokes.*"

"Ah," He grinned again. "I must study the classics."

"What do you want to talk to me about?" Gobi asked him.

"A moment in private. My office is just down the hall."

Gobi nodded and shook hands with the rest of the board members as they filed out of the room. George Weber said, "Glad you're on our team, Frank. We're counting on you."

Yuki Abe shook his hand. Her eyes were soft and luminous; her pale hand was warm. "I'm sorry about your son," she said.

"Thank you, Miss Abe."

She pressed his hand. "If there's anything I can do to help you, please don't hesitate to let me know." She gave him her card. It carried her scent, *Lady Murasaki.*

"Thanks."

"This way, Dr. Gobi," Action Wada urged. They stepped out into the hall, past the Japanese gardeners raking the sand in the atrium.

At a doorway, Action Wada adjusted his tie into a security camera. "Secret combination." He smiled at Gobi. The door slid open.

The room was not large. It had rice-paper panels, a ceiling mandala, and polished cement floors. A pair of brushed-stainless-steel sculptures stood at either end. It was lit by recessed lighting. Ascetic metal chairs surrounded an unvarnished pine table.

"Please sit." Action Wada gestured at one of the chairs. "I like simple things. Simple facts."

Gobi drew up a skeletal chair and sat down.

"Perhaps it has to do with the fact that my father was a Zen priest. You may be surprised."

Gobi waited.

"He was a very successful executive, a top shacho with one of the old keiretsus. After the Trade War with your hemisphere, my father retired from business and spent his remaining years in contemplation. So you see, Dr. Gobi, our sensibilities are similar. Only these days, we must cross the ocean to get the Western wisdom. Ha! Ha! Ha!"

Gobi looked at him blankly.

"Tea, Dr. Gobi?"

Gobi looked across the room. There was a small glass cabinet on a stand with some netsuke carvings on display. Wada's eyes followed his.

"You are interested, perhaps, in netsuke?"

Gobi's eyes flickered away. Those netsukes were dead. *Correction: They had not been activated yet. But the drives had been built into them.*

"Only certain type of netsuke," Gobi replied.

"I see. You are a connoisseur of Japanese art."

"Yes, I love the refined delicacy and all the subtlety. Now cut the crap, Wada. What's on your mind?"

Action Wada's eyes clouded. *He was genuinely offended. Good. Score one for Western wisdom.*

He opened his eyes and focused on Gobi. "On Station Seven, I believe you completed a certain transaction for us."

"Oh, you must mean with Miss Kato?"

"Yes, yes. That's the one."

"She was very good," Gobi said. "Thank you very much. I enjoyed her tremendously. To return the favor, I'd like to give this to you."

"Thank you, you are most generous," Action Wada said.

Gobi wrote something on a piece of paper and handed it to Wada.

Wada accepted it with a bow, read it, and frowned. "May I ask what this is?"

"Certainly. It's a 1-900 number—for a topless psychiatrist. You call this number, she comes to you wherever you are. You tell her your problem, she takes care of it right away. In living hologram, of course."

Action Wada crumpled the paper and laid it on the table. "This is not what I expected. You have a download for me."

He brought out a netsuke from his pocket. "Please." He nodded at it.

Gobi uncrumpled the paper on the table. "Dozo," he said, offering it to Wada again.

Action Wada rose from the table and pushed back his chair. He scowled. "Why are you not cooperating?"

"Because getting you the consciousness of Ryutaro Kobayashi wasn't part of the deal, that's why."

"You are a very difficult person, Dr. Gobi!"

"What do you mean? I just offered to share my shrink with you!"

Action Wada turned and strode out of the room angrily. "You'd better get busy. Find Harada," he barked. "You don't have all day, you know. Not in Neo-Tokyo."

● ● ●

Yaz was waiting for him in the hallway. "What would you like to do first, Frank-san?"

"This Sato, the programmer?"

Yaz's eyes waited. "Hai?"

"Did you ever meet him?"

"Mochiron. Of course."

"What can you tell me about him?"

Yaz thought for a moment, then wrinkled his nose in distaste. "He is a kamikaze-zoku."

"What's that?"

"In America, you say otaku-zoku. Same as hacker, neh?"

"That's right."

Yaz nodded. "Sato is kamikaze-hacker. Now you understand? He like to destroy."

"You're telling me he likes to destroy things?"

Yaz's laugh was more like a derisive snort. "Before he come, Neo-Tokyo okay, neh? After he come . . . *big* earthquake."

"That's a coincidence, isn't it?"

"Coincidence?"

"That means 'same timing' but not necessarily the same reason."

Yaz's expression clouded. "No." He shook his head. "Same reason."

"Do you know what he looks like? Is there a picture of him anywhere? That would help me get a feeling for him."

"Picture? Shashin?"

"That's right."

They went down the hall and took an elevator down several floors. "This way," Yaz grunted. He entered a room at the end of a long corridor of cubicles. Gobi followed.

"Wow," Gobi said, looking around the empty room. "The original paperless office."

"Hai," Yaz said. "No paper. No desk." He laughed. "No chair."

There was a long window with a view of the old Ginza, Neo-Tokyo's historic shopping street. The neons almost looked nostalgic until you realized they were daubs of living holo-color.

202 — — — Alexander Besher

"At least you have a window and some venetian blinds," Gobi remarked.

"Venetian blinds?" Yaz asked. He stepped up to the blinds and pulled the cord. The blinds came down and Yaz twirled the rod that adjusted them. With the blinds closed tight, the room became dark and a picture materialized on the screen.

Yaz laughed. "Satori blinds. Interior deco." He stepped back. "Sato, Kenji," he said softly.

The blinds flipped back on themselves as they searched the data base. While they waited, Yaz explained. "This is the last known picture of Harada's team when they were all still together. How do you say, it was their Last Supper?"

There appeared an image of an otaku-zoku hacker in a tight black jacket with a high collar and brass buttons. He had bad teeth, bad skin, and goggle-top glasses with show-off fiberoptics threaded through the transparent frames. He was sitting in a sushi bar holding out his chopsticks. A squid tentacle dangled from the end of them.

"That's Sato?"

Yaz grunted. "No. Not Sato. There." He twirled the rod in his hand and the picture scrolled out. Now Gobi could see a few other long-haired otakus in the frame. They were sitting together, obviously having a good time. At the end of the counter sat a young man staring straight into the camera. His eyes glowed like grey-black cinders in a hibachi. Next to him sat a young woman whose features were partially hidden by her long black hair, which tumbled across her face.

Her eyes awakened something in Gobi. *Something that he thought was dead a long time ago. Did his past life have a past life . . . ?* he wondered.

"That is Sato," Yaz said. "Do you want me to give you a close-up, Frank-san?"

"Yes, give me a close-up, Yaz," Gobi said in a funny, strangled voice. "But not of Sato. Of that girl sitting next to him."

— — —

They had gone back to his apartment in North Beach after they left Gobi's office on Green Street, the one with the shingle that read "Frank Gobi, Private Investigations."

They were lying on his futon bed. Gobi was the only gweilo living in the Chinese boardinghouse, and the old Chinese ladies were busy cooking their dinner in the communal kitchen. You could hear them arguing, discussing, invoking, and shouting at each other in Cantonese. The spicy smell of sesame oil sizzling in their woks seeped down the corridor and wafted under his door. Chinese opera played on a tinny radio.

The design on his quilt was something called "Rust Waves," and they had been floating on those waves for a while after making love.

The light in the room was translucent, dim. For a lamp, Gobi had a Chinese oil-paper umbrella set on the straw mat floor with a tiny spotlight clamped to the wooden handle. It cast shadows like petaled ideograms on the stucco walls.

With the foghorns droning out in the bay, they could easily have been swept away to sea in each other's arms . . . .

Kimiko sat up on the futon and stretched. God, she was beautiful! "How's your headache now?" Gobi asked her. Kimiko had told him she suffered from headaches a lot. She joked that it was because she imbued so much of her brain chi in her little paper origamis in order to give them life.

She leaned over to kiss him. It felt like the Kamo River overflowing its banks in Kyoto in the 12th century.

"Love medicine is better than herbal," she teased, as she pinched his nipple.

"Can I come visit you when you go back to New Nippon?" he asked.

She looked startled. "Things are very different in New Nippon now." She looked at the floating shadows on the wall as if she were trying to read something there. "Not like here, Frank."

"Things are different here, too, Kimiko, since I met you," he told her. He meant it. She had turned his life into a love factory—and production was going up every day.

Gobi traced the line of Kimiko's thigh with his hand, like he was dusting for fingerprints. Maybe she had a lover waiting for her in Neo-Tokyo? Maybe she had more than one. . . .

He could tell she was taking his request seriously though. He didn't want just to be her crazy gaijin lover in San Francisco. He wanted her yin and his yang to commute on a regular basis . . . alternate three months here in San Francisco, then three months in Neo-Tokyo. Whatever worked. Or they could meet in Thailand to get away. Or fly to Bali. Or find their own private temple somewhere in India, a temple dedicated to the goddess that had brought them together.

That was his fantasy anyway.

Kimiko felt a burning sensation on the bridge of her nose. The body, like the mind, is a sponge, she thought. It absorbs energies. Then when it desorbs, it's like a process of purification.

"Well, what about it, Kimiko? Can I come and visit you or not?"

She looked down at Gobi and giggled. "Maybe," she said in that tone of voice she had when she was contemplating lust in the fast lane.

He touched her hip and rocked her playfully until she lost her balance and fell against his chest with her breasts, her face, and her lovely eyes.

"Yes, all right, you can come," she responded huskily, as she began to search his body again. The fit came easily. "You come, Frank. Come, now!"

"I think you know this woman, Frank-san?" Yaz asked him softly. He had seen the pain in the American's eyes. Not the pain of loss, but the pain of discovery, which is sometimes much worse.

"When was this shashin taken, Yaz?" Gobi asked. Maybe he was mistaken. Maybe it was an old picture. Maybe it all made sense.

The young Japanese thought for a moment. "Early this year? These people are all members of Harada-san's private group. They are programmers. Sato was his chief programmer. That woman," Yaz nodded at her, studying Gobi's eyes, "is Kimiko-san."

"Yes."

"She is a friend of yours?"

"I thought she was dead."

If Yaz was surprised, he did not show it. He nodded. "Kimiko-san was very nice person. Yasashi. Gentle."

"Where is she now?"

Yaz frowned. "With Harada, I think. Sato left the group soon after this shashin was taken. After Harada discover Sato is selling tainted code to other keiretsus. Then the trouble start in Neo-Tokyo, and Harada take his team with him to find safe place to work on antidote. I *think* so."

So she was missing with him. In a way, her being missing had the effect of *restoring* her to Gobi. She was *still* out of reach, still in another dimension somewhere. Just like the Kimiko he always knew.

"Hmm," Gobi thought aloud.

"Yes, Frank-san?"

"Who took that picture?"

"Harada-san."

"Where was it taken?"

"In Chiba City."

"Can I get a copy?"

"Hai, chotto matte." Yaz twirled the rod and a holo-shashin printed out of the base unit. He handed it to Gobi.

That's when he saw it, when he looked closely at Kimiko. There, on the sushi counter. She must have made it while waiting for the sushi master to roll her a maguro or a tekka or a unagi.

Gobi looked up at Yaz. There was a gleam of hope in his eyes that Yaz hadn't seen a moment ago.

"I think I understand, Yaz."

"Yes, Frank-san?"

"I think I understand why a man like Kazuo Harada was willing to work with a man like Sato. He must have seen the evil in him right away, yet he kept Sato on his team."

Yaz studied the shashin, trying to discover the clue.

"It's the reason why Sato must have left Harada, in fact. He must have gotten wise to it."

Yaz shook his head. "You see something here, Frank-san? What is it?"

Gobi almost laughed. "Look, on the counter. She's been making her little origamis, her little paper power animals."

Yaz looked up, uncertain. "It's a frog."

"That's right, Yaz," Gobi grinned. "Frog medicine."

"Nan desu ka? What is it?"

"Kimiko was studying Mayan and Aztec shamanism and learning to incorporate their medicine into her artwork. Frog medicine is very powerful. It's used to clear out the negativity. From any environment. And from any person."

"Naruhodo." Yaz closed his eyes. He finally understood. "She was reprogramming Sato?"

"That's right, Yaz."

Yaz nodded. "Kimiko-san must be a miko."

"A miko? What's that?"

"Japanese shamaness. How do you call it in English—a medium? She cannot *write* program, but everyone knows she is a very important programmer for Harada-san. That must be why."

Gobi had to agree. "I'd be surprised if Kimiko ever wrote a single line of code in her life. She did it all with her hands."

MORAY

They rode the waterfall down to the garage on B-10 where Tomo, Yaz's maglev bike, was stabled.

"Dozo." Yaz gestured, as Gobi climbed into the sidecar.

Yaz revved up the engine. The Haniwa hovered like a cup above a saucer as it wobbled up the bridgeway to the garage exit.

Yaz briefed Gobi on his headset. "Otaku-zokus like to hang out at sushi bar where picture was taken. Maybe we can get some information there?"

"Sounds like a good place to start. Why do they like to hang out there? What's so special about it?"

"It's very famous for its interactive sushi. They also serve latest designer brain drinks. You like smart drinks, Frank-san?"

They were out in the grey-blue open space of the Satori roundabout. Yaz tilted the Haniwa in the direction of the maglev skyway. They caught a current and shot forward.

"Smart drinks?" Gobi replied. "Not really. When I drink, I prefer a stupid drink so I can just relax. I don't like a drink that's smarter than me."

Yaz looked at him and grinned. "Me too."

"What the hell is interactive sushi, Yaz?"

"You'll find out." He grinned again. "At lunch."

Yaz yanked Tomo's reins and the maglev steed shifted lanes, playing the traffic like a pachinko-meister. The traffic was moderate as they connected to the Chiba City gridway.

"Take a rest now," Yaz said. "We'll be there in half an hour."

As they traveled through the downtown canyons of Neo-Tokyo, Gobi could only marvel at how the sky-rises disappeared into the mist like so many ink paintings.

The sky was grey at the edges with swathes of darkening blue. An overall silence hung above the city like an unspoken thought.

Gobi noticed that the towers were connected by bridges on different levels. But when he looked more closely, he realized that the main links between the buildings were heavily armored drawbridges that could be raised and lowered at will.

"They look like castles," Gobi said, thinking of the copy of Osaka castle on the top floors of Station Seven.

"Keiretsu castles." Yaz nodded. "Over there, that's the Sumitomo group."

"Oh."

They passed under the drawbridge and spiraled past the Sumitomo banners flying from the castle walls.

"What's it like?" Gobi asked Yaz, as the cityscape boiled past them.

"What's *what* like?"

"What happens at night when the city changes?"

Yaz accelerated to a higher-level lane. He was silent. "Why do you ask?" his voice crackled on the channel. "It's different for everyone. Different for you. Different for me."

Tomo bolted forward as Yaz gave him a shot of power.

"Frank-san," Yaz called out hesitantly.

"Yes?"

"I think someone is following us."

"Don't turn around," Yaz warned Gobi. "Check your rear scan. It's that black Barracuda Miata behind us."

Gobi focused on the concave reflection above his right brow inside his bubble headgear.

Sure enough, a vehicle that looked like a 'cuda was neatly slicing its way through the traffic, first squeezing into the maglev grid of the vehicles in front, then leaping over them as if they were schools of tuna.

Suddenly the Barracuda was at their tail, scraping sparks off Tomo's rear fender. Startled, Gobi and Yaz both jumped in their seats. They saw two matching crew cuts and eyes as dead as pool cues. Muscles bulged in cheap Hong Kong silk suits.

"Yakuza," Yaz muttered under his breath, as he kept the maglev on a steady course.

He gunned Tomo forward.

The yaks dropped out of sight in the undercurrent, then resurfaced beside the maglev a moment later. They were racing side by side.

"Chikisho!" Yaz swore. He leaned forward and withdrew a moray whip from the saddlebag. It was long and black and spiny. In a single motion, he snapped it neatly against the 'cuda's windshield.

Gawking for a split second, the yakuzas ducked their heads. But the moray stunned their windshield, which snap-crackled into a thousand pieces, like an oracle bone being heated on the fire.

The 'cuda spluttered and slid along the safety rail in a sheet of sparks.

It took the yaks a minute of blind navigation to shatter the screen from the inside and to pry the pieces out of the frame so they could see where they were going.

By that time, Yaz had zipped through a tunnel that connected two keiretsu fiefdoms. He took an off-ramp chute and idled beneath the overpass.

For a few minutes, they watched as the exiting traffic circled out of the maglev grid.

Yaz punched into his keypad and Gobi saw the flickering images appear on the console. It was an aerial view of the skyway. Yaz had hacked into the surveillance system built into the tunnel so they could see the traffic coming and going. There was no sign of the Barracuda.

Until Yaz spotted it on the side of the embankment where the yaks had been parked, waiting patiently for Tomo to reappear.

"Chikisho!" Yaz swore again. He popped the brakes and the maglev slid off the directional current. It was a good thing Yaz's reflexes were so fast. The Honda Peugeot in front of them had crumpled to a halt—the driver knocked unconscious from the blast.

Yaz whistled. "They're using concussion grenades!" All around them the rubble of ferroceramic conductors and lane-change transponders lay scattered like broken toys.

The oncoming traffic was slowing where the yaks had left their explosive meishi calling card.

Yaz took advantage of the confusion to bring Tomo online again. He squeezed the maglev behind an 80-foot-long container truck that was carrying a full load of memory ramen.

In the adjoining lane was a bus loaded with country-bumpkin programmers headed for a sex tour of Chiba City's virtual vice dens. Gobi could see their anxious faces peering out the windows.

An impatient blast of yak fire aimed at Tomo brought the bus crashing down to its stumps. A greasy black pall of smoke poured out of the impacted side. Flames licked at its charred roof.

Yaz swore under his breath. "They're shooting wild!"

With a staccato pinging of laser bites, the 'cuda was now at their side, drilling holes in the body of their maglev.

One yak held out his laser magnum as if he were offering Yaz an opportunity to examine its ridged barrel before he blew him away.

Yaz lashed at him with the moray whip. The yak screamed as he was lifted out of his cockpit by the wrist, rigid from the 12,000 volts that charged through his body.

With another flick of the whip, Yaz released the yak into the air. He bounced a few times on the road until he soared off the elevated track like a carp blowing in the wind on boy's day.

There was another blast from behind.

"They've got a back up!" Gobi yelled to Yaz, who stole a backward glance. Two bullet-heads with wraparound shades and shoulders as big as sides of Kobe beef were gaining on them.

"Hold tight, please!" Yaz bowed apologetically as he gunned the maglev rotors to a fever pitch.

He tilted the bike so that they were suddenly riding the rail. The sidecar carrying Gobi lifted into the air and he was looking down at a 10-story drop to the streets of Neo-Tokyo below.

"Brace yourself!" Yaz shouted.

They lifted *off* the rail.

Yaz's machine vaulted across the line of traffic and skidded onto the roof of a container truck that was as long as a small runway. The bike and sidecar careened down its length.

Looming just ahead of them on the maglev grid was an intersecting skyway ramp that looked like it would rip them off the truck as if they were medicated plasters of Salonpas.

There was a roar as the bike raced down the moving runway—and lifted off into the air.

For a few moments, Tomo sailed through a number of uncharted mag vectors, then caught an individual current. With a metallic sigh, it spiraled in for a landing on the maglev grid of the upper skyway.

The two Barracudas in the depths below scrimmaged as best as they could. But they were soon lost in the swift currents, which carried them into the yawning jaws of the Void.

With two cylinders damaged, Tomo limped into Chiba City.

Yaz parked in an alley under a puddle of red and blue neons that dripped from a spluttering sign for Morinaga Mind Mints.

Tomo's sign shuddered and the muscles in its frame spasmed as Yaz switched it off.

"Are you all right?" Yaz asked his passenger. Gobi nodded. He was taking some deep breaths and running chi energy through his twelve channels. He had to get back into sync with his body after the ride.

"How 'bout you?" Gobi gasped.

Yaz scowled. "I'm fine." He knelt on the ground to take a closer look at the damage. A piece of cylinder crumpled off in his hand like a candy wrapper.

"One more hit and sayonara." Yaz grimaced as he tossed the cylinder on the ground.

"Who were those guys?" Gobi let out his breath.

Okay. He exhaled again. He was grounded now.

"Bad drivers," Yaz said in disgust.

"Why do you think they wanted to kill us?"

"Not kill you," Yaz shook his head. "They *want* you. Me, they kill, no problem. I'm just the driver. Not important."

"What makes you think that?"

"Two Barracudas working together. It's a professional job. First one engages the victim and neutralizes vehicle on maglev-way. Second Barracuda captures the target. There have been many such kidnappings."

Yaz adjusted the katana blades in his sash as he glanced at both ends of the alley.

"Usually, Frank-san, this *style* of kidnapping—" He looked puzzled.

"Yes?"

"It's yakuza trademark for kidnapping big Japanese boss. Like a chairman of a company, a director, or a big shacho." Yaz stared at Gobi and frowned. "You're not a big shacho, Frank-san."

No, I'm not, Gobi thought. *But I think I know where I can find one.* He had been directing some of his chi energy to Kobayashi, whose consciousness was throbbing inside the strongbox of his hara.

He'd have to do something about Kobayashi pretty soon. The trapped energy was beginning to fester.

Soon it would spread like gangrene across his soul.

AMA'S

This is Ama's place," Yaz told him.

Gobi stared at the wall of dead TVs at the end of the cul-de-sac. A compost pile of bio-chips mildewed on the ground, and a blinking gutter of fiberoptics ran the length of the alley-way before disapearing down the drain.

"Ama's?" At first, Gobi thought the wall was an advertising billboard whose meter had run out.

"The sushi bar where the zokus go. Shall we jack in, Frank-san? We must announce ourselves first."

Yaz brought out his bamboo flute from his duffel bag. "Shakuhachi synthesizer," he explained to Gobi. Then he bowed his head and began to blow. Amazingly, the blank wall responded to his playing.

Yaz's music conjured up marvelous images of birds, temples, clouds, goddesses, details of gold Muromachi screen paintings, clips of old black and white samurai films, an entire collective manga consciousness of a Japan that existed long before the creation of New Nippon.

When he was finished, Yaz stood there, a gallant figure, with his head bowed. He waited for the reviews to come in.

The screen wall dissolved and filled up with a giant image of a ruddy-faced Japanese woman wearing the robes of an 11th-century court lady.

She had long black hair streaming down her shoulders and rouge spots on her cheeks. Her eyes were a deep black but they were lit with a fire inside them. Her slightly opened mouth revealed her stylishly blackened teeth.

She clapped delicately with her powder-white doll's hands. "Only one man can play as wonderfully as that! Yazu-san, o-sashiburi desu-ne!" She bowed again. "It's been so long since we heard your flute!"

Yaz bowed in return. The wall of TVs slowly blanked out again except for the image of a door that appeared in the corner of the wall. Yaz pushed the image and the door swung open.

They stepped inside.

"Dozo irrashaimassen! Welcome!"

It was the woman they had seen on the screen outside. "Your performance will be added to the wall's memory bank for the future enjoyment of our customers."

"I am honored."

"Who is your friend?" Ama turned to Gobi with a broad smile.

"This is Frank-san. He's from San Francisco."

"My, you have come a long way! Please make yourself at home. This way, please!"

"You didn't tell me you were a regular here," Gobi whispered to Yaz, as they followed the proprietress into her establishment.

"I've only been here a few times, Frank-san. They have a very interesting image bank here. There's always something new to be found."

"Dozo." Ama sat them both down at the sushi counter.

The decor was "rustic cave"; fish tanks ran down the length of the walls.

A Buddhist nun with a pack of 'trodes on her back worked on a bowl of rice in the corner. A hairy guy who looked like he might be an aboriginal Ainu from Hokkaido was drinking by himself at the other end of the counter. Blinding white shades were implanted on his face like a visor.

A few otakus talked quietly at private tables in the back.

The sushi chef brought them a couple of steaming oshibori towels to refresh themselves. He was a skinny middle-aged man with a long face and a goatee consisting of a few sparse black hairs. He had a traditional sushi chef's band of 'trodes around his head.

"Hai." He bowed, wiping the counter. "What is your pleasure today?"

"What *is* interactive sushi?" Gobi whispered to Yaz.

"Ah, it's the house special," Yaz explained. "You eat fish, fish eats you."

"Huh?"

"Is everything all right, Yazu-san?" Ama asked.

"It's his first time," Yaz explained to her.

"Ah so." she nodded kindly. "Shall I explain the procedure to him?"

"No, that's all right, I'll do it."

Yaz turned to the sushi chef. "We'll start with some tuna, then some abalone, then some mackerel, then some eel. What's the special today?"

"Sea urchin."

"Excellent. We'll have some of that as well. And some hot sake."

"Hai." The chef bowed as he withdrew to prepare their order.

"Listen, Yaz, I'm not sure about this place. Is this a regular sushi bar or what?"

"Nothing is regular in Chibatown," Yaz told him. "But to answer your question. This is *karmic* cuisine. You have not heard of it in America? I am surprised. Customers who dine at Ama's do not simply 'eat' their dinner. There is an energy exchange. You assume the highest nature of the food you eat."

Yaz mixed the green wasabi paste in with his soy sauce. "In other words, Frank-san," he continued, "you agree to accept the living essence of the food into your own higher path, so that the fish accepts *your* path of evolution as the next step in its *own* evolution. Understand?"

"I see. And the sensors on the chopsticks?" Gobi had noticed that the chopsticks had flashing sensors. "They calibrate the fish's aura?"

"Oh those. They are nothing. Just for decoration."

"Yes, we got those cheap from Taiwan." Ama smiled as she brought them a steaming bottle of sake and some small cups.

She pulled her sleeve back and poured each of them a shot.

"Mmm." Gobi murmured his approval as the fire coursed through his system.

"Wait a minute," Gobi said. "If I eat this interactive fish, does that mean I'm going to absorb the *karma* of the tuna, abalone, mackerel, and eel?"

"Don't forget the grouper."

Gobi was stunned.

"Don't worry, we're on an expense account." Yaz laughed. "It is part of Satori Corporation's karma to pay for all of this. Kampai!"

"This place looks kind of empty," Gobi remarked, after he ate some sea urchin that obviously had suffered a rotten childhood.

"It is a little slow," Yaz agreed. "How do you like the eel?"

"A bit on the morose side. Shouldn't we ask about the picture?"

"You're right. Masta!"

The sushi master came over. "Hai?"

"Masta, can I ask you a question?"

The chef tightened the 'trodes tied around his head and wiped the counter with his cloth. His eyes were alert.

Yaz showed the chef the Satori print. "Do you recognize these people by any chance? I think they're regulars here."

"Sa neh . . . ?" the chef said, as he scratched his head. "I can't say if I have for sure. We have so many customers."

He called out to the otaku at the end of the counter. "Mamo, what do you make of this?"

"Eh?" It was the hairy guy with the silver visor. He lifted his head from his sake. His face was flushed and his pores were so clogged they looked like someone had poured cement into them. He wore a rumpled happi coat and a greasy red silk scarf around his neck.

"What do you want to know?" Mamo asked, studying the shashin. "It's been printed off a Satori Holo-Diary Super 22. Someone used a buttonhole lens to record it. It must've been part of their daily log. I won't ask how you guys came about it, seein' as it's obviously been decrypted."

He peered at it some more. "It's not a bad job, although you lost some data in the process. Gone to Filofax heaven, huh?"

Mamo returned the picture to the chef and smiled broadly, showing teeth almost entirely overgrown by purple gums. He addressed Yaz.

"You want me clean up this holo for you? Is that why you're here? Don't worry, you've come to the best there is. Mamo the Holo-Doctor at your service. I bet I can squeeze some audio out of it."

He gave them a shrewd look. "If you're interested, that is."

"Audio?" Yaz looked surprised.

Mamo took another look at the shashin. "It's on a 60 holo-track. There's sure to be an audio subtrack in there somewhere. See this fuzzy part here, sort of yellowish?"

"Yeah?"

"That's the color of the sound *before* it got erased. So, yes, it *did* have sound at one point."

"You mean you can amp it up?" Yaz asked.

"Hey, you want their baby pictures thrown in for free?" He grinned, his dark gums again on display. "I can go backward or forward in time as you like. Gender and species morphing's extra."

"Where's your lab?" Yaz asked. "Can we get going?"

Mamo chuckled. "You need it yesterday, right?"

"Right."

"You gonna pick up my tab?"

Yaz flashed him a New Yen chip. "We can arrange to raise the credit on this depending on your work."

Mamo perked up when he saw the chip. "I live near here," he said, rising off his stool. "It's about a five-minute walk. You guys got five minutes?"

SAYONARAVILLE

Mamo led them deeper into the back streets of Chiba City, away from the surf line of neon that broke on the reef of the Matrix. They heard a loud honking and looked up. It was a solitary Nintendo duck flapping its wings.

Boom! Boom! Boom!

They saw several thundering flashes in the sky and watched the bird fall like a dead manga.

"Duck hunt freaks!" Mamo spat contemptuously on the ground. "Someone ought to report them to the SPCH."

"SPCH?" Gobi inquired.

"The Society for the Prevention of Cruelty to Holoids—or is it the Society for the Preservation of Chinese Holograms?" Mamo wondered. "I can never keep it straight. Those Nintendo ducks are practically extinct."

"How much farther is it to your place?" Yaz asked anxiously. His hand tightened on his long sword.

"Not much farther," Mamo answered. "Why are you guys in such a hurry anyway? Oh, I get it. You don't wanna get caught in Chibatown after curfew, right? You wanna be safe at home when the Change comes?" He giggled. "Whatever gets you through the night."

They passed a smart ramen stall and a pet shop with genetically engineered pets. The puppy-birds were asleep in their crates on newspaper, wings folded as they dreamed. Otaku faces looked out at them through plate-glass windows. A dyke slut and her femme girlfriend were sharing an espresso in a kissaten, their nose rings linked by a silver chain.

A kiosk two feet wide and three feet deep sold grams of educational microsofts. The diode board offered slashed prices on everything, from channeled lessons in printmaking by Toulouse-Lautrec and Hiroshige to cram-course jukus that promised to get any village idiot admitted to Waseda University on a scholarship.

They crossed an alley where there were a few stuffed body bags zipped up lying on the curb. Fluorescent Japanese ideographs were printed on the bags.

"Defective body parts?" Gobi inquired. "From the transplant labs?" He had heard they grew artificial organs in Chibatown basements like bean sprouts. It was a local cottage industry.

Mamo paused, then prodded one of the bags with his toe. "No, these guys just didn't make it, is all. They didn't break through."

"Didn't break through what?"

Mamo grinned, showing his purplish Dilantin gums. "You American, first time in Neo-Tokyo, right? Thought so. These yojimbos didn't come through the Flux. Some people don't come back. Your friend here oughta tell you," he said, jabbing his thumb at Yaz.

"No, those dudes are gone, man. They're not comin' back. Not even to Sayonaraville," Mamo said, leading them down a narrow passage away from the bodies.

Mamo flashed his remote at a red eye blinking on a low doorway recessed in a fiberglass wall. The door swung open to reveal a narrow stairway lit by a naked halogen bulb.

"It's just up here," Mamo said, as he huffed up the steep stairway. "Just one thing, guys, I got a roommate, Marie. We share the loft. She's probably got her main squeeze with her, so we don't wanna disturb them, okay?"

"Don't worry." Yaz winked at Gobi. "We've just come to do our business, in and out, then we're out of everyone's way."

"Okay, come on in," Mamo said, as he punched the code to open the front door. "Don't mind the mess."

● ● ●

The loft was a tall concrete structure with canvas walls and terraced live-and-work sections on three levels.

There was a zabuton cushion on the floor of a small cubicle downstairs, and a low Japanese table piled high with stuff. Entrails of equipment, various disassembled computer decks, and spaghetti reams of fiberoptics, some of them still on their spools, cluttered the main work space.

A pair of floor spots were aimed upward at the grimacing face of the 12-foot-tall crimson-lacquered Dewa King who stood in a fervent pose, brandishing a short sword. It was a Niwo temple guardian from the Kamakura period in the 12th century.

"Where did you get that?" Gobi marveled. "It looks like a museum piece. It must be worth a fortune!"

"Think so?" Mamo asked cheerfully.

"How did you get it?"

"I traded it for some consulting work."

"So desu ka?" Gobi said skeptically.

Mamo laughed. "That Niwo's my buddy. He came back with me one day from the Great Digital Beyond. You'd be surprised what treasures pop up sometimes. Finders, keepers—ain't that right? Ha, ha, ha!"

Gobi wondered, *Is that* really *possible? Can you bring actual objects—historical objects—back from the past?* He could see it now: *Gobi the private eye sitting in his psychic P.I.'s office in North Beach. An attorney representing an art dealer in Zurich calls in for a consultation.*

"What can I do for you?" Gobi asks him.

"We have a client with 326 original Vermeers in his gallery."

"What seems to be the problem?"

"They're all the same painting, Mr. Gobi. The Lacemaker, oil on wood, c. 1669/70."

"I see."

"The Louvre in Paris, which owns the original, has filed a lawsuit to have our client's collection destroyed."

"What do you want me *to do about it?"*

"We wish you to authenticate our client's Vermeers. Each

one was transferred in time in a bona fide manner, meeting all legal requirements and paying all appropriate import duties."

"I think you'd better get to work now," Yaz told Mamo brusquely.

"Okay, let me see that picture again."

Gobi handed him the strip. Mamo took it and sat down on the zabuton cushion at the table. He lifted the silver visor from his face and they could see his eyes, or whatever passed for his eyes.

Thin membrane covered them. He dug his fingers under the webs and teased out the Olympus lensplants from his empty sockets.

"Sorry about that," he said, noticing Gobi's startled expression. "My electric contact lenses exploded a few years ago. They were early models, y'know. Had to rebuild my optics. It's a mail-order job, but it's good. Technically I'm blind as a bat, but don't worry, I always know what I'm looking at."

Sitting cross-legged at the table, Mamo loaded the picture onto a holo-deck and scanned it. He tapped something out on the keyboard and the image began to tease itself out into various audio-fonts.

"Hmm, let's see what we got," he began, talking largely to himself. "It's got a nice dingbat morphology. Notice the lispy greens and yellows. Need a nice phonic blue right here. Okay, okay. Let's remove this thing. What's that? Oh, that's the privacy tag. I'll-show-you-mine-if-you-show-me-yours type of thing. Cute. It's a standard holo-diary protection. Let me try this now. Wow, Lucky Goldstar's a lot tougher to break into. Need a stick of kimchi to blow it open. All right you guys. Just a moment. Hold on. Hold on. It's coming."

He lowered his visor again and smiled. "This'll only take a second. The program's running right now."

He scrutinized the screen again, then popped open an icon to check the subcode.

"Just as I thought, folks. That was a decoy program. *Tsk, tsk.* Clever, clever. Naughty, naughty. Okay, now we're going to get to the real stuff."

He punched some more keys.

"All right!!!" he exclaimed. "Like I told you, we're inside the buttonhole now. . . ."

"Inside the what?" Gobi asked.

Mamo gave him an exasperated look. "Inside the button-hole, man. Of the dude who took the picture. See this fuzzy stuff? It's lint. That other stuff is threads. Threads on his suit. See?"

There were magnified threads on the screen. Faces of people peered through the threads as though through heavy jungle growth.

Mamo frowned at the luminous globules, which looked like they were part of the Milky Way.

"What's that?" Gobi asked, studying the pearly globes intently.

"Looks like a string of white lights. Close enough to reflect into the lens. Could be jewelry of some sort. Sorry I can't make it out."

Mamo fiddled with the tuner. "Okay," he said. "The reso-lution's getting better. You can see his face now."

"See his face where?"

"In that glass on the counter."

The close-up showed the reflection of the man who had taken the picture of the group sitting at the sushi bar.

"Say," Mamo asked, suddenly getting interested. "Don't I know that yojimbo from somewhere?"

"No, you don't," Yaz replied.

"Yes, I do," Mamo insisted. "That's the Satori dude. That's Kazuo Harada! Hey, that's Ama's place! Shit! He was right here in Chibatown?"

"You said you could raise the sound on this still?" Yaz reminded him.

"Hey, don't rush me! That's Kazuo Harada, man! This is gonna cost you extra!"

"Just do it," Yaz ordered.

"Coming right up. Let's try this."

Mamo 'scoped the sound on the first try, but it was way too loud. The room boomed.

"Whoah! Sorry about that! That was his own programmed

volume control. . . . Sensitive eardrums, huh? I think the dude's got a cochlear implant. Yup, it's a Kawasaki J-32 earpiece, so it amped the sound up to where he can hear it himself."

"Can you turn it down?" Gobi asked.

"Sure, here goes. It's not real time, but it's the next best thing."

Mamo picked up a sound stripper and aimed it at the screen. "This here's my special scalpel," he explained. "It removes layers of old scar tissue from sound. I couldn't work without it. Listen to this. . . ."

They heard a man's voice. "It's Harada," Yaz whispered to Gobi. They listened to him address another man: *"Sato, why are you looking so glum? This is a celebration. Lighten up, that's an order!"*

A rumbling filled the speakers. Mamo fiddled with the sound filter and played it back. In the corner of the sushi bar, the young man with the coal eyes jerked open his mouth. *"Sensei, you cannot alter the nature of the virus. I have tried. Not even you, who are good—"*

"Nonsense, Sato-kun, we know it exists, now we're working on the antidote, all in good time—"

"—isn't any."

That's when Gobi heard *her* voice. He felt a tingling at the base of his spine, and when he looked up, Yaz was staring at him in a strange way.

"There is a man who will be coming from America. He will know what to do."

Yaz said to Gobi, "That's the voice of the miko, isn't it, Frank-san? The woman that you knew? What was her name again?"

"Kimiko," Gobi answered. "Her name is Kimiko."

Suddenly an electronic alarm went off in the loft. They all jumped up at the same time, startled by its shrill beeping.

"What's that?" Yaz demanded.

"Shit, man," Mamo yelped, as he disengaged from the

deck. He popped open a video icon on the screen that showed him the front of his loft.

"When it rains, it pours," he complained. "Looks like I got some clients dropping by. I better let them in before they wear out the buzzer."

"Wait a moment," Yaz said as he checked the screen. "You don't want to do that."

"You know them?" Mamo asked.

Yaz looked up at Gobi with a worried expression. "Those are the same guys who tried to take us out on the way over to Chibatown. I thought we'd lost them."

Gobi stared at the screen. "Shit."

Three crew-cut yaks stood on the front porch. The one who had tried to run them down with his partner in the Barracuda—and the two fresh hunks of Kobe beef. You could see their faces through the fish-eye lens, pockmarks and all, as they pressed their noses to the door frame.

"Frank-san, I think we better leave now," Yaz suggested.

Crew-cut No. 1 was fiddling with his pen-top wand, doing a bar-code analysis of the security system, running it up and down the frame. Nos. 2 and 3 were trying the more direct method, heaving their bulky shoulders against the door.

Yaz handed Mamo a New Yen chip. "Thank you. May I have the picture back?"

Mamo glanced at the chip but held on to the holo-shashin. "Think that'll pay for a new door?" Yaz gave him another chip. "Thanks," Mamo said, quieting down. He handed Yaz the shashin.

"Is there a way out of here besides the front?" Yaz asked.

"Through Marie's place upstairs. But I don't think she'd appreciate it if you guys walked in on her. . . ."

"Shee-it!" Mamo cried, as the yaks took the door off the hinges.

Gobi ran up the stairs, right behind Yaz. When Gobi looked down from the midlevel terrace, he had a clear view of the crimson halo attached to the back of the 12-foot Dewa King.

It had a nest of 12th-century cobwebs draped over its neck.

Judging from their plump hairy bodies, it looked like the spiders had eaten a meal recently.

It was a skinny box of a loft, but they found what they were looking for on the top level. A canvas flap served as a door, its clasps hastily tied. Yaz undid the knots without difficulty, and the two men entered Marie's boudoir.

It took a moment for Gobi to adjust his eyes to the darkness. A synthesized raga played on the speakers and the oil lamps cast a flickering glow on the two bodies making love on the platform.

They were entwined in what looked like a tapestry of coils and 'trodes. Gobi heard the rustling and clinking of the cables as the bodies thrust at each other.

An erotorama played on an air screen that was revolving 360 degrees around the circular love nest. The wires spilled over the bed and ran like green fiberoptic tendrils across a jungle floor.

My God, they're networked from head to toe! Gobi realized, as he traced the cables from the bed to a Sanyo Erosgizer console. He couldn't take his eyes off the scene. It was a frieze from one of the Indian love temples in Khajuraho.

Gods and goddesses, nymphs and devas, serpents and strange winged beasts were fornicating. There were beasts of uncertain appetite doing things that only beasts with uncertain appetites do to each other. . . ."Frank-san!" Yaz hissed into his ear. "Hayaku! Get moving!"

Gobi took a step and tripped over a cable. *Shit!* Sparks exploded across the room. He must have tripped over one of the connector cables.

The connecting circuits began to blow like a string of Chinese firecrackers. *Pop! Pop! Pop! Pop!*

"Ah, oh, ah, oh, ah, oh, ah, oh . . ."

The femme top began to buck frantically as she raced to the edge of her orgasm.

"*Yaaaaa! Yaaaa!*" Her partner jerked up. It was a woman with cropped hair.

As he hobbled over to the back door, Gobi saw her heavy breasts. Their pierced nipples jutted out from a latticework bra of fiberoptics.

"Who the fuck are you?!" the packer snarled.

"Oops, sorry . . . We were just leaving. The door's that way? Please don't mind us." Gobi apologized, his foot still tangled in the mess of cables.

Then the unexpected happened. Attracted by the sudden power surge around Gobi's foot, one of the fornicating winged monkeys flew off the erotic diorama, which had stopped spinning.

"Ch-ch-ch-ch-ch-ch-ch . . . " Its teeth chattered as it leaped across the room and attached itself to Gobi's left ear.

The monkey hung on to Gobi's neck with its powerful pinkoid fingers. Its wet mouth chattered into the side of his face as it tried to hump his head.

"Get off me!" Gobi screamed.

Yaz stood at the doorway, helpless. He had no idea what to do next. He had seen the beast fly off its pedestal, a flash of lower-level pink and brown erotic energy that had obviously short-circuited.

They heard the sound of heavy steps on the stairway. *The yaks would be there any second now,* Gobi thought. *What was he going to do with this infernal thing?*

"Hurry!" Yaz urged Gobi. They took two stairs at a time down the fire escape, the holoid ape still clinging to Gobi's neck.

Wop! Wop! Wop!

The ground in front of them erupted into dirt geysers. Gobi and Yaz looked up. A yak stood at the top of the stairs. He was aiming laser-shurikens at them in the alley below.

The monkey on Gobi's shoulder became desperate. It now realized that it was hopelessly adrift in the world of matter. Whatever was left of its programming—maybe 750 lines or so of its bio-code—began to consolidate into a demonic energy that clung to its new power supply. Unfortunately, that power supply was concentrated somewhere below Gobi's left ear, a few inches away from the lateral fuse of his cortex.

"That way!" Yaz cried, pointing to a tight space between two buildings.

The yak was now halfway down the stairs and in the process of hurling another shuriken at them.

Gobi now had an inspiration. He grabbed the holo-ape by its hairy ankles. With a burst of energy, he hurled it at the yakuza on the stairs. The flying monkeyplasm took the yak completely by surprise.

The monkey was now all over the yak's face. Its skinny holoid body wrapped itself around his neck, its sharp bony fingers began to dig deep into the sockets of his eyes.

"Aaargh! Aaargh! Aaargh!" The yak danced in circles of pain as he attempted to tear the nightmare from his eyes.

A second yakuza now appeared behind him. He let out a similar scream when he saw the chattering teeth and the gouging fingers of the demented monkey. His nunchaku sticks hung helplessly at his side. He could not bring himself to smash his partner in the face.

The man's life essence suddenly erupted from his empty sockets like gusts of wind blowing dead leaves off the ground. With a moan escaping from his blood-frothed lips, the yakuza leaped from the top of the landing into the alley below.

Gobi and Yaz heard the thud of his body as it hit the ground.

The brown-grey ectoplasm of the holoid monkey hovered over the yak's body for a moment. It was confused. Its host was gone. It was dying. It turned to look at Gobi, an expression of piteous horror in its eyes—as if it were beseeching him to do something.

Gobi knew exactly what to do. He ran the chi down to his hara. Quick, what was the combination to the lock on the strongbox? The numbers tumbled, the bolts slid back. Inside the blackness, the consciousness moved. It was sensate. It had been watching a little TV, an NHK documentary about a primitive tribe in New Jersey, an HDTV cargo cult of some sort. He heard the voice now. An old man struggling to speak.—*"Sato? Is that you? Is it time yet? Has the world been changed? Is my new body prepared? Who shall I be?"* And then—*"WHO ARE YOU?"*

    —*"Ryutaro Kobayashi?"*

    —*"Hai."*

    —*"I'm afraid you are going to have to be transferred now."*

    —*Silence.*

    —*The old man asked, "To my new body?"*

    —*"Yes. Please prepare yourself."*

    —*"Shall I be a man or a woman?"*

    —*"Neither."*

    —*A pause. "Do I have a choice?"*

    —*"No."*

    —*"This is a final karmic decision?"*

    —*"Yes."*

    —*A sigh. "I had hoped—"*

    —*"Good luck in your new existence."*

Gobi and Yaz watched as the monkey holoid scampered into the grille of the building's air-conditioning system and disappeared into a vent, its teeth chattering.

Gobi bowed. *"Kobayashi-san,* sayonara." And then he added, *"Please find him wherever he is and bring him enlightenment."*

SARUMAWASHI (MONKEY DANCE)

What, a monkey consciousness! With his thoughts a'blurring, Ryutaro Kobayashi extended his ephemeral chi into the envelope of this manga creature with long pink fingers and a pink cartoon cavity for a mouth. Where was his empire? Was this it? He saw cardboard shadows and silhouettes and beams of light. It was a long shaft. Up, up, up . . . . His thoughts willed the creature to climb—and it did! He peered through the grate into a room. A lone otaku sat at his desk with his console on. The light immediately attracted his monkey nature. It was his instinct to slip through the grille. He stood there on the floor for a minute—testing his balance—it was so odd, this non-body body. The otaku was on-line. God knows what, God knows where. It didn't matter. Anywhere was an opening. The pool of light looked so inviting. When the otaku turned his head to sip his mug of cha, the monkey essence of Ryutaro Kobayashi had already slipped into the stream and was swimming, swimming, swimming, deeper and deeper, into the It-of-It. He was returning to the source. The otaku saw the fractured shimmer of light on the screen. He stared at it until it disappeared, sighed, then returned to his game of S&M mah-jongg.

BURAKUMIN

The man in the inflatable overcoat stood by the recycling pits at the rear of the complex. He had watched the action from a distance.

Yaz and Gobi squeezed through the long row of otaku apartments and emerged into a clearing between the squatters' shacks.

Someone had a fire going outside. It looked like a small Bangladeshi community lived here.

"Gaijin burakumin," Yaz told Gobi. "They are foreign untouchables."

Of course, Gobi had heard about the foreign burakumin communities in New Nippon. This one obviously earned a meager living in Chiba City handling excess power surges for the otaku collective.

He felt a deep pity for them.

Gobi was aware that New Nippon technology thrived on a symbiotic relationship with the immigrant untouchables from the Third World. But, until now, he didn't really understand how they functioned as human filters.

Of course. By absorbing dysfunctional energies such as the energy of the holoid ape that had leaked from the Sanyo deck in Marie's loft, that's how.

Using a quick scan, Gobi saw that the Bangladeshis had perfected a technique for packing the energy effluents into long, sausage-shaped containers that they wore around their necks and down their backs.

The containers were transparent, and they glowed with the dark luminosity of discarded software karmas.

"My God, these people are human radiation shields!" Gobi exclaimed, as the realization hit him. "This place is a toxic dump!"

Yaz said apologetically, "No one asked them to come to New Nippon. They are glad to serve their adopted country. These are second- or third-generation energy packers."

"What are they doing?"

A tall and skinny dark-skinned Bangladeshi buraku was stirring the embers of the fire with a long pole. He smiled when he saw them. He had no teeth in his mouth. He wore a thin cotton jacket over a native skirt and cheap rubber zori sandals.

There was a sausage-tube device looped over one shoulder. Gobi saw that it contained a brownish-blackish energy. The man squeezed the end of the tube into the fire and squirted the tarlike substance into the flames. He was roasting a small animal. A thin column of greasy black smoke rose from the pit.

A few naked children were playing by the hovels, which were made of unrecyclable Mitsubishi materials. Bodies lay inside the makeshift shelters—old and young alike, hardly moving at all. Somewhere a baby cried.

Gobi felt sickened. "Energy packers?" he exclaimed. "You mean they've been hired to absorb the energy spills from otakus who OD on the virtual systems, don't you!"

"Unfortunately, there *is* an electromagnetic field that is disturbed when alternate realities are released into the atmosphere," Yaz conceded. "Someone *must* assume those virtual karmas. That is a new law of thermocybernetics that Japanese scientists have discovered. We never imagined such things were possible. The best scientists of New Nippon are trying to solve this riddle."

"How come we've never heard about this in the West? You've managed to keep a lid on it, haven't you?"

"Your technology hasn't reached our stage of development yet." Yaz smiled sadly. "By that time, hopefully we may be able to offer some practical solutions to the world."

"In the meantime, you're using these poor human sponges to absorb these software toxicities. That's criminal."

"We don't know yet how toxic the psyche is to the environment," Yaz protested. "This is still a brand-new field."

"But look at what they're doing," Gobi said. He raised his palms to the Bangladeshi man in a namasté greeting of co-spiritual recognition. "They're burning your damned karma and using it as cooking fuel!"

The Bangladeshi smiled back, a beautiful and vibrant smile, as he returned the greeting to Gobi.

There was only beauty and God in his smile.

"Namasté," he said, clasping his palms together. "Konbanwa, good evening." He bowed to Yaz without any malice.

Yaz bowed back.

Then the gaijin burakumin squirted some more bad karma into the fire as the man in the inflatable overcoat continued to observe them from a distance.

His silver face caught the reflection of the flames in the karma incinerator.

Yaz and Gobi circled the settlement of untouchables and cut through another long row of Chibatown lofts. They were backtracking to where Yaz had parked his maglev bike in the alley near Ama's sushi bar.

Tomo was still there, and the coast looked clear.

"What do you think?" Yaz asked Gobi. He had seen how the American ran his energy. He had heard the miko speak.

Gobi tried to feel it out, but he ran into a fog bank of fuzz that was as thick as iron wool. He shook his head. "Hard to say, there's too much static."

Neon waves were crashing against huge billboard reefs erected above the alley. A few blocks away, a life-size inflated Godzilla was doing a Kirin Bud commercial on a department-store rooftop, stomping on a rival brand's six-pack.

Dirigibles loaded with rush-hour traffic slowly navigated between the high rises, their beams 'scoping the streets below. People's faces appeared in the portholes, their caps pulled low, white gauze face masks for men and pink and green ones for women.

"We'll just have to risk it." Yaz pulled out his shakuhachi flute from his rucksack and blew a coded riff on it.

They watched Tomo come to life. The turbo-propulsers on the undamaged legs switched on. His head jerked back. With the bit clenched between his teeth, the maglev horse turned in their direction and slowly began to gravitate toward them.

"Hai yo," Yaz addressed his bike, which now stood at attention before them, poised to lift off.

That's when the cross-beams hit them.

One black Barracuda moved into the alley at the entrance. The other 'cuda pulled in from the back to cut off their retreat.

They froze in the sudden explosion of brightness.

Then Yaz leaped onto Tomo's saddle and Gobi followed, jumping into the sidecar. Tomo reared up as the two 'cudas closed in.

Above them in the narrow alley, a black Suzuki Sunspot chopper appeared, its rotors thundering as it blocked any vertical escape. They were boxed in.

Four yakuzas jumped out of a 'cuda and charged Yaz. They were swinging their nunchakus as though they were skipping rope. One of them bared teeth studded with pachinko balls.

"Tactical error," Yaz congratulated him. There was a flash as Yaz drew his katana from his sash and swung the blade. The yak's face twisted as the pachinko balls melted in his mouth, stifling his scream. The long blade sizzled. "Virtual katana," Yaz explained to Gobi, returning the blade to his scabbard.

Three distraught yakuzas danced around their fallen companion as Yaz tried to navigate Tomo around them. "No use." He reversed the bike; the spotlight from the chopper overhead stayed on them, as dogged as a nervous tic.

"The road is blocked ahead!" Yaz shouted. Tomo reared up, its turbos screaming as Yaz rose in the saddle, calculating their odds of escape.

A moment later, the Suzuki Sunspot dropped a net down over them.

They were lifted off the ground like salmon plucked out of the Kushiro River as they headed upstream to spawn in the mountains of Hokkaido.

The yaks got out of their cars and stood beneath the bird with its dangling cargo. Their suits had little ripples running down their backs as the chopper whacked the air above them for a few topsy-turvy moments.

Then the black Sunspot turned 360 degrees and headed toward Neo-Tokyo.

DEAD EX

Gobi looked up at the chopper and shouted to Yaz over the deafening roar. *"Who in the hell are they!?"*

Yaz studied the logo on the door of the black chopper. It was a stylized briefcase with a pair of legs sticking out of it. He sneered contemptuously. *"They're called the Death Express. . . . It's a yakuza shipping company. They guarantee overnight delivery of human packages anywhere in the world—or the customer gets one free hit."*

Yaz thought for a moment, then added, *"Someone's gone to a lot of trouble if they hired them. Dead Ex doesn't come cheap."*

Then Yaz bowed deeply to Gobi. *"Frank-san, gommen-na-sai! Forgive me! It was my duty to protect you! I have failed you!"*

Tears welled in his eyes. But they welled in Gobi's eyes, too, from the turbulent chop of the air.

"Forget it, Yaz! It's not your fault!" Gobi called back. *"Where are they taking us?"*

Yaz climbed up on the bike and stood spread-eagled against the wind as he grasped the net. He looked into the distance.

Chiba City was a blur of wind and bright lights as the chopper dragged its drift net over the rioting neonscape of giant kinetic billboards. A 50-foot-high inflated Godzilla was coming up starboard on the roof of Mitsukoshi Harrod's department store.

Gobi sat hunched in the sidecar, his knuckles white as they gripped at the windshield.

This is just great, he thought. *We've just been scooped up like goldfish at a fair. Now we're being carried away to God knows where, and there's absolutely nothing we can do about it. Or is there?*

Wait a minute.

Gobi felt inside his pockets. Yaz watched him curiously. *What was the American up to now?*

There! Gobi thought excitedly. *He still had it! It was worth a try. Anything was, if it would get them out of this airborne chafing dish.*

Gobi climbed out of the sidecar and clambered up beside the Japanese. He gestured at the vial in his hand and pointed at the open door of the chopper.

It was the vial of San Andreas 8.0 that the Latino yakuza had given him on the shuttle to New Narita. What had Carlos told him? *"I'll give you a word of advice about the 8.0, man. You'll know when it's time to use it. When you start to feel the tremors deep inside, that's when you drop the shit."*

Well, he *was* feeling those tremors now. His heart was pumping like a piston. It was time.

Gobi snapped off the head of the vial and carefully handed it to Yaz. *"Be careful, don't spill it!"* he warned. Yaz nodded. He had understood Gobi's frantic sign language.

Yaz pulled his shakuhachi flute out of his shoulder bag, and slipped the vial inside like a dart. He covered all the holes of the shakuhachi to turn it into a blowpipe. Then he stuck the bamboo instrument out of the net and fired.

One of the yaks appeared at the door to check on their netted cargo. He reacted immediately when he saw what Yaz was attempting, but it was too late. The 8.0 was on its way. The yak tried to block it. He caught the vial on his fingertips and juggled it for a moment, but it slipped through.

It fell inside the chopper and rolled on the floor toward the pilot's seat.

Within seconds the chopper was lurching and spinning out of control. There was an 4.2 tremor on board; the yaks didn't know what had hit them.

The chopper tilted crazily toward the Godzilla on the department-store roof. It swerved sharply on its side and a yak flew out of the open door. They heard him scream as he drop-kicked into open air.

The giant Godzilla took the chopper on the chin and the blades tore out the scaffolding that held the body of the giant ape up. The net that held Gobi and Yaz scraped the outside of the building at twenty stories.

A wall of neon exploded into a blue-green and red tidal wave that roared down into the street.

The chopper tried to lift off awkwardly, carrying Godzilla's deflated head on its tail. Godzy spun around like a tumbleweed of neon before he spiraled off the aircraft in a cascade of pixeled sparks.

Still thrusting out of control, the chopper now weaved crazily through the downtown canyons of Chibatown.

On the roof of another nearby department store stood a giant Nissin Cup O' Noodles. A gigantic pair of chopsticks dipped in and out of the cup in a kinetic advertising display.

"Oh my God!" Gobi cried out.

The chopsticks caught their net neatly as the chopper skewered into the roof of the department store. The net sheared open and their bike slid down the rails of the chopsticks and into the giant Styro-foam cup.

With Yaz back in the saddle and Gobi hanging on in the sidecar, Tomo tore right through the bottom of the cup.

For a single crystal-clear moment, the maglev bike hovered on the rooftop of the department store, teetering on the knife-edge of the twenty-story building.

Then Tomo roared back to life as Yaz spun the machine around.

The downed chopper crashed through a wall of neon, rotating on its twisted blades before crunching to a halt in the wreckage of the Cup O' Noodles display.

Four yakuzas in black garb leaped out onto the rooftop seconds before the Sunspot spun off the roof.

Explosive shurikens flew like punctuation marks above Tomo's head. One shuriken blew open the doorway behind them that led to the rooftop service entrance.

Yaz revved up Tomo. *Good, he was unharmed!* Then he spun around and they tore down the stairs on the bike.

The sidecar scraped the handrail, leaving a trail of sparks in its wake.

"Hold on, Frank-san," Yaz warned, as he steered Tomo off the stairwell. "We're going for a ride again!"

They blasted through a pair of wide swinging doors. Gobi shook his head.

It looked like they were in a lingerie department. The bike charged through a forest of clothes racks as the shoppers dove to the floor.

Gobi peeled a pair of fuzzy-logic panties from his face and unhooked an artificial intelligence bra from his ear.

Yaz swerved past the fitting rooms, blowing the doors off the hinges. It was a mixed crowd judging from the men, women, and transvirtuals who were trying on various ensembles.

One poor fellow got runs in his holo-nylons as he scrambled for cover.

"Straight ahead!" Gobi called to Yaz, as they entered the main aisle. "The escalators over there!" He pointed.

Yaz nodded and gritted his teeth.

One of the yakuzas suddenly appeared at the compassionate camisoles counter and swung his nunchakus as Yaz roared down the aisle.

He twirled his lethal sticks, but they got caught in a rack of garter belts and snapped back, smacking him in the face.

Tomo shot past him as they careened down the escalator tracks. Shoppers caught in their path threw themselves down as Tomo roared down over them.

Twelve stories and the men's ties and handkerchiefs department later, they roared out of the department store and into the street.

"Frank-san, you okay?" Yaz checked with Gobi, as he merged into the traffic and charted a steady course that would lead them to the elevated maglev-way.

"Nothing my size, I'm afraid," Gobi answered, tossing an interactive Hanae Mori evening gown into the Neo-Tokyo rush-hour traffic.

The wind tried it on briefly, then swept it off the overpass. A commuter who was handgliding between two keiretsu tower sectors caught it on his briefcase, and tied it to his handlebars.

Its blue chiffon optics caught the rays of the setting sun, turning the gown a royal purple. *"Thank you for putting me on,"* the Hanae Mori gown addressed the glider in a seductive voice. *"You look lovely tonight."*

"I think we're safe now," Yaz told Gobi over the headset after he ran a quick radar check.

There were no Barracudas showing anywhere on the 'scope within a four-kilometer radius. *Correction:* There was *one* Barracuda in the Yamanote 12 sector, but it was traveling in the opposite direction.

A review of its license showed that it was owned by the son of a shacho who worked for Itoh Tofu. The kid was 19 years old, and had a list of moving violations as long as the Izu speedway, but was otherwise clean. No known yakuza connections.

Yaz took the Marunouchi exit, which led to the heart of downtown Neo-Tokyo. He caught a current as they approached a keiretsu tower complex.

"It's been a long day, Frank-san," he said to his worn-out companion.

"Active," Gobi agreed.

"Here's your hotel," Yaz told him. "You'd better get some rest. We can get started again in the morning. Eight o'clock, okay? I'll pick you up."

Gobi groaned. "I'll be there. I *hope.*"

The Grand Interface Hotel was situated on the 34th floor of a keiretsu tower. It faced the old Imperial Palace, with a view of the algae-green moat and grey stone walls.

As the doorman collected Gobi's handgrip from the trunk of the battered maglev, Gobi lingered on the curb.

Yaz studied his American friend. "Yes, Frank-san?"

"Nothing, Yaz. Thanks." The Japanese looked at him with compassion. "Don't worry, the Change won't begin for another two hours yet. Everything will be okay. *Don't worry!*"

"No final words of advice, Yaz? I mean, on how to go *through* it?"

Yaz stared at him. This American would have to manage on his own. It was part of the unspoken consensus. "Death is the ultimate trade secret, Frank-san." He bowed.

Then he revved up Tomo—and master and maglev pulled away from the hotel platform.

THE GRAND INTERFACE

Gobi stepped into a cool white marble lobby. It was vast—in a minimalist fashion. At first glance, it appeared to be deserted. But as his eyes adjusted to the whiteness, he detected people hurrying through it. He wasn't sure whether that was because the witching hour for Neo-Tokyo was drawing close, or whether the Grand Interface attracted an elusive clientele.

He approached the front desk. "I'd like to check in, please," he said to the receptionist. "The name is Gobi."

"Ah, Dr. Gobi, welcome!" The smiling young man in the black frock coat and striped cravat bowed. He glanced at the screen. "You have been preregistered. Room 1508. If you'll just press your palm here, you can charge anything you like to your account."

"Any messages?"

"Let me check, sir. Yes, there have been several, all from the same person."

"Those must be from me, I'm afraid," a soft feminine voice addressed him from behind.

Gobi recognized her from her scent even before he turned around. The tangy velvet musk of *Lady Murasaki* swept over him.

"Miss Abe, what a surprise!"

Yuki Abe, director of Satori's multimedia networks division, had changed from her Western dress into an elegant kimono. It suited her. She wore white two-toed tabi socks and geta clogs, which gave her a slightly pigeon-toed stance that Gobi found quite charming.

"You remember my name?" she exclaimed with a trace of surprise.

"Of course I remember you. It would be difficult *not* to." He glanced at the messages in his hand. "You called me *three* times? It must be important. What can I do for you?"

Embarrassed, she clutched a little eel-skin handbag against her obi and looked down at the floor. "I hope you don't mind. I know I must seem presumptuous to you."

"Not at all," he said, touching her elbow. "Whatever it is, I'm sure it's important." He glanced at his watch. "Important enough for you to risk coming by so soon before the—*ah . . .* "

He felt suddenly tongue-tied.

"We usually refer to it as the 'Flux,' Dr. Gobi," Yuki aided him. "It helps if you give it a name. Sometimes we call it the 'In-Between Time.' Or the 'Shift.' Or even the 'Transformation.' You will get used to it."

She looked into his eyes. "Except in the beginning. The first time is always . . . "

She shivered. Her eyes screwed shut, then she opened them again with a bright smile. *"Different."*

"I see." Gobi pursed his lips. "Well, Miss Abe, can we sit down somewhere and talk?" He looked around the lobby. "That is, if we can *find* a spot?"

"What about that lounge over there?" she asked, nodding across the room.

"Lead the way," he said, his eyes still unaccustomed to the intense whiteness.

"Please call me Yuki. Miss Abe is too formal."

"Frank."

"Fine . . . *Frank."* She smiled shyly.

He followed her to a secluded well of white leather sofas at the end of the lobby. A keyboardist was tinkling a Kitaro tune on a white Yamaha grand piano.

They sat down, their knees suddenly touching. She nervously smoothed the hem of her kimono.

"Did you have a successful day?" she asked. "Yazu-san is a very fine person."

"Yes, he is. We had a very productive day. He took me to Chiba City." He studied her reaction. She squirmed a little in her seat.

"Ah, Chiba City." She nodded. "It is known for its many otakus. An interesting community. *Different."*

"That's right," Gobi agreed. "They don't call it 'Sayonaraville' for nothing."

She stifled a laugh and raised her eyes to his. "I suppose not."

"Now, Miss Abe—*Yuki,*" he corrected himself. "It is really most kind of you to visit me when you should probably be at home with your family."

"I don't have a family," she replied. "And I know you must be feeling . . . This *is* your first time in the new Tokyo, isn't it? Your first time passing into the Flux?"

"Yes, it is." He could see how awkward it was for her to get to the point. "I'm glad you're here, Yuki," he said softly, as he took her hand.

She smoothed her hem again as she struggled to express herself more clearly.

"You are alone in a strange city. If I can be of any service . . . "

"I think you can." His hand remained on hers, feeling the warmth grow between them.

She looked at him and whispered, "Which room are you in?"

As they crossed the lobby, Gobi bumped into the gaunt travel writer he had first met on Station Seven.

"Fancy running into you here, old chap!" The Englishman extended his bony hand. "Remember me? Simon Chadwick."

"What are *you* doing here?" Gobi asked, surprised to see him. "I thought you were up on Station Seven."

"I'm doing a piece on this marvelous hotel for *The Lobby Review.* Isn't this lobby absolutely grand, the way it seems to appear and disappear? It's all in the *optics,* you know. Really, it's one of the seven wonders of hoteldom. I say, are you a guest here?"

"As a matter of fact, I am," Gobi replied. "Well, nice seeing you again. Take care of yourself."

"Oh, dear me, you're always in such a rush, Gobi. Last time, you were with that delightful lady . . . what was her name? We never did have that drink I had hoped we would have. Perhaps you'd do me the honor this time. You *and* your charming friend here, of course." Chadwick bared his yellow teeth at her. "Madam." He bowed as he clicked his heels.

"Actually, Gobi," he continued, "I haven't any *immediate* plans, if you know what I mean, during the next hour or so, and I was wondering . . . *Oh damn,* why beat around the bush?"

"So far everyone here has given me the runaround when I ask them about this *thing* we're supposed to go through! Even the tourism office is of absolutely no help in that department; they're positively useless. They act so damned casual about it, as if it were nothing more than some sort of a moon-viewing festival! They're not informing the public about it as they *ought* to be."

Chadwick brightened up. "I *say,* Gobi, I've just had an idea! As one expatriate on the Road to Nowhere to another,

would you *mind* terribly much if we sat through this thing
together? The drinks will *all* be on me. It's my treat, old chap.
No, I insist. Strength in numbers and all that. What do you
say?"

"I'm *terribly* sorry, Chadwick," Gobi replied, disengaging
his arm from the Englishman's grasp. "I'd really love to, but I
can't. Maybe next time."

"Oh, dear. *Oh, my.* Next time. *Hummph.* Do you suppose
there *will be?* I mean a next time. Oh, well," Chadwick
huffed. "If that's how you feel about it. Have a pleasant
evening, miss." He nodded at Yuki.

Yuki nodded back at him in alarm.

Arm in arm, Gobi and Yuki crossed the lobby with
Chadwick looking after them like a sad sheepdog lost in the
moors.

They caught the elevator and went straight up to his room.

Yuki's breasts were like a twenty-year-old's, full and firm
with delectable little matsutake mushroom nipples. She had
left her Mikimoto holos on. They rippled around her neck.

At that moment, after they'd made love, Gobi would not
have minded if Neo-Tokyo *had* thrown the switch on him. It
would have been a lovely way to go.

Yuki plumped the pillows behind her. Her lips were open
and wet from their kisses. She smiled. "I think I'd like to have
a cigarette now."

She brushed her hair from her eyes and touched his nose
with her finger.

"I'm sorry, I don't smoke," Gobi apologized, as he rested
his cheek against her thighs and breathed in her scent.

There was a sweet spring of sweat beneath her navel,
which he licked very slowly.

"I don't mean a *real* cigarette," Yuki said, sitting up. "I'm
going to visualize one."

She closed her eyes, furrowed her brows, and inhaled
deeply. A few seconds later, she exhaled. Then she opened
her eyes wide and gazed down at his surprised face.

"I'm trying to cut down," she explained.

"Oh? How many do you visualize a day?"

"Nine or ten. That's not too bad, is it?"

"It's the thought that counts. If it gets to be too much, you can always visualize a nicotine patch."

From the window of his hotel room, Gobi could see a brightly lit cityscape of Neo-Tokyo, with its keiretsu megatowers and blazing holo-lights.

Across the broad avenue below, they looked down upon the Imperial Palace, its dark jade moat a bracelet on the wrist of time. The wooded hills and slopes hid the residence of the Emperor of New Nippon.

A yellow crescent moon hung above the city. Gobi glanced at the digital clock on the bedside table. It read 7:08:18 P.M.

There were about five minutes to go before the city began its transformation, he realized. *Not much time left.*

He glanced at Yuki. She was still puffing on her make-believe cigarette.

"Why did you come to see me tonight?" he asked.

She looked up at him in surprise, then flicked some imaginary ashes into an imaginary ashtray.

"You're not happy to see me?"

"You know I am. But that wasn't the main reason you came, Yuki."

"Mmm," she sighed, as she ruffled his hair. "Frank, does a woman need so many reasons to want to make love to you?"

"I can think of one other reason in your case."

"And what is that?" Yuki asked, as she settled back on the pillows, stifling a sleepy yawn.

"To find out what Yaz and I learned in Chibatown."

She opened an eye. "Learned about what?"

"You must have known that Yaz had a fragment of a shashin from Harada's Super Holo-Diary." He was testing her. "And that we were going to Chiba City to see if we could get anything more out of it."

Yuki smiled. "What's so important about that shashin? It's old news at Satori. After Harada-san disappeared, Action Wada had all his records and files searched. So they managed

to decrypt that fragment from a backup of his log? So what?
It's just a group picture of his team members."

Gobi leaned on an elbow and faced her. "Exactly. That's
what must have worried you."

Yuki gave him a half frown, half smile. "I'm afraid I don't
understand. Speak in Unix, will you?" she teased him.

"All right," Gobi said, sitting up. "I'll try. You were worried that we might find out you were part of his team. A secret
member. They've all vanished, but *you're* still here. So what
does that make you, Yuki? Do you work for Harada—or for
Action Wada?"

Yuki ground out her imaginary cigarette. She seemed dis-
pleased with him for the first time.

"Me on Harada's team? That's ridiculous. I'm not even *in*
that picture."

"Oh, yes, you are," Gobi said, as he reached for the
shashin that Mamo the Holo-Doctor had cleaned up for him.

He showed it to Yuki. She held it in her hand, and peered
into it from different angles.

"I'm sorry, Frank." She handed it back to him. "There are
five people in this picture. I'm not one of them. What are you
smiling like that for?"

"Maybe you weren't in the actual shot because Harada
would have taken pains to keep you out of it. But your *pearls*
were. You were sitting close enough to him that they were
reflected when he snapped the picture."

Yuki stared at him.

"See this milky blur reflected against the glass on the sushi
counter? We amped it up." He held the shashin up against her
breast, against the real holos. "Well, what do you know?
Look-and-*feel.*"

Yuki lit another imaginary cigarette. She glanced at the
time again. It was 7:14:20. Another forty seconds to go.

"Frank," she said, blowing imaginary smoke at him. She
was mildly irritated. "Excuse my language, but do you *really*
think I came up here to see if some otaku in Chibatown was
able to pick up a print of my tits on some cheap holo-shashin?
No, I wanted to be sure to be right here with you when you

went through to the Other Side. That's what we *also* call it, by the way—the *'Other Side.'*"

That's when it hit Gobi. *Of course. He was so stupid sometimes. He let his yang rule his yin when it was much wiser to maintain the center.* He heaved a plaintive sigh. *It was his sexual karma at work again.*

"It's the download, isn't it?" he said finally. "Everyone seems to think I have it."

"So you *do* have it then?" Yuki asked him sweetly, as she laid her hand on his hara.

But Gobi was unable to answer her. He attempted to steady himself on the nightstand, but his hand went right through the image of the table and he lost his balance completely.

"If you love your son, you must

let him travel."

—*Japanese proverb*

BARDO THREE

SHIFT

Frank . . . Frank . . . Dr. Gobi. . . ." He heard a voice address him as though from across a great distance. He felt someone shake his shoulders with a gentle insistence.

"Here, take this, it will make you feel better."

Someone handed him an oshibori, a steaming towel with a perfumed fragrance. He felt the steam rush into his pores as he inhaled the scent.

Aaaah. That felt good.

Gobi opened his eyes. He tried to accustom them to the blue light. It was unlike any shade of blue he had ever seen before. He was *seeing* in blue. He blinked his eyes.

He suddenly remembered where he was. Where he was *supposed* to be. Was he imagining things? No, it was real. He was *really* seeing through some sort of infra-blue filter.

Actually, it was more like he was *feeling* things with his sight. And that was a brand-new sensation.

Gobi stared through and *around* objects. He found that objects had no edges to them. Or was it his vision that no longer had any sharp edges?

The digital clock on the bedside table read 7:20:32. Five minutes and 32 seconds had passed since the Shift. But those minutes had no sides to them either. No tops and no bottoms. They seemed to float away.

Watching the bubbles of compressed time float away, he laughed. It was like watching a nonsectarian television commercial for eternity.

He began to laugh so hard that tears came to his eyes. He felt them, *tasted* them. They were real tears. Wet, warm, salty.

Time was not real. Tears were real. Gobi laughed again at the absurdity of it all.

He had fallen through—he had broken through to the Other Side. . . .

Yet he was still in the hotel room. There was someone on the bed beside him. He blinked again as he adjusted his vision.

It was Yuki.

"I am sorry," Yuki told him. *"But it is time for us to go now."*

It was Yuki, but it was not Yuki.

She looked different. She wore the ancient Japanese robes of a 12th-century court lady. She had several layers of kimono trailing to the ground beneath a flowing red silk hakama jacket. Her lustrous black hair was fixed in the ancient style and it hung down to her shoulders. Her skin was powdered white, and her brows were shaved with two black beauty marks painted high on her forehead. Her teeth were blackened according to the fashion of the era.

She walked across the room and stood by the window, her hands folded over the front of her robe. She held a fan. Her eyes were fixed upon something outside the window.

Gobi stood up. How did he manage to raise himself so effortlessly? And how did he come to be dressed in these clothes? These were not his regular clothes. Had Yuki dressed him? But it was all right. The clothes felt comfortable and all right on him. Everything was fine. He felt strangely elated.

Gobi looked into the mirror and saw that he was wearing some sort of loose, amorphous garb—a short white haori jacket, black gauze skirtlike trousers, and two-toed black tabi socks. He had a pair of wooden geta on his feet.

Gobi joined Yuki at the window. He moved as if he were the shadow of his own shen, like a man in a dream covering a great distance in a matter of seconds. He seemed to float, but his floating felt as if it were rooted in something solid.

She bowed in a kind of 12th-century deference to a late arrival from another world.

"It is beautiful, is it not?" she observed.

Neo-Tokyo's mega-towers were still there, but there was something different about the entire scene. It took an instant for Gobi to realize just what the difference was.

There, between the keiretsu towers, was a vista of pre-Tokyo. Gobi found himself looking at the 16th-century capital of Nippon, the capital that was once known as Edo.

But where was Neo-Tokyo?

Gobi gazed upon stretches of dark wasteland. There, among the sweeping tracts of land, he saw the mansions, the yashikis of the feudal lords, surrounded by the homes of their hatamoto bannermen. He saw the eaves of temples, and smoke rising from a thousand evening fires. Old-fashioned Japanese bridges arched across the Sumida River.

Here and there, steam rose from underground thermal springs. There was a strange dreamlike quality to the scene, as though he were watching a wood-block print come slowly to life.

The thought came to him from somewhere: *I have seen this before. I have been here before. But how? Where?* It was too overwhelming for him to think about right now.

"It is Edo, the old capital," Yuki said simply to him. In those few words, she described what hundreds of years of history had wrought upon a landscape that longer existed.

"Is it real?" Gobi asked.

"It comes and goes like a beautiful picture in the night. There is no ending to it, and no beginning. It exists in our minds. The Japanese mind. And now, in your mind, too."

"You mean, I am imagining *it,"* he said, trying to understand. *"Yet you are imagining it, too."*

"And it is imagining you."

Gobi wanted to ask her more questions. But instead his

attention was riveted by a scene unfolding among the neighboring towers.

He found himself captivated by a torchlit procession of a feudal Japanese lord being carried in a palanquin. An entourage of samurai horsemen thundered across a drawbridge that connected two keiretsu mega-towers. The banners carried by the hatamoto proclaimed the Kobayashi crest, a winged helmet in a red circle.

"Those are Lord Kobayashi's men," Yuki explained, as the procession entered a Japanese castle whose main gate was set into the 70th floor of a 250-story tower.

"Lord Kobayashi?"

"A powerful lord who seeks the ultimate power, power even beyond the Shogun or the Emperor. Power beyond life and death. He lacks only one thing."

"What is that?"

"He does not know the source of his own power. And that makes him very weak. And very dangerous."

"What is that source?" Gobi asked.

"It is an in-between place."

"In between what?"

"In between many realms. For those who dwell in many realms. Come." She smiled. *"You are expected."*

"By whom?"

"By my own lord. By the Lord Harada."

He followed her outside. The hotel corridor had been transformed into a broad passageway. Attendants waited with two kago, old-fashioned palanquins; they were dressed alike in blue hakama trousers and blue jackets.

The bearers knelt on the ground, waiting. One of the attendants slid open the doors to each of the palanquins and beckoned to Gobi and Lady Yuki. There was a cushion on the tatami floor inside the small interior.

As Gobi bent down to enter his palanquin, Lady Yuki touched his sleeve. *"One moment,"* she said. *"I must first warn you about something."*

"What is it?"

"We will be traveling through a part of the old town that is

heavily patrolled by Lord Kobayashi's forces," she told him.
*"My lord is being sought by Lord Kobayashi. His men will
hesitate at nothing to obtain any information they can about
my lord's whereabouts. Please, do not open the window of
your kago at any time. If we are stopped by guards at any
checkpoint, you must remain absolutely silent."*

Gobi nodded and climbed into the palanquin. The attendant slid the paper door shut behind him.

Gobi settled into the tiny traveling space as comfortably
as he could. There was a miniature gold-painted screen
behind his head with brush strokes of calligraphy on it. There
was a small video monitor to his right. He switched it on and
discovered he could watch everything that was going on outside.

Gobi felt the bearers lift his kago and he quickly learned to
lean from side to side in sync with their swaying rhythm.

"Washoi! Washoi," he heard them chant, as they hit the
ground with a padding stride.

The strangest thing was how natural it all seemed to him.
He was on his way to meet Kazuo Harada.

A blue mist rose from the upper levels of the mega-tower. The
kago bearers carried them across one of the elevated bridges.
As he watched the scene on the monitor inside the palanquin,
Gobi saw torches burning with a harsh black smoke and
pedestrians dressed in old-fashioned Japanese clothes.

"Washoi! Washoi!" The bearers continued their mesmeriz-
ing chant. Soon they reached a ramp that led them to a platform loaded like an elevator with other kagos and travelers.

The ramp descended to street level; once they reached the
ground, the bearers began to put on some speed. It was an old-
fashioned street, but Gobi couldn't quite put his finger on
what was different about it.

Part of it definitely belonged to the world of the 16th- or
17th-century Edo street life.

There were samurai, street peddlers, beggars, itinerants,
and hawkers of all kinds selling various sorts of goods.

Proprietors stood at the entrances to their shops, smoking their little brass pipes and enticing customers.

Monks with shaved heads carried staffs that jangled with Buddhist rings. Japanese women dressed in kimonos and wearing wooden geta clogs strolled with babies on their backs.

A 1930s Daimler automobile with tiny Rising Sun flags fluttering in the front roared past them. Farther down the street, a brigade of Imperial Japanese Army soldiers marched in their Kwangtung grey uniforms and leggings. From the looks on their scrubbed-clean young faces, they might well have been fresh recruits bound for the campaign in China.

With the apparent softening of the time membrane, Gobi was not surprised to spot Japanese from the latter part of the 20th century sprinkled in the crowd. They looked like ordinary commuters in dark blue pin-striped suits, wearing glasses and carrying briefcases. Their movements were clearly more stressed than those of their historical counterparts. A delivery-man on a scooter zipped through the busy traffic, his suspension system loaded with bowls of noodles in containers.

Wrapped up in these amazing sights, Gobi entered into the rhythmic swing of the kago bearers. On the monitor, he saw that Lady Yuki's palanquin was a short distance ahead of his. He failed, however, to notice the kago that was following them.

The kago bearers turned down a quiet side street. There were plenty of mansions and estates in this part of town. When they came to the end of the long street, they arrived at a samurai checkpoint with torches blazing. Gobi recognized the red-winged Kobayashi crest.

Two fierce-looking samurai in armor stepped forward with spears and ordered the palanquins to stop.

"Nanimono da!" the first samurai demanded. "Identify yourselves! State your business and your destination!" He challenged the kago bearers with his spear thrust forward.

Gobi heard Lady Yuki respond in her singsong court-lady falsetto. "We are from the household of the merchant Kazuma Dono, master of the Tamiya store in Suidobashi. I am his

252 — — — Alexander Besher

lowly consort, and that person in the palanquin behind mine is my daughter."

"What, the consort of a merchant, you say!" the samurai responded with an insulting leer. "In that case, let us examine your merchandise! Show us your faces!"

Lady Yuki slid open her door. The two samurai stared insolently at her beauty as she presented them with a demure yet properly downcast expression.

The other samurai now walked over to Gobi's palanquin and rapped on his door.

Gobi could sense his arrival before he even reached the kago. The energy of his stride was sulfurous black and smoky red. He could sense the man's bad humor and could almost hear the grinding of his teeth.

Gobi bowed his head and entered into a deep state. He entwined his fingers in the mudra of inner projection. Now he took a deep breath and his breath and his consciousness connected. A powerful rippling energy enveloped him.

Sitting in a half lotus position, he began to feel his toes tingle in anticipation.

Gobi knew exactly what has going to happen before it happened. His only hesitation was in deciphering the subtitles of the samurai's thought-forms.

As a consciousness footnote, it struck Gobi as curious that the man definitely had an authentic presence in time.

He was not an entity from the distant past. He existed in his own reality, which was some sort of a 17th century mindset of cultural, social, and martial arts mannerisms.

Gobi knew, for example, what the man had eaten for breakfast that morning: rice gruel and vegetables washed down with barley tea.

He was even able to pick up on the samurai's sexual thought-forms. The scent of the whore from the night before clung raunchily about his loins.

And then, Gobi found what he was searching for in the samurai's data base. There it was. He clicked on the icon and saw the image. The image of the samurai's worst nightmare.

Gobi rapidly downloaded that image.

Then he closed the file and pulled open his toolbox. That's exactly what he was searching for—the nightmare utility.

Those fright algorithms were a bit uncertain, but he just might be able to pull it off. . . .

The samurai rapped loudly on the door of Gobi's palanquin.

"Open up, sweet thing!" He laughed and winked lewdly at his companion. "Or, if you prefer, we can lend you a hand!"

"A hand—and maybe more!" The second samurai guffawed along with partner.

No reply came from within Gobi's palanquin.

"What's the matter with your daughter?" The samurai turned to Yuki. "She shy or what? Or maybe . . . maybe there is *no* daughter and you've been deceiving us! Is that it?"

The samurai grasped the door and slid it open, stepping backward with his hand on his sword, ready to slash.

Inside the kago sat a young maiden with a silk cloak over her shoulders and a shawl covering her head.

Her head was bowed.

"Show your face!" the samurai ordered. His partner stood poised behind him, his hand on his katana as well.

Lady Yuki pleaded. "Please, sirs, please! Please spare the young lady! Her face is not presentable! She is just recovering from a bout of the pox and her face has been ravaged. Please show some consideration for her feelings! Please!"

"The pox?"

Both samurai drew back. Then the more fearless of the two stepped forward again.

He drew closer to the figure that sat with stooped shoulders inside the kago.

"The pox, you say?" He sniffed at her. His face was inches away from the girl's.

"We'll see about that! Let me be the judge. . . . *Now, let's see your beautiful face, girl!*"

The figure lifted the shawl from her face.

Both samurai drew back in horror, dropping their arms to their sides.

The girl's face was hideously ravaged with ulcerated

wounds and pockmarks. A gaping cavity marked where her right eye used to be. She smiled sweetly and enticingly at them, her teeth exquisitely blackened. "If I can be of any service to you gentlemen . . ." she singsonged.

"Yaaa!" the samurai screamed and backed away as fast as their legs would carry them.

"Bakemono! A witch from hell! Begone! Begone!"

They gestured wildly for the kagos to be off. The bearers lifted the two palanquins and carried them off at a swift trot.

"Washoi! Washoi! Washoi!" Their chants echoed down the street.

The two samurai had barely gotten over their revulsion when the kago that had been following the first two kagos arrived at the checkpoint.

The two samurai guards were extremely wired now. Irritated, they waved the kago down. The bearers laid it on the ground.

"Akero! Open up!" They banged on the door.

The door slid open.

Inside sat a demonic-looking man wearing a long puffed-up coat, a head-wrapping of some sort, and what looked like opaque teacups over his eyes held in place by bands. The left side of his face was draped with a frieze of stapled silver chains.

The two samurai recoiled at the unearthly sight and drew their swords instantly.

The man pulled the sleeve down on his right arm and gave them a clenched-fist salute.

"Yaro!" The two samurai shuffled back a few steps. There was a weird contraption on the bakemono's arm.

"Yaaaaaa!" They charged him, their blades raised and slashing.

"Adios muchachos," Carlos said, as he zapped them with his channel-changer.

There was a bit of static, a little snow, and then the picture cleared.

Carlos rapped on the kago door to his bearers. "Hayaku! Follow that kago!"

They grunted as they lifted the palanquin. "Washoi! Washoi. . . !" They chanted, picking up their pace.

DOWNLOAD

The two palanquins arrived at the front gate of an old feudal estate with high walls. It looked abandoned. The head bearer rapped on a low side door in the main gate.

It opened almost immediately and a face appeared at the door. The gate creaked open. The procession continued down a white gravel path that wound its way between tall pines and cypress trees.

A pair of stone lions stood at the end of the path, guarding the entrance to the sweeping tile-roof Japanese residence.

A small group of servants and attendants waited there to receive the visitors. Lady Yuki was the first to emerge after the carriages were lowered to the ground.

"Frank-san, you may come out now," she called. He slid his door open and stepped into his wooden clogs, which had been placed on the ground for him. Everyone in the greeting line bowed as he approached the vestibule to the mansion.

"My master will not be disappointed when he hears of your skills," Lady Yuki congratulated him. "But you had me worried. You transformed yourself into that frightening apparition so masterfully. With just the right Japanese touch. How did you manage to do that?"

Gobi still felt disoriented. Something felt fuzzy somewhere. He heard a light ringing in his ears like a Tibetan bell. . . .

"It was like doing a flower arrangement," Gobi explained. "Only I used nightmares instead of flowers. That fearsome ghost—bakemono—was one image I sensed the samurai would respond to."

"Yes, it is part of our collective programming," Yuki agreed. "In our national data banks."

Gobi removed his clogs in the vestibule, then stepped into the foyer wearing his two-toed tabi.

"I've noticed how responsive this environment is to the power of suggestion," he observed. "It seems to be physical in its plasticity, yet its true form seems to be more, well, *mental*. . . ."

"*Mental*. Yes, precisely. That is an extremely accurate

assessment. It is a pleasure to meet you at long last, Dr. Gobi. Welcome."

Gobi looked up to see where the voice had come from. He and Lady Yuki had entered a central hall that was illuminated by flaming torches on cast-iron stands.

A distinguished-looking elderly man with white hair and glasses stepped forward. He was dressed in a dark kimono with a padded vest over it.

"I am Kazuo Harada," said the man who needed no introduction. "I have heard so much about you, Dr. Gobi. Your reputation precedes you. Ah, Yuki." He turned to Lady Yuki. "You did very well, my dear. My deepest thanks for bringing him to us safely."

She bowed delicately, like a paper fan folding upon itself, revealing the back of her powdered white neck.

Kazuo Harada's handshake was as crisp as old parchment. His eyes were bright and inquisitive. They burned with an unusual intensity. For a man in his eighties, he emanated the chi of a forty-year-old.

Gobi grasped his hand tightly. He felt a buzz run through him. "Harada-sensei, it is indeed an honor to meet you," he bowed his head. "I'm sure that at this moment you are probably the most sought after person in the world."

Harada glanced at Yuki. "Yes, it would appear so. By certain parties, at any rate."

"Harada-san," Gobi continued. "You have the key to Satori City. There is very little time left to get it back on-line. You must be aware of the fact that thousands of lives are at stake. We must act fast."

Harada frowned. "It is an unparalleled tragedy, Dr. Gobi. It is true that lives are hanging by a thread. But much worse things are in store for us if we succumb to emotional weakness and act too hastily."

"You don't *care* if people die?" Gobi was amazed.

"Of course, I care." Harada nodded. " But death is a relative term. It is a transformation, as you know. But a much greater transformation is now under way in the world. Something that you cannot yet understand. But you will soon."

Harada was coming into a different focus now. The image

swam before Gobi's eyes. Suddenly his white hair seemed too white, his eyes too intense. Gobi was losing his center. It was as if it were being slowly sucked out of him. . . .

"I'm afraid it's been a long, tiring journey for you, Dr. Gobi," Harada said, extending his arm to steady the American, who seemed to falter. "Just as you have been seeking me, I, too, have been awaiting you. But everything in its time. You must have some refreshment first. Some tea. Then we will complete the circuit."

He gestured for Gobi to follow. "This way, please. To my private apartments. We won't be disturbed there."

Harada led Gobi down a polished wooden hallway. As they walked down the long corridor, unseen hands opened sliding doors. The two men stepped through the interior of vast rooms to cross yet more corridors.

Gobi had the sensation of passing through countless chambers filled with art treasures, screens, paintings, scrolls, and sculptures. A subdued lighting system brought out the inner life of Harada's collection of rare Tibetan, Japanese, and Chinese holograms.

"I have been extremely fortunate to find this refuge," the feudal lord told Gobi, as they stepped through the chambers of his mansion. "It has enabled me to work in peace on improving Satori 2.0. Our post-virtual world lacks just one or two elements to make it work as it should."

Gobi sleepwalked past the treasures. A wooden voice— *was it his own? it was*—asked Harada, "You've got your programmers working here with you?"

"They are the finest, most dedicated group of professionals it has been my privilege to work with, Dr. Gobi," the white-haired man acknowledged. "And yet we seem to be missing something. An essential ingredient."

Gobi pressed him. "Is a woman named Kimiko here? *Kimiko Ono?* I believe she's a member of your development team. She's an old friend of mine."

"Kimiko Ono? Ah, yes . . . of course she is. Here we are,

Dr. Gobi. My modest quarters. We can discuss things in private here."

They had arrived in a small room, empty except for a low table and some zabuton cushions on the yellow tatami floor. There was a black lacquer tray with a small clay pot and several cups. A hibachi brazier glowed with coals and a kettle was on to boil.

"You must rest," Harada told him. "You have had an extremely strenuous journey. Your system has not yet had a chance to adjust to our rare atmosphere. Jet lag is nothing compared to crossing over the Flux." He made an attempt to laugh.

Harada poured boiling water from the kettle into the clay pot and rinsed it out. Then he took a few pinches of tea from a canister and sprinkled it inside the pot. He poured the water into the pot and waited, his hands folded on his lap.

Harada closed his eyes as if he were in deep contemplation. Or was he dreaming? He opened them again suddenly.

Now he rinsed their cups and poured the tea. They both waited for it to steep before savoring the brew.

"Domo." Gobi bowed as he brought the cup to his lips and tasted the frothy green cha. He wanted to ask Harada more questions, but he waited.

Still Harada did not speak. His eyes were closed and there was a funny smile on his face. It wavered on his lips before it went dead.

Gobi studied Harada's face. Something was happening here. Was he slipping into a state of samadhi? Of total absorption into a higher level of consciousness? What about his own feeling of light-headedness?

"Hello, Frank, how are you?" asked a feminine voice as the shoji door slid open.

He turned around, confused, half-expecting to see Kimiko.

But it was Claudia Kato, and she had a little black box with her. "We need that Kobayashi download now, Frank," she gave him a teasing smile. "We were just getting around to it on Station Seven, remember? Before we were so rudely interrupted. You still have it, don't you, Frank?"

"Claudia!?" It took Gobi a moment to register what was happening.

He turned to Harada, who was still sitting on the zabuton with his eyes closed. *"She works for you?"* But the man did not reply.

"No, Frank, you've got it wrong," Claudia replied. Two muscular Japanese technicians dressed in black hakama trousers with black jackets accompanied her as she entered the room.

"He works for us."

Claudia signaled to her two assistants. Each man seized Gobi by an arm and held him fast. They tied his arms back with a cord.

"This should really be quite painless, Frank," Claudia told him, bringing her face close to his. "Painless now—and painless afterward. You really have nothing to worry about. I told you how this thing works, remember?"

Gobi's ears were still ringing as the two men jerked him into a sitting position. One of them cuffed his ear to stun him. A hot coal burned on the side of his head and his brain began to spin.

The technicians secured the headband and connected the clips to the transfer pad at the base of his skull.

"You know a lot of things," Claudia said to Gobi. "But you *never* learned how to cooperate, Frank. That's what we really need more of in the world. Cooperation. And trust."

Gobi wasn't sure what he could do to resist the download. He had already freed the Kobayashi consciousness in the back alleys of Chibatown. But he now had Kobayashi's half of the algorithm. Each man had half. He knew that now. Harada had his half; Kobayashi had the other half. It was pure symmetry. He didn't understand it. He only felt its power, which pulsed like a beacon. It was—literally and virtually—the power to change the consciousness of the world.

He took a deep breath into his hara to stiffen his resistance to the probe.

Unghh!

One of the men punched his diaphragm, knocking the air out of him.

Gobi gasped and choked.

"Don't let him take any deep breaths," Claudia ordered her assistants. "He's trying to strengthen his hara."

He felt a hand lift his chin. It was Claudia's. "Was it difficult carrying him for so long? Don't be any more difficult, okay? It'll be over in a few minutes. Then I promise we'll leave you alone. You'll be free to go. You can go home again. Home to your son. He needs his father. Don't drift away, Frank!"

Claudia turned around. "Yuki!" she ordered.

Yuki entered the room, still dressed in her elaborate court robes but with a worried look on her face. She shuffled in on her knees across the tatami. She was carrying a tray with something steaming on it. It was an oshibori facecloth.

Yuki unfolded the steaming oshibori, then emptied a little vial into it.

She squeezed the cloth and brought it to his face.

Yuki had given him an oshibori back at the hotel, Gobi recalled with sudden a start. *But this stuff had a more bitter fragrance to it.*

In a moment he would breathe the vapor into his lungs and it would enter his bloodstream.

Gobi twisted his body away from Yuki's hand as she tried to bring the hot cloth to his face. He thrust his face away.

"Hold him!" Claudia ordered.

Kazuo Harada suddenly opened his eyes. *He hadn't moved a muscle the whole time until now. The bastard wanted to watch!*

Someone coughed. It was the guy holding him. Gobi felt the man's grip relax as he slipped to the tatami floor.

Claudia looked up. *There was a sound like a light pop. A sneeze?*

The other man toppled. His arm knocked the tray of tea off the table. Claudia's face froze as she looked up. Then she snarled, *"You!"*

The man with the silver face stepped into the room through the open shoji. He had entered by way of the garden.

He was draped in some weird get up, an inflatable overcoat

with pumped-up plastic cells. "Don't stand on my account," he said good-naturedly, as he stepped over the body of one of the technicians.

"Hello there, Gobi," Carlos addressed him. "They got you all in knots, huh? Be with you in a sec, okay, amigo?" He nodded at Claudia. "You'll have to 'scuse the boots," he said, pointing at his lizard-skins. "I shouldn't be steppin' all over these nice tatamis with them on, but seein' as I'm a little pressed for time, I'm sure you'll understand."

He barely gave Harada a glance.

"What do you want?" Claudia asked him in a harsh voice.

Carlos pointed his laser at her. "Don't move an eyelash, sweetheart. It might be hazardous to your health."

He waved the gun at Yuki. "You too, señorita. Put that towel down. On second thought," he winked at Gobi, still addressing the Japanese woman, "maybe you can give your friend an oshi-whatzit." He gestured with his gun.

Yuki hesitated.

"Hayaku!"

Yuki moved obediently across the tatami toward Claudia. She stifled a sob.

"That's it, hon, now you get the idea," Carlos encouraged. "Now give Miss Kato a taste of her own medicine."

Claudia sat there, a grim but defiant expression on her face. "You'll never get away with this," she said, steeling herself. Yuki brought the still-steaming oshibori cloth to her face. "Gommenna-sai," Yuki whispered an apology.

"The Kabuki sisters," Carlos replied, a grin spreading across his face as he watched the scene. "Have a nice flight, Miss Kato." He saluted her.

Claudia gasped lightly, then sighed as though a great weight were being lifted from her shoulders. Within seconds, her body became limp and she sagged in Yuki's arms.

Carlos stood behind Yuki like a referee at a match as he looked down at Claudia. As a final spasm ran through her body, Yuki wept.

"That's it, baby," Carlos said to Yuki with a strange gleam in his right eye.

"You got the right touch, honey. . . . Whaddyaknow?" He sniffed the air. *"Tetrodotoxin Orientalis.* The refreshment that pauses."

Gobi had watched the drama in a state of shock. So they were going to kill him first—*before* extracting the Kobayashi consciousness from him.

Carlos was not finished. "Okay, sweetie pie," he said to Yuki. "That's enough. Save some for yourself."

Yuki stared at him with a look of horror. But Carlos was unmoved. "You best be quick, honey. That oshibori's gettin' cold, and in just about two seconds you won't have any options left. Makes no difference to me how you choose to take it."

He placed the gun barrel between her eyes.

"Don't!" Gobi pleaded. *"Enough is enough! Stop it!"*

Carlos ignored him. "Say sayonara, honey. Uno, dos—"

Yuki trembled—then, with a final imploring look at Carlos, she brought the oshibori to her own face and breathed in deeply.

Her body went into an immediate convulsion. With a rattling gasp, she collapsed over Claudia's slumped form.

Her spasms continued for a few seconds. Then they ceased.

Carlos moved quickly to Gobi's side. He brought out his blade and cut the cord that tied Gobi's arms in the back.

Gobi rubbed his forearms to get his circulation going again. "Thanks," he said. But there was an accusing look in his eyes. "You didn't have to kill them, did you?"

"I did, I did," Carlos chortled. "You guys call it karma. I just call it 'in cold blood.' They were gonna waste *you,* hombre."

Gobi nodded at Kazuo Harada, who was still zoning out. "What are you going to do about him?"

"Don't waste your tears on this dude," Carlos said, as he stepped behind Harada.

In a movement that took a split second—Gobi's mouth fell open as he watched—Carlos drew his knife against the base of Harada's skull and slashed abruptly.

Harada's head jerked back as he fell to his side like a

Bunraku puppet who'd just concluded his final role at the National Theater.

Gobi felt sick again. *"You killed him!"*

Carlos dug his hand into the back of Harada's skull and pulled out a cylinder along with some optic wiring.

"Here," he said to Gobi, as he flashed the case at him. "You wanna pay your last respects?"

Before an astonished Gobi could reply, he dropped the cartridge into the deep pocket of his long padded coat. "Now let's vamonos," he spat out. "We gotta ticket to ride."

PICTURES AT AN EXHIBITION

They slipped into the garden through a shoji sliding door.

Gobi was still in his two-toed tabis. Carlos was wearing his lizard-skin boots.

"How . . . ?" Gobi asked, as he hurried to keep up.

"Save your breath, cojone," Carlos said. "There's an exit around here someplace."

They reached the far end of the estate. There was a low doorway in the wall hidden behind some bushes. "Knew it was around here somewhere," Carlos said, as he pushed the door open.

They heard an engine start up and a pair of headlights caught them in their beams. For a moment Carlos froze, then he relaxed again.

A long black Daimler with running boards pulled up to them. A pair of fluttering Rising Sun flags were mounted on the front. The door swung open.

"Jump in, amigo," Carlos said, as he held the door to the rear compartment open. Then he climbed into the front to sit beside the driver.

"I say, old chap," a familiar voice greeted Gobi from the driver's seat as the car began to move. "You *do* look a sight."

It was Simon Chadwick. He was still dressed in his khaki safari suit.

"You'll find a thermos of tea in the hamper," he said. "Along with some sandwiches."

"A real picnic." Carlos laughed as he rummaged in the basket. "Got any *real food* in there?"

"*'Fraid not,* my good fellow," Chadwick replied. "There's cucumber sandwiches and some scones. If you want beans, you'll have to go elsewhere."

Gobi sat in the back of the roomy 1930s sedan. He was doing a quick mental inventory. *Claudia. Yuki. Kazuo Harada . . . . But no, it wasn't Kazuo Harada, was it? It was a droid of some sort— of a quality he'd never seen before. Where was the real Harada? Was he still alive somewhere? He was back to square one.*

"What happened back there?" Chadwick asked Carlos. "I was beginning to get worried."

"Nuthin' much," Carlos replied, as he threw Harada's black box on the seat between them.

"*Oh, my!*" Chadwick exclaimed. "Is that what I think it is?"

"You're looking at a piece of hardware that's worth maybe a hundred, maybe two hundred mil, New Yen, amigo—retail. Wholesale, it's anyone's guess. Whatever goodies you can create out of it. Industries that ain't been born yet."

"I say, *good show,* old chap!" Chadwick congratulated him.

"You want to tell me what's going on?" Gobi asked. He turned to Carlos. "*Who* are you two? What are you doing together—here—on the Other Side?"

"The *'Other Side,'*" Carlos chuckled. "He's pickin' up the lingo faster than a dog picks up fleas. Whaddyaknow, our honorable passenger speaks Nihon-*gone!*" He laughed with Chadwick.

"You're such a tease, Victor!" Chadwick said, wiping a tear from his eye. "Honestly!"

"Victor?" Gobi wondered out loud.

The Latino extended his hand. "Special Agent Victor Velásquez at your service, Frank. Pleased to meet you."

"Special agent with *whom?*"

"The Virtual Bureau of Investigations. The *VBI.* Ever hear of us? I'm not surprised. We're a brand-new agency. We replaced Langley a while ago. But most folks don't know about that. Yet."

Chadwick guffawed. "Victor's a free spirit. One of the best, Victor is."

"And who are *you,* if I may ask?"

"Certainly not," Chadwick huffed, as though he were offended. "It would be highly inappropriate. Seeing as we don't exist either."

"He's been here before, you know," the Latino laughed. "He knows the ropes."

"You've been through the Shift before?"

"'Been here, done that, bought the T-shirt,' as you Yanks would say," Chadwick replied. He gunned the engine of the Daimler as he passed a retinue of samurai accompanying their lord on an official courtesy call to the Shogun.

"I don't believe it," Gobi said to the Latino. "You're not with any law enforcement agency that I know of. I saw the way you took out those people back there. You're a stone killer."

"Kinda struck you as cold-blooded, huh?" Special Agent Velásquez laughed. He opened his antique plastic case and offered a shabu stick to Chadwick.

"Three a day's my limit, thanks," the Englishman said, shaking his head as he steered through traffic. "I take it our friend's still operating under various archaic assumptions, paradigms as obsolete as the daily headlines. Can't say I blame him though. You practically need to be an archaeologist just to read the newspaper these days."

"What on earth are you talking about?" Gobi asked.

"Rules that apply *there* . . . where we come from . . . don't necessarily apply *here,* my good fellow."

"No," the Latino chimed in. "You can't pin a homicide on a guy for takin' out some droids in Shift City . . . or for erasing a nasty bit of graphics."

"Erasing graphics?"

"I'm afraid the poor chap still hasn't caught on, Victor. We may have to take him in hand. Hold on for Exhibit A."

Chadwick pulled the Daimler to a stop at an intersection where three or four Imperial Army officers were waiting for the light to change. They'd obviously been drinking.

Chadwick rolled down his window.

To Gobi he said, "Watch this now. A picture's worth a thousand words."

He leaned his head out the car. "I say there, sumimasen, old chaps . . . . Moshi, moshi."

That caught the military men's attention immediately. A weird gaijin sat behind the wheel of an Imperial Japanese Army HQ car.

"Keep in mind, it's 1941 as far as these chaps are concerned," Chadwick whispered to Gobi.

The major walked up to the car and peered at Gobi, then took a careful look at the man with the silver chains stapled to his face.

"I say there," Chadwick continued. "Do you know the way to the Imperial Palace? We seem to have gotten off the track. Where the *Tenno* lives? You know, the Son of Heaven. He's expecting us for tea. There's a good fellow. You can just point out the direction for us, won't you? Is it migi or hidari or masugu—left, right, or straight ahead? I'm afraid we're in a bit of a spot."

The major and his aides stood there on the curb, their faces red from the sake but becoming paler by the moment. Their eyes began to register systems shock.

"Nnnnn," the major finally bellowed, gritting his teeth. His hand went to his sword and he drew it out in a fell swoop. Its fine blade reflected the Daimler's headlights as he brought its arc to intersect with Chadwick's arm. He was going to slice it off at the elbow, perhaps even at the forearm.

"Yaaa!" The two lieutenants had drawn their swords and advanced behind the major. One of them had his hand on the car door.

Gobi heard Chadwick say to the Latino, "This might actually be a good moment, Victor."

The Latino nodded as he held out his little channel-changer and clicked it. The images of the Imperial Army officers flipped fast. Clicking backward, he riffed them into a montage of shots: samurai on foot, samurai on horseback, a monk, a woman, a child, a little dog, a cat, and finally a crow flapping its wings at the execution grounds.

Flipping forward, the major was a baby crawling, a schoolboy in uniform with a backpack, a university student with brass buttons on his black tunic, a giggling girl, a salaryman crammed in a subway train, then a manga in a comic book with the pages fluttering like cherry blossoms falling to the ground.

It had all flashed before Gobi's eyes in a matter of seconds.

"In living—or, I should say, in *dying* graphics," Chadwick declared solemnly, as he eased the Daimler back on the road. "Uncanny, isn't it?"

"What just happened?" Gobi asked.

Chadwick sighed. "It's the *Shift*, old boy. What on earth do you think this is all about then? Do you honestly think we've slipped off the edge of the world? Or that you're some sort of latter-day Christopher Columbus exploring the New World? Well, in a manner of speaking, you are, but. . . ."

"Make sense, Chadwick."

"Oh dear." Chadwick honked at a group of 16th-century Japanese pilgrims who were carrying packs on their backs, wide-brimmed sedge hats, and staffs; they wore leggings and straw sandals.

They stood at the roadside, gaping as the Daimler roared past them.

"One of these days someone's bound to get run over. Honestly . . . pedestrians! The ones from the Middle Ages are the worst!" Chadwick rolled his eyes as he turned back to Gobi.

"Yes, well, I don't suppose there's any harm in filling you in, old bean. Seeing that you probably won't be leaving this place anytime soon. We wouldn't want you getting back and alarming the public with your dispatches from the Inscrutable Interior, now would we? I can imagine the uproar. Demonstrations in front of the Euro Parliament, deranged E-mail to the White House, unrest on the Global Exchange. . . .

Good heavens, people may even start questioning the *fabric* of reality! Now where would *that* get us? Bad news, I'm afraid. No, none of this must ever get out. That won't do at all."

"Who the hell *are* you anyway, Chadwick?" Gobi snapped. "If that is even your real name."

"I'm just a nameless, faceless cipher doing my duty for God and the Euro Market. Keeping the shipping lanes clear. Holding up our end of it, if you know what I mean. The usual stuff."

"You're a spy?"

"Oh dear, *another* antiquated notion. Well, in a manner of speaking, I suppose you can say I'm the spy who came in from the operating system."

"Actually," Chadwick sniffed, "I don't mind admitting I was one of the first to get through in one piece. We were beginning to wonder, along with *your* chaps," he smiled at Gobi, "what on earth this was all leading to. Had to check out the possibilities, don't you know? See if there might be any nasty surprises in store for us down the road."

Chadwick drummed his fingers on the wheel. "Just where *were* the Japanese disappearing to? That was our biggest question. There was another possibility to consider as well. Was it some sort of scheme to isolate New Nippon from the rest of the world? Once *again?* Like the shoguns did? They shut everything down for more than three centuries, didn't they? It wasn't very hospitable of them, was it? It took your Commodore Perry to get them to pry their doors again. Black Ships and all that. Open the markets for free trade. Let the commerce flow."

"So what *did* you learn?"

"By George! What did we learn indeed? Well, as you must have gathered for yourself by now, things *aren't* what they seem to be. No, they're not what they seem at all."

"Meaning *what?*"

"Meaning, someone's actually *done* it, haven't they? They've turned it all upside down—all of human history and experience. *Existence,* old chap. It's not quite the same kettle of fish it once was."

"What is it they've done?" Gobi pressed. He had an awful feeling that he already knew the answer.

"Why, they've gone and *digitized* everything! At least, on this side of the planet. That's the trouble, old chap. They didn't do a very clean job of it. Half bungled it, I'd say. And now there's this dashed virus stalking the landscape. Most annoying really. A cucumber sandwich? No? Are you quite sure? Suit yourself then."

"Digitized everything? Everything here exists in *digitized* form?"

"That's what I've been tryin' to tell you, cojone, but you wouldn't listen." The Latino crossed his legs in the backseat. "Ain't the same as killing someone if you *zap* 'em. They don't go nowhere. They just pop up somewhere else in some other form. Some other state. It's sorta like recycling, in a way. You could turn out to be a rabbit or a stone or a samurai or someone's lunch. It's all just a bunch of *bytes,* man. Don't take none of it *personal."*

"But . . . *you* . . . and *me?"*

"Ah, that's where it *does* get a bit tricky, old chap, doesn't it?" Chadwick challenged him. "As they like to say here, *'What exactly is your Buddha nature?'* It comes down to that, doesn't it? You're a visitor in this fair land. You've bought the ticket, you've made the transfer. What are you *now?* The same Frank Gobi that you're familiar with, the original flesh and blood? Or are you just a digitized version of your former self? Or does it make any difference in the final analysis? Run *that* through your philosophy checker!"

They were crossing the Sumida Bridge, and entering the financial district. The keiretsu towers loomed ahead of them.

"I think the cojone's just beginning to get it." The Latino laughed. His laugh had a smooth texture. "It's rich, ain't it? When it finally hits you?" He punched Gobi in the shoulder. "Which are you now? Heh, heh, heh."

Gobi asked, sitting up, "Where are you taking me?"

Chadwick drove into the basement garage of a tower building. He went down several levels and pulled into a parking space beside an elevator.

"A place of refuge, old chap. They'll be looking for you now, won't they? You've got the Kobayashi algorithm. Or else why all the fuss? They'll be wanting that. But we'll protect you, won't we, Victor?" Chadwick said with a wink. "Shake a leg now." He opened the back door for Gobi. "Come on. *Come on.* There's not much time left. I thought you knew that already."

"You'd better tell me what's on your mind first," Gobi said, refusing to budge.

He felt a sudden hard pressure in his ribs. "You heard the man. Get going," Carlos ordered. He pressed his piece into Gobi's side. "Let me tell you something, cojone. I've done droids before and I've done humanoids. And I can tell you that humanoids are more fun."

PICCADILLY PERIPHERALS LTD.
NO SOLICITING

It was a seedy building by keiretsu standards. Dingy floors and walls, not so much as a Matisse in the foyer, and corridors of empty offices that went on for miles.

They took the elevator to the 45th floor. "All right, squire," Chadwick told Gobi. "If you'd be so kind, it's just that way." He motioned.

The halogen track lighting was down in most of the overhead strips. Gobi smelled ramen being cooked behind a number of closed doors. One door opened a crack—a face peered out, then quickly pulled itself back inside.

"Believe it or not, this was one of the grander office towers back at the turn of the century," Chadwick said cheerfully. "It's gone down a bit since the last bubble burst. But the rent's cheap and it suits our needs. It's just over here," he said, stopping in front of a door with a sign that read "Piccadilly Peripherals Ltd. *No Soliciting."*

Chadwick rapped on the door and listened. There was silence. He rapped again. They heard footsteps, then the door opened an inch and an eye studied them. In a moment, the door swung wide open.

A disheveled young Briton stood there without saying a word as Chadwick waved them in. The man was unshaven, with sandy hair, a round puffy face, and red-rimmed eyes.

"Ah, this'll be young Harris," Chadwick said, as he introduced them. "He just came over. Not quite adjusted yet, I'm afraid. How are you faring, old man?"

"Not feeling my best, sir. Had a bit of a rough landing. The parameters weren't set quite right. One foot's a bit shorter than the other." Harris shuffled awkwardly in his slippers.

"Ah, well." Chadwick nodded. "It's just a temporary inconvenience, I'm sure." He turned around to greet his guests. "Come in, come in." He rubbed his hands.

"Victor, kindly escort Dr. Gobi into that other room, won't you please? There's a good chap. We'll join you in a bit. I'll have a word with you, Harris, if you don't mind, before we get started?"

The Latino nudged Gobi along. "You heard the man. Move."

They entered a small, windowless room. Gobi looked around. There was a cot, a desk, a couple of chairs, and a dangling lamp shade. In a corner stood a large box that looked like a portable sauna.

Victor Velásquez waved his piece at him. "Sit down," he ordered Gobi. "Make yourself uncomfortable."

Gobi sat down on the rickety chair and looked at the man with the silver-link face. They were going to kill him, he had no doubts about it. That was one thought-form that required no subtitles here.

The Latino grinned, the silver links tinkling on his face like a rippling pie pan. "End of the line, huh, compadre? Who would have thought," he waved his piece around the room, "that you'd end up in a rat hole in a 'retsu tenement? You just never know. . . . When it's time to go, it's time to go. Ain't it so? That's what my mama 'tole me."

But Gobi had read him—and it was time to play that card. "You never had a mama. That's your problem, Victor, isn't it? Or is it Carlos? Whatever your name is—although it really doesn't matter a hell of a lot."

The Latino sighed and shook his head. "Now why you wanna tell me somethin' like that?" He looked at Gobi in a funny way. "You like to hurt people?"

Gobi studied him. He was a little man. A slight build, on the scrawny side, but fit like a bantam rooster. That chain-link fence on his face. That could be pure affectation, of course. A retro-postmodern-primitive body architecture inspired by the yakuza vogue. Or it could also be like some sort of a psychic Berlin Wall that intersected his two natures.

"Face it, Victor, you're a droid. You are what you hate the most."

The Latino sighed again. He patted the pockets on his inflatable-cell coat and brought out his shabu case. He opened it with one hand and transferred a crystal shabu stick to his lips.

"I forgive you," he said to Gobi, after taking a hit. "Because you are about to die and you are temporarily insane. *You are fucking temporarily insane!*" he shouted at Gobi.

"I say!" Chadwick came through the door, followed by Harris. "Is everything all right? Victor? What's wrong?"

"Nothing that can't be fixed. You'd better do your boy now. It's time to drain his brain-pan."

"Did Dr. Gobi say something to upset you, Victor?" Chadwick asked him.

"I merely pointed out to him something that must already be obvious to you," Gobi addressed Chadwick. "The man is a droid. Or rather the droid is a man." He shrugged. "I give up. Whichever came first."

Gobi didn't have time to duck. Victor slammed him in the face with his gun; stars popped in his head and blood trickled from his mouth.

"Victor!" Chadwick stepped between them as the Latino was about to lodge a second blow at Gobi's head. "Stop it!"

"Sensitive little bugger, aren't you?" Gobi groaned from the floor. His shen floated in the corner of the room, a neutral observer. A mass of dark energy was coiled above the Latino's cortex like an electrical storm. The Englishman was cool, like a rainy afternoon in Soho after a pint of bitters. He wore his aura like a dappled grey scarf around his fourth meridian. His hand was in his pocket.

"That'll be enough damage now, Victor," Chadwick said with a smile, as if he were indulging a favorite but undisciplined pupil. "I asked you to watch Dr. Gobi. Not to rearrange his brain cells. As it happens, we're *quite* interested in his brain cells. Help the man up, Harris."

"Oh," Victor said, stepping back as he saw the gun in Chadwick's hand. "Now what's this? Don't tell me that's meant for *me?* Or is that something the cat drug in from the bazaar in Akihabara?"

"Oh, dear me, it's nothing quite so tekky," Chadwick demurred. "This is a Walther P88. I'm much more partial to the old-fashioned mechanical firearms, aren't you? That way, there's no worry about anyone jamming your electronic firing system and causing no end of trouble. Happened to me once in Hong Kong back in '99. Two gentlemen from the Triads came at me carrying stilettos. Should've suspected something, they weren't put off by my Smith & Lazer. Sure enough, one of 'em's got this device, see, like a beeper. He squeezes it with a smile and it freezes my trigger. Damned awkward. Had to fight my way out of there tooth and nail. James Bond, what? Never made that mistake again. Not I. No, give me a *real* gun any day. Not like one of those kiddie toys." He nodded at the Colt Laser in Victor's hand.

Victor had his gun aimed at Chadwick's midriff. With a grin that faded fast, he squeezed the trigger. Nothing happened. "I did subsequently buy one of those little beeper things at the Golden Shopping Center in Kowloon," Chadwick went on without interruption. "I was quite surprised to find out how cheap they were."

With his left hand, Chadwick took a plastic infrared wand out of his pocket. It had been switched on. "It even muffles the sound."

The three shots carried Victor backward across the room. His overcoat immediately inflated and he lay on a little raft on the floor like a toppled totem.

"Damned shame, that." Chadwick's eyes returned from Victor's spread-eagled form back to Gobi. "You definitely pushed the wrong button, old chap," he said, with a look of reproach. "It really doesn't do to insult these hybrids, you know. They're awfully thin-skinned."

He tut-tutted. "Still, the bloke almost risked the entire operation. Amazing hubris they're coming up with these days. . . . I can recall when their egos were nothing but vaporware. Still," Chadwick sighed, "here we all are—minus one, of course—and there's a job to be done. Harris?"

"Yes, sir."

"Have you got everything ready?"

"*Sir!*"

"Then let's get cracking, shall we? It's almost dawn. We get the best reception about now." He explained to Gobi with a smile, "That's when the energies are most active. When the two Matrixes are closest to each other."

"Pity about poor Victor," Chadwick pined, as Harris rolled a little trolley with a black box on it toward Gobi.

Gobi sat in the chair with his hands cuffed behind him.

"Excuse me, sir, I'll just need to secure this on your head," the young Briton in the white lab coat apologized. He brushed Gobi's hair away from his forehead and laid the contraption on his head. It looked like a crown of 'trodes with clips.

"He was a droid, yes, it's true, but it was a pleasure working with him," Chadwick reminisced. "Actually, you hit the nail on the head, Gobi. You've got a good eye, if I don't say so myself. Not many people would have picked it up. Victor came out of a secret research program that led to the launching of the VBI. He was incubated in a Toshiba Cray system. . . . Never *did* know his mum, although she knew *everything* about him, you can be sure of that . . . enough to give the poor child a frightful complex when he was growing up. The father, who inseminated the *remembryo*—you know, the 'read-only embryo'—was quite highly placed in the old Agency. A genetic clone himself, actually. You can imagine the effect all this had on young Victor's upbringing. His mum's a Cray and his Dad's twice-removed. . . . I say, Harris, what are you fussing with now?"

"Sorry, sir." Harris' face reddened. "I've just been running a test. We seem to be experiencing a slight technical difficulty. I think it's due to the same factor that I encountered during my entry."

"And what's that?"

"There appears to be quite a strong fluctuation in the energy field. I think the problem lies right here in this building. Energy's being drained at a frightful rate. If you'll check the ohmmeter, sir, you'll see what I'm talking about."

Chadwick glanced at the device. "I say, that needle does seem to be having a fit, doesn't it? Can't you do something about it? Use the auxiliary power? Do *something,* won't you, Harris? We haven't got much time left."

"I'm *trying* sir."

"Well, *that's* encouraging," Chadwick said, peeved. "Anyway, where was I?" he asked Gobi, who sat there watching wordlessly.

Gobi had gone into Master Yang's approved hibernation breathing protocol and his shen was in the hallway looking for escape options. He passed through many, many empty offices.

In one office space, a family of a ronin salarymen lay sprawled on scattered futons. Children lay dreaming in rows, like little sparrows on a yakitori skewer. It was the "katta takaki" syndrome. The executive had been nominally laid off by corporate headquarters due to the Big Downturn of '22.

*But he had faithfully remained in the office and his family
had moved in with him, establishing residence on the 45th
floor.*

*Gobi went down one level in the 'retsu-scraper. This was
different. This was interesting. A colony of burakumin squatters had taken possession of a floor housing old unused mainframes from a bankrupt real estate corporation. It was a grey
market operation. The two dozen or so Bangladeshi and
Indian untouchables were downloading software effluents into
one of the mainframes, stoking it like a furnace.*

*They were recycling software toxicities onto the New
Nippon Net! This was a far cry from the primitive operation
Gobi had witnessed in Chiba City. There, the untouchables
had been burning the waste in fires. . . .*

*An info-untouchable dressed in a grunge sari stopped in
her tracks. She was carrying portable hard drives in either
hand like buckets filled from the village well. "Hari om!" she
muttered out loud. She must have been a sensitive to feel his
presence hovering nearby.*

*Gobi's shen floated up to mainframe. So this was what was
sucking up all the energy in the building. The mainframe was
like a pressure cooker, ready to blow. . . .*

"Victor went up through the ranks, did you know that?"
Chadwick grunted to Gobi. He was dragging the Latino's
body from where it lay to the box that looked like a sauna. He
opened the box and arranged for Victor's body to slump on
the bench inside. Then he closed the box, which left only
Victor's head sticking out of the opening at the top.

Chadwick twirled some knobs. "Harris, what are these
coordinates set for? London or Brussels?"

"Home office, sir."

"That ought to do. We'll just fax him over there. Let them
deal with it. I'll send a note along later."

"Very good, sir." Harris looked doubtful. "Must you do it
now, sir? The power supply being uncertain?"

"Dash it, you're sounding more like a Luddite every day,

Harris. Don't you have any faith in the overwhelming superiority of our technology?"

"Sorry, sir, it's the leg, sir. The right one's at least three inches shorter than the left. Something was lost in the transmission. I'm feeling a bit handicapped now, sir."

Chadwick slapped the machine for Gobi's benefit. "British Telecom. *Bio-Fax*. What will they think of next, eh?" He winked. "Good-bye, Victor, I salute you."

He stood at attention for a moment, then flicked the switch. Victor's face was bathed in a green glow. His mouth opened. The gold ridgework peeped through the green mist. His silver-green face mask crinkled. A shot of steam erupted from his collar. Then he was gone.

"He's on his way. File transfer complete."

Chadwick sat on the rickety chair opposite from Gobi, and leaned back. "Oh, he worked freelance for a while. For the INS actually. The Immigration and Naturalization Service. Victor was a bounty hunter." He laughed.

"Just like in the old Westerns." He laughed. "He worked the maquiladora belt—all the way from the Tijuana-San Ysidro to the Matamoros-Brownsville border. That's how he came to our attention actually. He was one of the best. I say, Gobi, you look a bit grey. Would you care for a cup of tea? No? Harris, what *is* it with you? Stop fidgeting."

"Sorry, sir, almost there. We'll have to improvise with the power cables, but this should do the trick. . . . "

"Carry on, Harris. This is all going into my report, by the way. Anyway, Gobi, it *wasn't* widely reported—" Chadwick giggled. "In fact, it wasn't reported *at all*. The INS put a lid on it and your media gratefully obliged. They were given some rather choice scandals to sink their teeth into instead."

The Englishman grinned. "But there was a *horrendous* traffic in droids starting up across the border, y'know. From the Kobayashi Droidworks in Baja. At first, the quality was rather low-end. Pool attendants. Servants. Gardeners. Migrant workers. Disposable droids . . . "

He sniffed. "Victor spent quite a lot of time honing his skills hunting them down. Collecting their chi boxes. Then he discovered a brand-new generation coming across. These were different. These were droids with résumés, credentials, Ph.D.s. M.B.A.s. Some of them even had *political* ambitions. Data bases loaded with lists of wealthy supporters. Your chaps really sat up and took notice about then."

Chadwick continued, "Some of these droids were getting elected to local city councils. Others were eyeing state senatorial races. It was all beginning to look rather dicey, if you know what I mean. That's when Victor got recruited by the Virtual Bureau of Investigation."

Chadwick leaned back in the chair again, its legs creaking. "The bureau got formed rather in a hurry, almost like Dulles' OSS during the Second World War." He waved his Walther P88 in the air.

"This Neo-Tokyo exercise was meant to be our little joint operation, don't you know. The boys from Brussels working hand in hand with the chaps from Washington. Go behind enemy lines and all that. Now I'm going to have to report that Special Agent Velásquez has fallen in the line of duty." Chadwick looked depressed at the prospect.

"Ready, sir."

"Thank you, Harris! Well done. It'll only be a moment now, Gobi. Awfully glad you've decided to cooperate with us on the download. It should be quite painless really. Take heart, old chap." Chadwick slapped him on the shoulder.

"I say, Gobi, I have a confession to make and I don't know whether I'll have another chance, so I'd best do it now. You know it was *me,* back there on Station Seven, who tried to do you in. I was the one who tried to harpoon you in that gondola when you were with the lovely Miss Kato. I thought you were a hired gun working for the opposition. Victor had to set me straight on that one. I didn't know you were a hidden asset. Hidden from yourself, too, apparently. Poor Victor! You will forgive me, won't you, Gobi? *I say, Gobi?*"

"Stand by, sir," young Harris declared. "I'm about to throw the switch—"

That's when the mainframe on the 43rd level of the 'retsu building blew and Gobi went spinning into the Void, taking his shen with him. He had found a way out and he was taking it.

"I think we lost him, sir."

"Damn."

"Sir?"

"What is it, Harris? I'm trying to think."

"There's someone knocking at the door."

"What? At this hour? Go see who it is. If it's one of those wretches from next door, tell them to go away."

Harris came back a moment later. "It's a woman, sir. She's dressed in a sari."

"Confound it, Harris. Is that what you've come to tell me? We've just lost our chap in the system here—he slipped right through our fingers—and you've come to tell me what some blasted woman is wearing. In a *sari,* you say?"

"Yes, sir. She appears to be one of the untouchables from the floor below."

"What of it?"

"I'm not quite sure, sir. But she's got some sort of a tube with a noxious-looking substance in it."

"Tell her we don't want any. *No soliciting.* It says so clearly on our front door."

"Yes, sir. But she says it belongs to us."

"What? She's not one of those recyclers, is she? Peddling something?"

"She may be, sir. They've been working those mainframes downstairs. She says she was loading one of them and there was a blowout. It may all be *connected,* sir."

"Let's have a look, Harris. One never knows, does one?"

Both men stepped into the anteroom and glanced out in the hallway. "I thought you said she was wearing a sari, Harris," Chadwick said, looking around cagily.

"She was here a moment ago, sir."

A young Japanese man stepped out of the shadows. "I believe you may be interested in this?"

He held out a tube with a glowing brackish substance in it.

"I say, who are you?" Chadwick asked, staring at the tube but wary of the man's self-assured manner and presence. "And what's that you've got there? What *is* it!"

There was a crumpled greenish-silver object sitting in a pile of ashes inside the clear plastic tube.

Victor.

"I regret your fax did not go through." the young Japanese bowed. "You must try to resend it."

Then he brought out his virtual katana and held it in his right hand. It was a priceless family heirloom. A Mitsubishi Munemasa. "May I come in?" he asked politely.

WEST OF THE VOID

It was just so much cyber-chutney. Gobi heard the humming sound of Tibetan bowls. He felt the roll of the Void and the thunder as soft as a feather tickling his ear. All the emotions of this planet, like dreams in amber, were resurrected in pulses of color. He heard snatches of sound. Bits of cellular conversations from the last century, like digitized lace curtains fluttering over the windows of long-ago lives. Sturm und Drang, the roll of drums and the furious trumpets. Here was a snatch from Adolf Hitler's address at the Nuremberg rally followed by the nasal drone of William the Conqueror and the mellifluous tones of Queen Isabella of Spain whispering through a scented handkerchief to a lady in waiting . . . .

Layers and layers of voices, music, streams of data, images cast off like heat from the potbellied stove of the imagination.

Unfinished symphonies fished out of the trash. Wrong numbers. Orders for take-out food. Dial tones of passion, call-forwarding of desperation, angry hang ups, long intimate strolls down memory-wires, the voice-mail of aborigines in Dreamtime . . . .

It was all inside this envelope with a great big stamp on it sailing into space.

The angels toiling in the fields leaned on their hoes as he sailed past. The little devils playing games by the riverbank dove for cover in the bushes. The lowing cattle lumbered on the rutted road and the turtledoves cooed in the shade of the plantain tree.

Gobi was on a roll. He turned west at the far end of nothing-ness 'till he saw the spires of Satori City, unlit and shut down. He saw empty boulevards, corroded traffic lights, sightless data banks, and abandoned packets on the Information Turnpike: Memory Mazdas, Cyber-Chryslers, Touchscreen Toyotas.

Gobi kept on going, past Satori's Adult World with its livid landscape of coitus interruptus, its unliberated lingams and unyoked yonis, the unregistered orgasms of the dead rever-berating in unsung karezzas . . . .

He felt the searing atomic blast of that death park, and almost lost his foothold in space.

He passed Karaoke Country, a giant drive-in of silent per-formances, voices in limbo, the breath that named the songs now a frozen whisper locked away in a lower key.

Still, Gobi could pick up a buzzing somewhere. From far off—but not that far—just a weak signal, still broadcasting.

". . . this is yours truly, yours ghoully, King Alfonso Aserioso, broadcasting on the Wasteland NetFM . . . All you hardy souls out there who're still listening, we're gonna be shutting down soon, soon as we're done playing this last set . . . Yup, it's shoo-time!!! Anyway, it was great while it lasted, wasn't it? All good things, you know. . . .

"Here's one last bulletin from V-town, Sectors 11, 12, 18, and 19 have gone into disconnect. Yeah, sorry guys. I appre-ciated getting your feedback. Wishing you the best wherever you've migrated to. Hope you find much happiness there.

"I also got a final weather report to give ya . . . mild and sun-shiney in the lowlands of Gametime, snow and precipita-tion in Virtual Bhutan and the Him-and Her-a-Layas, and this just in, kinda gives me the heebie-jeebies to have to say this, but there're more ro-langs sightings, they're coming down from the mountains in droves. Can't keep a good virus down, can't keep a bad one down neither, huh . . . ?

"Just watch your flip sides, happy campers, bladers, and

V-trekkers, if any of you are still up there—them living-deads are meaner than Earthshoes with rabies. . . ."

Gobi saw the snow-capped Himals on the horizon. He felt the sun shining like a giant reflection from the wound of fading fire. Night would soon be setting on this land.

He touched down on a trail. He began to walk.

THE KUNDALINI KID

The Kundalini Kid had been flat-spotted by the tsunami. He'd been caught totally off guard by an avalanche of light, along with his buddies Tony Allabanza, Zack Ganbaggio, Skater, and Druid Dan.

Now he was on his own.

The Kid had been V-boarding with the gang at the Interfaceland Annex. Tony had been pulling super-hot switchstance frontside noseblunts, while Zack'd been alleyooping 360 degree frontside noseslides like they were going out of fashion. Druid Dan was goofing off as usual.

The ramp was slick and without a lot of flats, so when it was his turn he landed his board on a parachute jump, burning in hard on his ankle.

At that precise moment, the whole world exploded on him. He remembered going through the concrete like a knife through Mazola.

The guys had been blown out of the freeze-frame. He never saw where they got to. And now *this*. He glanced around. Where was he? Mountains. Snow. Valleys. Oh shit.

The Kid wished he still had his board. He'd *never* felt gravity shudder in Gametime before. He'd been wearing his forklift-tire shoes and when he landed—whew! He still felt the burn on his pads.

Hey, you weren't supposed to feel pain *in Gametime! Except in your head.*

Now he had a headache like a leaky faucet dripping marbles on his raw brain.

How was he going to get back? This was *really* stupid. So the system had crashed. It had its moments of being screwy, but never like this before.

Wait a minute, was he ever going to get back? This wasn't like that Channel Emmanuel thing, was it? The one his Dad had been giving him a hard time about?

Cool it. Of course, you'll get out, he thought. It's just a matter of time. They're gonna miss you. And then they'll send someone in to look for you.

And what was that music? It sounded like a cool electronic waterfall. Like a glacier humming. . . .

Don't look back, he told himself.

For a while now, the Kid had the feeling that he was being followed.

I don't know what this game is—or even what level I'm on. Wish I had my Satori Genie with me. It'd tell me what sector I was in, what the rules are, and what little surprises are in store. But I lost it coming through that burn.

Damn! The Kid stopped in his tracks.

"WHAT IN THE BEJEEZUS!?" The Kundalini Kid freaked.

"Don't worry." He heard a voice address him from behind. So someone *had* been following him after all.

He spun around. It was a girl. She was maybe thirteen or fourteen years old, but he couldn't tell for sure. She was carrying a mountain climber's ax and had a bag slung over the shoulder of what looked like a yak-skin coat. Her cap had earflaps. She wore Doc Dalais, boots with a firm grip on the afterlife.

"Sorry, I didn't meant to startle you," she said. "I just had to make sure you weren't one of those."

"One of those *what?*" She had made him jump and he didn't like that.

"You haven't seen any of them yet? You must be new."

"Excuse me," the Kid said, as politely as he could. "But what are you referring to? And why have you been following me?"

"I'm *sorry,*" she repeated, removing her thermal gloves and extending her hand. "I'm Sherpa. Sherpa O'Shaughnessy. Actually, Sherpa's my handle here in Trek Land. Back home I'm Devi. Say, you *are* new."

"I'm Trevor Gobi. But they call me the Kundalini Kid. So this is Trek Land?"

"That's right. It's got some action elements—find the Yeti, that sort of thing—but it's mostly adventure travel. See those peaks?" she turned around and pointed them out like a tour guide. "You know what those are? I know them all by heart. Dhaulagiri. Annapurna. Shishapangma. Cho Ou. Everest. And, of course, Kanchenjunga. It's that one over there."

"That's great," the Kid said. "But what I want to know is—what on earth are *those* things?"

"Not a pretty sight, is it?" Sherpa said, with a pensive look. "This place is changing. It's not trekker-friendly anymore."

A huge grey cobweb hung across the trail. It looked like there were rubber masks hanging from it. Faces with frowns, cheeks stretched, mouths gaping.

"Yuk!" Trevor grimaced. "They look like shrunken heads to me."

"They're human screen-savers," Sherpa observed.

"What!"

"Actually, they're all that's left of a party of trekkers. I saw them a couple of days ago on this path. I think they were lost."

"What are you talking about?" Trevor asked, horrified. "What happened to them?"

"I thought *you* were new. You're not from these parts, are you? All kinds of strange people have been drifting in from other sectors. Anyway, to answer your question, ever since this thing happened—y'know, the *crash*—they've been coming down from the high country."

"What've been coming down?" Trevor asked, dumbfounded.

"The ro-langs, Kundalini. The walking mutants. They're moving into the neighborhood."

A roar in the distance drowned out everything. The light on the horizon flashed stroboscopically, releasing huge vertical slashes of orgone currents that rocked the mountainside. Boulders from the precipice above careened down the slope and dropped into the chasm below.

Sherpa stood like a frozen statue. Her eyes were fixed on a point centered on the horizon. "Oh my God, there goes Kanchenjunga. This whole place is going down the drain. It won't be much longer now."

Sherpa used her pick to disengage the cobweb from the path. Trying to overcome his deep revulsion, Trevor Gobi stepped past the remains of the trekkers.

"It's horrible," he said. "What do we do now? Where can we go?"

"This whole sector is going to go any time. That's what just happened over there," Sherpa pointed to where Kanchenjunga had stood. "The graphics are all coming apart. Our only chance is to try to get over to the other side. See over there?"

Trevor shielded his eyes against the glare. He saw a mountain range and a bubble behind it glowing like an ice cap. "That's the boundary of Gametime?"

"Yup, beyond that, we can begin our descent into Virtualopolis. Provided there's anything left, of course. This is probably happening everywhere."

"What do you mean?"

"Don't you know what's going on, Trevor?"

"I'm . . . I'm not sure," he said, as he looked down at his sneakers.

"How old are you?"

"Ten and three quarters."

"Well, you're old enough to know the truth. This isn't fun and games anymore. This is like the Endtime. Do your parents know you're here?"

He shook his head.

"I'm sure they must."

"They wouldn't know *where* I am. *I'm* not even sure where I am."

"C'mon, Trevor, I know where there's a pay phone farther up the trail. You can at least try to get a message across. There's a switchboard in the Wasteland that's probably still on-line. They'll net your calls over via a bulletin board. That's how I did it. I sent word out to my sister."

They walked in silence for a while. "I know I must be dreaming," Trevor said. "I had a dream like this once when I had a fever."

"You're not dreaming."

"But my *body's* over there. This is my *mind* walking."

"I guess it all depends on your definition of dreaming."

"I know what my definition of a nightmare is. This is it. How come you know this place so well?"

"I've been here before."

"Are you a trekker?"

"Goodness, no," Sherpa replied. "I come up here to collect specimens."

"What sort of specimens?"

"The herbs and plants that grow up here."

"Why would you want to collect those?"

"Mostly for their medicinal properties." She patted her knapsack. "I've collected a bunch of them already. *Semecarpus anacardium,* for instance. It's the nut of the bhayalo tree. It can cure cancer."

"Wait a minute. None of this stuff is real. It's all *virtual*-generated. How can it be any good in the real world?"

"Hey, I'm interested in the DNA algorithms of certain rare plants that only grow in the higher altitudes of Gametime. You never heard of virtual biotech?"

He shook his head. "You got any virtual aspirin?" he asked her. "My head is splitting."

"That's a pretty cool name."

"What is?"

"The Kundalini Kid. I like that."

"Thanks."

"Like the energy that shoots up the spine, huh? Powerful." Sherpa tried to lift his spirits. "It won't be long now. The pay phone's just up ahead a bit."

"You sure about that?"

"Your head still hurting?"

"No, it's better."

Sherpa had tried some virtual reiki on him, passing her hands over his head meridian like she'd seen her sister Tara do. It was the nerves—the nerves and the altitude. Somewhere on the other side, they would think they were dying.

Come to think of it, she puzzled, maybe they were.

"I don't believe I just saw that." Kundalini shook his head.

"What?"

"I think I saw a pair of sandals or something run across the path. Look, look, there's more of them!" he pointed excitedly. "In the brush over there!"

"Don't worry, you're not imagining things," Sherpa reassured him. "This is Earthshoe country."

"What!"

"Those're Earthshoes."

"There they go again!"

"A size six, maybe a size eight. There's colonies of 'em up here."

"Are you nuts!"

"They're really quite harmless. See . . . c'mon guys, c'mon." Sherpa knelt on the trail and extended her hand. *"Ts, ts, ts, ts . . ."* she called to them.

One of the more courageous shoes, a dark brown suede model (left foot, size $8\frac{1}{2}$) padded over, but remained within bolting distance if things got too uncomfortable. Its right-brained twin stayed away.

"C'mon boy, c'mon boy, or are you a girl? Hard to tell. . . . C'mon, I won't hurt ya . . . you're not my size anyway."

That seemed to reassure the Earthshoe. It ventured close

enough for Sherpa to touch it gently on its head. "There you are, there you are." She caressed it. *"Prrrt, prrrt."* It let out a contented sigh as it rolled over on its back to have its tummy done.

"No, I don't think so," Sherpa said. "I don't know *where* you've been."

"Wow!" Kundalini marveled. "This place is weird!"

"Run along now," Sherpa said, rising to her feet and brushing off her yak coat.

The Earthshoe shuffled away to join its chattering brothers and sisters in the bush.

"They've been breeding pretty fast," Sherpa remarked. "Like I told you, things've been changing around here. I think some trekkers might have left a pair or two behind on the trail, then—" she shrugged. "It's all conjecture, of course, but the parameters have been mutating. There's a virus running through the system."

"The walking mutants?"

"Yeah. Keep still, Kundalini—*listen,* can you hear that?"

He listened for a moment. "No, I don't. What do you hear?"

"Nothing," she said. "That's just it. Everything's suddenly so quiet. All the little Earthshoes have disappeared. They're not moving, not making a sound—"

Then they both heard it. The swishing, like arms swinging, and the loopy feet trying to keep up with a thought that was out of sync with the operating system.

Ohmygodohmygodohmygodohmygod . . .

Kundalini's heart skipped like a pebble skimming the surface of a pond before it sank into its own miasmic reflection.

"Ro-langs!" Sherpa warned.

They came around the bend. They had a loping gait and empty expressions, but they were dressed like long-gone Tibetans, ghouls from the last century, predating the Communist Chinese invasion of 1950. They were waving their hands in a come-hither gesture.

"Just our luck!" Sherpa swore. She studied their slow back-and-forth weaving and their rolling eyes. "Those are gdons!"

"Gdons?" The Kid's legs froze. He couldn't move them.

"There are different kinds of ro-langs. Those look like epi-demic ro-langs. They're carriers of spirit sickness. Oh damn, look what's coming up ahead! It's their advance team of mini-rimis!"

The ro-langs' front guard all looked different. They were a motley crew of little demons and goblins. Some of them looked like chihuahuas in turtlenecks riding on little wheelchairs, beaming half-witted smiles and scimitar teeth, bared like can openers. Others were cartoonlike sprites, incu-bii, succubii, and a procession of cerebral meningococcii in little white tuxedos and cummerbunds who were making wet smacking sounds with their lips.

"Sherpa!" Kundalini cried. "I can't move!"

Sherpa closed her eyes and went into a fast semi-trance. Her fingers were entwined in the mudra of protection. She downloaded the prayer for liberation from evil that her sister Tara had taught her.

"By the strength of the Three Noble Jewels, by the strength of the spell, the mantra, by the strength of the peaceful and fierce high patron deities, and especially by the strength of the twenty-one noble Taras whose essence is compassion . . . "

She put more energy into it, calling up the power from the base of her spine.

"May all the evil schemes of harm by lha and lu, by ghouls, spirits, and flesh-eating demons, by polluters and demons of madness and forgetfulness, by mamo demonesses and evil dakinis, by all misleading demons, by king demons and demons of death, by gongpo and fliers in the sky, by nyen and sadag, by serpents and ogres and nojin, by all ghosts and hungry spirits . . . May they be pacified! May they not arise!"

"Sherpa!" Kundalini shrieked. The chihuahuas in their mini-wheelchairs were coming up fast, leaving little trails of dust in their wake.

"NAMO!!!" Sherpa cried out, opening her eyes to face the onslaught.

"Sherpa! *Help!*" The thing was sniffing his face. But it was looking at him with a weird sort of recognition, as though he were known to it.

It was a pinkish holoidlike monkeyplasm, and when the chihuahuas arrived, it rose on its full hind legs on the boy's shoulders and hissed, baring its yellowish-pink teeth and hurling holoid insults and threats at them.

The mini-rimis beat a hasty retreat.

The loping gdons wagged their fingers, and lolled their tongues out at them. The mini-rimis cowered behind their gdon hosts, but they kept on coming.

B-O-O-M!!!

An explosion took out the lead ro-lang and it dropped to its knees, tried to rise, got up again.

B-O-O-M!!! The second explosion took it out for good.

The pink holoid monkeyplasm was gone. It had been on Trevor's shoulder for one split second. The next moment it had disappeared into the bush, leaving a vague pink trail.

It was almost as if he had imagined the whole thing. But he could never forget its eyes. That look of recognition. It was too weird.

Trevor and Sherpa looked behind them. Three kids now appeared on the trail. One of them was dressed in an oversize quilted coat with a backpack. He lobbed what looked like a slightly curved spinning stick into the air.

B-O-O-M!!! The explosion tumbled the two remaining gdons.

Another kid stood there—wide-legged on power skis—holding a pair of dynamic ski poles. He wore goggles and his ebony face was smeared with white antiglare cream. He was aiming one of the poles at the ro-langs.

Trevor saw him squeeze the firing mechanism high up on the pole handle. He was firing orange thunderbolts into the mini-rimis, who scattered in all directions.

The first kid twirled another explosive stick into the air.

B-O-O-M!!!

"Hey, catch!" The second kid tossed Trevor his other ski pole.

Trevor caught it gracefully in the air and instinctively began to fire off rounds of thunderbolts at the retreating mini-rimis.

"That's it!" his new ally shouted. "Keep shooting!"

The third kid did not participate in the defense. He sat slumped on the ground, shivering. He appeared to be breathing heavily and sweating.

"Well, we kicked their butts, what do you think!?" the first kid declared grandly. "Looks like we got here just in time. You guys aren't armed, huh?"

Sherpa asked him, "Where did *you* come from?"

The first kid, the biggest of the three, said, "Hey, no need to thank us! Those brain-deads would've smoked your membranes by now!"

"Sorry, I didn't mean to sound ungrateful," Sherpa apologized.

"It's all right. I'm Larry, this here's Mozambique. That's Phil. He's not feeling too well."

"I'm Sherpa. This is Kundalini. What's wrong with you, Phil?" Sherpa walked over to him and felt his forehead. It was hot and his eyes were dilated.

"I dunno. I crashed bad," he said weakly.

Kundalini returned the ski pole to Mozambique. "That was neat. Thanks."

Mozambique gave him a wide grin. "It's a Vajra peashooter. Fires Tibetan thunderbolts. Glad to be of service, mon."

"And that—" Kundalini pointed at Larry's gizmo. "I've never seen one of those before. What is it?"

"Oh, yeah? Where you been trippin'?" Larry studied Kundalini for a moment. "You look like a V-boarder, man. You fell into this sector, huh? Like Phil. He don't belong either. We picked him up on the trail. He says he got separated from his girlfriend when it crashed."

He brought out his sticks. "See these?" he said, showing Kundalini the combos. "They're Haikichis."

"Haikichis?"

"Yeah, they're a Guatemalan-Japanese design. Go ahead, try it. This one's not loaded. You've got to move the spinner stick a bit off center, see, then you toss the other stick into the air. It can really fly."

Trevor rotated his arm in a circular motion, then flung the other stick straight up. It spun like a propeller halfway down the meadow.

B-O-O-M!!!

Larry laughed. "Oops! Sorry. I guess that one *was* loaded after all!"

"You guys are really equipped." Trevor was super-impressed.

"Yeah, well, me and Mozambique have been working our way up through the game levels," Larry explained. "Racking up points, winning all kinds of prizes, like life-giving incense, magic thunderbolts, astral credit cards that award you karmic merit, you name it."

"Cool. What game is it?"

"It's a game called 'Rim: The Wheel of Life.' See, you start on the outer edge of the wheel. You gotta work your way through the twelve interdependent stages—which are the causes of life and misery, y'know, from ignorance to death. It's real Tibetan. Then you go through the six realms, starting with the realm of hell. Then there's the realm of yidags, which are the tantalized ghosts. Then you got the realm of animals, the realm of human beings, the realm of the demigods, and finally the realm of the gods. The spokes of the wheel divide the different realms. The axle is what holds it all together."

"Gee," Kundalini asked, "which realm are we in now?"

"Well, kid," Larry said. "It beats the heck out of me. This was *supposed* to be a game. Then these gdons started showing up meaning business. It's not a game anymore. I mean, this is the *real* thing. You live or you die. It's as simple as that. And it makes not one iota of difference if you do *either*. I ask you, what kind of a game is that? Whoever designed it must have led a really deprived past life."

"Which way are you headed?" Sherpa asked Larry.

Larry was about fifteen or sixteen. He was a big-boned kid with a square jaw. He rubbed his chin and looked serious. "I think we might be headed the same way. This place is ready to go any minute, I reckon. We're gonna try to make it to Virtualopolis and the lowlands."

"I think you're right," Sherpa sighed. "I figure that's our only chance. We can travel together if you like. But—" she lowered her voice to a whisper, "your friend, Phil. He's infected. That looks like a gdon bite on his neck. It's festering. I don't know if he's going to make it."

THE CALL

Sherpa had led them to a little white pay phone up the trail. Phil was the first to leave a message—for his girlfriend, Norma. First, he dedicated a song to her on King Alfonso Aserioso's pirate station broadcasting out of the Wasteland. Then he got ready to transmit to the Outside.

Larry and Mozambique helped him up and propped him in front of the pay-eye.

"How do I look?" Phil asked, matting his hair down. He looked like a corpse in drag.

"Byootiful," Mozambique told him. "Like you been pumpin' virtual."

"Thanks, guys . . . okay, drop the quarter."

Sherpa slid her mag-card through and the call went live to the Wasteland for the reroute.

"Hey, Norma girl, I miss you honey, I don't know if we'll ever see each other again," Phil said. "Tell my sister Rose I love her, and my Mom and Dad. . . ."

Sherpa whispered to Kundalini, "It's really tough." She brushed a tear away from her eye.

"Due to the heavy use of this bulletin-board line from the Wasteland to the Outside and in order to accommodate other customers wanting to use the line, your call is being cut short. . . ." An operator's talking head came on the screen.

"Kundalini, it's your turn now," Sherpa told him.

"Okay, Sherpa, thanks. You sure this is gonna get through?"

"Don't worry, it'll be rerouted."

"What time is it over there?"

"We're in different time zones, Kid," Larry informed him. "Between here and the Wasteland, well, there ain't much of a difference. But between here and home—you got to cut through all the compression layers, then time plays tricks. . . . You could be days ahead or days behind. Either way."

Trevor stepped up to the pay-eye and brought his face up close to it.

"Hi, Dad!" he beamed. "I know you're probably really worried about me, but don't be. I'm fine. I know I can't get back to you right now. But it's okay, I'll come home soon. I promise. There's just a few more levels I need to complete before I can get out of here. You won't believe this game, Dad! There're all these weird things that come at you. Demons, zombies, gdons, ogres, all kinds of hungry ghosts. . . . It's like nothing else you've ever seen! Oops! I gotta go now! This is costing me!" He smiled wanly. "You owe me a couple of thunderbolts, Dad! I love ya! 'Bye now! I'm outta here!"

He stepped away from the cam. "How did I do, Sherpa?"

"You were great, Kid. Very convincing. Now, c'mon, you guys, we'll all take turns helping Phil, but we've got to get moving. It's going to get dark soon."

THE GO-BETWEEN

Gobi heard the thunder from the horizon and looked up. A massive peak—it looked like 8,000 meters of pure granulated white pixels—collapsed like a sugar bowl being emptied. The snow erupted into the sky and hovered—a shimmering cloud in a thanka painting—before the brilliant blue emptiness siphoned it away.

Now the ground trembled under Gobi's feet. He felt the complementary vibration run up his yin heel vessel like a spidery drumbeat, torquing his step so that he had the illusion of stumbling.

He had to pause and steady his shen with deep chi breathing.

Remember this is all samskara, illusion, he told himself. *An on-line samskara.*

He halted when the trail reached a fork that crisscrossed in different directions.

Which way to go?

He felt strangely excited. *Soon, soon,* his senses told him. He could feel his destination looming now like the sun on the back of his neck. But he had to temper his anticipation. He could still take the wrong turn at any time.

Calm yourself, Gobi. Don't lose it now. Use the second sight of your second sight.

When he refocused his eyes, he saw the markers that had been left for him.

There was a trail of little paper origamis. Some of them had been twisted onto the branches of trees, like prayer offerings to the gods. Others had been placed on stones along the way.

When he reached the top of the trail, he saw a figure waiting for him. She stood outside of a hermit's cave. The woman wore a padded jacket with a belt and had her black hair tied back in a ponytail. She took off her sunglasses as he approached.

"Hello, Frank," she greeted him, with an anxious smile. "You found the trail." Then she added, "it's been a long time. You look good."

"Hello, Kimiko," he replied. "You look good, too. I thought you were dead."

"I *had* to do it, Frank. I had to make it look real."

"Is that why you hired me as your bodyguard? So it would look like I had bungled the job? So I could be properly remorseful and spend the next few years of my life looking for love and God in all the wrong places?"

"I'm sorry, Frank."

"Who was she? The woman who died in your place?"

"She was a go-between. In the same way that I hired you to protect me, I hired this person to be my double. I didn't mean for her to die. You *must* believe me. She was just a decoy. Doing my errands, taking part in my daily routine. So I could be free to work without interruption. She just happened to be in the wrong place at the wrong time."

"Doing your dirty laundry?"

"Please don't put it that way, Frank."

"Was I part of that work, too, Kimiko? Was I part of the charade?"

"No, Frank, you were part of my love life. I *wanted* to let you know that I was all right—but I couldn't afford to. That would have tipped off my father's enemies. With me out of the way, they couldn't threaten Ono NeuroIndustries. They couldn't blackmail my father."

"They got him anyway."

"I know, Frank. I was the one who hired you to try to find him. You didn't know that, of course. You did your best. But it was too late for Father."

"Why didn't you tell me *then?* That you were still alive?" Gobi still wanted to believe in her. At least, on some level.

"By that time, I was already working for Kazuo Harada on Project Satori. You don't know how important it is to the world. We were racing against time to set it straight. We *still* are." She looked at him with soulful eyes, still warm in their elusiveness.

"I hear voices, Kimiko," a man called from inside the cave. "Who's out there?"

"It's Kazuo," Kimiko told Gobi. *"I'll be right there, sensei!"* she called back to him.

"Let's go in, Frank. You must meet him."

At the entrance to the cave, Kimiko laid her hand on his arm. "Frank, I know it's probably very difficult for you to forgive me. So much has happened. So much is in the past. But you know—" she gave him a wan smile. "If you wanted to, we could get to know each other again. You've heard of the wish-fulfilling tree? All we need to do is ask."

"I know, Kimiko," Gobi replied, his heart heavy. "I've heard of that tree. But frankly, at the moment, I think we've used up all our wishes."

● ● ●

He was much thinner, more frail than his holoid had been. But his trademark white hair and designer glasses were the same, as though they'd been lifted out of the Kazuo Harada Catalog, items 67 and 68.

He had a cup of tea at his side. There was a little kettle steaming on a hibachi brazier—the bytes whistled. He was seated at a terminal.

"Ah," Harada said when Gobi walked in behind Kimiko. "You must be—"

"This is Frank Gobi, sensei," Kimiko introduced them.

"Naruhodo." Harada's shrewd eyes penetrated the form of Gobi's shen, admiring the way it had been compiled. He was a visionary all right. He knew the difference between a Kmart ectoplasm and a Mitsukoshi Harrod's walk-in aura.

"Welcome to Satori Gametime, Gobi-san." He rose to give Gobi a bow.

"What's left of it," Gobi said, studying the cave.

It had been comfortably refurbished. They were in the work area. From the outside you would have expected a dark, dank cavern. But there was a cleverly designed skylight with a snow-cover. Worktables were scattered throughout the cave—but they were empty. A corridor ran toward the back of the cave, where the individual bedrooms, communal o-furo bath, and canteen were located.

"Yes, it's true," Harada acknowledged. "You must have heard the thunder not long ago. That was Kanchenjunga," he said. "But don't worry, there is a backup."

"Where is everybody?" Gobi asked.

"Everybody?"

"The other members of your team. I thought they were with you."

"They were."

"It's just us, Frank," Kimiko explained. "They were foolish not to take precautions when they went out."

"What happened to them?"

"He got them."

"Who?"

Harada frowned. "Sato. Tashi Nurbu. The Rimi."

"He is insane, of course. But people like him are not usually judged by their sanity." Harada took off his heavy black-frame glasses and wearily rubbed the bridge of his nose.

"Insanity almost becomes a moot point, like the color of his hair or his eyes. What he has done is to transform the world. We cannot judge him by standards that no longer exist." Harada sighed.

"He is a thief."

"Oh, are you aware of his past? Yes, he is a common thief, too. He is *so* many things. He stole the program. Yet that is what Prometheus also did, is it not? He stole the flame from the gods. And he delivered it to man."

"Yet you continued to do business with him. Why?"

Harada pursed his lips. "I did not know the true facts at the time. I would have preferred to deal directly with the Tibetans, of course. But they would never have offered me what Tashi Nurbu did. He dared to break the old taboos."

He sighed. "Now, of course, the old taboos are haunting us. That's karma, I suppose." Harada's eyes brightened with a flash of wry humor. "Of course, I would have preferred royalties instead."

"When did you find out about the virus?"

"Before the Mega-Quake happened. You must understand, the 'Quake was *never* meant to happen. Not the way it did. It was supposed to be a smooth transition."

"A smooth transition?" Gobi asked. "Into what?"

"The next stage of mankind's evolution," Harada declared. "And the end of the old cycle as we know it. Of birth, childhood, maturity, old age, death—and, of course," he added sadly, "of rebirth."

"Unfortunately, Sato got greedy," Kimiko said. "He went to the Kobayashi Group and offered them the same program."

"Yes, Ryutaro Kobayashi never had any scruples." Harada nodded. "He was willing to release this Tibetan program on the market the way it was—complete with virus. A very tragic mistake indeed. With tragic consequences, as you can see for yourself."

Just then the floor of the cave shifted on its axis, the mountain groaning and grinding its molars. A shower of debris rained down on their heads.

Harada brushed the dirt off his console and peered at the screen. "There goes Annapurna," he said, looking up. "And Shishapangma. And Manaslu. Everest may be next."

"How was it done?" Gobi gritted his teeth. "How did he *digitize* Neo-Tokyo?"

"You start small," Harada said, "then you work your way up. But not Tashi Nurbu. He did it the other way around. I told him, 'Sato . . .'"

"Please answer my question."

"It was the first real breakthrough in consciousness compression. I won't bother to give you the technical details. I always say, leave the engineering to the engineers. I'm a hands-on management person myself. But let me just tell you this: It is now possible to store a city of a million human-scale inhabitants in a storage space of, say, 10^{24} bits. Provided they are properly encoded, of course, you can store a hundred cities the size of New York inside of a matchbox."

Gobi stared at him and at Kimiko.

"What he's telling you is quite true, Frank," she said to him. "In fact, a human brain can now be encoded in less than 10^{15} bits."

"You can downsize the entire universe and still have room for backup copies," Harada added.

"I'm not sure who's crazier, you or Tashi Nurbu," Gobi told him.

"Normally, I would take that as a compliment. It's an occupational hazard for geniuses to be considered crazy," Harada replied. "But in this case, I think I will have to defer to him. *He* started it."

"You call this the next cycle of human evolution? A new world order?"

"No, it's not catchy enough. I call it *'Taming the Untamable, Owning the Unownable.'* How does that sound?"

"Just one last question," Gobi said, as he rose to leave.

"Yes?"

"Where is he now?"

"Tashi Nurbu?"

"Yes."

"He's out there. He's become the virus now. He *is* the Rimi. I suppose he's always been that. He's had to evolve, too. He's waiting for you, Mr. Gobi. I believe you've got something he wants."

"Good-bye, Frank," Kimiko squeezed his hand outside the cave. It was getting dark. The few remaining peaks caught the rose glow of the sky and reflected a deep marble quietude.

"Good-bye, Kimiko."

"I'll be waiting here if you want me to."

"Good luck," he said to her, and he began to walk down the trail. When he turned to look back, she was already gone.

LOWLANDS

How are we going to get to the lowlands from here?" the Kundalini Kid wondered out loud.

As far as the eye could see stretched the rippling backbone of the Himalayan mountain range, sheer and menacing, with no shortcuts except for the gods.

Sherpa looked grim. "It would take a few days to walk down to the pass—on this trail, at least."

Larry peered down into the blackness of the crevasse. "Not necessarily."

"What do you mean?" Sherpa asked him.

"You guys afraid of heights?"

"Why do you ask?"

"There could be a quicker way."

"What do you mean by that?"

"Moz, what do you think?"

Mozambique looked down into the void. Phil was leaning on Sherpa's shoulder. He was in a bad way. "You want my honest opinion?" Moz asked.

"Yeah. Maybe. Go ahead."

"I think we got no choice."

"Okay, gang," Larry said. "This is your lucky day, all of you. You, too, Phil."

"How's that, Larry?" Sherpa demanded.

Larry got his pack and undid the straps. "Like I said, we didn't come here to pick flowers like some people did. No offense, Sherpa." He grinned. "Just kidding. But lookee what we got here. Moz, how much you got left in your pack?"

"'Bout 300 miles, seems like."

"Okay, let's do it."

"Do what, you two?"

"Bungees," Larry said, showing them the coil. "This is what you call brain bungees, see? Virtual bungee-jumping."

RIMI

Rimi's tongue is lolling from left to right. Its face is the side of a wall that you can never quite reach the top of. It hands are like levers. You can stand on them and then drop through the trapdoor. And, of course, the feet are like heavy rollers that crush the sap of the spine to make the spirit juice that makes the Rimi's eyes shine.

Rimi is a prose poem to death that never ends, but only vacillates at the end before it skips to the next line. It is a hunger that can never be filled, an eye that can never be plucked, and a memory that can never be absolved—much less forgotten.

Rimi does sketches with its brain. Long, slow sketches as it pans the thought. It is happiest when it is sketching the dead and the dying because that can only mean one thing. That it is not dead itself.

That is a comforting thought to the Rimi, although sometimes it wonders what the fuss is all about.

Its feet are a size 60. The little Earthshoes that scatter when it approaches are like cockroaches of desire. It wants to be small sometimes, but it can never be. It can only be big.

Its frustration is slow to build. Lately, the children have been escaping it.

Earlier, on this path between two sheer precipices, where the wind is howling and the rock offers no comfort except the hope of slipping, it came across the group of children.

When they saw it, as usual, they vibrated their excitement at a fever pitch. This only encouraged the Rimi to approach them. It wagged its tongue and waved its right hand back and forth. That is the universal Rimi language that says, *Stay. Do not move.*

But earth-children, like Earthshoes, are incorrigible. These children had long cords attached to the harnesses on their backs. The cords are long, elastic. They are attached to rings the children quickly hammer into the slippery rock face.

The Rimi barely takes a step—and it is only a single step for the Rimi to reach the children—before they leap from the ledge.

These are mountaineering bungees. The children drop thousands of feet into the lost crevasse.

Rimi is so clumsy. It sinks to one knee and feels the first bungee, strumming it.

As it strums the cords, the drone builds: *Dmmm, dmmm, dmmm, dmmm, dmmm. . . .*

What a sound it is! Somewhere deep in its heart, the Rimi is touched, so touched.

A toxic Rimi tear falls on each cord and swims down woefully, all those thousands of feet, where the acid of its beautiful grief will soon touch the spine of each dangling musical note.

Dmmm, dmmm, dmmm, dmmm, dmmm. . . .

The Rimi hears something else now. It is a download. A silent whirring at first, then faster and faster, louder and louder. A rumble of snow, an earlier avalanche from somewhere high above reaching it now. A curtain of sound.

Rimi raises its arms protectively, then lumbers away from the ledge.

It does not know its enemy, but it *feels* its enemy. As the whiteness of the snow spirals downward, a patch of it touches the Rimi's cheek and its tongue acts like a windshield wiper, twelve inches long and corrugated. It wipes the burning snow off its face.

The Rimi now knows that it is a hunter being hunted. Rimi touches its cheek, where a hole has been burned, and its eyes, with a hurt expression, look up, red-rimmed.

They are deep, deep red. Like a hot coal yearning for a lover's touch. The Rimi likes to kiss, too, with that great big lolling tongue.

The man is standing at the other end of the ledge. He has glanced down the crevasse where the children have fallen. Why is he standing there? The wind is howling like a lullaby, the dark blue shreds of sky starting to fall away like the snow into the chasm.

He is holding something in his hand, and spinning it. The sound of the avalanche. In his other hand—*is it his right or is it his left hand?* The Rimi is sometimes a little cross-eyed—he is holding something else.

Now the Rimi begins to think in Tibetan again. It is so tiresome to express in human language what only the muttering void can describe so eloquently.

It is a three-bladed object. It is a phurbu. A ritual dagger.

It comes back to him now. From a dream a long time ago. The Old Monk has been lecturing the dge-bsneyn, the apprentice to the sorcerer. Of course, it is for him that he has come. He has come to slay the virus.

"You are the heretic whom I have been expecting," Tashi Nurbu says to Gobi simply.

The heretic faces the slender Tibetan, who stands on the ledge. Around them, on all sides of the illusion, the twinkling lights of New Nippon are ablaze. It is the shift time of the Matrix, when one dream expires into another. The towering peaks are crumbling into the gorge, sigh after sigh, mandala after mandala, one sand painting merging into another.

There is no way back now.

"It is I."

"Where is your master? Or have you come alone?"

"I have come alone."

"This is fated then."

"It is fated."

"You cannot stop me. That is fated also."

"It is so. I cannot stop you."

Tashi Nurbu is surprised at that remark. "You come to die then? A graceful death I will give you. You are an honorable man. Come here, let me lay my hand upon you gently. Like this."

He is the Rimi now, forefather to the Yeti. He is lolling his tongue and wagging his hand in the come-hence mudra.

"I cannot stop you, but I can summon what will stop you."

Tashi Nurbu frowns. "What is the meaning of those words?"

"I am only the dge-bsneyn. The go-between."

"The go-between between *what* and *what?*"

The Tibetan warrior stands in his wine-red monk's robe, his long black hair hanging down to his shoulders, his cheekbones high on his face and his mouth set in a firm line. He is whirring the mani.

"You think that prayer wheel can stop me, dge-bsneyn? Or that phurbu in your hand? You have not strength enough to strike me. Nor do you know where my secret mole is. For I am mole ro-langs. That is my lineage."

"I know what you are. And no, I do not need to know where your weak spot is because you are weakness incarnate. It covers you."

"Brave words," Tashi Nurbu scoffed.

The dge-bsneyn kept whirring the wheel. *Would it not hear him? Would it not come? Would it not fly from Mt. Kailas, if it had to? He had so ordered when he gave it its freedom.*

"Enough of this precipitation from your mouth," Tashi Nurbu sneered. "You are wearing out the mantra and my patience."

The Rimi took a step toward the dge-bsneyn.

It came upon him suddenly, like a pink blur out of the blue.

The dge-bsneyn merely handed it the phurbu. And so it flew upon the Rimi's shoulder. Of course, he recognized it. It was the human, the industrialist to whom Tashi Nurbu had once given such mighty powers.

But he did not recognize him in his present form, a pink holoid monkeyplasm with fiercely chattering teeth. It held the phurbu high, as if it were examining it, clearly sensing the syringe that would send the serum into the neck of the Rimi.

The Rimi's eyes sought the dge-bsneyn's. Not begging for mercy, for it had already received mercy. It was seeing the light, the light in the darkness, the light in the miracle of its own undoing.

The Rimi turned now, as the mountains disappeared. It hurried across the ledge, to follow those peaks. There was time enough for the valleys.

The monkey chattered maniacally. It was freeing itself of its holoid karma. *It had come to destroy the world, to own it, and to sell it. And now. . . .*

Go in peace. Gobi bowed. *Both of you.*

MORNING

He began to stir from his reverie. *When conscious dreaming meets conscious waking, that is when the creative energy of the morning meets the lord of karma. . . .* Gobi's thoughts raced ahead of his body.

Gobi opened his eyes and blinked. "Yaz!" He smiled.

He was lying on the cot in an office. Now he remembered. He was in Chadwick's office in the keiretsu tower.

"Don't get up too suddenly." Yaz's hand restrained him.

"What—?" he looked around.

"O-hayo, Frank-san. Good morning." Yaz handed him a steaming cup of some pungent brew. "Drink this."

He drank. The weakness was lifting. He felt a new strength. He sat up. "What—what happened? What are you doing here?"

"I followed you, Frank-san. But only to this place. I think you have gone far, far away from here."

"Where's . . . Chadwick?"

Yaz glanced at the saunalike biofax box in the corner of the room. It was empty.

"He had to make long-distance collect call to his home office." Yaz grinned. "His assistant, also."

"I see—"

Gobi blinked again. "Is . . . is anything different, Yaz?" he asked.

"Different, Frank-san?"

"About this morning?"

"Hai." Yaz grinned again. "You have awakened at last."

They rode the waterfall elevator to the thirtieth floor of the Satori Building. The raucous parrots and mynahs echoed from the atrium and the ribbon of the Iguaçú Falls shot a spellbinding mist into the air.

The two Satori security guards dressed as gardeners in blue happi-coats and their two-toed tabis scanned him with their hands.

"Hai," they grunted, as they let him pass.

"Can you wait for me here, Yaz?" Gobi asked him.

"Okay, Frank-san, but don't be too long, neh? You have flight to catch."

"Wakarimashita. I understand."

He went down the hall past the executive boardroom. He passed a cubicle where a salaryman was working. He paused. The man looked up at him curiously.

"Excuse me," Gobi said. "Can I borrow your necktie?"

The Japanese gave him a perplexed look. "I am sorry? Nandesu-ka?"

"Your necktie. Can I borrow it for—," he looked at his watch, "three minutes? I promise I'll return it to you."

The bewildered Japanese processed the request, then handed his necktie over to Gobi with a bow. "Dozo."

"Domo arigato."

Gobi stepped in front of a doorway with a security camera. He put the tie on, knotted it, then adjusted it in a certain manner.

The grey metal door slid open automatically.

Action Wada looked up in surprise when Gobi entered the room. He was sitting at his pine desk.

"Secret combination." Gobi grinned, as he adjusted his tie again. The door slid closed behind him.

Action Wada frowned. "I thought you would be on your way to the airport by now."

"I wanted to stop and say good-bye first."

The burly Japanese was wearing a Pierre Hayashi suit of burnished copper, over a California roll-colored shirt with pink and avocado hues and a loud Scriabin tie.

"Good-bye, Dr. Gobi. Have a pleasant flight home."

"I heard the news."

"What news?" He frowned again.

"Kazuo Harada has come back in from the cold."

"Ah yes, I have heard that. It was on Asahi CNN this morning."

"And he's made a takeover bid for the Kobayashi Group. Especially after Satori City came back on-line."

"That is correct." Action Wada allowed himself the thinnest of smiles. "That is business, Dr. Gobi. But you are a scholar, you would not understand that perhaps."

"Save it, Wada. Your humor's wearing a bit thin. What are you going to do with all the stock you've been accumulating?"

"Stock, Dr. Gobi? What stock?"

Gobi brought out an interactive meishi business card. "This belongs to your man Kimura in San Francisco. I held on to it. It's a bit ragged looking but still quite revealing."

"What about it?" Action Wada's eyes narrowed.

"These are clever little things," Gobi said. "They keep a real-time accounting of Satori shares on the Global Exchange. See, they were at 10067, down -93, an hour before the crash. Right after *that* happened, they bit the dust. I mean, they *really* went down. . . . See how fast they dropped?"

Gobi clicked the chronometer on the meishi. "Down to

70062. He whistled. "That's a drop of 3005 points in two hours. Phenomenal."

Gobi looked up from the meishi. "Funny, it keeps going way down."

"Yes," Action Wada said, as he laced his fingers together and leaned back in his chair. "It is only natural. When a disaster such as the crash of Satori City occurs, it impacts everything. A terrible tragedy. But you are fortunate now, I think. Your son is all right?"

"Yes, he is, thank you for your concern," Gobi replied. "But tell me something, as the shares were dropping, how come you were buying—through intermediaries, of course—as much stock as you could possibly lay your hands on? You bought two million shares of Satori stock at fire-sale prices, Wada. How much is it worth since Harada's return? And how much is it *going* to be worth when Harada announces that Satori will be launching Satori City 2.0?"

Gobi eyed him. "The word's first post-virtual environment, guaranteed consciousness-safe and holistically correct." He shook his head in wonder. "How are you going to guarantee that? Canaries in cages? If their minds get blown, you pull everyone out fast?"

He sat on the edge of Wada's desk. "You pulled the plug on Virtuopolis, didn't you, Wada?" Gobi leaned and spoke in a soft voice to the Japanese. "It *wasn't* the Kobayashis, although they were naturally interested in taking over Satori. It was you all along. You had your eye on the Kobayashi Group as well. Didn't you? The new shogun of the global 'retsu network. Pretty ambitious of you."

Action Wada kept staring at him.

"I hear there's a Satori board meeting planned for next Wednesday. That's when Harada is going to formally announce the merger of the Satori Corporation and the Kobayashi Group. Unless something should come up to disrupt that announcement."

Suddenly Action Wada looked complacent. "What is it that you want from me, Gobi?"

Gobi looked at him for a moment. "You need to do a lot

of penance, Wada. A lot of penance and a lot of transformation."

"Name your price."

Gobi brought out a sheet of paper and handed it to the Japanese. Wada studied it for a moment. "What is this?"

"Just what it says. It's all pretty clear. I figure you made about 1.2 billion New Yen on your little speculations. This is a list of international nonprofit organizations that could benefit from your generous financial support—totaling roughly that amount, by the way. The other page identifies a new organization—'Victims of VR'—which will disburse damages and reparations to all those who suffered from the Satori crash. Starting with a certain Chukchee village in Eastern Siberia."

Action Wada let that sink in. He nodded. "Very well. Anything else?"

He followed Gobi's gaze across the room.

"Ah," Action Wada said. "I understand."

Action Wada got up and walked over to the shelf where his collection of neuro-netsuke carvings was on display. He picked one up. It was a Kyocera carving of a monkey holding a chestnut. He caressed it.

"There is an honorable keiretsu custom whereby the top executive who is responsible for tragic circumstances takes full responsibility for the event. In the old feudal days, of course, they committed seppuku. Ritual suicide."

"I'm aware of that custom." Gobi nodded.

"This is an empty netsuke," Action Wada said. "Tomorrow, it will be full of a saddened consciousness."

He closed his hand over the netsuke.

Gobi got up from the table and walked to the door. He stopped there and bowed. "Sayonara, Mr. Wada. May you benefit from many fruitful meditations."

Action Wada remained standing stiffly, his hands at his sides, as Gobi left the room. "Sayonara," he said, as he bowed deeply. "Have a safe journey home."

THE END

EPILOGUE

Yes, the Keiretsu Wars had been bloody by virtual standards. But after the New Edo was born—the new meta-environment they called Satori City 2.0—a new era of peace, tranquility, and refinement was ushered in. The arts flourished. Tibetan masters refined their karmic softwares, the public was generally enlightened, and consciousness became the currency of the land. It had its rise, it had its fall, but it held steady. My father Gobi commuted between the realms with Tara, his consort on the Rim. The compassion they shared for all sentient beings was known to all, especially to me, his son.

On this day, affixing the hanko (seal) of The House of Gobi, I remain with love and respect, for all the worlds that are contained in the known and the unknown, in the familiar and the unfamiliar, in the imagined and the unimagined, all part of the One, the Whole, and the Interconnected, with this memoir of the Age of Unenlightenment.

(signed)
Trevor Gobi
from "The Keiretsu Monogatari"
("Annals of the Mega-Corporate Wars")
Vector 16, Matrix Two
Taihei 43 (2067 A.E.)